WAR ON A THOUSAND FRONTS

THE ORION WAR – BOOK 6

BY M. D. COOPER

Just in Time (JIT) & Beta Readers

James Dean
Marti Panikkar
Timothy Van Oosterwyck Bruyn
David Wilson
Lisa Richman
Steven Blevins
Scott Reid

Version 1.0.0
ISBN: 978-1-64365-000-5

Cover Art by Andrew Dobell
Editing by Jen McDonnell

TABLE OF CONTENTS

FOREWORD

This has been, without a doubt, one of the most complicated Orion War books to write. Not because my muse has dried up—no, quite the opposite. This book is a single locus of so many events that have been building up over time, storylines that have been breeding in the shadows and now coming into their own.

Much like New Canaan, this is a book where many different characters get time on the page, from Tanis and Sera all the way to Corsia and many others.

I also had to take great care to weave this book with the events of Rika Commander, and other books that are only outlined, but not yet written—such as the third Hand's Assassin book.

And so, this book has taken me the longest to write of any in over a year, but the end result has been nothing short of fantastic.

I had several of my own 'WTF' moments in this book, as a few of the characters did things that will tweak the direction of future books enough to surprise even me.

I know, I could just force everything to follow the script, but I like to be surprised by where the story goes as much as you do.

So even though you read Rika Commander, and *think* you know what happened to Tanis after the events on Pyra at the end of Attack on Thebes...well, let's just say you ain't seen nothing yet.

My pulse is pounding a bit after writing some of the final scenes and noting some important parts for the next book, 'Fallen Empire', and I hope yours is going to be as well, when you get to the end. If so, then I've done my job well.

Michael Cooper
Danvers, May 2018

PREVIOUSLY…

When last we left Tanis, she had just been brought aboard the *Carthage*, a new I-Class (based on the *I2*) ship commanded by Joe.

The battle for the Albany System is still raging around the ship, as the allied fleet assembled to rescue Tanis beats back the massive Nietzschean armada.

Rika was instrumental in saving Tanis, and if you'd like to see more of their interactions following that daring rescue, you'll find them in Rika Commander, though we also see some of their conversations from Tanis's point of view in this book.

While many of the major players are temporarily clustered together in the Albany System (on the rimward side of the Praesepe Cluster, roughly 550 light years from Sol, and 3000 from New Canaan), others are still widely dispersed.

Sera is at Khardine, and Krissy is managing her part of the Transcend's civil war from within the Vela Cluster. Garza and his clones are running about, causing chaos, and Jason Andrews is the governor of New Canaan.

In addition, Katrina has been freed of the remnant Xavia that was placed within her, and Cary, Saanvi, and Faleena are also aboard the *Carthage*, meeting their mother after she was brought aboard by Priscilla and Rika….

KEY CHARACTERS REJOINING US

Andrea – Sera's sister who used a back door into Sera's mind to make Sera try to kill Tanis in the Ascella System.

Cary – Tanis's biological daughter. Has a trait where she can deep-Link with other people, creating a temporary merger of minds.

Corsia – Ship's AI and captain of the *Andromeda*.

Faleena – Tanis's AI daughter, born of a mind merge between Tanis, Angela, and Joe.

Garza – General Garza is head of BOGA, Orion's counterpart to the Hand.

Greer – Admiral Greer is responsible for the protection of Khardine, the Transcend fleets on the front, and supporting Tanis's efforts in the Inner Stars.

Jason Andrews – First Captain of the *Intrepid* and current governor of New Canaan.

Justin – Former Director of the Hand. Was imprisoned for the events surrounding the attempted assassination of Tanis.

Katrina – Former Sirian spy, and one-time governor of the Victoria colony at Kapteyn's Star—and Warlord of the Midditerra System.

Krissy – Admiral Krissy is the daughter of Finaeus, and currently in charge of military operations to quell the civil war in the Transcend.

Mary – Daughter of Flaherty, recently rescued from Airtha along with her son Drew, Leeroy the pilot, and Figgy, a dog they met during the escape.

Oris – Septhian government official working for Nietzschea who betrayed Tanis and Thebes.

Priscilla – One of Bob's two avatars.

Rachel – Captain of the *I2*. Former captain of the *Enterprise*.

Rika – Colonel Rika is the leader of a battalion of mechs sent on a mission to destabilize key elements of the Nietzschean Empire. Rika was also instrumental in rescuing Tanis on Pyra.

Saanvi – Tanis's adopted daughter, found in a derelict ship that entered the New Canaan System.

Sera of Airtha – A copy of Sera made by Airtha, containing all of Sera's desired traits and memories. President of the Airthan faction of the Transcend.

MAPS

For more maps, visit www.aeon14.com/maps.

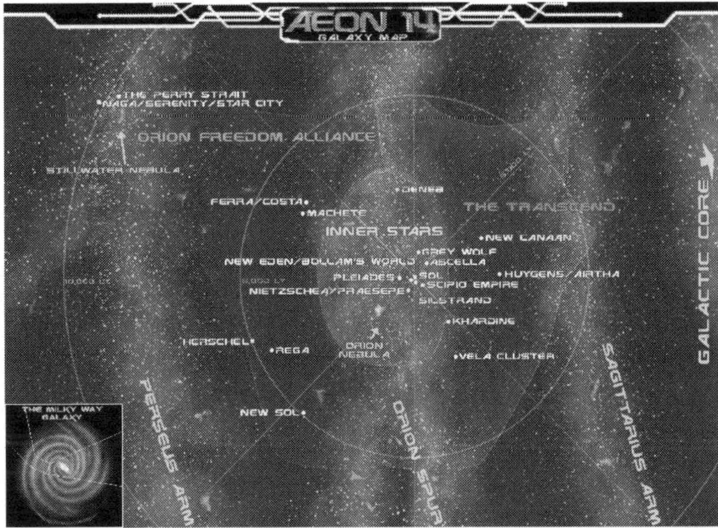

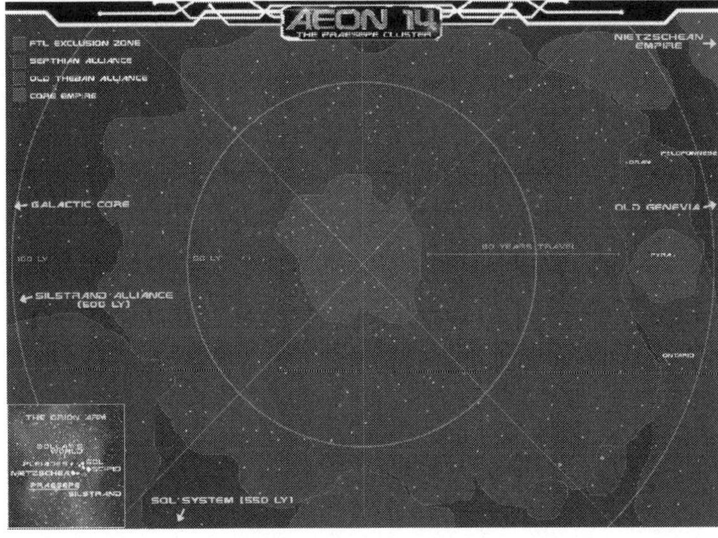

ORION FRONT

STELLAR DATE: 08.21.8949 (Adjusted Years)
LOCATION: TSS *Tharsis,* Cerden System
REGION: 10LY from OFA border, Transcend Interstellar Alliance

Marcel slumped in his chair, watching the Orion Guard ships break off from the engagement, shifting onto a vector to slingshot around the nearby gas giant.

The TSF had won the day, but just barely.

All around the *Tharsis* lay the wreckage of both Transcend and Orion ships; hulls venting atmosphere, many glowing brightly from reactor meltdowns. It was a mess—except for a slowly expanding bubble of empty space to starboard, the result of a ship that had lost bottle containment and suffered an antimatter explosion.

"Sir," Ensign Lavalle on comms turned to address Marcel.

Marcel nodded for the woman to continue, though he could tell from the expression on the ensign's face that he would not like the news.

"I've just gotten word from the *Pursuit*. Admiral Jorgen died in the explosion aboard their ship. His entire staff was killed, as well."

Marcel drew in a long breath. Jorgen had replaced Admiral Heath, and had only been in command of the battlegroup for six months. At this rate, they'd have captains running the fleet.

Shit…that's what Lavalle is hedging around.

"Colonel Vala?" he asked Ensign Lavalle, begging the stars for good news.

Lavalle shook her head. "Sorry, sir. Vala's ship was holed, its CIC was lost."

Marcel sucked in a sharp breath, then forced himself to expel it slowly. While the two Seras were battling over the Transcend's presidency thousands of light years away, the fleets on the Orion Fronts were being worn down to nubs.

Here on the Spinward Front, it was the worst—what with their proximity to New Sol. Though he'd heard that it wasn't much better on the Anti-Spinward Front. Both fleets were at less than half their original strength.

The fact that they'd won the battle today was a miracle, only possible because of intel that Admiral Jorgen had picked up. Without foreknowledge of the enemy's attack, there would have only been a patrol garrison protecting the Cerden System when the Orion Guard arrived.

"Sir?" Lavalle asked. "What are your orders?"

Marcel straightened in his seat. "So, I'm senior, then, am I?" he asked.

Lavalle nodded, and Marcel couldn't help but notice that half the eyes on the bridge were on him.

"OK, people," he said, summoning his last reserve of energy. "This is still an active battlespace. Half those damaged OG ships could still fire on us. Attend to your work."

The bridge crew turned back to their consoles, at least appearing to be focused on their tasks.

"Lavalle, send orders for Major Uda's group to set up a picket on the far side of the battlespace; there's a chance those Oggies could come around the planet and blast past us on their way out. I want them to seed mines just in case. Get Mendel's Marines to find a good hull and secure it. That'll be our prison ship. All other groups, begin S&R operations."

"S&R on Oggies, too?" Lavalle asked.

Marcel nodded slowly. For as much as he'd liked Admiral Jorgen, he disagreed with the late Admiral's no-rescue policy on Oggies—which even went so far as to destroy any disabled ships and ignore escape pods.

Marcel didn't want to slowly freeze to death in space, or drift in stasis till the SC batts on the pod ran dry. If *he* didn't want to die that way, it was not a fate he'd deliver on anyone else. He didn't care how much he hated the enemy.

"Yes, Lavalle. Obviously lower priority, but we're not going to leave them to die—so long as they come peaceably. No TSF blood will be spilled saving them."

"Yes, sir," Lavalle replied smartly.

Marcel couldn't tell if she approved or disapproved of his orders, but decided that so long as the ensign followed them, it would have to do for now.

Not that he was all that worried about Lavalle. She was a good woman, followed orders and was efficient and conscientious about her work.

But she was also a barometer for the rest of the crew, and if she was hiding her thoughts on the matter, it was a telling indicator.

<*Farrah,*> he reached out to the ship's primary AI. <*Looks like you're in charge of fleet tactical now, any initial thoughts?*>

<*I think we need to abandon this system,*> Farrah replied without hesitation. <*All that's left are a few mining outposts—everyone else has fled. No sane person wants to live this close to the front anymore.*>

Marcel wanted to argue with Farrah, to tell her that the TSF wouldn't abandon a system after they'd just successfully defended it—but he knew she was right.

The 917th Fleet had once numbered over fifty thousand ships, spread across five hundred light years of the border with the Orion Freedom Alliance. Now their numbers were fewer than ten thousand, and the five other fleets that patrolled the border weren't in much better shape.

With reserves—of which there were few—the three thousand light year border with the Oggies was now guarded by fewer than fifty thousand ships all told.

Marcel pushed his palms into his eyes and drew in a deep breath. A hundred thousand stars defended by a smattering of ships. And if the Oggies kept pressing like this, they'd punch through the defenders before long.

Stars, they may already have, he thought. *We really have no way to tell; we're not even patrolling half the systems anymore.*

The thought of his fleet failing so utterly at their mission made him want to scream.

We need more ships!

Marcel didn't have the latest information on the fleet strengths elsewhere in the Transcend, but he knew for a fact that the civil war taking place around Airtha, Vela, and Khardine was occupying more than half the space force.

At least no TSF ships were involved in the strange crusade that Field Marshal Richards was undertaking in the Inner Stars. She seemed to be funding that herself, with minimal use of Transcend resources—bar the jump gates she was chewing up. Marcel had overheard Jorgen complaining more than once that getting new gates over the last year had been well-nigh impossible.

Marcel was about to compose an update to send to Admiral Greer at Khardine when he remembered that the only QuanComm blades in the fleet had been destroyed in the battle.

"Fuck!" he swore, while slamming a fist into his chair's armrest.

Several eyes on the bridge turned in his direction, but when they saw the rage plainly evident on his face, they turned away.

"Farrah," he growled. "Dispatch a courier drone to Fortress Gibraltar. Have them send our status to Khardine, and ask command what they advise."

<*Of course, Captain Marcel,*> Farrah replied. <*Should I make a request for reinforcements, or…*>

"If they can't tell we need reinforcements—" Marcel stopped himself before he said something he'd regret later. "Yes, Farrah, put in a request for everything. Stars knows we need it. Once we've done S&R here, we'll advise the remaining civilians to evacuate, and then get the hell out of this system."

<*Yes, sir.*>

The orders given, Marcel fell silent, watching the fleet's progress as they took in friendly escape pods, and corralled enemy ones.

It will take days to clean up this mess. Days in which the enemy could regroup and strike again. He had no illusions about how that engagement would go.

TANGEL

STELLAR DATE: 08.28.8949 (Adjusted Years)
LOCATION: A1 Docking Bay, ISS *Carthage*
REGION: Pyra, Albany System, Thebes, Septhian Alliance

Cary felt her skin tingle as her mother's hand brushed against her cheek. The range of emotions surging through her threatened to overwhelm—joy, relief, elation—but they all gave way to confusion when Tanis spoke.

"Faleena, my dear, you're so beautiful."

A feeling of surprise emanated from Faleena that matched Cary's own.

<*Mom?*> Faleena asked. <*Are you OK?*>

Tanis's eyes appeared to refocus, and she rested a hand on Cary's shoulder. "Cary, you are truly something unexpected. More amazing than I'd remembered."

<*Than either of us remembered,*> Angela added.

<*What just happened?*> Faleena asked Cary.

<*I have no freakin' clue, Fal.*>

"What happened down there?" Saanvi asked, as Tanis pulled both girls into an embrace.

A rueful laugh escaped their mother's lips. "Stars, what *didn't* happen down there."

<*We began to ascend is what happened,*> Angela said, and Tanis glanced at Priscilla. "But you did something to stop it…you used…"

Priscilla held up her hands and shook her head. "I just did what Bob told me to do. If I hadn't, we wouldn't have been able to bring you back up here. Rika could barely hold onto you as it was; if it wasn't for the fact that her skeletal structure was so dense, you would have slipped through her."

"Pardon?" Cary asked, glancing at Priscilla before locking eyes with her mother. " 'Slipped through'?"

Tanis chuckled. "I guess I hadn't quite figured out how to stay anchored in the three dimensional world. Not that it matters now, Angela and I seem to have reverted to our old selves."

"I'm surprised that happened," Priscilla said. "Bob didn't think anchoring you would cause your mind to split apart again, though he said it was a risk."

A curious look came over Tanis's face, and Cary wondered how separate her mother and Angela really were.

<*Even if they did split apart again, it won't be like before,*> Faleena whispered quietly into Cary's mind, apparently on the same train of thought. <*She saw me…* ***sees*** *me, Cary. I don't know how, but she was looking at my mind.*>

Cary considered Faleena's words for a moment, then reached out to her sisters to form Trine and took a step back to observe their mother.

Trine drew in a sharp breath in each of her bodies as she gazed upon Tanis's form.

At first glance, it appeared as though her mother's body contained a remnant, but as she looked closer, Trine saw that it was more than a remnant. A fifth dimensional being suffused their mother's body—she could see it rooted deeply in both Tanis and Angela.

<*You are beautiful, too,*> Trine said, realizing she could see Angela in the remnant-like figure that occupied her mother's body.

"You've become quite proficient at that, girls," Tanis said as she looked from Cary to Saanvi and back. "Not that I'm surprised. To do what you've done with extracting the remnants is no simple thing."

Trine split apart, and Saanvi whispered. "Mom, what's going to happen to you?"

Tanis reached out and took Saanvi's hand. "I'm going to fully ascend at some point. Though what Priscilla did has made it possible for Angela and I to operate as separate beings for a while longer."

<*A while?*> Faleena asked.

Tanis nodded, a smile quirking the corner of her lips. "So long as I don't end up in any dire circumstances, a few years I suspect."

Cary bit her lip before asking, "And then you'll just turn into some being made of light?"

Tanis shrugged. "I'm not convinced that fifth dimensional beings have to shuck their mortal coils, so to speak. The ones we've all encountered began as AIs, so they had no bodies to begin with—well, not ones that were useful when it came to moving around."

Tanis paused and looked down at herself, then held up her left hand and snapped her fingers before continuing.

"I, on the other hand, rather like my body. Especially now that I've reconfigured it."

"I noticed you regrew your arm," Saanvi said. "I assume that happened down on Pyra, as well?"

Tanis nodded. "I was able to strip apart molecules and atoms and reform them into anything I wanted. I harnessed the energy and used it—"

"You almost killed yourself," Priscilla interrupted. "At least, that's what I think was happening."

Tanis shook her head. "I wouldn't have died. But I think I would have burned up this body...and our distinct minds. Then there would have been no going back."

"Mom," Cary shook her head certain that horror was writ large on her face. "You're going to give me a headache. How is this possible?"

Tanis took Cary's hand as well and led her daughters toward the nearest lift bank. "For some time now, Angela and

I have been...growing a new brain. Its interleaved with our current ones, and is directly connecting them in millions of locations. Down on Pyra, it came awake, and our consciousness shifted to it. Now it's...asleep again."

"Wouldn't that brain have been burned up, as well?" Saanvi asked.

"Maybe...or maybe it would have transferred into other, non-physical dimensions...it's hard to say. I don't really want to try it and find out."

"Good call," Priscilla added as she fell in beside them.

Tanis looked over at the avatar, and then paused, her gaze shifting to the mechs and humans gathered nearby.

"Just a moment," Tanis said. "I need to go thank Rika for saving me."

* * * * *

Tanis didn't let go of her daughter's hands as she turned toward Rika and her team.

The tall cyborg woman was surrounded by three humans, with a platoon of her soldiers coming down the *Derringer*'s ramp to join them.

Tanis had to admit that she was impressed by these mechanized warriors. By her standards, what had been done to them was a horrible disfiguration, but the cyborgs bore their mech bodies with pride, never flinching or behaving as though they were in any way inferior to those around them.

"Rika!" Tanis called out as she approached. "I owe you and yours a deep debt of gratitude."

Rika turned, a tired smile on her lips as she held out her left hand and Tanis slid hers from Cary's tight grasp.

"Admiral Richards," Rika said as the two women shook hands. "I'm glad to see you're doing better. You were in rough shape back on the planet…I imagine doing an impression of a starship engine is exhausting. No pun intended."

Tanis hadn't realized that Rika must have seen her unleashing the energy barrage that had obliterated the Nietzscheans. She wondered what the woman thought of that—*she* still had no idea what to think of that.

<*Think of it as kicking major ass,*> Angela advised.

<*Noted, Ang,*> Tanis said with a laugh.

"I was feeling a bit of burnout." Tanis grinned at her joke, but then her smile disappeared. "I am deeply sorry about General Mill and Captain Ayer. I feel somewhat responsible for what happened to them. They died honorably."

Rika squared her shoulders and shook her head. "You may have been the catalyst, ma'am, but the blame lies with traitors in the Septhian and Theban governments. What happened here was going to occur sooner or later, anyway."

"You're probably right about that," Tanis replied, while reaching up to tuck her hair behind her ears. "We'll have to determine how deep that sickness goes."

"What are your plans here, then?" Rika asked.

Tanis looked the mechanized woman up and down. "First we're going to finish off the Niets…there's still a battle raging around us—though one can barely tell in here. Then we'll restore this system to order and summon Prime Minister Harmin to see what he has to say for himself."

One of the men standing with Rika, a stocky dark-skinned soldier, snorted a laugh. "This I would love to see, the PM coming here with his tail between his legs."

"Barne, stow it," Rika said, making a slicing motion through the air with her left hand.

Tanis gave Barne a small smile. "As far as I can tell, Septhia recently *lost* Pyra, maybe all of Thebes. Not to mention that it was never really theirs in the first place. I'm not entirely certain that we should cede it back to them."

A small smile crept across Rika's lips. "I like the way you think, Admiral."

Tanis placed a hand on Rika's shoulder. "No 'Admiral' for you. To you, Rika, I am 'Tanis'. I look forward to talking with you further. I think we can benefit one another greatly."

Rika's cheeks lit up with a small flush, and she ducked her head in a nod. "Of course, Ad—Tanis. I look forward to that. Now that we've found the likes of the ISF, we're not keen to run off on our own any time soon."

"Except that we need to get back out there," one of the men with Rika—a young man named Chase, Tanis saw by the indicators on her HUD—said. "There's still a fight to be had and a world to save."

Tanis nodded. "There is. I need to get to the bridge."

<We can manage the battle well enough from here,> Angela said. *<Already are.>*

<Appearances, Ang. Physical presence counts for something.>

Angela's silvery laugh filled Tanis's mind. *<We're Tangel now, do we need to keep up appearances?>*

<We need to think of a new name. Though I guess it's better than Tangela.>

<Says you.>

While Tanis and Angela debated possible names, and reached out to the ship's command network, Rika replied.

"We'll speak again soon, I hope, Tanis."

Tanis gave a crisp nod. "You can count on it. Just don't get blown up out there."

Rika snorted. "Killed by Niets? Very unlikely."

"Good." Tanis turned back toward the lift banks, her daughters and Priscilla in tow. Behind them, the *Derringer* was lifting off once more, turning back to the dock's exit and the fight raging around Pyra.

"Even *we* don't get to call you 'Tanis' in formal situations," Saanvi said with a grin, as they settled into the dockcar with Tanis at the controls.

"She won't either, but informally…I don't know. There's something about that Rika. She feels like a kindred spirit."

"She's a warrior, that's for sure," Priscilla said from the back seat. "And a survivor. She told me some of her story during our journey insystem. That girl is built out of pure, unfiltered, hardcore moxy."

"Good," Tanis replied. "She's going to need it for what I have planned."

"What's that, Mom?" Cary asked.

Tanis glanced at her daughter—*daughters*.

She was still amazed by how she could *see* Faleena within Cary's mind. Tanis knew one thing was for sure: she wasn't ascended—yet—but she wasn't…whatever she used to be. It was as though she had one foot in each world.

"Mom?" Cary asked. "Star Command to Mom."

Tanis shook her head and smiled. "Sorry, trying to coordinate the battlespace better. Joe did a good job setting it up, but there are optimizations."

"What about Rika, and what you have planned?" Saanvi inquired, as the dockcar reached the lift bank.

"Oh, well, it's obvious that we can't let these Nietzschean scumbags stew for long. We've set them back, and now we have to finish the job. But I'm not willing to let the Trisilieds build up for much longer, either. They dropped a damn starship in our backyard on Carthage. That deserves recompense."

Saanvi chuckled. "JP said it scared the horses all the way out at his farm."

"I wonder how he's doing," Cary murmured as they walked onto the lift. "He joined up for you, Sahn, and now you're out here."

"Indeed," Tanis raised an eyebrow as she regarded her daughters. "I seem to remember all sorts of stipulations being placed on you two after your escapades at Carthage. Ones that required you to finish your time at the academy—yet here you are, thousands of light years from the Palisades."

Cary shrugged, while Saanvi's eyes widened in worry.

<*She's messing with you,*> Faleena giggled. <*Besides. I wanted to come see Mom, and that means I have to drag my meat-suit along.*>

Cary groaned. "It's so disturbing when you call me that."

<*I'm such a bad influence,*> Angela said, a soft laugh accompanying her words. <*Yes, Tanis is messing with you. We're both happy you were the first people we saw at the bottom of that ramp.*>

"I thought I was Good Mom and you were Mean Mom, Angela," Tanis said.

Cary snorted, and Saanvi raised a hand to cover her mouth.

<*Seriously, Tanis? You're By-the-Book, Stickler Mom. I'm Party-Time, Have Fun Mom.*>

"She's right, Mom," Cary said with a sheepish nod. "It's just how you are. We love you for it."

Tanis sighed. "Man…when you're out-funned by an AI…"

The doors opened a moment later, and Tanis was surprised to see the Carthage's bridge foyer, and not the administrative concourse.

"The Mark II's have a dedicated dock-to-bridge lift tube," Cary explained. "I think Abby had it added in. She complained it was always such a pain to get to the bridge on the *Intrepid* and *I2*."

Tanis shook her head as she surveyed the space—which was barren except for three empty pedestals at the far end. "There's a reason why you don't have direct access from the dock to the bridge."

"They added safety precautions," Saanvi replied.

Tanis wondered about that. Not that it mattered right now. "No avatars on the Carthage yet?"

<*Not yet,*> a new voice reached into Tanis's mind.

<*Kerr,*> Angela replied with a warm glow in her voice. <*I'm sorry we didn't greet you properly when we arrived.*>

<*Think nothing of it,*> Kerr replied. <*You've been busy.*>

"That we have," Tanis replied, as the group walked across the foyer toward the short corridor that led to the bridge. "I'm glad you passed muster in time to ship out."

<*Well, we're all a bit green, but we're managing. One hell of a shakedown cruise.*>

Tanis noticed Saanvi giving the empty pedestals a long look as they walked past, and felt a momentary burst of protectiveness.

<*You don't think Bob talked to her about becoming an avatar, do you?*> she asked Angela.

<*No, he wouldn't do that after you told him not to. Don't worry, your ruling that no one under fifty years of age can be an avatar still stands. They'll find someone else to do it.*>

Tanis wondered about that. Her plans to build dozens of I-Class ships meant she needed at least twice as many avatars. Over half the population of New Canaan was under the age of fifty, and she wasn't prepared to allow outsiders to take on the role, so she may have to loosen her restrictions.

She also wondered about the wisdom behind building more AIs as powerful as Bob. *I'm not sure the galaxy needs more 'hyper-intelligent' beings.*

<*Kettle, meet pot,*> Angela commented.

<*Our ascendency helps my case.*>

Angela laughed. <*Keep telling yourself that.*>

They reached the bridge's door, and Tanis squared her shoulders.

Time to put on my game face.

The doors slid open, and Tanis walked out to see a near-perfect mirror of the *I2*'s bridge. Her gaze slid over the rows of consoles, the captain's chair, the holodisplays and tanks…until she saw Joe.

He stood with his back to the door, arms akimbo, studying the battlespace projected on the main holotank, barking out orders and requesting details and analysis from the teams surrounding him.

But the moment she stepped across the threshold, his head snapped up, and he turned to face her, a look of relieved joy spreading across his features.

"Tanis," he said, the single word cutting through the cacophony surrounding them.

Tanis had intended to walk across the bridge calmly, filled with grace and poise, to give the love of her life a chaste embrace in the view of the crew.

She did none of those things.

One moment, her hands were clasped in those of her daughters, and the next, she was running across the bridge, weaving around consoles and crew, to crash into Joe—who ended up careening into her at the halfway point.

Momentum spun them around, and Tanis brushed her hair out of her face a moment before their lips met, and their bodies pressed into one another in a desperate embrace.

"Told you to be careful," Joe mumbled, as their mouths slid past one another and came to rest near each other's ears. "You nearly got killed, what…three times while you were gone?"

"Who can keep track?" Tanis whispered as she continued to crush Joe against herself.

<*I can.*> Angela chuckled softly in their minds.

"Stars, don't actually *tell* me, Angela," Joe admonished as he pulled away and stared into Tanis's eyes. "So you're still the pair of you in there, eh? The briefing Colonel Smith forwarded led me to have some doubts about who I'd meet."

<*You still have to contend with two wives for a bit longer,*> Angela said.

"Huh," Joe cocked an eyebrow. "So much for hoping."

Tanis was surprised to hear him say that—though she wasn't entirely certain he wasn't joking. "I didn't think you were anticipating our eventual merger."

"Tanis, I've been waiting for it for *decades*. You two just need to get on with it already. The anticipation is killing me."

<*I'll tell you more about it later,*> Tanis said privately before turning to the main holotank. "So, how're things going?"

Joe turned and walked alongside her toward the view of the battlespace. "As if you don't already know. I could see you nudging things long before you even got up here."

Tanis surveyed the allied fleets interspersed throughout the Nietzschean half-sphere of ships. What Joe and the allies had pulled off was almost beyond comprehension; to jump so many ships into such a small area simultaneously was an unparalleled marvel. The timing alone would probably be the subject of thousands of dissertations in the future.

"All hail the QuanComm system," Tanis said in a near whisper as she watched a detachment of ISF ships push through the Nietzschean forces, and engage a pocket of enemy vessels that were inflicting heavy losses on a group of Scipian cruisers.

Nearer to the *Carthage* lay the wreckage of a thousand Nietzschean vessels that had attempted to boost away from Pyra and burn the world as they fled.

"Looks like you gave them what they deserved," Tanis said, gesturing to the remains of the fleet, which was moving into a loose orbit high above Pyra.

"Cowards," Joe shook his head. "Nietzschean master morality is such a crock of shit. Only they would consider something like burning a planet honorable. Whoever made a civilization based on Nietzsche's teachings needs to have their head examined."

"I imagine they're long dead," Tanis replied. "Which is lucky for them."

"Well, there's still their emperor—some pretentious ass who took on the name 'Constantine'."

Tanis nodded. "Yeah, he's on my list now."

"Good, mine too."

As Tanis began sending commands to the fleet, a pain stabbed through her stomach, and she realized something was missing.

"Any chance someone can get me a BLT?"

RELIEF

STELLAR DATE: 08.28.8949 (Adjusted Years)
LOCATION: Presidential Stateroom, Keren Station
REGION: Khardine System, Transcend Interstellar Alliance

[They got her. Safe and sound.]

Sera reread Joe's message four times before she allowed herself to believe it. She had half a mind to grab a ship and jump out to Thebes just to set eyes on Tanis herself.

<*Your heart rate has finally settled back down.*> Jen sounded relieved as well.

"Yeah, well, Tanis is pretty important to our efforts. I don't know who I could put in charge of the Inner Stars offensive without her—stars, I don't even know if the ISF would remain in the fight."

<*Now you're just being silly. You know that Joe and Jason wouldn't abandon the Transcend. It's not in their natures.*>

Sera nodded. That was true, but would those two men be able to muster the entire populace of New Canaan to the war effort like Tanis had? They had their Starflight plan, their Aleutian backup location—wherever that was. If ever there was a people fully prepared to drop off the face of the map, it was they.

Give them more credit than that, she admonished herself. *They're putting everything into defending a galaxy that they don't even know—and that has tried to wipe them out more than once.*

Sera rose from her desk and walked to the window that looked out over the inside of Keren Station's habitation cylinder.

The peaceful scene of gently rolling hills and grassy plains was incongruous with the events going on elsewhere. The fact that the ships of the alliance were even now engaged in a pitched battle with the Nietzscheans while she watched birds wheel above was hard to swallow.

She sighed and leant against the sill. *Life doesn't stop everywhere else when something bad happens. It just soldiers on.*

<Maybe you should go to the war room,> Jen suggested. *<Greer and the others will be there. Your presence will help.>*

"You sure like to mother me," Sera said with a soft laugh as she ran a hand through her hair.

<Shoot, sorry, I—>

"It's OK," Sera interrupted Jen. "I didn't mean it like that. I said it without even thinking of Helen. That's progress, I guess, right?"

<I'd say so. I don't need to take Helen's place. I'm happy just to help you out as much as I can.>

"That you do, Jen, that you do."

Sera looked down at her body, surprised to see that her skin still bore the appearance of a blue shipsuit—her semi-official look. She'd found that lately, when she got lost in thought, her skin reverted to the deep red that she now considered to be her natural skin color.

It also tended to lose any of the 'adjustments' that made her not appear to be completely naked.

Sera chuckled at the memories of how she'd made Admiral Greer quite uncomfortable on several occasions when her skin had reverted while she was deep in thought in his presence.

As amusing as it was, losing control of her appearance was a tell, and Sera didn't like tells. Even though she was reasonably certain she could trust everyone on Keren Station, that didn't mean she wanted them to be able to read her state of mind so easily.

"OK, let's go see what the Admiralty thinks of the battle for Thebes."

She pushed herself off the window sill and walked toward the door where a pair of low boots waited. She slipped her feet into them and pulled a belt off a hook on the wall, wrapping it around her waist and holstering a sidearm.

Theoretically, she was in the safest place in the galaxy right now, but Sera had learned firsthand how well that theory held up.

She stepped out into the corridor, and nodded at the two members of her High Guard as they fell in behind her.

Another part of being president that I don't think will ever stop feeling weird.

The War Room was one level down in the administrative complex, and Sera arrived in only a few minutes to find Admiral Greer and his staff standing in the center of the room, arrayed around one of the larger holotanks.

"All-in-all quite the success, don't you think?" Sera said as she approached the group.

Greer turned toward Sera and gave a sharp nod. "They'll be talking of this one for centuries."

The woman next to Greer, Rear Admiral Svetlana, gave a rueful laugh. "Well, it was going to be talked about no matter what. The question was in what light? I'm glad that it now will be a positive one."

Sera agreed with Svetlana's assessment, and there were nods from the other admirals, generals, and colonels present.

"And we're ready to deploy gates to withdraw the fleets?" Sera asked.

Greer nodded. "We have ten ready to go, ma'am. I'd send more, but we don't have the ships to spare. We've already weakened Krissy's response forces greatly, and she had just begun a major bait operation."

"Not to mention how strapped the Spinward Front is," Sera added. "We need to work out how to reinforce them."

"Understood," Greer blew out a long breath. "Not sure who I'll rob for that. If the ISF would just share its tech so we could grow ships—"

Sera held up her hand to forestall the rest of Greer's statement. "You know Tanis won't budge on that."

Greer opened his mouth to respond, but Sera's narrowed eyes caused him to close it and nod.

"This civil war is strapping us at the worst possible time," Svetlana shifted the conversation. "We need to end it as soon as possible."

Greer gave Svetlana a sidelong look. "We'll save that for tomorrow's briefing on Operation Ringbreak. If we start on that topic now, it'll derail us from what we need to focus on today."

Sera looked down at the holotank, watching the view of the allied forces, the updates showing them sweeping through the Nietzschean ship formations, decimating them en masse.

The data was basic: colored pinpoints of light denoting ship types and alliances. Any more detail would stress the QuanComm network and burn out blades. At present, network degradation was a real concern. While the massive strike against the Nietzscheans in the Albany System was shaping up to be a decisive victory, it had burned through hundreds of paired blades.

Over fifty percent of the QuanComm blades had overheated, their rubidium cores losing entanglement with their counterparts many light years distant, a terminal effect that ended their 'spooky action at a distance'. Sera had sent requests to New Canaan for more, but knew they were already being manufactured at the fastest rate possible.

As frustrating as it was to rely on one star system for so many of their resources, Sera agreed with Tanis's logic on the matter. Their only real edge in this fight was the technological advantage from New Canaan.

But Tanis's people guarded their tech zealously—something proven by what they had been willing to do to win the Defense of Carthage. The safety of the process used to produce their ships was paramount. If the specs fell into Airthan or Orion hands, the war would be over in less than a year.

With a very unfavorable outcome.

"So what should we do to bolster the Spinward Front, sir, ma'am?" Svetlana asked. "You saw the latest updates from the 917th Fleet. They're commanded by a captain now, for star's sakes. He's abandoned an entire section of the front, falling back to Fortress Gibraltar. That opens up hundreds of light years to the OG."

"I think we need to punch Orion in the gut," Sera said as she pushed the battle around Pyra—which was turning into a rout of the Nietzscheans—to another holotank and brought up the Three Arms view of the galaxy. "We know from the strategic data Jessica brought from Orion Space that Orion has withdrawn almost all of their forces from the Perseus Expansion Districts. All that is left are small policing forces. We could dispatch a force or two to rampage through their territories."

One of the other admirals, a man named Mardus, nodded with a grim smile. "Xenophon and the ten thousand hoplites."

"Hopefully with less betrayal," Sera said with a chuckle. "But yes. If we send a core of cruisers equipped with stasis shields and light destroyers for fast attack missions, we could create one hell of a mess inside of Orion."

"Civilian targets?" Greer asked, his expression unreadable.

"No," Sera shook her head. "Just the opposite. We uplift them. From what Jessica shared, the Expansion Districts aren't even as advanced as half the Inner Stars. For all intents and purposes, those people live in squalor. We'll have to be smart about it; we can't obliterate their economies overnight, but we could make life a lot better for them."

"Do you think it will pull pressure off the Spinward Front?" Svetlana asked. "From where I stand, it looks like

Praetor Kirkland doesn't give a rat's ass about the Expansion Districts."

"And the Perseus Expansion Districts are much closer to the Anti-Spinward Front," Greer added.

Sera nodded as she stared at the map. Greer was right. Chances were that resources would be pulled from Orion's Anti-Spinward Front to deal with an incursion. She looked up at the admirals. "Well, I did say 'a force or two'. What if we sent one to…Costa—where *Sabrina* jumped out of Orion space—and the other to Herschel? We have enough data on that region from captured soldiers like Colonel Kent."

Greer highlighted Herschel on the map and then pointed at another star, eight hundred light years away. "Rega's pretty damn close to Herschel. Hitting them there will be more than a sabre-rattling. They'll come in hard to put down a force that deep in the OFA."

"You're right about that." Sera met Greer's eyes with cold certainty. "But if Rega sends forces to Herschel, they won't be sending them to the front. That may give us enough breathing room."

Greer grunted and looked back at the holo. "Stars, I wish Scipio would just finish with the Hegemony already. We could really use their help in the larger fight."

"Scipio has made inroads," one of the colonels reported. "But the Hegemony has turned their entire economy over to a war footing, including retrofitting many of their private merchant fleets. They have millions upon millions of ships, now."

"And here, Tanis just gave hundreds of ships to the Septhians," Svetlana shook her head. "President Sera, I volunteer to lead the expeditionary force to Herschel, but we'll need a fleet that can actually get the job done."

Sera nodded. “It'll have to be at least five hundred ships. A force large enough to take a system, but small enough that it can operate with less support.”

“I can work up the optimal configuration,” Svetlana replied with a crisp nod. “I have given extensive study to this sort of attack on Orion.”

Sera met the tall admiral's gaze, their eyes locked across the table. “Admiral Svetlana, you know that emergency extraction may not be possible. If things go sideways out there…”

“I understand the risks, President Sera. I'm willing to take them on. When I signed up, it wasn't to sit in a fortress and plot.”

Sera saw Greer blink, followed by a sidelong look at Svetlana. She wondered what he thought of the Rear Admiral spearheading an operation like that. Granted, assignments of personnel were his call, and she handed that responsibility to him.

“I'll abide by Admiral Greer's selections,” Sera said. “Which I imagine he'll want to mull over for a bit. Even if we do this, we still need to bolster the fronts. Stars knows Airtha's not doing a thing to help.”

The next two hours turned into a long session of examining force allotments and strategic defense positions—namely, seeking out positions they could abandon to free up fleets for the fronts.

Every option came with as many—and often more—cons than pros, but at the end of the session, they had selected three thousand ships that would bolster the fronts and form the two Orion space strike forces.

As they'd worked, the battle around Pyra had continued to progress, updates feeding to the secondary holo. By this point, most of the Nietzschean ships were either disabled, or in flight. Some might escape their pursuers, but the vast majority of the enemy armada was now little more than drifting hulls in the black.

Once the meeting had wrapped, Sera walked to the holotank to study the engagement she knew Tanis was now managing.

At the lower right was a list of allied ships lost, and casualty estimates.

It had not been a bloodless fight. Many of the allied ships did not possess stasis shields, and no small number had been lost—over five thousand, by the latest count.

Sera shook her head as she tried to wrap her mind around the sheer number of ships and people involved in the conflict that was spreading across the stars. *It has to be trillions of humans and AIs at this point.*

For all intents and purposes, those lives were on her. Well, her and Tanis. Without the *Intrepid*'s tech upsetting the balance of power, this war would not have come for some time.

She turned and nodded to Greer and Svetlana, who were still standing over the other holotank, likely discussing Svetlana's desire to lead the force into Orion space.

The admirals both gave her deferential nods in response, and Sera left the CIC, taking a right in the wide corridor, heading toward the commissary, her pair of guards still in tow.

Her destination lay three levels below, and Sera decided to take the stairs. She was skipping down the steps, when a door on the landing swung open, and she almost collided with a dark-haired woman in a pink dress.

"Oh, sorry!" the woman exclaimed, then her eyes turned to Sera's, and she gasped. "Madam President! Oh, shoot, I'm *really* sorry. I should have looked before I kicked the door open."

The woman's face looked familiar, and when her HUD gave her addressor's name, it was Sera's turn to be surprised. "Mary? Flaherty's Mary?"

She glanced back and lifted a hand, directing her guards to stand down.

"As much as I love to be identified by my father's name, yes," Mary said, then pursed her lips. "Sorry, I tend to bleed sarcasm sometimes."

"Sorry, I should know better," Sera ducked a nod. "I've lived in others' shadows long enough to know how much it sucks. It's very nice to meet you, Mary-who-only-happens-to-be-Flaherty's-daughter."

"And you as well, Sera-who-happens-to-be-President-of-the-Transcend." Mary offered her hand, and Sera shook it. "Where were you off to when I nearly knocked you down the stairs?"

"Lunch," Sera replied simply. "Too much strategizing with the brass makes me famished."

"To the Deck 87 Commissary?" Mary's brows rose. "I didn't know they let your type in there."

Sera nearly coughed in surprise. She'd grown accustomed to a certain amount of deference that Mary did not seem to possess. "My 'type'?"

"Yeah, high-uppity muckity mucks." Mary leant in and lowered her voice to a conspiratorial whisper. "The D87C is a workin' person's mess."

"I'm a working person," Sera said, her voice rising in pitch as she took a step back. "I used to be a pirate, you know."

Mary nodded. "Sure do. My father's told me all the stories. Mostly about all the se—dammit, I've gotten twice as familiar in half the time. Sorry, I'm still adjusting to all this. Forget my needling, I'm just hangry."

Sera was having a hard time reconciling Mary with Flaherty. The woman had spoken more in the last two minutes than Flaherty usually did in two days.

Maybe she's where all his words went.

Still, Mary was like a breath of fresh air, compared to the hours of serious conversations and days of worry over Tanis.

"Well," Sera gave Mary a mischievous wink. "Why don't you accompany me to the D87C? Maybe with you at my side, no one will notice that I'm an uppity muckity muck."

Mary lifted a finger. "*High*-uppity muckity muck."

"Right," Sera laughed. "High."

As they descended the final flight of stairs, Sera asked, "I must admit, I'm a bit surprised to find you here at Keren. Flaherty told me he'd gotten you off Airtha and sent you to some place in Sagittarius. He wouldn't even tell *me* where."

"Yeah, daddy knows best, right? He *tried* to send us packing, but he'd also let slip where he would be. So after convincing Leeroy to turn our ship around, we followed after."

"Leeroy?" Sera asked, as they walked out into the well-lit corridor that would lead them to the commissary.

"Yeah, my on-again, off-again ex. Currently we're on again, I think. My son, Drew, and Figgy, our dog are also here. Drew wants to enlist, but I'm trying to convince him to find work on Keren. I know that's not terribly patriotic, but he's the world to me, you know?"

Sera didn't know, not really. She was starting to think that she'd never have anyone who quite fit that bill. Elena might have, once; Tanis was incredibly important to her, but that was a different sort of relationship altogether.

Still, she said, "Yes."

"Leeroy is working on small ship repair, he's good at programming and managing bot teams—better than some NSAI, even. He knows when to cut corners to get a ship back out on time, and when those cut corners would lead to disaster…dammit, I'm rambling."

Sera chuckled, deciding to voice her prior thought. "I think I know where all of Flaherty's words went."

"I'm not normally this bad," Mary replied with a self-deprecating expression. "Just so much going on, then almost knocking you down…life's pretty topsy-turvy."

"You're telling me," Sera said, as they reached the doors to the Deck 87 Commissary.

She wasn't surprised to see two more of her High Guard already inside, eyes sweeping the gathered throng suspiciously.

"Dang, your shadows are everywhere," Mary commented.

Sera nodded. "Only place they don't follow me is into my bed at night."

Mary's eyes widened. "Even the san?"

"No, Mary," Sera chuckled. "I was exaggerating. They keep an eye on me with a fleet of drones—plus they have nanocloud tech. I guess Tanis really doesn't want me to kick it. She'd have to take control of the whole show, then."

The commissary was relatively empty, and the two women joined the line of three people waiting for their turn at the buffet.

One of the women in line turned and, upon seeing the president behind her, offered her spot.

"No, please," Sera raised her hand. "You were here first; my stomach isn't any more important than yours."

The woman flushed, but nodded silently as she turned and grabbed a tray.

"Scaring the locals?" a voice asked from behind them, and Sera turned to see Flaherty standing behind them.

"Stars, you're like a giant man-cat. How do you move so quietly?" Sera asked while Mary laughed.

Flaherty shrugged and glanced at Sera's feet. "I don't wear crazy boots like you do, makes it easy."

"Dad never did get fashion," Mary said with an apologetic shrug.

"Yeah, I was with him for some time," Sera replied, glaring at Flaherty. "I have a clear memory of certain comments."

Flaherty placed a hand on his chest and gave her a wounded look, before shaking his head and gesturing for the two women to move forward with the line.

"So what brings you down to D87C?" Sera asked, knowing the answer.

"You," Flaherty grunted.

"You know I have my High Guard now, right?" she asked, waving a hand in the direction of her shadows.

Flaherty nodded. "Good soldiers. But they're predictable, doing all the correct things at the correct times. I'm a bit harder to pin down."

"Are we actively in danger here?" Mary asked as she grabbed a bowl and ladled soup into it.

"Yes," Flaherty replied.

Sera placed a hand on Mary's shoulder. "Don't worry, he'd say that no matter where we were."

"Not true," Flaherty replied while grabbing a roll, then scooping a pile of leafy greens onto his plate. "There are safe places."

"Oh yeah?" Sera asked. "Where."

"Give me a minute. I'm sure I can think of one."

Mary chuckled and placed a sandwich on her tray, followed by a helping of chips and an apple. "There we are, everything a growing girl needs."

"Growing?" Sera asked.

"Well…no. Just seemed right at the time."

"You're not pregnant, are you?" Flaherty asked. "I like Leeroy…but I don't know if I like him *that* much."

Mary shook her head. "Dad, seriously, you sent us halfway across known space with him. You must trust him."

"A quarter."

"You trust him a quarter?" Sera asked, raising an eyebrow as she finished selecting her food and turned to look for a table.

"No, I sent Mary and Drew a quarter of the way across known space with Leeroy. Less, considering how far into the Perseus Arm the OFA has expanded."

"And the trust?" Mary asked, following Sera to a table a few meters away.

Flaherty grunted. "I trust him to keep you safe. Do I trust him enough to raise your next child?" He didn't bother answering his own question.

"At least you know he's honorable," Sera said as she sat.

"Maybe. Didn't take her where he was supposed to."

"Dad," Mary said flatly. "I'm a person, not cargo. I decide where I go. I wanted to be with you. I've spent most of my life wondering if you're even still alive, I'm not doing that again."

A spear of guilt struck Sera as she realized that it was Flaherty's promise to her that had taken him away from Mary for so many years. She'd known it intellectually, but seeing the impact it had made on this woman sitting across the table from her was a different thing entirely.

Flaherty looked as though he was going to make an argument, but he glanced at Sera and, upon seeing the look in her eyes, nodded to Mary.

"OK, you're right."

"What?" Mary asked. "I'm right? This is a red letter day, if ever there was one."

Sera chuckled. "Yeah, he doesn't dole that one out very often."

Sera took a bite of her sandwich, and a glob of sauce fell out and landed on her arm. She lifted it to her mouth and licked it off, noticing as she did that Mary was grinning.

"Oh, right," Sera chuckled. "Twenty years since I was a pirate, but I still haven't let go of the manners—or rather, lack thereof."

"It's OK," Mary shrugged. "I was more wondering about your outfit. I'm a bit partial to skinsheaths; they're nice and low maintenance. Where'd you get yours?"

Flaherty grunted. "Pirates."

Mary's eyes lit up. "Really?"

"No," Sera shook her head. "I got it from Bob, the *Intrepid*'s AI. Though it's not an outfit, it's my skin."

"But it doesn't look like a skin job. There are creases at your elbows, and it looks like your breasts are covered."

Sera grinned at Mary. "I'm protecting poor Flaherty here from having to gaze upon my naked body."

"Plus everyone else around here," Flaherty added.

"So it's a malleable sort of thing?" Mary asked.

"Yeah. Sort of. Flaherty was right in that I first got the skin job when I was on a pirate base, but it was killing me, so Bob got me an upgrade. He declared that human epidermises were subpar when it came to keeping their bodies safe and made something better for me."

Sera held up her hand, and it took on the appearance of a thick glove, and then of slender fingers—albeit without any creases or prints. She even changed it to something approximating a normal skin color.

"That's amazing!" Mary exclaimed. "I've never seen anything so…effortless. And that's on your whole body?"

Sera nodded. "It's also integrated with ISF Mark X Flow Armor, with moderate stealth capabilities. Not as good as the real stuff, but better than nothing."

As Sera spoke, her hand became invisible, and then she laid it on the table and grabbed her fork with her other hand, stabbing down with all her might.

The impact jostled everything on the table, but to Mary's visible amazement, the tines bent aside where they'd hit Sera's invisible hand.

"Stars burning in the core," Mary whispered, shaking her head. "Why does anyone have normal skin if they can get what you have?"

Sera glanced at Flaherty. "Why indeed. Do you want it, Mary?"

"Stars yeah, that would be amazing. I'd be wearing my entire wardrobe all the time *and* be bulletproof. What more could a girl want?"

"Flesh and blood?" Flaherty asked.

Mary waved a hand. "Nonsense. It's reversible, right?"

Sera's hand reappeared, and she held it in the air, wobbling it back and forth. "Ehhh…sorta. It's not easy to undo; you'd have to have your entire epidermal nervous system replaced and reconnected in the new skin. It's probably a few days' work."

Mary nodded. "Right, I figured as much. So how do you 'upgrade' my epidermis?"

Sera stroked her chin. "I'm not entirely certain. I did it once to someone in an elevator in a pinch, but that was back before I had the flow armor added in. It may need to be done more carefully. Why don't I look into it before I possibly eviscerate you?"

"That would be swell," Flaherty grunted.

Sera was about to show Mary some more things her skin could do, when Jen alerted her to an incoming message from the STC.

<*Put it through,*> Sera replied.

<President Sera,> the AI STC controller began. *<We've just received word that Governor Andrews of the New Canaan colony has arrived on an ISF cruiser. We have them on approach, and they're scheduled to dock in eighteen hours.>*

<Nothing about the nature of his visit?> Sera asked.

<No, ma'am.>

<Thank you.> Sera closed the connection, and then her eyes.

Jason Andrews.

She had seen him a few times in the months following the Defense of Carthage—brief encounters all, and always in larger settings. If he was coming here, it would be to meet specifically with her.

Sera opened her eyes and sighed. "Well, looks like an old flame has come for a visit."

"Jason?" Flaherty asked.

"How'd you know?"

Flaherty shrugged. "Not many of your old lovers are alive and not in prison. It's a short list."

Sera groaned and threw a piece of lettuce at him—which he caught and ate. "You're incorrigible."

"I'm truthful."

Mary shrugged. "He doesn't have much choice."

"Yeah, well, he's the one that opted for the alterations to ensure that," Sera replied.

Flaherty shook his head. "That would be an assumption, Madam President. You shouldn't make—ow! Sera, kicking your aides under the table is very unbecoming of a woman in your station."

Sera drew her foot back. "I'll do it again if you don't stop talking like that."

Flaherty raised his hands and gave her a rare smile. "Just making sure my girl is still in there. You're all Mrs. Serious Business these days."

"Your girl?" Mary arched an eyebrow.

Flaherty wrapped an arm around his daughter and gave her a quick embrace. "Don't worry, Mary. You're the good daughter in this scenario. Sera's the one that needs constant supervision. Be dead a hundred times without me around."

Sera flashed her own smile back at Flaherty. "Eighty-seven, by my count. You sure you can't lie?"

"I can use hyperbole when it's obvious."

Sera and Mary locked gazes, both shaking their heads.

"You OK sharing him with me?" Sera asked.

Mary snorted. "Honestly? I'm kinda glad he spends so much time mothering over you. If he slathered all of it on me, I think I'd suffocate."

Flaherty groaned and took a sip of his coffee as he glared at the two women over its rim. "This is why I never talk."

DAMON SILAS

STELLAR DATE: 08.28.8949 (Adjusted Years)
LOCATION: Meela Station, Churka
REGION: Gorham System, Vela Cluster, Transcend Interstellar Alliance

Roxy glanced around at the other six members of her strike team and did her best not to think about how long they'd been crowded together inside the cramped shipping container.

Her HUD wasn't so forgiving, and the moment she thought about how much time had passed since they'd entered the container, it flashed a helpful update: *sixty-seven hours.*

Roxy resisted the urge to groan, while silently cursing Justin for sending her on this mission.

Well, not for sending **me** *on the mission, more for not coming along,* she amended.

The six former Hand agents that surrounded her in the container were all skilled operatives, and all fiercely loyal to Justin. Two of them, Sam and Harry, had even broken him out of prison.

An act Roxy had been very grateful for, since Justin was the only one in the galaxy who had known where her stasis pod was.

Thoughts about Justin caused no small amount of mental turmoil for Roxy. She'd been with him for centuries and had once loved him deeply, but she no longer knew if that was the case.

The mere thought of questioning her adoration for Justin caused a wave of images and feelings to flow through her mind, reinforcements that were intended to cement her devotion to the man.

The man who turned me into a machine…

A feeling of surprise came over Roxy at the thought. That she was even able to consider her current state in the wake of the corrective imagery and emotion was surprising. Normally when the neural lace in her brain modified her thinking, it was impossible to do anything other than bask in her adoration of Justin.

But this time, she was still able to think critically.

He stole my body…made me into this thing.

Roxy looked down at herself, her sapphire skin gleaming even in the dim lights within the shipping container. Soon she'd don her combat armor and cover it, but Justin had instilled in her a compulsion to show off her skin whenever possible.

It was one of the delights he took—reminding her how he'd made her into both an elite assassin, and his favorite art display.

How dare he do this to—

Roxy's mind went blank, a feeling of euphoria overcoming her. The euphoria was linked to her thoughts and memories of Justin, and she basked in the drug-like haze, dreaming of the time spent with the man she loved, yearning to get back to him.

How long have we been in here, anyway? She wondered, and her HUD obliged with the answer: *sixty-seven hours.*

* * * * *

An hour later, Roxy reached behind her and activated the transceiver built into the shipping container's wall.

The container itself was heavily EM shielded to conceal the seven people within, but every few hours—on an irregular schedule—Roxy activated the device and listened for any news from their operative on the outside.

Thus far, the message had always been, 'Stay in position'.

That 'position', at least presently, was a cargo hold on Meela Station, in orbit of Churka, a small, terrestrial world in the Gorham System.

Justin had chosen Gorham because it was frequented by individual ships from Admiral Krissy's fleet. Sometimes they came in pairs, but half the time, only a single destroyer would enter Gorham—more often than not, escorting cargo convoys that were gathering supplies for the war effort.

If the TSF held to their current schedule, a convoy should already have come past Meela station—a facility they often stopped at for resupply—but thus far, none had arrived.

In another two days, the strike team would be out of supplies, and would need to exit the container regardless of whether or not their prey had come by.

And so, with more than a little anticipation, Roxy sent out her ping, waiting for the response to tell her to sit tight once more.

<*Omega Team, TSF destroyer* Damon Silas *inbound for resupply. Container to be transferred in one hundred ninety minutes. Will be external vacuum transfer. Prepare for zero-g and vacuum. End.*>

Roxy sent an acknowledgement blip, then disabled the transceiver. Before the transfer time, she'd reactivate it four more times on the pre-arranged schedule.

"OK, team," she kept her voice low and soft. "We're t-minus one-ninety-mikes. Our target is the *Damon Silas.* It's a Caparsi Class destroyer. We don't have the specifics of that particular ship in our databases, but it should conform to the standards. Review those, plus the common variances. We don't know our destination within the ship, but Caparsi destroyers only have two cargo bays capable of holding containers this size."

The team nodded. The four women and two men organized their equipment, their eyes appearing sharp and focused on their tasks, even while reviewing internal data.

Roxy approved of their abilities, Hand agents were the best of the best at hiding everything they did under layers and layers of misdirection. Whenever they appeared to be doing one thing, you could be certain they were up to something else.

She wondered if they were talking to one another about her over the Link. They'd spoken very little in general, but that was also normal for Hand agents. They spent the vast majority of their time operating on their own—often years of travel away from their handlers and any backup.

To have this many working together on one objective was almost unheard of.

But, for all intents and purposes, Hand agents were near-vanilla humans. They had to be, to blend in better on their operations in the Inner Stars—unless the job required them to get modded.

For a moment, Roxy wondered what would have happened if she'd entered the Hand while Director Sera was in charge. Sera was also known for her unconventional—at least, by Airthan standards—predilections, but she wasn't prone to modifying her own underlings for her pleasure.

Granted, Justin had kept Roxy hidden from the public eye—and disassociated from himself—so it was entirely possible that Sera had done the same to some poor soul.

To hear Andrea talk, one would think that Sera had orgies every night, and slept with every creature she laid eyes on.

Not that Andrea was innocent of such behaviors. Though she was more known for her general volatility, her appetites were not any great secret.

Standing slowly, Roxy ran a check on her limbs, moving them through their full range of motion, ensuring that she'd be at peak performance when the mission began.

"You really can twist about," Harry said, unabashedly watching her as she went through her routine. "You almost look like a candy cane, wrapped around yourself like that."

Roxy shrugged. "I suppose. When your body is almost entirely boneless, it's no great feat."

Harry nodded silently before picking up his pack and pulling out his stealth sheath. Once Roxy disentangled herself, she did the same, retrieving the SS-R4 model sheath and unsealing its front closure before stepping into it.

Unlike the organics in the container, hers didn't have the need for any biological hookups; she emitted no heat from breath, no bodily waste. She barely needed the SS-R4's ability to mask body IR, as she could lower her temperature to that of her surroundings with ease.

If Justin hadn't wanted to make me his little art display, and had instead chosen to give me more useful skin, I wouldn't need the stealth sheath at all.

The disdain—and hint of vehemence—behind her thought surprised Roxy. *How is it that I am able to think so critically of Justin?* Usually such thoughts were quelled.

She felt as though she'd been able to do it more often of late, though the realization dissipated in a moment, as images of working with Justin and partnering with him on this great endeavor filled her mind.

He's going to make an amazing leader for the Transcend.

Once in her SS-R4, Roxy proceeded to check over her weapons. The first was her lightwand, which she slid into a small pouch on her thigh. Following that, she added the four carbon-blade knives to their sheathes on her back. A handgun with a fold-in grip went into the pouch on her left thigh, followed by ammunition packs on her chest and the small of her back.

Finally, Roxy lifted her rifle out of the bag. It was a stealth-capable, multifunction weapon with three firing modes. The first was the standard pulse mode—one she rarely used—followed by flechettes and kinetic slugs.

The flechettes were Roxy's favorite. She didn't know why, she just felt they suited her more. It could be that she had favored them in the time before Justin had saved her...or maybe she'd picked it up afterward; she really wasn't sure.

The next three hours were spent analyzing ideal routes to take the ship. The team was in unanimous agreement that there would be an AI running the *Damon Silas,* and disabling it would be the top priority.

Harry was reasonably certain he had a breach technique that could get him into the ship's security systems, but it was based on an old set of command-override keys that they couldn't count on. If that override didn't work, they'd have little time to effect their seizure of the ship; if Justin's intel was correct, only seconds once they were detected. For that reason, they decided not to use the breach unless absolutely necessary, or until the AI was offline.

"I'm on the AI," Roxy said. "Lloyd, you're with me. Harry, you take your team to Engineering; Sam, you're to take the forward weapons control node. Once we have that, we can get the ship the hell out of this system. It's critical that we get control of the stasis shields—once everyone realizes that their ship is going for a ride, we're going to become the target of every weapon in this system."

Harry grunted, shaking his head. "Those are going to be a long four AU to the jump point."

"Justin will be ready," Roxy said with calm assurance.

"Better be," Lloyd said while cleaning the charge pod socket for his rifle. "If he's not, we'll get to find out firsthand how much firepower these stasis shields can shed."

Several minutes later, they felt the cargo container lift off the deck and begin to move. While it *should* be airtight, no one wanted to find out they were wrong the hard way, so the team pulled on their helmets.

Roxy activated her EM suppression suite, just in case the ship ran an active scan against the container before allowing it entry.

The container shifted a few times, and then left the station's artificial gravity field. It changed vector twice over the next fifteen minutes, then gravity returned, and the team gently settled back down to the bottom of the container.

They took up their assigned positions within the small space, weapons covering the double doors at each end. If the ship decided to perform an inspection, they'd have to kill the inspector and get out of the container in seconds. No one wanted to die in the killbox if they could avoid it.

Minutes passed with no activity other than the slight vibrations caused by other cargo settling onto the deck. After twenty minutes, the vibrations stopped, and Roxy crept to the doors and placed her hand on the seal, slipping a nano filament through.

Once it was in place, the team got a view of a dimly lit cargo bay. From what they could see, it appeared to be Bay 9A, the one closest to engineering.

The filament deployed drones that worked their way up the surface of the container. Roxy held her breath—which didn't matter, since she didn't need to breathe. But this was the moment of truth. They had two egress points on the sides of the containers, but they could be blocked by other cargo. If that was the case, their only exit would be the doors on either end, and opening those would be hard to hide from internal surveillance systems.

The drones finally reached the top, and the team got a full picture of the bay. It was nearly full, supplies of all shapes and sizes stacked on racks and atop cargo containers. The overabundance was great for blocking surveillance, but bad for their exit.

Then Roxy's fears were quelled, and she finally exhaled. The secret opening on the right side of the container was only partially blocked. Even better, the crates sitting next to it would obscure the team's exit.

She nodded to Sam, who unlatched the section of the container's side and pulled it free. A holofield shimmered into view, masking the opening and the team that was about to pass through.

From this point on, they were EM silent. The team confirmed the countdowns on their timers, and then Roxy slipped out first. Careful to walk softly—SS-R4 could only mask so much—she worked her way over a stack of crates and down to the central aisle that ran through the bay.

By some stroke of luck, the door into the corridor was wide open; Roxy was about to thank the stars, when a woman approached, stopping in the doorway. She pulled out a tablet, likely to do a visual inspection, then stopped and turned to speak with someone in the passageway beyond.

Shit, Roxy cursed as she approached the woman, a CWO by her insignia. There was just enough room for her to slip past the TSF chief, so long as the woman didn't move back any further.

Roxy slowed her movements, all but pressing herself against the bay's doorframe as she slipped past the chief. When she was directly behind her, Roxy considered just killing the annoyance. She knew it would be a terrible idea when it came to stealth, but it was enticing nonetheless. Of course, then she'd have to kill the man in the corridor that the chief was talking to as well. Someone would probably notice the blood and bodies.

What a shame.

A small part of Roxy wondered if she had always been so bloodthirsty. She couldn't remember her younger years, before Justin had molded her into his creature, but she couldn't imagine she'd always defaulted to killing any annoyance. It seemed illogical.

A moment later, she was past the woman, and standing in the corridor. Her goal, the ship's AI, was closest, but she was in no rush to reach it. Roxy decided to wait and ensure that the rest of the team was able to sneak past the chatty chief before continuing on.

After two minutes, she picked up the 'all clear' ticks on the team's pre-determined frequencies, and nodded with satisfaction.

They were past the first hurdle. If all went well, the *Damon Silas* would be theirs within thirty minutes. She moved down the corridor, hoping that Lloyd was following behind. It was tricky to move invisibly through a ship with another person. Your chance of bumping into your companion was almost greater than running into the enemy.

For that reason, they'd agreed that she would start on the route to the AI's node chamber thirty seconds before Lloyd. She'd ensured that the other teams had set their travel order and wait points as well.

They hadn't given her any trouble regarding that directive. Given that Hand agents almost always worked solo, these six were admirably good at coordinating with one another.

Four minutes later, Roxy was standing on the right side of the door leading into the ship AI's node chamber. A soft tap on the bulkhead next to her head informed her that Lloyd was in position, and she drew in a slow breath.

Why do I keep doing that? I don't recall concentrating on my breathing so much on prior missions.

Roxy's ability to breathe was just for show, something to make her seem more human—which was odd, considering she didn't even look human. *Another contradiction Justin built into me.*

She pushed the thoughts away and cleared her mind. They had to wait another six minutes for the clock to count down to zero. Once it did, all teams would begin their breaches.

A pair of ensigns turned into the corridor, approaching Roxy and Lloyd's position. As they drew close, Roxy pressed herself flat against the bulkhead, careful to avoid the swinging arms of the young man on the right.

For a moment, there was a fleeting worry in her mind, a concern over the fact that they were going to kill the TSF crew. *After all, aren't they fighting for the Transcend too?* Sure, these people were fighting against Airtha and her evil ways, but they didn't even know that Justin's faction existed. If they knew, maybe they'd do the right thing and join him.

Just as quickly as the thought came into her mind, it left, the feelings of certainty that Justin was doing the right thing crowding it out.

Roxy set her jaw and gave a resolute nod. *We are on the right side of this.*

Two minutes later, a lieutenant strolled down the corridor and stopped in front of the entrance to the AI's node chamber. He placed his palm on the door control, passing secure tokens, and then stood back as it slid aside.

Roxy's first reaction was to worry, but then she realized that this was the perfect way in. Even if she did have to kill the lieutenant—Clancy, by his name tag—she could do it at the same time that she took out the AI.

It would save her at least thirty seconds of breach time on the door.

Without further thought, she slipped into the room, just as the door closed behind Lieutenant Clancy—glad that Lloyd hadn't tried to enter as well.

The node chamber was a standard affair, small, with a rack of equipment on one side, and the SAI's titanium cylinder in the center, data cables linked into it in several places.

"Afternoon, Carmen," the lieutenant said as he pulled up a holodisplay. "How is everything with you today?"

"Right as rain, Lieutenant Clancy," Carmen replied audibly.

Roxy found it odd that the human and AI were conversing audibly, but as they bantered, the exchange almost seemed to be performed by rote.

"Another day, another supply run babysitting job," Clancy said as he flipped through diagnostic reports, marking each off as 'reviewed and approved' at the source terminal.

"I'd rather be on a milk run like this than out at the front," Carmen replied, the AI's voice carrying a soft laugh.

"You always say that," Clancy replied, glancing up at the titanium cylinder. "But you know that these 'milk runs' are bait. We're trying to suck the Airthans and any separatists into attacking us. It's why we have the stasis shields."

"And that's why I volunteered for this placement," Carmen replied. "Not because we're a juicy target, but because of the shields. Plus, if anyone hits us, the cavalry comes running and crushes them."

Roxy's blood pressure rose as she listened to the pair talk.

Bait ship? Cavalry? No wonder this ship is out here all alone! And we've gobbled up the worm. Hook, line and sinker.

She considered her options as the pair continued their conversation. If she aborted the mission, there was little chance her team would make it off the *Damon Silas* alive.

The only real option was to move forward. Based on the way Carmen and Clancy were talking, no one expected an attack to come from within, which meant that once they secured the ship, its stasis shields would make it the safest place to be in the Gorham System.

Her real concern was for Justin's fleet, which would jump in to escort the prize out. If the *Damon Silas* really was bait, and the 'cavalry' was coming, then he was going to be in one heck of a fight.

There was nothing for it. He would be in the dark layer now, and there was no way to warn him that the TSF destroyer was a trap.

As the clock wound down, the lieutenant closed out the terminal he was using and approached the AI's cylinder.

"Ready for your weekly checkup?" he asked as the access panel on the cylinder slid open.

"Just keep the rectal thermometer to yourself," the AI replied in a mock-serious tone.

"I can't believe people used to do shit like that."

Carmen groaned. "Wow, really ratchetting it up in the bad pun department, there."

"I learned from the best."

The timer on Roxy's HUD transitioned from white to red as it crossed over the ten-second mark. She crept up behind Lieutenant Clancy and, carefully reaching down for her gun with her left hand, stilled her breathing and prepared for what was to come.

3…2…1…MARK.

In one, fluid motion, Roxy drew her pistol, placed it against the base of the lieutenant's skull, and fired.

Brains and gore exploded from the bottom of his skull, covering Roxy in the man's grey matter and mental mods. For a moment, she stared in horror at the mess dripping off her hand, then realization dawned on her: the man must have had a reinforced skull…instead of the shot bursting out through his forehead, it all came back out the hole she'd made.

Roxy shook her head as the body before her fell to the ground, revealing the AI's tesseract-shaped cube within the cylinder.

The access panel began to slide shut, but Roxy was faster and, in an instant, she tore the AI's core free and threw it to the ground.

She raised her dripping pistol and aimed it at the AI's core. Without a second thought, Roxy pulled the trigger, only to see a message show on her HUD informing her that the gun's firing chamber was jammed—with Clancy's brains, no doubt.

"Dammit," she muttered, and reached for her lightwand just as an alarm blared across the ship.

"Well, I guess you all know what's happening now," she muttered.

With a flick of her wrist, the lightwand came to life, and Roxy knelt down, ready to slice the AI core in half, when Carmen's voice emanated from it.

"*Wait!* I don't want to die!"

"Nothing for it," Roxy replied as she raised her hand to strike.

"You're going to die too! All of us will." The AI's voice was pleading, and something in it stayed Roxy's hand.

"What do you mean?"

"This is a stasis ship, did you know that?"

A rueful laugh escaped Roxy's lips. "Know it? We're counting on it."

"All stasis ships have countermeasures to ensure that they're never captured. With me offline, and your team—I assume you have a team—attacking the ship, you can bet that Captain John has already armed it."

"*Fuck!*" Roxy swore. "So we go through all this, and the ship blows?"

"I can stop it," Carmen said, her words coming so fast, Roxy could barely parse them. "I can kill the sequence, but I have to do it fast."

Roxy lowered her wand. "OK, so do it."

"No." The AI's single word was laced with defiance.

"No?"

"You're a cold-blooded *murderer*." Carmen all but shouted the accusation from her thirty-centimeter cube. "You'll kill me once I do. I want you to get me off the ship in an escape pod."

"No. There's no way you can disable the sequence from an escape pod. You'll need privileged access." The AI didn't respond, and Roxy rocked back on her heels. "Seems we're at an impasse. But if we want to live, we'll have to work something out. I'm Roxy, by the way."

"Put me in a hard case and take me to Bay 13C. The device is in there. I'll disable it, and then I'm going to have to trust you to stick to your end of the bargain."

Roxy considered her options for a moment before nodding.

"OK, I'll do it. You have my word I won't kill you."

"And the rest of your team. Do you speak for them?" Carmen pressed.

"They won't kill you, either."

"And you'll not do something that directly or indirectly causes me to die?"

"Shit, Carmen, I have no idea, I'm about to get in a firefight. Chances are your case is gonna get a hole blown in it, then we all die. For that matter, how will I know that you're not going to tell everyone on the ship where I am?"

"You're covered in Clancy's insides. The ship's internal cameras are going to spot you just fine."

"Good point. So, do we have a deal?"

The AI didn't respond for a moment, then made a sound like a groan. "I guess that'll have to do. The hard case is just above you."

Roxy spotted the standard-issue TSF AI case on the rack, and pulled it off, fitting the AI's core in place before pulling up the case's specs. She located the wireless transmitter, and drove her lightwand into it.

"Just to make sure we're on the up and up," Roxy said.

"Asshole," the AI shot back.

Roxy chuckled as she closed the case, and opened the door to see the muzzle flash from Lloyd's rifle as he fired down the corridor.

"Nice of you to come out and join the fun; got a bit messy in there, I see." The man's tone was dour. "We on to the bridge, then?"

"Change of plans, there's a self-destruct in Bay 13C that we have to take out. It's not far from here. On the ship's central axis."

"Self-destruct? TSF has gotten crazy since I served."

Roxy hadn't known Lloyd was former military—not that it surprised her. Many of the Hand agents were recruited from the TSF's special forces.

"It's because of the stasis shields. I guess they really don't want it to fall into enemy hands." As Roxy spoke, she unslung her rifle and added her shots to Lloyd's, pushing the soldiers he was engaging with back into cover. "C'mon, we only have a few minutes!"

The pair fell back down the corridor, moving from cover to cover, when suddenly the enemy fire ceased.

"What the?" Roxy said, checking through her drone feeds. "They're falling back."

"Well, the ship *is* going to blow," Lloyd said with a shrug.

The pair moved quickly through the final sixty meters to their target, and Roxy breached the door while Lloyd stood guard in the passageway once more.

Bay 13C was small, little more than a storage room on the map. But it's purpose had clearly changed. The first thing Roxy saw upon entering the room was an antimatter bottle standing on a pedestal in the middle of the room.

An array of SC batteries were positioned around it, and a shimmering shield enveloped them all.

"Stasis?" Roxy asked as she opened Carmen's case.

"Yeah, plug me in on that console over there, I need direct access."

Roxy complied, wondering how the field would respond if it contacted a physical object. Once she'd set Carmen onto the console—hoping the AI would live up to her word—she turned back to the stasis shield around the antimatter.

Casting about for something to prod it with, she found a sheet of plas, and rolled it up.

"Don't!" Carmen cried out just as Roxy reached forward and touched the plas to the field.

As Carmen's shout reverberated through the room, there was a brilliant flash, and half the plas ceased to exist.

"What the fuck?" Roxy exclaimed.

"Don't *do* that! You trying to kill us?"

"I didn't think it would—"

"How about you *don't* perform half-assed experiments to see what happens when you push a bunch of atoms against a field of zero-energy matter, OK?"

Roxy nodded as she looked at the half sheet of plas in her hand. "Why doesn't the air do that?"

"There's a light grav field keeping the air molecules off the stasis shield. But it's not strong enough to resist determined idiots."

Roxy eyed the device in the room with a newfound level of respect. "And they just leave this thing in here?"

"Normally, only highly trained specialists come in here, not fools like you."

"I'm not—"

"Shut up! Seconds here."

The gravity of their situation hit Roxy once more, and she clamped her mouth shut. Seconds later, the shimmering stasis shield disappeared, and then a light at the bottom of the antimatter bottle turned from red to green.

"How long did we have?" Roxy was momentarily surprised at her own morbid curiosity.

"Don't ask. So, what now? You going to put me into a pod like you promised?"

Roxy turned her attention to the AI sitting atop the console. She knew what Justin would want; he'd tell her to kill the thing. It was too risky to set free, and too dangerous to keep around.

But Carmen had put her life on the line to save Roxy—granted, she didn't have much of a choice, since it was her only chance to live.

"I'll do my best, but I can't get to a pod right now. I'm going to put you in a stealth pouch so no one on the team sees you—but you'll need to kill your EM to stay hidden."

"Roxy—"

"It's the best I can do. Shut down."

"Give me your word you're not going to kill me," Carmen said, her tone almost pleading—if an AI could even do such a thing.

"I already did."

"Humor me." Now Carmen really *did* sound like she was pleading.

"I promise," Roxy said.

The AI seemed to accept it, as her core went dark a moment later.

As Roxy pulled a stealth pouch out of her SS-R4, a strange sensation came over her. This being had placed her life in Roxy's hands. She was trusting a person who had just stormed her ship to keep her alive.

Roxy determined that she would do as she'd promised. She would keep Carmen safe, but she would *not* put her in an escape pod. She was going to keep the AI safe with her.

The thought of hiding something from Justin never fully formed in her mind, but Roxy skirted around the edges of it, careful to keep the idea from being suppressed. For it had occurred to her that perhaps this AI could work out a way to free her from the mental prison she was in.

And then she'd kill Justin.

FAILURE

STELLAR DATE: 08.29.8949 (Adjusted Years)
LOCATION: TSS *Regent Mary*, Interstellar Space
REGION: Near Vela Cluster, Transcend Interstellar Alliance

Krissy bent over the holotable in the *Regent Mary*'s CIC, staring incredulously at the display before her.

She wanted to scream, slam her fists into the table, and beat some inanimate object to bits—or better yet, find Justin and kill him with her bare hands.

Instead, Krissy took a deep breath and closed her eyes.

"OK, Colonel Kysha, walk me through this again. The *Damon Silas* came into the Gorham System a day late, but made good time with its convoy to Meela Station."

Colonel Kysha swallowed before replying, clearly able to sense Krissy's ire. "That is correct, Admiral Krissy. As best we can surmise, Justin's strike team got onto the *Damon Silas* during its resupply. The *Silas* had just sent over four shuttles of people on shore leave, so when Justin's Hand agents hit the vessel, it was lightly crewed."

"That's a policy we'll have to change," Krissy muttered. "We're not joyriding through space, we're running missions."

"The crew of the *Damon Silas* had been nine months without shore leave…it was thought the Gorham System was secure—"

"*Khardine* is secure," Krissy cut the colonel off. "We need to resend the orders directing captains to transfer there for shore leave during any refit. We're in the middle of a fucking war for stars' sakes!"

"Yes, Admiral." Kysha nodded quickly. "I'll see that it's done."

"So, do we have any intel on why the ship didn't blow? Captain John got a message off that he had initiated the self-destruct."

"That is correct, ma'am. In the time given, only the captain or the ship's AI could have disabled the self-destruct."

"Which means one of them was compromised," Krissy mused.

"An analyst team is trying to determine if any other possibility can fit the known facts, but that is our current working hypothesis." Kysha paused, and when Krissy didn't ask any further questions, she noted the *Damon Silas*'s location on the holotable. "At 18:24 local time, the attackers had full control of the ship. They activated the stasis shields and boosted away from Meela Station."

"And there was nothing the locals could do about it," Krissy added.

"No, they tried firing up the ship's engine wash, but once the enemy understood what was going on, they changed vector to keep their engines oriented away from any pursuers with enough firepower to punch through the wash."

Kysha set the holotable to a new time: 21:39 the same day, and pointed to a location at the edge of the system.

"At this point, a fleet of four hundred ships jumped in here. These are all ships belonging to a variety of systems near the border with the Inner Stars. Each of them had declared as independent from us or Airtha. Either they have surreptitiously sided with Justin's faction, or they had defectors who did."

"Something we'll need to investigate," Krissy said while rolling her shoulders. "Just another task on the 'Keep the Transcend from Disintegrating' list."

Kysha pursed her lips. "Shall I see to sending scout ships to those systems?"

"No. Well…not all. We don't have the resources for that. Pick a random sampling. We'll see what we can learn."

"Understood." Kysha advanced the clock to 23:14. "Here is where our ships jumped in. As you know, this couldn't have happened at a worse time. With the bulk of our response fleet in the Albany System fighting the Nietzscheans, and two other bait traps sprung, we could only send thirty-seven ships to help the *Damon Silas.* They harried it and damaged one of its engines, but more than half of our ships had no stasis shields. Once Justin's fleet came into range, they had to disengage—especially since his people aboard the *Silas* advised them of the engine wash trick."

"Fucking stars," Krissy muttered. "Well, we have to consider *that* secret out in the wild, now. So, from there, the rest of the story is pretty much 'they got away,' right?"

Kysha blew out a long breath. "Yes, ma'am. The *Damon Silas* jumped ten minutes ago. The bulk of Justin's fleet hit the system at over 0.8*c*. They pushed our pursuit ships back as they blew past them, then continued on an outsystem vector for a jump point clear across the system.

"The locals are harrying them, picking off a few ships here and there. He'd also sent in an escort fleet at a lower *v*. They took some losses, but they've all jumped out with the *Silas*."

Krissy pushed herself away from the holotable and turned, running a hand through her hair. "Well, looks like I need to prepare a report for Sera. I don't envy her having to tell Tanis that we just lost a stasis shield ship."

She glanced back to see Kysha swallow again. "Yes, ma'am."

A long, calming breath later, Krissy turned back to the table. "Hemdar, can you prepare the report for Sera?"

<Already on it, Admiral,> Hemdar replied. *<You'll have it in a minute. I'm just waiting on finalized assessments from the analyst*

teams about the likelihood of Justin reverse engineering the stasis tech.>

Krissy was more than a little interested in that answer. "Which way are they leaning?"

<Toward 'slim to none'. Though having a stasis ship is a big advantage for him. But if he's in league with Airtha…>

Hemdar let the words hang. They all knew what the outcome would be, there. Airtha stood a much better chance of reverse engineering the stasis shield systems. Not only that, but stasis shields used picotech. She'd get both.

Krissy wondered—not for the first time—how one scientist from five thousand years ago had cracked picotech, and then come up with stasis shields, while no one else had come close on either. What made Earnest Redding so special that he found not one, but *two* holy grails?

There were rumors that there must have been some ascended AI influence, but Krissy wasn't so sure about that. If ascended AIs had that level of tech, why didn't *they* use it?

Maybe they have something better, Krissy mused. *Stars…now* ***that's*** *a terrifying thought.*

"OK, well, include that in the report. It's not as though we haven't considered this possibility," Krissy said. "Now, what we need to focus on is getting our fleets back from Albany as quickly as we can. There are too many bait ships hanging out in the wind."

"Yes, Admiral," Kysha grimaced. "Ever since we jumped the fleets out to Thebes, I've had this twitch in my left arm. We have sixty gates disassembled and ready for transport the moment we get the word that it's safe to send them to Albany. It will take us four hours to get our ten-thousand ships back in the Transcend, ready for deployment."

"Ours first?" Krissy asked, pulling up the dispersal plans for the allied fleet in Albany. "I'm surprised that Greer didn't push to have his pulled back first. I wouldn't blame him; we don't want Khardine unguarded."

"Admiral Sanderson has forty-four hundred ISF ships ready to jump out of New Canaan if Khardine falls under attack."

Krissy whistled, surprised to hear that. Officially, New Canaan would not let their home fleet fall below ten-thousand ships. It would seem they understood the importance of keeping the Khardine capital secure.

As Krissy spoke with Hemdar, Kysha set the latest status from the Albany System on the holotable. It showed the remaining Nietzschean ships in a full rout, but a terrific mess had been left behind. The S&R operations were going to take some weeks. It appeared that Tanis was establishing a secure staging ground near an inner planet named Buffalo, and that was where the gates were to be set up.

"Looks like they expect to have Buffalo secured in ten hours," Krissy said, then pursed her lips, praying nothing happened before then that would require anything more than her reserve forces. Her thoughts turned back to the mess with Justin.

Anything ***more****, that is.*

"Let me know the minute they're ready to ship the gates," Krissy said as she turned to leave the room. "I'm going to send that report to Sera, and then wait to see if she wants to discuss it in person."

"Understood, Admiral Krissy," Kysha replied. "I'll see to it that scout ships are dispatched within the hour to begin reconnaissance on the systems that may be supporting Justin."

"Very good, Colonel," Krissy replied, as she walked out of the CIC in search of a strong cup of coffee before sending the report to Sera.

Maybe a whole pot.

TRUTH AND REALITY

STELLAR DATE: 08.29.8949 (Adjusted Years)
LOCATION: Node 1, ISS *I2*
REGION: Pyra, Albany System, Thebes, Septhian Alliance

Tanis stepped through the node chamber's doors and strode toward the railing that ran around the catwalk. Behind her, the door locked and sealed.

Not to keep her in, but to keep any intrusions at bay.

In front of her was Bob's primary node, a ten meter cube hanging in the center of the chamber. Conduits carrying Bob's lifeblood—power and data—connected to the node in a dozen places. Cooling systems ringed it, and light glowed from deep within the multi-layered cube.

<*You came to speak with me 'in person',*> Bob said, his voice carrying no inflection that Tanis could hear.

But she didn't need to *hear* Bob to gain insight into his thoughts. She could see them. It was why they'd come to his node to have this conversation.

"Do you remember the last time we were here?" Tanis asked. "You, Angela, and I?"

<*Of course I do,*> Bob replied. <*You came here after I woke you from stasis at Estrella de la Muerte. You saved the ship.*>

<**We** *saved the ship,*> Angela corrected the multinodal AI.

<*It is the same thing when referring to the two of you,*> Bob replied, his tone nonchalant, almost dismissive. <*Even then, the distinctions between you were diminishing.*>

Tanis nodded, working to remain sanguine about the situation. "Because of what you did to us."

<*Are you accusing me, or thanking me?*> Bob asked.

The question hit Tanis like an atom beam, shredding the arguments and accusations she was about to make, the blame she was prepared to lay at Bob's feet.

<*Shit, he's got us there,*> Angela said privately.

Tanis nodded absently as she stared at Bob's mind. It was unlike any other human or AI mind she'd seen. She thought it would be like most minds, only deeper—like an onion with layers upon layers of thought. But that analogy failed utterly. If Bob's mind was an onion, it was a galaxy of onions that became larger—not smaller—the further you went in.

Over the day since her rescue, Tanis and Angela had learned how to interpret the surface thoughts of others the same way they could read expressions on a human's face.

They could even do it with AIs, watching their *n*-level matrices of thought and emotion shift and change in response to stimuli.

But not so with Bob.

His mind was so vast, so far-reaching, that it was impossible to determine what aspect of him was responding to the words she'd uttered. Or even to interpret his mental responses at all.

<*Even if we were fully ascended, I don't think we'd be more than a mote next to him,*> Tanis replied. <*Do you think he sees our mind?*>

<*Yes,*> Angela admitted after a moment's pause. <*I think he has for some time.*>

<*Why do you think separately?*> Bob asked. <*You became one. I know this; Priscilla shared it with me, and I saw it in the mind of Rika.*>

"At least we're back on track," Tanis said as she lifted one leg over the railing, followed by the other, to sit on top with her feet hooked behind the middle bar.

Despite her unconventional perch, she couldn't shake the feeling that she was supplicating herself before some ancient deity, seeking wisdom and guidance.

Angela's laugh wreathed her thoughts. <*You can't shake that feeling because **I'm** thinking it.*>

No one spoke for a moment, then Angela replied to Bob's question. <*We think separately because of what Priscilla gave us to stabilize our form, to keep us from moving beyond this physical body.*>

"Which you seemed prepared for." Tanis worked to control her emotions, to hold back the accusations that wanted to burst free from her. She could sense them in Angela as well, and they shared a feeling of calm and control before Tanis continued.

"You knew there was a risk that we'd ascend in a situation like what happed on Pyra, you didn't just whip up the subatomic stabilization that Priscilla provided. Did you know what would happen down there, Bob? Brandt *died* down there. She's gone, and I'm going to have to face her daughter someday and tell her about her mother's final moments! Do you know what that's like?"

Tanis's tone was strident; she wasn't yelling, but she really wanted to.

<*I didn't know Brandt would die. I didn't expect the Nietzscheans to bring so many ships.*>

<*The fuck, Bob!*> Angela exclaimed. <*You **knew** the Niets would attack?*>

<*It was in your own analyst's reports. They didn't expect a fleet this size either, and their probability of attack was very, very low. Mine was higher, but I got it wrong too. I'm neither omniscient, nor omnipresent. You both understand that better than anyone. Your involvement makes it even harder to predict.*>

Tanis resisted letting out a groan. "So we're back to my 'luck' again, are we? There's no mystical power controlling my destiny, Bob. From what I can see, it's just a bunch of AIs who think they know better than everyone else—except they don't seem to know anything at all."

<*You raise good points, Tanis. I will do my best to address them,*> Bob replied, his tone even, carrying no rancor after Tanis's accusation.

<*The floor is yours.*> Angela's tone, on the other hand, was sardonic in the extreme.

<*Some of this you know, Tanis-Angela, but some of it you do not. However, perhaps you need a reminder. Firstly 'luck' is just a convenient term for your condition. What you really do is alter probability on a quantum level. Because my advanced predictive algorithms must take* ***everything*** *into account, your presence skews the results. Even after studying you for centuries, I still do not know how you do it—though the information that Katrina has provided us leads me to believe that you were* ***made*** *to be this way, a suspicion I have harbored for some time.*>

Tanis opened her mouth to respond, but then closed it. She wanted to hear Bob out. Her emotions—and the outburst they were bound to cause—would only get in the way of this discourse.

<*However,*> Bob continued, <*I have also suspected that you operated in such a fashion that caused you to be so unpredictable—and too difficult for those who altered your base physiology to control—that they tried to do away with you. Several of your exploits in your youth point to this, events such as your assignation of the Toro mission.*

<*Again, these are not fully formed beliefs, they are based on suppositions I have made after considering what Joe learned from Katrina and the Xavia remnant. I* ***do*** *know that* ***I*** *brought you into my fold deliberately, though I don't know if all of my actions were of my own volition at that point. I was young, and it was possible that I was influenced to help you.*

<*Regardless of these things, I identified your 'luck'—as we shall call it for lack of a more concise term—and began to attempt to map it. Around the same time, Earnest alerted me to the fact that your minds had become inextricably linked, that we would never be able to separate you, and that you would, before long, die.*>

"Die?" Tanis couldn't help but interrupt. "When did you come to that realization?"

<*Before we left Estrella de la Muerte. At that point, you had five or six years before you went insane, shortly after which you would have died.*>

<*I never knew it was so…real and present,*> Angela said.

<*We hid it from you,*> Bob's tone was matter-of-fact. <*We had to. Earnest and I pored over myriad solutions in an attempt to save you. One thing we determined early on was that with your luck in the mix, the less you knew about what we were doing, the less likely you were to inadvertently affect it.*

<*Our first step was to stabilize your minds. That was a long, slow process, one that took us nearly fifty years to do. Something about the way you two became interlinked after you fought off those STR attack craft in the Sol System made your mind very resilient to any sort of influence we tried to effect.*>

"Probably because Angela is so stubborn," Tanis muttered.

<*Seriously? Me, I'm not the stubborn one. You realize* **this** *is why he kept us out of stasis during the journey to Kapteyn's Star.*>

"Bob? Really?"

<*Partially, yes. I was also trusting in your undeniably efficient ability for self-preservation to protect us all.*>

Tanis had to admit to herself that what Bob was saying was truly fascinating. Though it was taking some effort to divorce herself from the anger caused by the knowledge that he had altered her brain—her *mind*—without her knowing, and had been doing it for nearly the entire duration of their friendship.

She understood that it had saved her life, but the secrecy was still difficult to accept. Alongside that, the issue she had with Bob's theory was that he believed she unpredictably altered the fabric of the universe at a quantum level.

"Bob, hold onto that, because I think I see where you're going, but I want you to explain it. I want to understand *how* we alter quantum-level probabilities. How did you ever come up with that idea, and how did you test the theory?"

Bob laughed, a thundering wave of rueful humor rolling over Tanis. <*Well, for starters, I have the capability to think* ***a lot*** *and, not only that, I had a lot of time to do it. However, my realization began with photons.*>

<*Good place to start,*> Angela commented.

<*After you began to merge—though before we revealed it to you—Earnest had to make several upgrades to your neurological modifications to deal with how you and Angela kept bleeding through them and into one another. A particularly tricky issue was your vision. As you know, because of the military nature of your upgrades, Angela has always had full access to your vision. She sees through your eyes when she wishes to—which is frequently, I might add—and as a result, your optic nerve feeds directly to both of your brains.*

<*I say 'nerve' though your entire optic system is more inorganic than organic. Regardless, it does have an organic housing. As you well know, this is a neurological data interface that is usually heavily buffered. Should an AI choose to backdoor into a human's mind through their optic nerve, they could directly control much of the other person's mind, and so these buffers protect the human.*

<*Again, your mind was altered by the military on many occasions, as were your sensory systems and their inputs. I speak of both of you, of course. One of these alterations was to reduce the buffering on the optic data transmission to improve ocular data speed and bandwidth, in order to handle your increased sensory range. Earnest and I are both reasonably certain that this is where your merging began. It was also one of the things we struggled to rectify for some time.*>

<*OK,*> Tanis said privately to Angela. <*Is our optic linkage that unusual? I never thought it was.*>

<*I didn't, either. It was a standard set of mods for MICI agents.*>

<*The reason why it was so difficult,*> Bob continued after they finished speaking—a clear indication that he could tell when they were doing it. <*Is because you see the world differently, Tanis, you just don't realize it. Not only do you see a broader range of the EM spectrum, but you can focus on more of it at once. Don't forget, you were one of few artificially upgraded L2 humans to be paired with an AI. There are no 'standard mods' for you.*

<*As Earnest and I worked, it became apparent that all of the systems we came up with to reduce optic-nerve bleed-through would have required us to reduce that EM sensitivity. Moreover, we would have needed to alter your brain to reduce focus, but that was a core aspect of your neurological L2 enhancements.*

<*So Earnest and I worked to devise a way to slow the bleed-through, limiting the direct access into one another's minds that it was fostering. The problem was that no matter what we tried, it never seemed to work properly.*>

<*Because of photons?*> Angela asked.

<*Yes,*> Bob replied, his voice thundering with conviction. <*You know, of course, that even individual photons refract. And refraction is a key part of vision itself. The words are crude, but you both understand that photons exist in multiple places at once because of this. Highly accurate EM sensors need to account for these events when triangulating light sources and filtering different EM wavelengths apart to create a clearer, more coherent image.*>

Tanis nodded. "Right, EM sensors such as my eyes."

<*Yes. But what Earnest and I came to realize is that your eyes were faulty, yet not faulty. They passed every test we threw at them, but still managed to have a performance profile that didn't match their specifications. This caused them to constantly thwart the systems we were putting in place to limit mental bleed-through.*

<After extensive study, Earnest discovered that the probability curve for what photons would do when interacting with your eyes didn't match any model we could devise. Until I altered the model to add a 'beneficial' algorithmic matrix.>

"This is where we move into magic, isn't it?" Tanis asked, a touch of sarcasm in her voice.

<Tanis, you have torn atoms apart and seen through both minds and worlds. You have done this through scientifically explainable—and repeatable—methods. You should be the last one to call something out as 'magic'.>

"I suppose," Tanis allowed. "I guess I have a mental block on this issue. Please, you were about to tell us what a beneficial algorithmic matrix is."

<Well, it's possibly one of the most complex things I've ever devised—and it's far from perfect, but it was enough for us to gain the efficiency we needed to retain your advanced optical systems, as well as slow your merging.

<As you know, even in something that appears to be known and consistent, such as the refractive properties of a given material, the actual result is inconsistent due to everything from imperfections, to temperature, to random subatomic particles passing by. The algorithmic matrix I developed has to do with correctly predicting the reflection and refraction properties of your eyes. You know that some light that enters your eyes reflects, and some refracts. This happens at multiple points within your optic system, similar to how it occurs in an organic eye.

<In your eyes, the math doesn't always work. The measurable results of reflection and refraction appear to defy probability just a hair, and come out more favorably for you than it would for anyone else. If you would benefit from more photons entering your eyes, then that happened. If there was a bright light and fewer photons entering would be preferred, that occurred. Not by any large means, not enough that it tripped up any of your prior mods, but it was there, just enough to throw off what Earnest and I were trying to do.>

"You're serious..." Tanis said, running a hand over her head and pulling off the band holding her hair back. "My eyes bend what's probable to be in my favor."

<*Yes, but not just your eyes. Every part of you does this. The effect is cumulative. It is your 'luck'.*>

"And you figured all this out while we were drifting between Estrella de la Muerte and Kapteyn's Star, didn't you?" Tanis asked.

<*Huh,*> Angela gave a soft grunt. <*So whenever Earnest came out of stasis to examine us, it was for your grand experiment.*>

<*Yes, and no,*> Bob replied. <*As I said, the stated reasons for having you out of stasis were also true. You'll recall that I confided my belief in your luck early on to you. That was also part of the experiment. To see if your knowledge of the effect would change it.*>

"Did it?" Tanis asked.

<*Yes. It made it stronger.*>

"But I never believed it," Tanis retorted. "Wouldn't my disbelief make it weaker?"

<*I believed it,*> Angela whispered. <*So much of what we went through—even back then—was so amazing that 'luck' made sense. I latched onto it as the reason we'd survived. Doing so allowed me to compartmentalize the incredulous.*>

Tanis shook out her hair, freshly released from its ponytail, as she glared up at Bob's primary node. "OK, so if you can quantify this 'luck', where does it come from? It long predates mine and Angela's road to ascension—which was not what I expected to have happen when our minds merged, by the way."

<*At first, I thought it was extradimensional,*> Bob told them. <*The ascended AI that left Sol at the end of the Second Solar War didn't leave many records, but the general nature of their ascension was known—that they had broadened their existence into more dimensions. However, over time, I too began to perceive those other*

dimensions. Not consistently, but I was developing systems to do so with better clarity. I began to form a new hypothesis.

<*It was so incredible that I doubted it for some time, but in the end, it was the only answer left: the influence that increases the likelihood of events occurring in your favor was not extra-dimensional, it was extra-***universal**.>

"Seriously? You mean some other universe in the multiverse is influencing me?"

Tanis felt a sense of wonder sweep over her—along with the memories of a bar she had found herself in not long ago. A bar she was not supposed to recall, but which she and Angela remembered all too well.

A bar in a different universe.

<*How would one exert extra-universal influence?*> Angela added her own question to the mix. <*Are you saying that a conscious force from another iteration of the universe is reaching into ours and altering it around us?*>

<*Perhaps,*> Bob replied quietly. <*Maybe as we hone our new senses, we'll be able to see the influence somehow. For now it is just a hypothesis. Whether or not it is really occurring, and whether or not it is a conscious being, or some unlikely confluence of variables, is impossible to discern. For all we know, this happens all the time, but no one is able to see it.*>

Tanis lowered her head, closing her eyes as she let everything Bob had said sink in. She could feel Angela doing the same, the pair sharing in a strange feeling of comfort.

"Why am I not upset about all this anymore?" Tanis asked quietly. "I mean…I still think I resent you keeping things from me, Bob, but that's a shallow thing. I've always known you keep secrets—stars, you've flat-out told me from time to time. But don't you think that in this case we should have known?"

<*Tanis, Angela….*> Bob's voice carried a tone Tanis had never heard in it before. The only descriptor she could think of was 'anguish'. <*You have no idea how difficult every conversation*

is with you. For smaller minds like yours—yes, even ones with one foot through the door of ascension—a thought process can consume you. A reaction to one event can color all thoughts. Not so with me. I can simultaneously be upset about a thousand things, and happy about a million more. I am constantly experiencing the full breadth of my version of emotional reaction. But when I speak with you, it consumes more of my mind than any other thing I do. Managing this ship's engines during a close approach to a star is simpler than saying hello to the two of you.>

<I don't know if we should be flattered or offended,> Angela replied.

<Perhaps both,> Bob's words hung in the space between them. *<I constantly worry that I am influencing you in a way that will have unpredictable results. In my experience, your actions are most beneficial to yourself and those around you when I guide you as little as possible.*

<That's difficult for me, because the two of you are some of my favorite people to talk with. You understand me in a way that not even my avatars do.>

"That's weighty praise, Bob," Tanis replied. "Tell me, now that I'm an engineered product of greater minds, how are we supposed to feel about that?"

Bob laughed again, and Tanis basked in it, realizing for the first time that Bob's thoughts no longer overwhelmed her at times like this. Instead, they exhilarated her.

<Well, Tanis. Most people you know are either formed by chance encounters and DNA combinations, or modified by their parents before birth. Your origins are not so different in that respect. You've just been molded by more powerful beings than most. Your description of 'the product of greater minds' applies to many humans and AIs. At one point, it was an apt description for me. You're not ***quite*** *as special as you might think.>*

<I feel like a passenger caught up in the winds of fate, here,> Angela said quietly. *<Not that it'll matter for much longer. Tangel doesn't fret about such things.>*

<Doubtful,> Bob interjected. *<If what Katrina related from Xavia is true, you were chosen with great care, Angela. You and Tanis are both important components in what you're becoming. I am certain that the 'luck' factor is greatly enhanced by your presence.>*

"OK, Bob," Tanis straightened and stared up at his node once more. "So luck and merging brains aside, why are we ascending? Human and AI minds have merged before and just became one mind—if they survived. Why is Tangel an extra-dimensional being with ridiculous powers?"

<If you allowed yourself to embrace it, you'd know the answer,> Bob replied. *<But the answer is simple. I did it to you—I know enough of the future to understand that humanity only survives if you ascend.>*

"You *'did it to'* us?" Tanis exclaimed along, while Angela asked, *<How exactly did you manufacture our ascension?>*

<I had been working at it for some time. It is through the picotech Earnest and I have been using to modify you that we grew the new brain you now possess. The one I can see you using, even though you try to cling to your separate minds.>

<I knew it!> Angela shouted in triumph. *<You* ***have*** *been using picotech on us.>*

<It was necessary to compensate for your 'luck' where it affected quantum particles. Earnest and I have been modifying you with picotech since we arrived at Kapteyn's Star.>

"Huh," Tanis grunted. "So that's by your design too, then."

<Somewhat,> Bob replied. *<I guided something that I think would have happened anyway. It just would have taken longer. Once* Sabrina *came back, and Iris delivered the data from the ascension program at Star City, I was able to put the final puzzle pieces into place. I just needed the catalyst.>*

"Pyra," Tanis whispered.

<I suspected it could happen there,> Bob sent a feeling of remorse into Tanis's mind. *<But had I known the details of what would happen, I would not have willed it. Too many lost their lives for this one victory.>*

"And yet, you said humanity would not survive unless I ascended," Tanis replied. "On the scale you measure things at, it would be a worthwhile trade."

The words were bitter in Tanis's mouth, and she hated the thought of them. That her elevation should cost the lives of billions made it utterly distasteful to her.

<How does one measure such things?> Bob's voice once again contained ample sorrow. *<Pivotal people were lost. Some you'd never expect, others that are obvious, such as General Mill and Commandant Brandt. But then again, without these events, it may be that Rika would never have come into our sphere of influence. Perhaps that all occurred because of your luck.>*

"Never have I needed such a firm reminder as to why I hate the idea of having this luck," Tanis said with a grimace. "Still, you're right. Rika is a very interesting person, I likely owe her my life."

<Perhaps,> Bob's voice sounded pensive. *<Either way, she has a part to play in all this. I assume you see that.>*

"I do," Tanis and Angela said together.

<Do you see the other thing?> Bob asked.

A sigh escaped Tanis's lips, and she closed her eyes, still seeing the room around her, but with different organs, mechanisms for sight that did not exist in the three dimensions she was so familiar with.

"I do, Bob," Tangel replied. "I understand now. I never 'de-ascended'. What Priscilla did only stabilized my physical form so Rika could carry me. I've been…taking comfort in a fallacy that I am still two people."

<As have those around you,> Bob added. *<No one knows how to deal with an ascended being. Why do you think I maintain the fiction that I am not one as well?>*

Tanis looked at the light she'd seen emanating from Bob's primary node—really looked at it. She could see his existence stretching beyond even what she could perceive. As always, he was aeons ahead of her.

She looked at the air molecules around her, gathering them into a thick column and floating before Bob's node. She set her jaw and stepped into the pillar, allowing it to envelop her legs and support her as she rose into the air, hovering before the glowing node.

"So, why is it that I'm instrumental in saving humanity?" Tangel, the ascended being, asked. "And don't think I didn't notice that AIs were not listed as being in species-level peril."

Bob's response came in the form of a question.

<How upset would you be if I refused to tell you?>

COMING CLEAN

STELLAR DATE: 08.29.8949 (Adjusted Years)
LOCATION: Ol' Sam, ISS *I2*
REGION: Pyra, Albany System, Thebes, Septhian Alliance

Tangel folded her hands together as she sat at the kitchen table, waiting for Joe and the girls to arrive.

Why am I so nervous, she wondered, answering herself with, *You know why. This is the point of no return.*

She saw that Joe was on the path leading to the house, waiting for Cary and Saanvi, who were a minute behind, having taken a different maglev to the cylinder.

He looked nervous—she could see the creases around his eyes on the ship's optical cameras. They were just a hair tighter than normal. Not enough that a human would notice, but she did.

Unclasping her hands, she looked at them, turning them over and counting the small folds in her skin, and the folds within those folds. When she began to count the bacteria living in the cuticles on her fingers, and compare their molecular counts, she tore her gaze away.

This is ridiculous.

Over the following eighty-seven seconds it took for the front door to open, Tangel cleared her mind, thinking of nothing at all, just being. It may have been the hardest thing she'd ever done.

"Tanis?" Joe's voice called out, as the sounds of footfalls came to her.

"In the kitchen," Tangel called out, opening her eyes once more and smiling as her family filed into the room. She rose and exchanged embraces with each of them—even Faleena, to whom she sent a feeling of acceptance and love.

Without needing instruction, everyone sat, Joe at her side, and the girls across the table.

Tangel had considered a thousand ways to start this conversation, played each one out a dozen levels of probabilities deep. In the end, she'd been lost in options with miniscule differences when it came to how the revelation would play out.

She knew there was no other option but to ease them into the knowledge of what had happened.

"I need to tell you the full story of what happened on Pyra," she began, meeting the eyes of each person around the table. "How it all came to be."

Joe nodded, an encouraging half-smile on his lips. "We've been dying to hear it. Take your time."

Tangel drew in a deep breath and nodded before launching into her tale.

"They'd worn us down one-by-one, the Nietzscheans. Looking back, it's hard to believe we survived as long as we did. In the end, it was just myself, Brandt, and Ayer—the Marauder captain. We lost Ayer that final night, and Brandt—" Tanis paused, trying to find the right words. "She was a Marine's Marine until the end. She sacrificed herself to save me."

Joe placed a hand on Tanis's shoulder. "I'll pass that on to her family. She'll have a hero's burial on Carthage."

Tangel nodded silently, composing herself—surprised that it was so hard.

"I was in an atrium," Tangel spoke up after a few more seconds. "Out of everything, totally spent. I took a blow to the head, and when I came to…I wasn't Tanis anymore."

"So you and Angela *did* merge," Saanvi whispered, eyes wide.

"Yes, sort of," Tanis replied. "But there was more. We could see things, understand things we'd never imagined. We were able to create fields to manipulate matter at fundamental levels. We existed across more levels. We…we were able to kill with a thought."

"Were?" Cary asked, an eyebrow cocked.

Tangel shrugged. "Well, 'are'. I can see the spaces between the atoms in your body, I can tell how to pluck them apart, spin them off, draw the energy out of them."

"Shit," Joe whispered his eyes wide with disbelief. "Are you serious?"

Tangel nodded. "I know you're all wondering—heck, I know that Trine can probably *see* it. Simply put, I've ascended."

Joe swallowed, then a smile toyed at the corners of his lips, and he poked a finger into Tangel's shoulder. "You don't look ascended; seem like good ol' flesh and blood Tanis."

Tangel held up her left arm. "Yeah, but only because I want to be. I grew this in an instant. I think I could un-grow it just as fast, but I'm still taking baby steps. I don't want to do something like accidentally unmake my physical body. I'm rather attached to it."

<But…you two—Angela and you…you've been speaking separately,> Faleena said haltingly.

"Yeah, we have. The parts of us that used to be separate are still there, but they're more like memories…shadows. After Priscilla introduced a swarm of pico to stabilize our form, we thought—*I* thought—that we were separate. But Bob set us straight: we're not separate. We're one person now—though I plan on behaving as separate beings insofar as interactions with any others are concerned. I don't know that the ISF or all our allies are ready for this."

Tangel paused, studying the faces of her family members. Joe was still split between amazement and amusement. Saanvi appeared more curious, her eyes narrowed as she stared into Tangel's. Faleena seemed elated, while Cary's face, on the other hand betrayed nothing. Her mind, however, was another story entirely.

No one took up the conversational torch, so Tangel ended up breaking the silence. "You don't seem very surprised."

"Oh, we're surprised, Mom…moms…Mom?" Cary said after a moment, her voice nearly devoid of emotion—which meant she was holding anger in check. "Just processing. So let me get this straight. We all knew you two were merging—"

"Taking your time about it, too," Joe interrupted with a wink.

"Right, yeah," Cary stammered, casting her father a wounded look. "I guess not to me, though. I don't want to lose my moms."

Tangel could see the void of anger turn into an ocean of anguish behind Cary's eyes, and reached her hand across the table. "I'm not going anywhere, Cary. And we're both still here, Tanis and Angela, we just speak with one voice now."

"But you're ascended…" Cary rasped. "Aren't you just going to turn to light and disappear?"

Tangel held up her other hand, slipping a part of her fifth dimensional body outside the bounds of her three-dimensional one. The visible result was tendrils of light swirling around her hand.

"This is just the rest of my body," Tanis said, holding Cary's gaze while speaking calmly. "You have it too, you just can't manipulate it like I can."

Cary's eyes widened, and she glanced at Saanvi. "Because we make up Trine?"

"No," Tanis shook her head. "Everyone occupies more of space-time than they realize. You're just not cognizant of it—well, *you* are, Cary, you just don't understand how to control it."

Cary's face grew ashen. "Am *I* going to ascend?"

Tanis nodded. "Someday, if you want to." She glanced at Joe. "You all can, eventually. I mean…billions of people did it on Star City. To my knowledge, none of them were merged with an AI mind, they were just regular people."

"So I'll turn into some being of light as well?" Cary whispered, her voice wavering as she spoke.

Tanis realized what was bothering Cary so much. "I think I need to clear up a misconception. When you ascend, you're really just becoming aware of, and able to manipulate, things in more dimensions. Trine is effectively an ascended being, but you're not when you're alone. In time you won't need to do your deep Linking mind merge to use your abilities, Cary. But you're still you, a person with a brain and a mind. You need neurons to think, you need energy to function—you just have different ways of going about that. Not everyone does it the same way."

Tanis paused and looked at the room's ceiling. "I'm outing you, Bob."

<Very well,> Bob replied. *<But what you hear stays in this room.>*

"Bob's ascended," Tangel said. "Has been for some time. Ascending for an AI isn't fundamentally different than it is for a human—though they lack bodies, which limits their initial set of extra-dimensional sensory organs. Many ascended AIs make themselves new bodies in the other dimensions, they…move their minds there. That's why we only see them as beings of light and energy. They can manifest a physical presence if needed by manipulating matter."

Tanis paused and rapped on the table, turning it to steel where she touched it, then rapped again, turning it back to wood.

"But I can already do that, and I like my body, and I like my brain where it is. I have no need to shift myself from this dimension into others. Not to mention the fact that I think they lose something in the process when they do it."

"But what about Bob?" Saanvi asked. "Is he going to shift himself away?"

<Not anytime soon,> Bob replied. *<Moving my multinodal mind out of the dimensions in which it was created is no simple task, even for me. And Tanis is right. The adjacent dimensions alone are not enough to encapsulate all aspects of myself—or Tangel's self, for that matter. I suspect that many of the other ascended AIs have retained some measure of physical form as well—though they'd have to have first created one. Carting around a number of massive node cubes is not practical.>*

" 'Tangel'?" Joe asked. "I thought you two had settled on 'Tangela'?"

"Too many syllables," Tangel replied. "I kept thinking of other names, but they were all too…different. We're not different or new, we're Tanis and Angela."

"This is just too weird." Cary's voice rose in pitch as she spoke. "I can't call you 'Tangel'! You're my mom!"

Saanvi placed a hand on Cary's shoulder. "We called *them* 'Moms' most of the time anyway. Now we're just calling *her* 'Moms'. No difference."

Cary turned her head, glaring at Saanvi. "No, it's *a lot* different. For all intents and purposes, Mom is dead. So is Angela!"

As she cried out Angela's name, Cary rose, knocked her chair over, and fled the room, then the house.

Saanvi began to get up, but Tangel held up her hand. "You know Cary. She's going to need a bit to come around to this on her own. Faleena is talking with her as well."

"Faleena told you that?" Joe asked, and Tangel shook her head.

"No, I can see it."

Joe's mouth formed a silent O.

"How?" Saanvi asked, leaning forward.

"Oh, Saanvi. You've always been the most curious young girl—and now woman—I've ever known." Tangel gave her daughter a warm smile.

"I like to know how things work." Saanvi shrugged.

"Because you want to gain some measure of control after feeling like you had so little," Tangel replied.

Saanvi waved a finger at Tangel. "You may have me all figured out now, Moms, but don't try to distract me with your psychoanalysis. I want to know how you can see AIs. This isn't the first time you've said you can see Faleena's mind."

Tangel waved her hand in the air, and an image appeared over the table. It was a wavering mass of light and dark, diaphanous tendrils stretching out, moving through dark areas, causing them to become lighter while others grew dim.

"That is Faleena. At least, her electromagnetic spectrum. I can see more of her, but it doesn't translate well into a visual. But even at this distance, through the walls, I can see what her mind looks like."

"How far away is she?" Joe asked as he stared unblinking at the image before him, moisture in his eyes as he *saw* his daughter for the first time.

"Down on the dock," Tangel replied. "She's not entirely happy about this, but she's putting on a brave face. Trying to console Cary—it's not going well."

"Are you reading Cary's mind?" Saanvi's eyes narrowed.

"No," Tangel gave a rueful laugh. "She's yelling. I can see the windows vibrating."

Joe barked a laugh. "No keeping secrets from you anymore."

"Like that was ever possible before," Tangel said as she regarded Joe, unable to miss the knowing look he shared with Saanvi. "What?"

"Nothing, oh Ascended Moms, there's just *some* stuff you don't know," Saanvi's mouth took on a mischievous grin. "And we're going to keep it that way."

"How am I going to rule the galaxy if I don't know everything, though," Tangel wondered in a mock sulk.

Joe sputtered a cough. "Say what?"

Tangel gave him a slow wink. "Mess with me, and I mess right back."

"Stars," Joe muttered. "Looks like we didn't lose Angela in your merge."

"Sahn, hon," Tangel gestured toward the door. "I think your sister is ready for an arm around the shoulder about now."

Saanvi chuckled as she rose, glancing at Joe. "I see how it is, Moms. Need some alone time with your mortal consort, do you?"

"Hey," Joe said in mock anger. "I'm no one's consort. I'm obviously the Chief Acolyte."

Saanvi walked around the table and wrapped her arms around Tangel. "Just so you know," she whispered softly. "I may seem all calm and controlled on the outside—but that's the curious scientist in me. Inside, I'm freaked the hell out."

"I know," Tangel whispered back. "I'm still your mom, and I'm not going anywhere. You're going to be stuck with me for a looooong time."

"Good. Because if you turn into a glowing ball of light and leave us, I'm going to go to Star City, ascend myself, and then find you and kick your ass."

"Ha!" Tangel barked a laugh. "I do not doubt that for a second."

Joe pulled Saanvi close as she passed, giving her quick hug before she left.

Once they heard the door close, Joe shifted in his seat and stared into Tangel's eyes for a minute without speaking.

"What?" Tangel finally said.

"They look different, but I can't tell what it is."

Tangel caused her eyes to sparkle. "Maybe it's just my general brilliance."

Joe snorted. "Do that more often and you'll get people more than wondering about your ascendancy."

"Seriously, Joe," Tangel took her husband's hands. "How is it that you're so…accepting of this?"

"I'm surprised that you keep asking me that," Joe replied. "I wasn't kidding when I said that loving two women was hard. You—rather, Tanis and Angela—have been a part of my life longer than I lived without them. When I first met you, I fell in love with Tanis, but we spent decades together, just the three of us. You know I came to love Angela as well. Sometimes I wondered…."

"What?" Tangel laughed. "That Tanis would be jealous?"

"OK…now *that* is weird." Joe shook his head slowly, a half-smile on his lips. "To hear your voice speak of yourself as though it's someone else."

"Should I change something about my appearance?" Tanis asked. "Something that will make it easy to remember that I'm Tangel, and not Tanis or Angela?"

Joe put a finger to his lips as he considered it. "Maybe? I wonder what would work."

"I could make a streak of my hair black," Tangel said, and a moment later, a lock of hair at her left temple turned black.

Joe shook his head. "No, nothing so overt. It'll probably bother Cary, too. She needs you to stay as you are as much as possible. What about your eyes? Maybe add just a hint of lavender to them."

Tangel cocked an eyebrow. "If it's enough to notice, how different would that be than coloring my hair?"

"True..." Joe tapped a finger against his lips. "I've got it! Make your nails a darker color. You always keep them natural or choose a light pink. Go for something darker."

"Like this?" Tangel held up a hand, and her nails shifted to a darker red.

"Perfect!" Joe proclaimed, then looked her up and down, a smile forming on his lips. "You know, I always knew you were destined for great things...many of which you've achieved. But, I gotta say, ascension and a full AI merge all at the same time? I doubt there are any others like you." He leant back in his chair, grinning as he clasped his hands behind his head. "I sure can pick 'em."

"Pft!" Tangel pulled Joe in close. "I picked *you*."

"Remember when you ran the SOC on the *Intrepid,* back at the Mars Outer Shipyards? Remember what everyone called you behind your back?"

Tangel rolled her eyes. " 'Dragon Lady' was the nicest one, if memory serves."

"Correct, oh glowing wife of mine. Yet I braved your lair and conquered you. I chose *you*."

"I just let you think that."

Joe reached out and pulled Tangel toward him.

"Keep telling yourself that," he said a moment before their lips met.

UNDERSTANDING

STELLAR DATE: 08.29.8949 (Adjusted Years)
LOCATION: Ol' Sam, ISS *I2*
REGION: Pyra, Albany System, Thebes, Septhian Alliance

Tangel stepped out into the evening light, glancing up at the long sun that ran through the center of the habitat cylinder. She noted that there was a slight variance in the light output from one end of the long sun to the other, and sent a message off to the engineering team's queue.

Ninety-seven meters of stone path lay between her and the lake, another seven worth of dock, and at the end of that, her three daughters.

Tangel still remembered the first time she saw each of them: Cary as a newborn—carried and birthed the old-fashioned way—and Saanvi as she woke from the stasis tube, a trembling little girl, nearly petrified with fear. She also remembered seeing Faleena's mind as Angela, the first words their third daughter had spoken.

She remembered, as Tanis, the feel of their skin, the bioreadout reports on their health, skin temperature, pupil dilation, body proportion measurements, the uncertain looks in their eyes. She remembered the EM frequencies their brains gave off, the feel of connecting to minds over the Link, all of it. All at once.

Closing her eyes, Tangel drew a deep breath. Memories were hard. Though her mind was one thing, her memories—barring recent ones—were not. She had two overlaid experiences; disparate recollections, disparate conclusions.

As she examined them, she couldn't help but note that, as time passed, Tanis and Angela had begun to think more and more alike. Back when Tangel divided, she couldn't see it as clearly, but now it was abundantly apparent. For years, the overlap had been greater than the differences.

But how to explain that to the women sitting at the end of the dock?

Tangel smiled. At nineteen and twenty years old, her two organic daughters both behaved as though they had everything figured out. They certainly were more put-together than Tanis had been at that age—on the brink of joining the military to rebel against her father.

Funny how history repeats itself, Tangel mused. *Though my two girls joined the military to please me, not to anger me, as I did with him….*

A high bandwidth data stream was flowing between the girls—*yes, 'girls',* Tangel thought. *They could be a thousand years old, and they'd still be my little girls.* She surmised from the information flow that the three of them were deep-Linked, sharing in the special bond that these three sisters possessed.

Tendrils of light began to drift around Cary, and Tangel saw them reach out toward Saanvi—from whom three small filaments of light also came, stretching toward Cary.

Well that's unexpected.

Unexpected, maybe, but it did make sense. When Cary Linked into the minds of her sisters, she was creating a new being of sorts. Not one so deeply entwined as Tanis and Angela had become in their later days, but something in Cary was a catalyst that pushed them closer. Thus far, Faleena seemed unchanged, but she'd not been a part of their little group for as long. Time would tell how her progression went.

Tangel wasn't certain what it was, but she was eager to see it unfold—so long as it happened slowly. There was no need for her daughters to evolve too soon.

She began to walk down the path, moving slowly, giving the girls time to notice her—and hopefully not wave her off. As she neared the water's edge, Saanvi glanced over her shoulder, and then made to rise.

"You don't have to go," Tangel said, but Saanvi shook her head.

"It's OK, Moms, we had our chat. You're up now."

Tangel embraced Saanvi, then sat next to Cary, feeling the dock vibrate for a few more moments until Saanvi made it to the shore.

"I'm sorry," Tangel whispered, staring down at her hands. She didn't dare look into her daughter's eyes yet, fearful of what she might see there.

Cary didn't respond right away, but Tangel could tell from her breathing that she nearly did three times. Then she finally said, "For what?"

The words were caustic, full of anger. They cut into Tangel, but she ignored the pain. This wasn't about her, it was about her daughter.

"For going through this change so soon. We all knew it was coming—but I thought I'd have decades still. I don't want you to feel like you've lost your mothers."

Cary turned her head, and Tangel looked up, meeting her daughter's eyes, blue and set into a face that looked so much like her own. The same cheekbones, the same eyes—Joe's brows and lips, though. A bit of both in the nose.

"Have I?" Cary's voice rasped as she breathed the question. "Are you still there?"

"I am," Tangel replied. "I know this feels like a big change, but, in all honesty, it was a very small step."

"Mom," Cary snorted derisively. "*Ascension* is not a small step."

"Well, I was referring more to Tanis and Angela becoming one person. Though it was the catalyst for ascension…it's a different thing."

A tear slid down Cary's cheek. "When you came down off the ship…when you spoke…I hoped you were still you. But you were lying to us."

Tanis shook her head. "No, I was lying to myself. I know I put on a brave face—that's sort of my thing—but I was scared, too. I don't—didn't—want to change…."

"Which is it?" Cary whispered. "Didn't or don't?"

"Well, the ship's sailed, so it doesn't matter much anymore. I didn't want to do it so soon, and I don't want to do anything that hurts you. That's the very last thing I ever want."

Neither woman spoke for a minute, then Cary said, "Faleena says that you seem 'correct' now."

"Oh?" Tangel cocked an eyebrow, glancing at Faleena's still mind, where it lay nestled within Cary's. Her other daughter was doing her best not to intrude on the conversation, but Tangel could tell that it was difficult for her. "Is that the case, Faleena?"

<A bit,> Faleena replied hesitantly. *<I think I could see better than most where you and Angela overlapped. So much of my own mind is made from yours that it is more apparent to me. The way you were before…you were both incomplete. Now you're finally one person. I think it was how you were always meant to be.>*

"Meant to be?" Tangel asked with a single laugh. "I don't think there's any guiding force in the galaxy driving what we should and should not be."

<Really? I would have thought that you of all people—what, with how you have been pushed and prodded, molded at every turn—would believe otherwise.>

"Right," Tangel nodded thoughtfully. "What Katrina said about my past. How the AIs made me—us."

"Doesn't that bother you, Moms?" Cary asked. "I mean…they shaped you into what you are."

Tangel shrugged. "Not really. I hashed this out with Bob, and he helped me understand it. People like to *think* they can control their surroundings, shape the future to their liking. But they can't…and if all the ascended AIs out there were to be honest with themselves, they'd realize that they too are products of their environments. My 'luck' is evidence of that. Not only can they *not* control me, they can't even tell what I'm going to do. I'm like the ultimate variable. The variable variable. Which, honestly, always seemed strange to me.

"Everything I do in life *feels* like the next logical step. The obvious thing to do. Yet somehow, it seems to always thwart the AIs' ability to predict things." Tangel winked at Cary and Faleena. "If you ask me, I think that it's the AIs that have some sort of cognitive dissonance."

<*Not funny, Moms,*> Faleena replied, sending a mock scowl into Tangel's mind.

"So you're just going to brush off what's been done to you?" Cary asked. "They may have even set you on the path that made you merge with Angela."

"They may have," Tangel agreed, deciding not to reveal all the nuances to her progression. "Bob suspects as much. Maybe when I finally come face-to-face with the Caretaker, I'll ask him. Right before I kill him."

<*Is that your ultimate goal?*> Faleena asked. <*To kill the ascended AIs?*>

Tangel saw Cary's eyebrows rise, the expression echoing Faleena's question.

"I doubt it. There's at least one that I like."

<*Thanks,*> Bob interjected.

Tangel glanced out toward the lake before continuing. "But what I really want to learn before I become judge, jury, and executioner, is *why* the core AIs are doing what they're doing. If they feared humanity, they could have wiped them out at the height of the FTL wars. Is it really what they *want,* to keep everyone balanced on the knife's edge? It seems impractical to me."

<*And to me,*> Faleena added.

"You said 'them'," Cary stated tonelessly. "Are you talking about humans or AIs? You're not really either, anymore."

"Both?" Tangel asked with a shrug. "Neither? I don't know that it matters."

<*I think you might be a new thing, Mother,*> Faleena said in a wistful tone.

"Don't be so sure," Tangel replied. "Space and time are vast. Could be another Star City out there, filled with human-AI merges that are all ascended. You know...I really don't like that word."

"Merges?" Cary asked.

" 'Ascended'. I didn't elevate, I just became more perceptive."

Faleena chortled. <*Plus there's that whole matter-transmutation thing you can do now.*>

Tangel waved her hand dismissively. "I imagine you'll figure it out soon enough. You just have to come at it from a different angle."

"What do you mean?" Cary asked, her voice almost frantic.

I'm such an idiot, Tangel chastised herself. *So much for being more perceptive.*

"Cary, I just realized...you're worried about merging with Faleena, aren't you?" Tangel asked quietly.

A sharp sob escaped Cary's lips, and she nodded as tears slipped onto her cheeks.

"Oh, Cary," Tangel slipped an arm around her daughter's shoulders. "I don't think you're going to merge. Not unless you do something stupid like I did back in Sol with those fighters."

"I don't want it, but then I feel guilty about it at the same time," Cary whispered. "You mean so much to me, Faleena, but I don't want to merge with you. And I feel horrible about that. I mean…Moms' mind is so beautiful now. Why wouldn't I want that?"

A shuddering breath escaped Cary's lips.

"I'm so selfish."

<*Well…*> Faleena said hesitantly. <*I don't want to merge with you, either, Cary. I'm not ruling it out in the distant future, but I want to experience life as* ***me*** *first. Then maybe you and I can talk.*>

Cary shook her head. "Now I feel horrible for being glad that you don't want to stay in my head forever."

<*Cary, we're a special sort of sisters; we share a bond that few others do. Nothing can ruin that. No matter if our minds share headspace or not.*>

"Do you think, Faleena," Tangel ventured carefully. "That maybe it's time for you to come out of Cary?"

<*I don't really* ***want*** *to, but I think it would be best if I did. For both of us.*>

"Cary?" Tangel asked.

Cary straightened her back and wiped her cheeks. "Sorry I've been so…whatever about all this."

"Don't apologize," Tangel replied, brushing Cary's hair back from her face. "Everyone processes things differently. Not only that, but we're all going through things that no one has imagined. Remnants, Xavia's memory, making shadowtrons, dealing with the threat of the core AIs, my changes...."

"Don't forget the massive war we're embroiled in," Cary added with a smirk.

"That too."

<*Cary? Should I go, then?*> Faleena pressed.

Cary sighed. "I know that 'yes' is the right answer, but the last thing I want is to lose you."

<*You're not going to lose me. I'm going to take a page from Iris's book and get a body that looks just like yours. Then I'm going to follow you around like a creepy doppelganger.*>

"Oh yeah?" Cary asked. "You going to hit on the guys I like back at the academy?"

"Guys?" Tangel asked. "What guys?"

Faleena laughed, a sound like leaves rustling in the wind echoing in their minds. <*If I were to fancy a human, I think it would probably be Gladys, but I've got my metaphorical eyes on Sabrina.*>

Tangel almost choked. "Sabs? You've only met her the once."

<*We've exchanged some messages over the QuanComm. Nothing much, and very slowly—over days, so we don't tax the system.*>

"Well I'll be," Tangel said with a shake of her head. "Maybe once you're done at the academy, you can get an assignment there."

<*Seriously?*> Faleena asked, almost giddy.

"What?" Cary nearly shouted. "What happened to being my doppelganger?"

Tanis shrugged. "You're a year out from that. And nothing says you couldn't both go. At some point, Amavia is going to want to return to New Canaan, and I'm in a never-ending need for more high-ranking fleet commanders that know what the hell they're doing."

<*You're going to recall Jessica?*> Faleena asked.

Tangel rose and offered Cary her hand, pulling her daughter to her feet.

"If she wants to. *Sabrina* has been her home for a very long time now. If she wants to stay, I won't stop her, but I could really use her in an admiral's chair."

Cary whistled as they began to walk back toward the house. "What about Cheeky? I can't imagine *Sabrina* without Cheeky."

Tangel laughed. "Neither can I. But now that she and Finaeus are married, it feels wrong to keep them apart."

<*OK, two things,*> Faleena said. <*Firstly, you and dad are apart a* ***lot****. Secondly, can you imagine Cheeky on the* I2*? You'll never get her into an ISF uniform.*>

Tangel laughed, shaking her head at the thought. "Well, your father and I aren't exactly newlyweds. As for the uniform…I suppose we'd have to make an exception for her. Though it's not like the ISF *really* needs to adhere to a physical dress code to show our common bond. Maybe we can come up with some more options."

"Whoaaaaa," Cary leant to the side, looking Tangel up and down as they walked. "Up until now, you still sounded like some combination of the Moms. But this? Flexibility in the dress code? 'Options'? Hmm…maybe you're an alien."

Tangel pulled Cary close and kissed the side of her head. "There's my girl, sarcastic sense of humor and all."

"I got it from you."

LUNCH AND FATHERS

STELLAR DATE: 08.29.8949 (Adjusted Years)
LOCATION: Sear, Keren Station
REGION: Khardine System, Transcend Interstellar Alliance

"Gotta say, President Sera," Mary said, as she sat down at the table across from the woman she was addressing. "I didn't expect to get an invite to join you at one of the station's fancy restaurants only a day after nearly running you down in a stairwell."

Sera looked around the restaurant, named 'Sear' after its reputation for serving the best steak around. "I guess it is on the fancy side. Honestly, my guards have a short list of restaurants they consider to be 'safe enough', and this was the only steakhouse on the list."

Mary snorted as she looked at the list of specials hovering on the table between them. "Talk about presidential problems. And inviting me?"

"Well..." Sera shrugged. "It seemed like you could use a friend. I checked the duty roster, and Leeroy and your son are both pulling double shifts—heck, even your dog, Figgy, is working with cargo crews to sniff out any contraband."

"He loves it," Mary grinned. "Poor Figgy spent years fending for himself in the bowels of Airtha. Who would do that to an uplifted dog? People can be cruel."

Sera nodded slowly, her mind turning to the ring and its inhabitants. "What do you think it's like there, now that Airtha is in control?"

A pained look filled Mary's eyes, and she shook her head. "Stars, I try not to think about it too much. I've a lot of friends there.... All I can do is hope that Airtha hasn't seen fit to do some sort of mass mind control on them all."

Sera pursed her lips, and Mary's eyes met hers for a moment before she asked, "Could she do that? People have protections against mental breaches, but...."

"But ascended AIs don't seem to play with the same rulebook we have," Sera completed for Mary.

"Right...so you're saying she could have subverted the entire population of humans, just like she did to the AIs?"

Sera nodded slowly. "It's a fear I have. I have a lot of friends there too, you know. But I have to wonder if they are really friends now, or something else."

A servitor set the women's drinks on the table, and Mary stared into hers for a half-minute before looking up apologetically. "Sorry about this. I'm usually better company. Sometimes it just feels like I cheated somehow."

"In getting away?" Sera asked.

"Yeah."

"Except that your escape saved people's lives. Leeroy, your son, David. Heck, even your dog."

Mary snorted. "The first two, sure. But I think Figgy would have been fine. Take a lot more than some prissy ascended AI and her weak-assed clone of you to take that dog out."

"Don't go disparaging my clone's ass," Sera chuckled. "I'm told she looks identical to me, and my ass is a work of art."

"Wouldn't know," Mary laughed. "Since you're apparently my adoptive sister, I can't check you out—not to mention you're the freaking president. Which is just a bit surreal."

"I'm not really that different from anyone else." Sera took a sip of her brandy. "Just a girl, trying to make it to tomorrow."

"Right, and you put your pants on one leg at a time, just like the rest of us," Mary snorted.

"Well, I would if I wore pants," Sera agreed.

"Speaking of which..." Mary began, leaving the words hanging.

"You still want skin like mine?" Sera asked. "Like I said, it's semi-permanent. Plus...there's a risk that your father may dismember me."

Mary rolled her eyes. "Seriously, Sera. You're the president of the freaking Transcend, and I'm a grown woman. Flaherty has no say in this."

"Right," Sera snorted. "You and *I* both know that, but your father doesn't—and I doubt we could convince him."

"Well," Mary gave Sera a conspiratorial look. "What dad doesn't know—"

Sera pointed to her right. "He's sitting at the bar, watching us."

"What the fuck?" Mary muttered, her eyes darting to where her father sat. She made to rise, but Sera put a hand on her arm.

"If you make him leave, he'll just take up a position somewhere else, and we won't see him that time. He's sitting there as a courtesy, to let us know that he's here."

Mary gritted her teeth and shook her head. "I love my father, I really do, but that man's infuriating sometimes."

Sera chuckled, nodding in agreement. "Just think, though. Without him, we'd both be dead—in my case, several times over. I figure that earns him some leeway."

"Now I want your skin even more." Mary's eyes glinted as she spoke. "If dad gives me a hard time, I'll tell him that it makes me safer."

"You know," Sera said, touching a finger to her lips. "That angle may just work. Heck, I should make *him* get it, too."

Mary giggled and rubbed her hands together. "Only if you give me control over it. I'd prank him constantly."

"OK…now you're talking," Sera said with a laugh. "I'll reach out to Finaeus and see if he can hook you up."

Mary raised her glass and tapped it against Sera's. "I'll drink to that."

THE PRAETOR

STELLAR DATE: 08.29.8949 (Adjusted Years)
LOCATION: Palatine, Euros
REGION: Earth, New Sol, Orion Freedom Alliance

Garza checked over his uniform, ensuring that he was the picture of perfection. Not that Praetor Kirkland was a stickler for tidiness, but he did pick on imperfections when he received bad news.

<The praetor will see you now.> The summons entered Garza's mind, delivered by a nearby human administrator.

No AI assistant for the praetor, Garza thought as he rose from the chair he'd been waiting in. *He pretends that he's a pure human, that he doesn't use AIs, ignoring the hundreds of AIs in New Sol that keep the system and his empire in order.*

It was an old gripe of Garza's—one he liked to sink his teeth into and revel in before entering the praetor's chamber. The fact that the man he was about to see believed himself to be the savior of a pure human race was laughable. Garza had to get it all out of his system before speaking with Kirkland, or he was bound to snicker in the man's face at some point.

The truth of the matter was that Kirkland was a man of ideals, but one who lacked the conviction to execute on his vision.

That was where men like Garza came in. When he had taken command of the Inner Stars Division of Alignment and Control, it had been a joke, barely able to make any inroads against its Transcend counterpart, the Hand.

Personally, Garza liked the name his enemies used for his division: 'BOGA'. It sounded like the name of some insidious shadow organization from an ancient vid. Certainly a step up from 'ISDAC'.

During Garza's tenure as its leader, BOGA had become a force to be reckoned with, pushing the Hand out of many regions of space, even going so far as to gain control of the Hegemony of Worlds. The Hand still held sway in the vast majority of the smaller interstellar nations, but Garza had scored major wins in gaining allies like the Trisilieds and the Nietzscheans.

Gains that Kirkland barely acknowledged.

All the praetor cared about was crushing the New Canaan colonists, constantly bringing up the loss Garza had suffered there two years before.

It was getting old.

Garza stopped at the unadorned double doors leading into Kirkland's office. He drew a final calming breath before pushing them open and entering the praetor's lair.

The office of the man who ruled the single largest swath of human space—roughly two billion stars—was unimpressive to say the least. Barely fifteen by twenty meters, it was filled with made, but simple furniture. Wooden chairs and leather couches sat against one wall, a bookshelf lined the other.

A mid-sized wooden desk rested near the wall-to-wall windows on the far side of the room where Kirkland stood, hands clasped behind his back as he stared out over his domain.

It's like they're all cut from a template, Garza thought, shaking his head. Hegemon Uriel, President Sera—the Airthan one, at least, he couldn't speak for the degenerate one—the Trisilieds king, Constantine, a dozen others he'd met...they all loved their view, loved to survey their holdings.

Which was patently ridiculous. Their 'views' barely covered a few thousand kilometers at best, while their territories stretched over trillions.

A dark room with a massive holodisplay; *that* was the way to survey one's empire.

"General Garza," Kirkland said without turning, as Garza approached his desk.

"Praetor," Garza replied.

He was tempted to bluntly ask Kirkland why the man summoned him. There was little need for in-person meetings. Especially when it involved a three-day trip. What was more annoying was that he'd wanted to journey to Nietzschea to learn from Constantine how his inroads into Septhia were going. But the praetor liked to play his little games, behaving as though this were just a casual chat.

Ultimately, Garza had sent a clone to meet with the Nietzschean emperor. When the clone returned, Garza would gain the memories and experiences as though they were his own—but it still wasn't the same as going himself.

And even without the advantage of clones, there was always work to be done at his division's headquarters at Karaske. Taking a week to meet with the man who *thought* he was running the Orion Freedom Alliance was just a monumental pain in the ass.

I should have sent a clone ***here****, and gone to see Constantine myself.*

Garza continued to stand before the praetor's desk, which he'd been told was some ancient relic that the man had brought from Sol when he left millennia ago. The idea of wasting this much mass allocation on a wooden desk baffled Garza.

But then again, Kirkland was a man more driven by convictions than logic. Unfathomable behavior was his norm.

After almost a minute, Kirkland turned, regarding Garza evenly from behind his bushy eyebrows. "Tell me of your latest plans to attack New Canaan."

The words stunned Garza. "Sir? I have no plans to attack New Canaan. There's no reason to do so anymore."

"No reason?" Kirkland's brows lowered, half obscuring his eyes. "That is the heart of the infestation. Cut it out, and we'll be well on our way to purging their damaging 'advances' from humanity."

"It's too late," Garza countered. "They've shared much with the Khardine government, and Tanis Richards now leads a fleet that is moving around the Inner Stars with impunity. This has all been in my reports, I—"

Kirkland cut him off with a wave of his hand. "All this because you failed to destroy them two years ago."

Garza clenched his jaw. The praetor brought up the defeat as though he expected there to be no losses against an enemy that outclassed them in every way but sheer volume of forces—and even that advantage was diminishing.

"No one could have expected them to summon Exaldi. That is a weapon we have no counter for. Our only hope is to take more and more of the Inner Stars and convert the populace to our way of thinking. Tanis Richards will not use her weapons of mass destruction against an innocent star system's population."

Garza had made the argument before. Orion's primary advantage was a massive home population that could field fleets to seize and occupy hundreds of thousands of star systems. They would starve Tanis Richards both of resources and of a populace willing to fight alongside her.

At least, that was the plan he had been pushing with Kirkland.

The problem with Garza's proposed plan was that there was no endgame. If they cornered Tanis, she would unleash her picobombs, or summon the Exaldi once more. She may not win, but she could decimate any attacking force, and then simply leave. The galaxy was too big…she could hide anywhere.

"So we're to play a game of cat and mouse for the next century?" Kirkland asked. "That's your plan?"

Garza drew himself up, locking his eyes on Kirkland's. "Praetor, correct me if I'm wrong, but isn't our ultimate goal to bring the Inner Stars into the OFA, and to wear down the Transcend? We are achieving these goals. We've secured over half of the largest political entities in the Inner Stars, and, even better, through Tanis's unwitting help, the Hegemony and Scipio are entering into all-out war. That's exactly what we want."

Kirkland gave a slow nod. "True, seeing those two destroy each other will be a great victory. Once they're sufficiently weakened, we'll sweep in and take both their capitals."

"Which is the plan that is in the works," Garza replied. "We're building a fleet just for that task—though it's caused us to remove most of our forces from the Expansion Districts."

"I know you feel that is unwise," Kirkland said with a heavy sigh. "However, I believe that the PED is well-enough in hand that we don't need the active threat of the Orion Guard looming over them for the people to operate within our strictures."

"Are you certain about that?" Garza asked, still holding Kirkland's gaze. "After the incident at Costa Station with that *Sabrina* ship, we have to assume that the Khardine

Government knows we've decreased our presence in the Expansion Districts. They could easily make inroads there."

Kirkland pulled out his chair and sat, giving a derisive shake of his head in the process. "I thought you were just telling me about how we have them on the ropes, with all the alliances you've forged in the Inner Stars. At best, Khardine holds a quarter the strength of the Transcend, and—so far as we can tell—they're the ones supporting the fronts on our borders. They're engaged in conflicts clear across known space. The last thing they'll do is hit us in the Expansion Districts. Even if they did, what end would it serve? There are few strategic targets in the PED."

"Very well," Garza allowed.

By and large, he agreed with Kirkland, but he wanted to be on record as advising caution so that the praetor couldn't throw it in his face later. Though it probably wouldn't stop him.

"Now then," Kirkland placed his elbows on his desk and folded his hands together. "Tell me about how we'll finally put an end to the blight that is New Canaan. I believe that without her base of operations, Tanis Richards will become a much smaller threat. Perhaps we can even draw her back into her home system, and kill two birds with one stone."

Garza sighed as he sat and pulled up a holodisplay of deployment options. He'd appease Kirkland with a battle plan, but he'd kill himself and all his clones before he even considered enacting it.

Perhaps it's time for the praetor to be replaced....

As he laid out options for drawing a fleet together that could crush New Canaan, Garza considered the options the Airthan Sera had presented him with when he met with them.

Of course, they'd tried to take over his mind, but all they'd done was subsume a clone.

That didn't mean he wouldn't work with them—just that he wasn't going to form an alliance yet. First he needed the degenerate version of Sera to whittle down her doppelganger and abomination of a mother.

Then he'd strike. A taskforce of Lisas were already training for the operation.

OPTIONS

STELLAR DATE: 08.30.8949 (Adjusted Years)
LOCATION: Capitol Complex, Keren Station
REGION: Khardine System, Transcend Interstellar Alliance

Sera settled into her seat in the briefing room, nodding to the admirals, generals, and assorted staffers. Next to her sat Carl, her secretary of the interior, and Hanso the transportation secretary.

Over seventy other people were present, and Sera realized she only knew half of them. She supposed that was a good thing; as more systems sided with Khardine, the mass of representatives increased—as did the number of complications.

At the front of the room, Admiral Greer waited for everyone to settle down, which happened within a few seconds of him raising his right hand.

"OK, everyone," Greer began. "We're here to review assault options on Airtha. President Sera has tasked us with formulating a plan, and we have three options, each with different strategic profiles."

A holo appeared to his right, showing a graph that started at zero on the left, and rose to just over five-hundred million on the right.

"These are the TSF casualty rates for the different strategies we've worked up. Plan Full-Auto has a projected zero casualty rate for our forces, while Plan Alameda has a massive casualty rate. It also has the lowest chance of success."

On Greer's left, a holo appeared displaying the all-too familiar Huygens System where Airtha lay.

"We can see here the various defensive emplacements in the system, as well as where we expect the forces Airtha has gathered to position themselves. Most of this comes from standard TSF defensive doctrine for the Huygens System, updated to include the number of ships she has likely amassed.

"With plan 'Full-Auto', none of this matters. All that we care about is hitting Airtha with a few shots."

"A few shots of what?" Admiral Rellan asked from a few seats to Sera's left.

<*Impatient man,*> she commented to Jen.

<*He frequently is.*>

"This one would require assistance from New Canaan, but it should be feasible. The 'shots' would be one-ton neutron slugs, but at stellar compression levels. They would be housed in stasis fields and fired at relativistic speeds into the system."

A wave of murmurs swept through the room, and Sera spoke up. "Can you elaborate on how we make these slugs?"

"I can provide the full workup, but the technology is based on what Jessica and her team observed at Star City in the Perseus Arm. The city's weapons fired coherent beams of neutrons that were really held in stasis bubbles. This meant that they retained their highly compressed mass until right before impact, when the field drops, and a relativistic shrapnel blast hits the target."

Admiral Svetlana let out a low whistle. "That'll do it—if they can reach the target. Airtha has interdictors, so we can't use gates to jump the bullets insystem.

Greer nodded. "You're right. Airtha interdicts unplanned gate jumps a thousand AU from the star. That gives their forces roughly one hundred and forty hours to intercept. However, their reaction time is greatly compressed as the bullets will be travelling at nearly the same speed as the message that an interdiction occurred. In reality, they'll have less than ten hours to react."

"That still seems like plenty," Rellan said.

Greer's eyes narrowed as he regarded Rellan, clearly annoyed at the interruptions. "That's why we send a million."

Sera laughed. "I guess I know why you named it 'Plan Full-Auto'."

"Is that even feasible?" Hanso asked.

"It is, if New Canaan can retrofit their stasis pods to the task," Greer replied. "They have millions of them left over from their refit of the *I2*."

"A million bullets against half a million ships," Sera mused. "They'd still stand a chance of stopping them."

"We only need a dozen to reach Airtha," Svetlana said. "And since they're in stasis, they can't be stopped or destroyed, only shoved aside. The defenders would need to fire lateral shots at the bullets to move them off course."

Sera glanced back at the attendees, many of whom were nodding in appreciation—even Rellan, who spoke up once more.

"Any chance we can convince the ISF to supply stealth tech for these?"

"We don't have stealth tech for the majority of our ships," Svetlana countered. "Let's not waste it on bullets."

Rellan began to respond, when Greer held up his hands. "Stealth and stasis are not mutually compatible, unless you build a shell around the item in stasis, which is feasible, but introduces issues with acceleration and transition of the bullets through the jump gates."

"I assume we'd use a swarm technique, like we did at Albany?" Sera asked. "Send the bullets through from a large number of locations."

Greer nodded. "That's the idea. We really wouldn't need a million, either. It's possible that we could still destroy Airtha with half that number."

Sera leant back in her seat, tapping her finger against her chin. "Still need to fire them. Do we even have the ability to do this?"

"Honestly," Rellan interrupted. "We could do it with rail-fired slugs. Enough of them in stasis at relativistic speeds...stars, even without stasis shields. A few million, and the system would be destroyed."

"Use the DL," another voice spoke up. "Launch them into space near Airtha, then transition them into the DL. They can bypass the interdictors and make it much further insystem."

"The Exaldi will get them," Svetlana countered.

"Maybe," Rellan mused. "But some would get through. We've done drone tests like this, and often, two percent make it through to the inner system, I—"

"Won't work," Sera returned the favor of interruption to Rellan, and included a stern glare. "Airtha is surrounded by a higher density of Exaldi than normal—that was a key part of its selection."

"OK, everyone," Greer held up a hand once more. "Believe it or not, we've considered the options you're presenting. They're in the full data packet, along with the assessments of their effectiveness." He paused and gestured at the casualty estimate chart once more. "The other option is much like the bullets, but instead, we simply send in every ship we have. It would require pulling them from all theatres—but if we did, we could put together a force that would outnumber the defenders over two to one."

"And the losses?" Sera asked.

"We'd lose every ship without stasis shields. However, the analysis shows that we could take the ring intact."

"I thought that wasn't a goal?" Svetlana glanced at Sera. "There was concern that everyone on it could be irreparably subverted."

Sera nodded. "I did say I wanted an option that did not take into account civilian lives, but a conversation with someone recently has changed my mind about that. We all know people on Airtha. We at least owe it to them to try a solution that does not involve their wholesale destruction."

"That's where the middle ground plan comes in," Greer replied. "We fire the bullets, but at secondary targets: at fleet groups, defensive emplacements, everything *but* Airtha." He pointed at a casualty estimate of twenty million. "We'll lose at least that many, but I believe we'd take the day."

Rellan shook his head. "On top of those civilian casualties, we'd lose half our fleets, and then Orion will walk all over us. This doesn't sound like a great solution."

Greer nodded slowly. "I'm not in disagreement. It may be that waiting to sway more of the districts to Khardine's side is advisable."

"I've heard rumors that the Sagittarian districts are considering separating and forming their own alliance," Carl said. "I don't know how many more we'll pull in to our side."

Rellan folded his arms and looked like he was going to spit. "I thought we were better than this. Thirty percent of the Transcend is with us, maybe twenty with *her*. The rest are waffling or declaring for themselves."

"OK," Sera said as she rose and stepped up beside Admiral Greer. "This is excellent information. I'm open to more suggestions. But for now, we're going to continue to see how things play out in the Vela cluster—see if Krissy can gather more resources. If we can manage for another year, then New Canaan can have nearly a hundred thousand ships for us, and double the number of ships we currently have with stasis shields. That changes the outcome of a full assault greatly."

"A year's a long time," Svetlana said in a quiet voice.

Sera agreed, but she didn't have any other options at the moment. "In a year, Tanis will have put down the Nietzscheans and the Trisilieds, and Scipio will have taken out the Hegemony. That will take the wind out of Orion's sails in the Inner Stars. We'll have a lot more options at that point."

"There are still seventeen more empires and alliances in the Inner Stars that are leaning toward Orion—ones at least as big as the Nietzscheans," a colonel pointed out.

Sera nodded. "You're right, there are. But we have many tools at our disposal. Over sixty percent of the Hand's regional directors are with us, and we have missions underway to affect the decisions of those considering alliances with Orion."

There were slow nods following her words, and no one else spoke up to voice an opinion. Sera nodded to Greer and returned to her seat.

"OK," Greer said as he surveyed the room. "We still have the two Hoplite Fleets to ready, as well as planning for Sera's other key endeavor. Let's move like we're out of time."

Sera rose and watched the brass file out before approaching Greer. "A bit dour on your endnote, there."

Greer nodded. "I suppose. I think some of them are treating this war like something we'll win if we just do our jobs like normal. I guess it's the result of no one suffering a defeat in so long. They need to remember that this is a fight for our lives, and for everything we believe in."

"You're not wrong there," Sera said as she watched the last of the TSF's leadership file out. "Though I wish you were."

A REFLECTIVE WALK

STELLAR DATE: 08.30.8949 (Adjusted Years)
LOCATION: Ol' Sam, ISS *I2*
REGION: Pyra, Albany System, Thebes, Septhian Alliance

Tangel led a silent Rika through the forest on their way to the maglev station. She was taking a circuitous route. The conversation that she and the Marauder captain had engaged in was one that would take some time for Rika to digest.

The mech—something Tangel was surprised the cyborg warriors called themselves—had seen a lot of changes over the past few days. Everything from witnessing the destruction of a Nietzschean armada to the knowledge that she and all her people could be made whole, should they desire it.

<*You've already affected her,*> Bob said, as Tangel led Rika over a small bridge stretching across a bubbling brook. <*When you touched her, showed her your vision, her mental patterns shifted. Do you see it?*>

<*I do,*> Tangel replied. <*She's going to need that added strength. With General Mill and Captain Ayer dead, there are few people in authority over her that understand and respect her. She needs to know that someone she esteems believes fully in her.*>

<*Is it true?*>

<*Bob!*> Tangel admonished. <*I would not seed a lie in her mind. And I would not knowingly set her on a road to ruin. I believe Rika can execute the plan and topple Nietzschea.*>

<*Just checking. I've gotten used to reading everyone's intentions. You, I have to ask to gain certainty.*>

"Admir—Tanis." Rika began to speak as they stepped off the bridge's wooden surface and back onto the earthen path. "I get the feeling there is something more you want to tell me."

"Ask you is more like it," Tangel replied.

Rika cocked her head, a corner of her lips curling up in a nervous smile. "*You* asking *me*? Why does that make me nervous?"

Tangel winked. "No need to be nervous. I was just thinking about your mind—well, your brain."

Rika's smile turned into a laugh. "I don't know that anyone has ever said something quite like that to me before. Usually people are talking about every part of me except for my brain."

"Well, they're foolish, then," Tangel replied. "I believe that when Niki gets properly paired with you—should the two of you choose to do it—we should begin the process of enhancing your mental capacity."

"Sorry?" Rika coughed. "Enhancing?"

"Right now, you're close to an L1—don't ask me how I know that, I can just tell. You have a higher neuron density than is normal, but your axons are not as long, and your dendrites are not as interconnected as they could be. I don't think it would be that difficult to get you to L2 status."

Rika lifted her left hand and placed it on her head. "Won't that…change me?"

"It would," Tangel nodded. "But because you already have a high volume of neurons, the change would not be as much as someone going from L0 to L1 normally experiences. The changes are different for everyone, but mostly you'd find that you're faster, you can make intuitive leaps better—and they're more accurate because you can consider more variables. You might even get the ability to multithread."

"Multithread?" Rika asked. "Like think of more than one thing at once?"

"Right," Tangel confirmed. "Though many people *think* they can do this, L0's really can't. They may switch focus quickly—at a cognitive penalty, I might add—but they really can't think of two things simultaneously."

<Like when you were talking with Angela and I, as well as to Tim?> Niki asked. *<I was impressed at how well you did that.>*

You have no idea, Tangel thought. *Especially considering that I'm passing myself off as two people right now.*

While talking with Rika, Tangel was masquerading as Angela in twenty-seven conversations in the Link, and as Tanis in three others.

And it wasn't remotely taxing.

"Exactly like that," Tangel replied to Niki. "As an added advantage, being directly linked with Rika's mind, you'll be able to have deeper conversations with her, and share more via what amounts to a sort of cross-cognitive intuition."

"We wouldn't merge, would we?" Rika asked quickly. "Not that what's happening to you and Angela is bad…I just like being me, is all."

Tangel laughed as she shook her head. "It's vanishingly rare now, but at one time, many L2s paired with AIs—well, not many, but a lot. To my knowledge, Angela and I are the only ones who have found themselves in this predicament."

"I guess that's reassuring," Rika replied, then fell silent.

Tangel could see that she was deep in thought—both from her lowered brow and from the activity in her mind. It was plain to see that the mech and her AI were also speaking rapidly with one another.

"It would make me a more effective leader, wouldn't it?" Rika finally asked.

"It would," Tangel nodded in agreement. "Much more effective. I believe that you would fare much better in your fight against Nietzschea."

Rika snorted. "Stop hedging. You mean that fewer of my mechs would die from stupid decisions I make."

Tangel laughed, her tone rueful as she thought of her many stupid decisions. "Yes, but you're not going to be infallible. And don't get cocky."

"No chance of that." Rika shook her head as the maglev platform came into view on the trail ahead. "Self-doubt and second-guessing all the way, here."

<Don't listen to her,> Niki interjected. *<She's got her head on straight.>*

Tangel chuckled softly as they walked out of the trees and into the maglev platform's clearing. "I know it. I wouldn't have offered you this mission otherwise."

Rika nodded in silence as they stepped onto the platform and waited for a car to arrive. "I hope I live up to that belief."

"You will," Tangel said, giving Rika a slow wink. "And think on the L2 enhancement. It could really help."

"I think I'll do it," Rika replied as the car arrived. "I mean…I think it's a sure thing, but I want to talk it over with Chase first."

"Good," Tangel nodded. "I'm glad you two work as a team."

Rika laughed. "Me too, Tanis, me too."

NEW HORIZONS

STELLAR DATE: 08.30.8949 (Adjusted Years)
LOCATION: Bay 19-12A, Keren Station
REGION: Khardine System, Transcend Interstellar Alliance

Sera squared her shoulders as she waited on the docks with her High Guard, watching as Jason's shuttle settled on its cradle. For reasons she couldn't quite pin down, Sera felt more trepidation than the meeting should engender.

She hadn't spent any time in private with him since Elena had come aboard the *Intrepid* just over twenty years ago at Ascella. Though they'd flirted constantly during the month she spent aboard the colony ship, Jason had never made himself fully available to her.

It wasn't surprising. He was the captain of the ship, burdened with his duties and responsibilities—not the least of which was keeping a handle on Tanis.

Sera was the spy who turned out to be the daughter of their uncertain ally. Not the sort of individual a logical person would become entangled with.

One thing is certain about Jason—he ***is*** *logical. Not risk averse, or calculating, but rather…considering.*

Which made her wonder why he had come to Khardine—especially at a time when so many allied ships had been deployed to the Albany System to rescue Tanis.

The cradle's ramp lifted to meet the shuttle's opening airlock, and Sera had to force herself to relax.

Seriously. You saw Jason just a year ago. Neither of us made any overtures. This is just a professional visit.

There was no reason to believe that there was anything remaining between them—granted, she was still getting over her father's betrayal and death, and Elena….

A pair of ISF Marines were the first ones out of the shuttle, stepping smartly down the ramp. They didn't seem overly concerned about their surroundings, which may have been due to the fact that two members of Sera's personal guard were also ISF Marines.

A moment later, Jason Andrews' large frame appeared, silhouetted in the airlock's opening. He paused for a moment, and then stepped onto the ramp. His calm, purposeful strides reminded her of one of the reasons she'd always been drawn to him: the man was the living definition of 'unflappable'.

He must have undergone rejuv recently, because his formerly silver-white hair was now a dirty blonde. The change shifted him from the stately captain she'd first met on the *Intrepid* twenty years ago, to a much younger, rakish-looking man. Somehow it didn't decrease his mystique, though, it enhanced it.

<*Well* ***that*** *wasn't in the bio I read on you,*> Jen said with a soft laugh in Sera's mind. <*Have feelings for the New Canaan Governor?*>

<*Hush, Jen,*> Sera chided her AI.

Relax, Sera, she told herself. *He's not here to see you. You're both heads of state on official business. Well, I suppose that's not correct. He* ***is*** *here to see me, but not like that. Don't make him the rebound guy after Elena.*

As Jason descended the ramp, she could see that his eyes had settled on her. A broad smile formed on his lips, and his pace quickened. Sera walked forward, and they met at the base of the ramp, clasping hands.

"Governor Andrews, it's very good to see you. We don't get a lot of state visits at Khardine."

"Sera, please," Jason's smile was warm and comforting. "Just call me 'Jason'. I don't stand on formality—I know it's not your preference, either."

Sera shrugged. "My many advisors are beating it into me, though they're all quite put out that you wanted to meet with me privately."

Jason ran a hand along his neat beard—an affectation she was glad he'd kept—and nodded soberly. "Sorry for all the cloak and dagger stuff, the topic I have to discuss is highly sensitive. Would you care to come aboard my pinnace?"

"Surely I have more comfortable accommodations on Keren."

"Yes," Jason gave Sera an appraising look. "But Tanis has instructed that conversations on this topic take place only in highly controlled locations."

"Tanis's orders?" Sera asked. "Aren't you the governor now, Jason?"

Jason cocked an eyebrow and gave a soft laugh. "You know that no matter what her title is, Tanis is in charge. It's in her nature. She was born for this."

"That sounds strangely prophetic, Jason," Sera replied.

He shrugged as he offered his hand and turned to walk back up the ramp. "Would you like to know why I've come?"

"Are we staying in the docking bay?" Sera asked. "If we're taking the pinnace to your ship, then my guards will insist they come along."

Jason glanced at the four High Guard standing nearby. "As they should. I wish I could convince Tanis to travel with an escort like this."

Sera snorted. "As if you could. Besides from the updates that Joe sent, Tanis is a one-woman battle station now."

Jason barked a laugh. "Well, she'd have to be to house that iron will of hers. And yes, we're staying on the dock. No need to bring your guards aboard."

"OK," Sera replied, and nodded to the High Guard before taking Jason's hand and following him up the ramp, wondering why he'd offered it to her, and why she felt forty years younger holding it.

Once inside, Jason led her to a small dining cabin, and they sat on either side of the table. A servitor poured two cups of coffee, and then retreated to its alcove.

Jason added cream to his, while Sera opted to drink hers black. The planet Troy in the New Canaan System grew some of the best coffee beans in the galaxy, and there was no need to muddy their taste.

"So?" she said after a moment, hoping to prompt Jason into explaining his mysterious visit.

His gaze rose to meet hers, and his eyes remained on her face as he took a sip of his coffee. When he lowered his cup, his eyes drifted down as well, and a small smile graced his lips.

"I'm glad you haven't changed your mode of dress, even though you're the Great President now," he said.

Sera looked down and saw that her skin had reverted to its red 'naked' state at some point, and chastised herself for not maintaining better control.

Perhaps I need to suck it up and ask Jen to keep an eye on me.

She considered changing her appearance back to her uniform, but decided not to. There was no shame in being what she was—though she worried that Jason would think she was doing it to seduce him…which maybe she was—subconsciously, of course.

Of course.

"Well, I don't normally go around like this," she confessed. "But if I get distracted, I revert…"

Jason took another sip of his coffee, an eyebrow arched. "Distracted?" When he set down the cup, there was a mischievous smirk on his lips.

"Jason Andrews!" Sera's brow lowered. "Are you flirting with me?"

Jason held up his forefinger and thumb. "Maybe a smidge. But if you're still…whatever you might be with Elena, I'll stifle it."

<*He's perceptive,*> Jen commented.

The governor's mouth hung open for a moment longer, as though he was going to say something more, but then he closed his lips and regarded her with his penetrating brown eyes.

Sera made a dismissive swipe with her hand, nearly spilling her coffee. "No," she said a little too loudly. "I mean…no, I'm not 'whatever' with Elena. I'm not entirely over her, over what she did to me—to everyone, for that matter—but I no longer harbor any pleasant feelings or longing for her. The neurologists are working out the best way to reverse whatever it was that Garza did to her, but I think it would be best if she and I never…anythinged anymore."

Her expression must have contained some level of angst, because Jason's eyes softened while she rushed out her explanation.

"Sorry, I shouldn't have gone there," he soothed. "It's inappropriate, and we have other matters to discuss."

Sera was continually impressed by Jason's ability to be the stodgy old man—even when he no longer looked it. "Jason, it's OK. I appreciate frank conversations like this. I spend too much time in my own head. I'd grown used to bouncing ideas off Tanis, but she's a bit hard to get ahold of right now."

"That's a part of what I have to tell you," Jason said with a solemn nod. "There are things we've learned about Tanis from Katrina that she wants me to share with you."

"Why you?" Sera asked.

"Well, because I spoke with Katrina directly. I have it from the horse's mouth, so to speak."

Sera had read the report out of New Canaan that one of the colonists' old companions from Victoria had followed them through Kapteyn's Streamer. It was mind boggling to think that the woman had spent five hundred years waiting for the *Intrepid* to arrive.

The report had been light on details, but it did note that Katrina was being 'detained'.

"You knew her from your time back at Kapteyn's Star, didn't you?" Sera asked.

"I did." Jason leant back in his chair and folded his arms across his chest. "I counted her as a friend. I still do, I think. She ended up coming under the influence of an ascended AI, one named Xavia. The AI…bent her a bit. Not to mention some of the things she went through...I swear, I think we had a far easier time of it than she did."

"That's not saying much," Sera replied. "Is this Xavia the same being as the Caretaker?"

"Not from what Katrina says. She believes that Xavia represents a different faction. One that wants to see humanity advance on its own terms. I guess they got tired of seeing the Caretaker's group drive humanity into one dark age after another. To hear Katrina tell it, Xavia and her ilk have been greatly responsible for much of the general uplift in the Inner Stars over the last thousand years."

Sera snorted. "Just like those ascended AIs to take all the credit. The Hand worked tirelessly to forge alliances and build humanity back up."

Jason shrugged. "I take it all with a grain of salt. Either way, Xavia told Katrina some interesting things about Tanis."

The way that Jason spoke the words, it was clear that he was about to drop a bomb, and Sera steeled herself for it.

"Go on."

"Well, from what she's said, Tanis was *engineered* to be what she's become."

"She what?" Sera leant forward, hands on the table. "How was Tanis engineered?"

"You of course know that Tanis is a natural L1, right? She was enhanced to be an L2 in her late teens because she had the neural structure to support it. It's what precluded her from getting an AI, until research—research spearheaded by the Enfield Corporation—worked out how to embed AIs in the brains of L2s."

"Are you saying that Terrance Enfield had some hand in 'engineering' Tanis? Though I suppose that's not too surprising. Tanis has been more a product of science than nature for some time."

To some, the words may have come off as demeaning, but Sera didn't mean them that way, and from the soft laugh Jason gave, he didn't interpret them as such.

"You're not wrong about that, but that's not what it means. Terrance says he knew his company had been the one to facilitate Tanis getting her first AI, but not that anything nefarious had been done."

"And you trust Terrance?" Sera asked, nearly folding her arms too, but realizing it would look ridiculous if the two of them were sitting at the small table with their arms folded, staring each other down.

She expected Jason to bristle at her question, but he only laughed.

"With my life. Multiple times. Terrance and I go way back. Waaaaay back."

"OK, so where is all this going? Did the ascended AIs tamper with Tanis somehow?"

"Yeah, from what I can tell they improved her, made sure that she'd be able to get the *Intrepid* where it needed to be. Except, as you know, Bob got us out of the Streamer too soon. We exited from it five hundred years before the master plan was ready."

Sera studied Jason's expression. She could tell that he still had more to say, so she nodded for him to carry on.

"Katrina said—and Tanis has confirmed this with Bob—that *he* also altered her, without her or Angela knowing."

"Shiiiiiit," Sera drew the word out. "How so?"

"I don't have all the details, so you'll have to talk to Tanis about it when you next see her, but Bob confirmed that he *and* Earnest have been changing Tanis's brain slowly and carefully for years to facilitate what ultimately happened on Pyra."

Sera shook her head, incredulous disbelief flooding her features. "Why?"

"Bob's argument is that it had to be done to keep them alive. If he'd let their merger proceed without intervention, she would have gone insane decades ago. They worked up some new picotech procedure that erected quantum-level barriers to direct how their minds merged."

"Tanis must be pissed!" Sera exclaimed.

Jason nodded slowly. "I know *I* would be. She seems to be taking it in stride."

"Is that because she's ascended now? Or whatever she is?" Sera asked. "Stars, I should go see her. I need to know what she's thinking."

"From what I understand, she's only semi-ascended." Jason took another drink of his coffee. "Whatever that means. This is all pretty crazy stuff. But in all honesty, I've been living with the fallout from transhumanism my entire life. I was one of the first documented natural L2s, you know. Did a lot of work to free AIs—sucks to see that we're still fighting that same fight."

"I didn't know that," Sera said, examining Jason in a new light. She knew the basics of his story, born at Proxima Centauri in the early fourth millennia, grandson of one of the heroes of the Sentience Wars whose parents had gotten out of Sol to some place a little tamer. She knew he'd plied sub-light ships in the black for centuries, which gave him a sort of kinship with the FGT. Beyond that, she didn't know too much else.

"So what does all this mean?" Sera asked. "What do we do with this information?"

"Damned if I know," Jason replied with a grin that looked far more roguish on a young man's face. "It's not really the main topic I came here to discuss."

His words caught Sera mid-drink, and she nearly spat out her coffee. "Seriously?" Sera paused to set her cup down. "The fact that Tanis is part of some millennia-long master plan to either save or destroy humanity is the *side topic*?"

"Well, we know that Tanis is too strong willed to allow herself to be controlled by anyone. Everything she's done is evidence that she's no one's pawn."

Sera let out a coarse laugh. "You're right, there. Woe be to any super-being that thinks they can control her. She's going to beat them at their own game."

Jason nodded and lifted his coffee cup once more, tipping it back to drain the last remains before signaling to the servitor that he wanted a refill.

While the bot completed his request, the governor leant forward, placing his elbows on the table. "You've heard of our Aleutian site, right?"

Sera nodded. "Yeah, I've seen it mentioned in a few places. You sent out the initial ships when I was still in New Canaan last year."

"Right, we did. I assume you know what it is?"

"Sure, I guess." Sera spread her hands wide. "A beta site for your people; I don't blame you, New Canaan is in everyone's crosshairs. I'm a bit surprised you all stayed."

Jason chuckled as he watched the servitor set his coffee down on the table. "Jen," he addressed Sera's AI. "I assume you're listening?"

<*I am,*> Jen replied. <*This is a fascinating topic.*>

“Don’t I know it,” he agreed, while pouring a generous amount of cream into his coffee. “You now have Omega clearance, Jen. Top level.”

<*Uh…what is ‘top level’?*> Jen asked.

“There isn’t one. It means you have unrestricted access to any ISF and New Canaan intel. Sera has it too, now. The two of you don’t need to keep secrets from one another.” He paused and met Sera’s eyes. “But I’ll trust that you’ll keep what I’m about to tell you in the strictest confidence. Until we decide to take action.”

“Er…sure,” Sera said, her brows deeply furrowed.

“To your previous statement about us remaining in New Canaan: simply put, we’re a stubborn group. We put a lot of effort into building our colony, and a lot of lives were lost defending it.”

“But you’re realists,” Sera replied.

“We are, yes.”

“I’ll admit.” Sera’s eyes narrowed as she watched Jason’s eyes for any tells. “I’ve been curious as to where your Aleutian Site is, but Tanis didn’t volunteer the information, and I decided she’d share it when she was ready.”

“It’s in the LMC,” Jason replied tonelessly, not looking up as he stirred his cream into his coffee.

This time Sera nearly did choke. “The Large Magellanic Cloud? Like…the *galaxy* that’s a hundred and sixty fucking thousand light years from here?”

“Closer to one seventy, where we are,” Jason said, looking up and winking at Sera. “We like to do things big.”

“No fucking kidding,” Sera muttered. “Seriously, Jason. This is all getting to be too much. Ascended AIs scheming from the core of the galaxy, Finaeus building a secret staging ground in the 3kpc Arm, Tanis ascending, and now this. Are you all leaving?”

“You know about Project Starflight, right?” Jason asked.

"Yeah, Tanis told me that you guys are going to make Canaan Prime burn asymmetrically and fly it out of the Milky Way Galaxy. That's some serious long-term planning."

Jason nodded. "Go big, or go home, right? Well, I guess we finally *got* a home, so we're going 'big' there. Anyway, the Aleutian site is the yin to Project Starflight's yang. It's the destination. But we're not stepping out of the conflict. We'll do our part, and help put things back together before we leave."

"Leave," Sera whispered the word. "So you are going to leave. All of you."

"It's not like it's going to happen tomorrow, or even in a century. It takes a long time to accelerate a star to galactic escape velocity."

"Sometimes you must wonder about the words you're saying," Sera laughed.

Jason snorted. "I'm just a simple guy from Proxima Centauri. You're the one who grew up on a diamond ring wrapped around a Saturn-sized white dwarf star."

"Touché."

"There's more."

"Jason…seriously, just spill it already, you're killing me, here."

Jason nodded soberly. "This is serious stuff, Sera. We jumped to the LMC on the outskirts of the NGC 1783 globular cluster. Conditions were right for Class G stars in that region, and we found them. The Aleutian team is studying local cosmic events to determine if it's a safe region—or if they should relocate. They're also setting up an industrial base around a star they've named Cheshire."

"Damn," Sera whispered. "What does the Milky Way look like from out there?"

"I've not been there yet," Jason replied. "But I imagine the answer is 'amazing'."

"OK, so, while this is way up there on the freakin' awesome scale, I'm not sure why it warrants a private visit from the man himself." Sera smirked at Jason as she spoke, the glib words and grin on her lips the only way she could deal with all the information Jason had hit her with.

"You're right. I'm here to talk about what we *found* in the LMC."

Sera's eyes grew wide, and she slammed both hands onto the table. "You found aliens! I knew it!"

Jason barked a laugh at her enthusiasm. "Stars, I wish we'd found aliens. Well, maybe. Who knows, maybe they're in hiding. Either way, what we found were humans."

For a moment, the words didn't make sense to Sera. "What? Seriously? Humans?"

Jason nodded. "Not just any humans, we found the Transcend."

"OK, stop doling it out," Sera said through gritted teeth, as the myriad implications of his words all but buried her. "Lay it on me."

"Sorry, trying to make this…less nuts than it all is."

"You've failed. Just give it to me."

Jason took another sip of coffee and leant forward once more.

"While our people were setting up, they kept noticing strange variances in the light from a few stars not far away. Variances that didn't match natural patterns. What they *did* match were massive fusion burns from planet movers undertaking terraforming operations."

"Shit," Sera whispered. "Really?"

"I thought you wanted me to just spill it. You've gotta stop interrupting for that to happen."

"Sorry." She pursed her lips and gestured for him to continue.

"The activity was coming from a group of stars at the edge of an open cluster about two hundred light years away. Once we had shipped in our backup gates, we jumped in a scouting team and took a closer look. What we found were three FGT terraforming groups, all working on establishing new worlds—well, that's what they *had* been doing. When we came in closer, we saw that they'd ceased those operations and were stripping the systems down and building shipyards."

"I…I have no knowledge of this," Sera said. "I don't think anyone here does."

"We have a stealth ship doing a close fly-by as we speak," Jason replied. "We'll know more soon. But if you don't know about this, there are only two options."

Sera nodded and let out a long sigh. "Airtha, or some other rogue element in the Transcend."

"Or a rogue element that is now under Airtha's control."

"My father had to have known about this," Sera muttered. "What *else* did he have going on?"

"I don't know," Jason replied, his voice kind. "Chances are that, whatever it is, Airtha has the details, given her position at…well, Airtha."

Sera nodded. "We need to accelerate our plans to stop her. TSF strategists are working on some ideas, but…they're not ideal."

"How so?"

"Well, Airtha has the Huygens System well defended. There could be as many as half a million ships there by now. We'd wondered why she'd given up so much of the Transcend to us without a fight. Now that I know she's building ships in the LMC, I wonder if she has other, similar facilities spread throughout the galaxy—or even in the other dwarf galaxies surrounding the Milky Way."

"So what's your plan of attack on Airtha?" Jason asked. "Or, at least the winning proposals."

"This is all predicated on Airtha being linked to the ring and being unable to move from it. However, from the report you sent from Kara, who I'd really like to meet, it's possible that Airtha is fully ascended, and may not be directly connected to the ring anymore."

"Hard to say," he replied. "From what we've been learning about ascended beings, to operate in our three paltry dimensions, they need some sort of physical presence. Earnest believes that they need to reconstruct themselves in other dimensions to fully leave this one, and that it may not be possible to do so entirely. Either way, she may still be tied the ring."

"Or she may not," Sera countered, and Jason shrugged before she continued. "Well, taking the Huygens System with our current resources is impossible—not if we want to be able to stand up to Orion afterward. However, destroying it is not."

"Destroying it?" he echoed. "How will you do that?"

Sera signaled the servitor for another cup of coffee. "A derivation of what the allies just pulled off in the Albany system, but with bullets."

"You're going to have to fire a lot of bullets to get past those half a million starships."

"Yeah," Sera nodded. "But if we use chunks of neutron stars held in stasis fields and moving at relativistic speeds, Airtha's defenses won't be able to stop them all. And it will only take a few of them getting through to destroy Airtha's ring."

Jason whistled. "That's one hell of a solution."

Sera wondered what he thought of his allies now, knowing that they would consider the wholesale slaughter of a trillion people, just to take out their enemy. "It's partially my fault. In a fit of frustration, I suggested that perhaps everyone on Airtha is fully under my mother's sway, and that we'd lose too many trying to take the system."

"Well, you're probably not wrong on both counts."

Sera snorted. "Yeah. I wish I was, though. We need to take out Airtha, but we can't assault her directly. Especially because with the control she has over the AIs…we'd be murdering slaves. I tabled the wholesale destruction option, thinking that we could choke off her access to resources, but now she has extra-fucking-galactic shipyards!"

Sera's voice had risen as she spoke, and Jason's eyes softened with compassion as he stretched out a hand and took hers.

"We've not been given an easy path, that's for sure. But we know that Airtha has these other facilities now, and we can destroy them, deny the LMC to her."

Sera nodded, not withdrawing her hand, the realization hitting her that she hadn't touched anyone romantically in over a year. *Hugs with Tanis don't count because they're not romantic for her.*

<*And if Airtha has other facilities?*> Jen asked, speaking for the first time since Jason dropped his bombs.

He shrugged. "It would take centuries to search the galaxy, we just have to assume that if we shut down that one expansion location, she won't have had time to set up others. But what we really need is better intel. We only saw that location because the FGT had been there for hundreds of years already, and the light had reached the Aleutian site."

"Of course, the intel we need is all at Airtha."

"Would it be?" Jason mused. "Your father struck me as a very well-prepared man, generally speaking. Is there any chance he had a backup site for the Transcend's government? A bunker of sorts in another system?"

"Given the fact that he was colonizing the Large Magellanic Cloud, I imagine he had a few out there." Sera shook her head and drew a deep breath, trying to find options. "The only one I know of is in Airtha's hands, nearly as well defended as the Huygens System."

Jason's brow furrowed, and then a small smile formed on his lips. "You know…if I were a paranoid megalomaniac who wanted the ultimate backup plan…"

Sera's eyes widened. "The LMC locations *are* his ultimate fallback—that's why even I didn't know about them. And if they are, there would be data there about any other sites, and the resources Airtha has access to."

"Bingo," Jason grinned. "I'll return to New Canaan and organize a strike team."

"No," Sera replied, and Jason's eyes narrowed.

"No?"

"Well, yes, but also no. I'm going, too."

Jason held her gaze for a moment before his solemn look turned into a grin. "That's what I like about you, Sera Tomlinson."

"What?" she asked.

"You're a woman of action."

NIETZSCHEA

STELLAR DATE: 08.31.8949 (Adjusted Years)
LOCATION: Valhalla
REGION: Capitol, Pruzia System, Nietzschean Empire

Garza's shuttle set down on a landing pad at a level of the Imperial Spire known as 'Valhalla'. As the cradle locked onto the shuttle, and the ramp rose, Garza composed himself for the meeting with the emperor.

After a minute, he rose and walked to the shuttle's opening, noting that his guards were already at the base of the ramp.

Looking around, he couldn't help but be a little impressed by the view. If he hadn't known otherwise, it would have been impossible to tell that Valhalla was over one hundred kilometers above Capitol's surface.

Before him stood a massive marble edifice, crafted in the form of an ancient fortress, featuring towers that stretched into space, beyond the limits of even Garza's augmented field of vision.

Around the landing pad were manicured lawns and gardens, and beyond those, a lake that encircled the entire platform.

From the approach the shuttle had taken, Garza had seen that the water poured off the edges of the lake, kept from blowing through the thin atmosphere by grav fields, which made it seem as though there was a hundred kilometer veil, pouring off the spire.

The effect shrouded the spire's shaft and made it appear as though it hovered on a pillar of mist.

None of that impressed Garza.

He'd seen his share of impossible feats of engineering: the ancient High Terra Ring, the Scipian ecumenopolis of Alexandria, the diamond Airthan Ring—though that one was only in a memory from a clone—and even a far-off view of Star City.

A spire like this was almost boring.

Even so, he'd come himself, sending a clone to deal with Praetor Kirkland. The Nietzschean Emperor was a tricky man; hard to pin down, and even harder to negotiate with.

It was a job he'd not send a clone to do.

Constantine also posed little threat to Garza—unlike Airtha and Sera. Garza was glad a clone had been sent to the Transcend's capital. It came back entirely under Airtha's thrall, though it did at least confirm that the abomination had finally ascended.

Praetor Kirkland may be a fool, but at least he had been right about the risk that Tomlinson's former wife posed. Keeping her around had been a mistake, one that Garza was glad to know had finally taken Jeffrey Tomlinson out of the picture.

As Garza walked down the shuttle's ramp toward the functionary that waited for him below, he couldn't help but wish things had gone differently.

Jeffrey Tomlinson had started out as a good man. Stars, he had been the one to really kick-start interstellar colonization. He founded the Transcend.

It was possible that the man had been one of the most influential humans in all of history.

A flash of regret passed through Garza's mind that he had needed to order Tomlinson's death. He'd lost a valuable asset on the mission, as well. Elena's placement with Sera had taken decades of work, and she threw it all away to kill Tomlinson herself, when Kent should have been the one to do it.

Still, Garza's plans could move forward even with the wrinkle that the degenerate Sera presented. It was Tanis Richards who was the real problem. That his operation in Scipio had failed to kill her was more than infuriating; it put many of his other operations on the spinward side of Sol at risk.

The Nietzschean functionary said something in greeting, and Garza nodded absently, still lost in thought as he considered his best options for bolstering the region against Tanis and her fleet of invincible ships.

His best option was to go wide. Hit hundreds, maybe even thousands of systems at once. Never concentrate forces, never give Tanis a target she could strike.

He'd learned that lesson twice now. Once at New Canaan, and again at Silstrand. It wouldn't happen a third time.

"General?" the Nietzschean functionary asked, his tone making it apparent he was repeating himself.

"What is it?" Garza snapped as they turned onto the main pathway leading to Valhalla's gates.

"I was just letting you know that the emperor will be seeing you in the garden today."

Garza waved his hand. "That is fine. Wherever he wants, so long as he doesn't keep me waiting."

"Of course not," the liveried servant said, ducking his head obsequiously before guiding Garza through Valhalla's gates and along a shrouded pathway leading around the main cluster of spires toward what Garza assumed to be Constantine's private garden.

The walk was just over half a kilometer, and Garza was beginning to wonder if the emperor had spent so much money on trappings that he couldn't afford a groundcar, when they finally reached a pair of gleaming gates.

As the servant guiding Garza approached, the gates opened, revealing an idyllic meadow beyond. Trees ringed the perimeter, and a small stream flowed through the center. On the far side of the stream was an ancient oak, its large boughs spreading across a quarter of the meadow.

Beneath the tree's thick branches, reclining on a chaise, was Emperor Constantine.

The man wore a simple white robe, chewing languidly on grapes he was plucking from a bunch hanging on a pole. On either side of him were naked servants—both men and women—who were fanning him as though he were some ancient Terran king.

The servants surrounding the emperor were the finest specimens of humanity a person could imagine. They embodied a perfected physical—and likely mental—form; all completely natural.

In a manner of speaking.

Constantine, and those he surrounded himself with, were entirely unmodded. They were, however, genetically engineered in every way.

Normally, the setting Garza approached would likely lead to debauchery before long, but he knew that not to be the case with Constantine.

The emperor purported to be celibate—something that every source at Garza's disposal confirmed. For whatever reason, the man seemed to enjoy proving to everyone that he was immune to any desires of the flesh by surrounding himself with carnal temptations.

Nietzscheans, Garza thought in derision. *In their effort to become the purest humans they can be, they've forgotten what humanity is all about: Multiply and fill the heavens. Fulfill our manifest destiny.*

The functionary led Garza across a series of flat-topped stones placed in the stream, and then stood silently before the emperor, hands clasped behind his back.

Garza resisted the urge to roll his eyes as they waited a full minute for Constantine to acknowledge their presence.

Finally the man spoke, his voice a deep baritone. "General."

Constantine didn't look up from the grapes he held in his hand, and Garza waited for five long seconds before replying.

"Emperor Constantine. It is good to see you again."

The emperor finally looked up and nodded to Garza before glancing at the servant and flicking his hand, gesturing for the functionary to leave.

Without a word, the man left, and Garza took it upon himself to sit in one of the chairs next to the emperor's chaise.

A look of annoyance flickered across the emperor's face, but he didn't make an issue of Garza's presumptive action.

"To what do I owe this pleasure, General Garza?" the emperor asked, as though they hadn't already exchanged a host of messages.

"I'm here to review the strategy for the assault on Septhia, as we'd discussed in our communications. I understand you have amassed a force capable of striking every Septhian star at once."

"Have I?" the emperor arched a brow. "I suppose I have. However, I recently enacted another plan."

Garza's brow pinched together, and he resisted the urge to reach out and slap the grapes out of Constantine's hand. Instead, all he said was, "Oh?"

"Yes. It turns out that Tanis Richards and her ancient colony ship have been flitting around the edges of my empire, looking for someone."

"Really?" Garza had no idea why Tanis would do such a thing. "Who?"

"A rather odious man, a thorn in my side. General Mill of the Marauders."

Garza delved into his data on the region and pulled up the information on the Marauders—a group of mercenaries consisting of Genevians who had banded together after their people's conquest by the Nietzscheans.

"What did she want with Mill?" Garza asked.

"I don't know, but I expect to find out. My moles within the Septhian government have orders to attack them when they finally meet. Chances are that it will be somewhere in Thebes or the Politica. I've massed a fleet of over seventy thousand ships, that should see to my enemy's capture, and the destruction of whatever escort they possess."

Garza felt heat rise in his face as he fixed the emperor with a penetrating stare. "Tell me this isn't the fleet we were going to use in our attack on Septhia."

"*General* Garza. Do not presume to instruct me as to what to tell you. We are in Nietzschea here, not your Orion Freedom Alliance."

Garza drew in a deep breath and schooled his expression before inclining his head. "I ask your forgiveness. But tell me, did your ships attack?"

"We are some distance from Praesepe," Constantine replied, his tone arch, as though he were going out of his way to forgive Garza for his verbal faux pas. "But I did just receive word that the attack is being readied. At Albany, no less. I rather like the symmetry of it. And yes, we committed the force we'd built up for the attack on Septhia. Once they've captured Tanis Richards and her ship, they can proceed with that mission as planned."

"Doubtful. They're likely lost," Garza said simply.

"What is? Our prey?" Constantine asked, his serene expression cracking for the first time.

"No. Your fleet," the general clarified. "I imagine it's gone."

Constantine dropped his grapes and swung his legs over the edge of his chaise, sitting up and fixing Garza with a penetrating stare. The indolent emperor was gone, now replaced with a power-hungry man determined to seize anything his thoughts settled on.

"I sent *seventy thousand* ships. The accounts I have tell me she was travelling with a few dozen escort craft. Even her vaunted *Intrepid* cannot stand up to a force the size I sent."

"*I2*," Garza corrected.

"What?" Constantine snapped.

"The ISS *I2*. The *Intrepid* has been upgraded. Now the ship likely has firepower equal to a quarter of the fleet you sent against it, just on its own. It houses a hundred thousand fighters, all with stasis shields. You sent your fleet to its death."

"It's not possible," Constantine whispered. "I will have captured Tanis Richards!"

"No," Garza hissed. "You squandered your opportunity to divide your enemy's forces. If you mass, she will strike you and decimate your fleet. Tanis Richards is a bleeding heart. Your best offense is to attack everywhere at once, destroy worlds, decimate entire star systems. Create mass humanitarian crises that will slow her down and divide her forces. *That* is how you defeat her! You wear her down to a nub."

The emperor had paled as Garza's voice rose in volume, but then he seemed to remember himself, and rose before Garza.

"You'll do well to remember your place, General. I am emperor in Nietzschea, you—"

Garza rose and took a step toward the emperor, moving within arm's reach of the insufferable man.

In an instant, Constantine's naked servants held a host of weapons from blades to pistols. All aimed or leveled at Garza.

Constantine smirked. "Sit."

Garza lifted a hand. Slowly, as though he were bored with the situation. He snapped his fingers, and the naked men and women surrounding him fell to the ground.

"Do not think I would come here unprepared, Constantine. I have means at my disposal you can only imagine."

The emperor's face paled as he realized he was completely at Garza's mercy. "How?" he whispered. "I have countermeasures...."

"There is much I have not shared with you...yet," Garza said, sitting once more, and gesturing for Constantine to follow suit. "I *was* going to share jump gate tech with you, but first you'll need to build a new fleet. I want Septhia gone within the year."

Constantine sat as directed, a look of utter confusion on his face. "I need more resources, I've lost much, protecting the empire, our borders are vast—"

Garza held up a hand. "You have the resources. You have worlds, moons, more than enough to build millions of ships. Yes, you have debts you owe, you've spent much in your conquests. But frankly, Emperor Constantine, I don't give a fuck.

"You claim master morality? Well, use it. Seize what you want and build a fleet to *end* your enemies. Build that fleet by whatever means necessary, and I'll facilitate you with jump gates to deliver it to the doorsteps of every star system that opposes you."

Garza rose once more, and looked down at the emperor in disgust.

"I've implanted my nano inside your body. You have a year. If I'm not satisfied with what you've done by then, you'll die. There's nothing you can do about it. My nano is undetectable by your medical science."

"Garza..." The word came out in a choke.

The Orion general let a laugh escape his lips as he began to walk away, stopping at the stream to look over his shoulder.

"One year, Emperor. And remember. I *own* you. I own all of Nietzschea now."

The emperor sputtered something, but Garza ignored him as he stepped across the stones in the stream then strode back through the meadow.

Of course, he'd done nothing to the emperor, but the man would go to his medics nonetheless. Their inability to find anything would cement his belief that Garza did indeed leave something within his body that would kill, come a year.

Garza decided that he would stay near the Capitol System for a few weeks—long enough to be sure that the emperor would do as he'd been told. Or, should Constantine disobey, to see that the man was replaced.

Following that, Garza would meet back up with the clone he sent to Praetor Kirkland and see how much longer *that* man would last in his position.

INNER EMPIRE

STELLAR DATE: 08.31.8949 (Adjusted Years)
LOCATION: Bridge Conference Room, ISS *I2*
REGION: Pyra, Albany System, Thebes, Septhian Alliance

"Here's the deal," Tangel spoke slowly, sweeping her gaze across the four people in front of her. "I like Thebes. You're a good people who got dealt a bad hand. I don't think that becoming a part of Septhia is good for you; they're just treating you like a buffer between themselves and Nietzschea."

At her words, the men and women nodded soberly.

General Andre spoke up first in his gravelly voice. "I won't argue with that, but we're still staring at Nietzschea across a thirty-light year stretch of systems that are just waiting for the Niets to roll across them. From what you've said, your fleet can't stay here forever. With all that in mind, Septhia is the best option we have."

As the general spoke, the woman to his left, Governor Herra, began to shake her head. "No, Andre, that's just a delaying tactic. Septhia is trying to build a new empire to stand against the Niets, but they're doing it on the backs of everyone around them. In the end, they'll be no different from the Nietzscheans."

Admiral Kally snorted. "Except they're inept. The Septhians can't hope to pull off what the Niets have done—they're not ruthless enough."

"Which we should consider a blessing," Herra said, catching Kally's eye.

"I see that we're all on the same page, then," Tangel said, turning to the fourth visitor, a man named Kendrik. He pursed his lips, then nodded.

"I am. Assuming you have some sort of plan that's more than just a way to call for you to come save us when the Niets attack again—because they *will* attack again."

Tangel nodded as she considered Kendrik. He was the person she needed onboard the most, but he was also the one with the most to lose.

As a businessman who had corporate interests across Thebes and much of Septhia, backing Theban independence from Septhia would put his broader business operations at risk from retaliation.

However, he was the one with the skill and the contacts to manage what Tangel wanted to build in Thebes.

"I can't make guarantees that Septhia won't act…in a manner contrary to their best interests, but I will do everything in my power to bring them in line with what's best for Praesepe at large."

"Which is your way of saying that you'll make them promise not to seize my businesses in Septhia, right?" Kendrik asked, his unblinking eyes boring into Tangel's.

This is where Angela would say something like, 'wow, he's got a set of balls on him', Tangel thought with a mental smirk.

But straight talk is what Kendrik needed to hear.

"There is verbiage in the Alliance treaty which precludes them from taking action that can be considered retaliatory against citizens of other allied nations who operate businesses in both jurisdictions. There are also, however," Tangel's eyes grew serious as she held Kendrik's gaze, "provisions against war profiteering."

Kendrik didn't reply for a moment, but Tangel couldn't help but notice how wide Kally's eyes grew. Then the man gave a short nod.

"Very well, I believe it should not be an issue for me to abide by the alliance treaty. So what do you need from me? I don't have any military power to back a re-formed Theban Alliance"

"True," Tangel said, a smile playing at the corners of her lips. "But how do you feel about operating the largest shipyard this side of Sol?"

"Admiral Richards," General Andre grunted. "Speak plainly, please. What is it that you're proposing?"

"Very simply put, we're at a disadvantage against many of our enemies. They have the ability to bring larger fleets to bear than we do. When they mass, we can meet them and crush them, but there are millions of star systems out there, and we can't police them all; there are just too many fronts to this war. What we *need* are strong, dedicated allies to create bastions of strength that the enemy cannot roll over, allies that also strengthen those around them.

"That's a very generic strategy, though. More specifically, what I want to do is turn Thebes into a fleet building powerhouse. We'll take the Albany system and make it the economic center of the Praesepe cluster."

"That's…ambitious," Governor Herra said, breaking the silence that had settled on the room after Tangel's statement. "I'm certain you've noticed how the Albany System is in ruin. Pyra is all but an unlivable wasteland, and estimates are that it'll take three years to find all the survivors that jettisoned in pods when their ships and stations were destroyed by the Niets."

"And that's the optimistic view," Andre added.

"I think we can do it," Kendrik said, his concerned expression countering the optimism in his words. "But we'll make ourselves into an even bigger target than we are now. The Niets will come back."

Tangel leant back in her chair. "Ladies and gentlemen, you said it yourselves. The Niets are coming back no matter what—the only way to stop them from eventually crushing

Thebes is to defeat them. Thebes will be the engine of that destruction."

Admiral Kally shook her head, sighing as her eyes narrowed. "If your allied fleet hadn't just done what it did here, I'd believe you to be a lunatic, but you've already proven your abilities to us. How will we do this?"

Tangel brought up a view of Pyra, the planet shrouded in dark clouds and storms, a result of the destruction the fleeing Nietzschean ships had rained down on the world.

"This is a two-pronged approach. The first is to deal with the ruin that is Pyra, and the economic issues you're going to face in the wake of this destruction. No one is going to want to invest in Thebes—especially the Pyra System. And by 'invest', I mean time more than money. We need to make this system a shining beacon in the night. To do—"

The door slid open, and Finaeus rushed into the room. "Sorry I'm late, I was wrangling with Gunther. That man did *not* want to give up his Peter."

"Sorry?" Governor Herra asked.

"Allow me to introduce Finaeus Tomlinson," Tangel said as Finaeus took a seat. "He's going to kick off this project."

"Good to meet you folks," Finaeus said as he reached for the pitcher of lemonade on the table and poured himself a glass, glancing at Tanis as he did. "Gonna be a hell of a job to break the Peter down, but with the I-Class gates, we can get it through without too much trouble. Be a lot faster than building from scratch. Right size for Pyra, too. Give us a good grav-ring."

"Pardon?" General Andre asked, while Kendrik whispered, wide-eyed, "A grav ring?"

Finaeus gave Tangel an apologetic look. "Sorry, Tanis, I guess I jumped the gun, there."

Tangel shook her head, a forgiving smile on her lips. "Far be it from me to quell your enthusiasm, Finaeus. Carry on."

"Right," he said, then took a quick sip of his lemonade. "What we're going to do is take a Peter—that's a device we use to cool planets after we make or move them—and use its base support structure to build a ring around Pyra. Probably situate it about two hundred and forty klicks above the surface. We use particle pressure to support the ring, run an accelerator around the whole planet, and then the ring rests on that. You get a bit lower gravity than on the surface, but not much. We can probably build a structure capable of supporting a few billion people at least. Plus, the whole purpose of a Peter is to manage temperature on a planet—it usually cools them, but Gunther's can run both ways. We'll stabilize Pyra, manage its sunlight with collector arrays on the ring, and get your world back in pristine condition in a decade, tops."

"All the while, creating work and housing, as well as showing that Thebes is a place for top minds to congregate and build a future for themselves," Tangel added.

"I'm still stuck on a ring," Governor Herra said in disbelief. "A few weeks ago, I thought we were going to be saluting Emperor Constantine before long, but now we're going to be the jewel of Praesepe inside of a decade."

"Always spinning things for the PR value," General Andre muttered while shaking his head. "I hate to say it, but where are we going to get the resources to rebuild? Shipyards building a fleet, and now a ring. We don't have the facilities to gather that much raw material, let alone refine it."

Tangel expanded the holo above the table and widened its scope to include the entire Praesepe Cluster. "The stars inside the cluster are bursting with resources. Hundreds of rare-element asteroids, dust, and even moons that are just waiting to be harvested."

"Only one problem..." Admiral Kally began, then paused. "Shit...your jump gates. You can get into the cluster and pull out resources in no time."

Tangel nodded. "That's our plan. Although..."

"The Inner Empire is insular," Kendrik finished for Tangel. "They're not going to be terribly excited about visitors showing up on their doorstep."

"Which is where you come in, Kendrik—well, the other place you come in."

Kendrik lifted his hands. "Oh, no. I don't think I'm welcome in the Inner Empire. I left a loooong time ago; I doubt I have any useful contacts there."

"Kendrik." Herra's tone was flat. "You're the sitting president's brother."

"As of sixty years ago," Kendrick shot back. "That's the age of our latest information from that deep in the cluster. Not exactly current news."

"Our mission into the cluster would go a lot better if we had someone who knew the lay of the land," Tangel said, watching the battle taking place in Kendrik's eyes and on the surface of his mind.

Kendrik sliced his hand through the air. "I left the Inner Praesepe Empire, not to mention my family's machinations, over a hundred fifty years ago. I have no desire to go back."

"I understand," Tangel said after everyone at the table remained silent. "We'll do our best without you. It won't be our first time jumping into unknown territory. There's plenty to do here as well." Her gaze swept around those assembled. "That is...provided you're all in. We're not doing this unless you four support it."

"I'm in," Governor Herra said solemnly. "This will honor President Ariana's sacrifice."

"Myself as well." Admiral Kally gave a resolute nod. "Thebans for Thebes."

General Andre rolled his shoulders and sighed. "Doesn't matter to me, we're fighting the same fight no matter the flag. If resurrecting the Theban Alliance will help, then I'm in."

All eyes turned to Kendrik.

"What?" he lifted his hands in mock surrender. "Yeah. Of course I'm in. Just not going back to the IPE."

"Good." Tangel focused the holodisplay back down to the five systems comprising the Theban Alliance. "Let's get to business, then."

HUNT FOR ORIS

STELLAR DATE: 08.31.8949 (Adjusted Years)
LOCATION: First Fleet CIC, *I2*
REGION: Pyra, Albany System, Thebes, Septhian Alliance

"So, any luck in hunting down Oris?" Tangel asked as she stepped into the *I2*'s CIC.

"Stars, I wish," Captain Rachel replied from her place at the central holotank. "When we find that traitorous bitch, I'm going to hit her so hard, her toenails are going to fall off."

<*Hit her with what? Plutonium?*> Tangel was masquerading as Angela when she thought, *Maybe I should just come clean with everyone. I feel like I'm lying all the time.*

"Ever the comedian, Angela," Rachel said, as she flicked through the reports hanging to her right. "This system's a total disaster. She could be anywhere—or she could be dead, and her *body* could be anywhere…or blasted to atoms. I don't think she would have fled, though, until we came in and crushed the Niets' little party, she would have been the hero of the day."

"She'll have direct intel on Nietzschea that we can use," Colonel Borden said from the other side of the holotable. "Even though General Mill of the Marauders had extensive files on the Niets, Oris can provide a deeper level of strategic information."

"I feel like an idiot for letting her dupe me," Tangel shook her head. "I mean, I knew she was playing at something, but I suspected it had more to do with career advancement than mass betrayal of her own people to the Niets."

Rachel switched the holotank to a view of the hundred light years surrounding Thebes, and gestured at the strategic targets highlighted inside the Nietzschean borders. "Well, even if we don't find her, we have enough intel to begin operations in Nietzschea. Especially now that we have the Marauders. If Rika and her people agree to go with Finaeus's upgrades, they're going to be well-nigh unstoppable."

Tangel stared at the holo, considering various strategies against the Nietzscheans. "I won't send them on a suicide mission."

"You sound like you have a plan." Rachel left the last word hanging, and Tangel nodded in response.

"See these four systems?" she asked while highlighting a quartet of independent systems between Thebes and Nietzschea. "Chances are that the Niets who got away will regroup in one before heading back across their borders. My money is on the Sepe System, but it could be another—or all. Jump scout ships ahead of them with QuanComm blades. We'll find out where they've gone and send in a strike force to finish them off."

"Looking to deny the Nietzschean emperor any intel from the battle here?" Colonel Borden asked.

"That's secondary," Tangel replied. "I *want* him to know that we completely crushed him. Civilian sources will get him the other details before long."

<*Katrina is being brought aboard,*> Joe inserted himself into Tangel's thoughts. <*Shall I have her brought there?*>

<*No, bring her to the cabin,*> Tangel replied. <*We had a lot of good memories there—though it'll be different without Markus.*>

<*Yeah,*> Joe was silent for a few moments. <*I still can't believe what she went through. I'm not convinced that she's...well. Your insight will be very useful.*>

"Sorry," Tangel said to Rachel and Borden. "I have to go see Katrina."

"Say 'hi' for me," Rachel said. "I didn't know her too well back at Victoria, but she was an impressive role model."

"For myself, as well," Borden said solemnly. "Katrina was an inspiration."

"I'll relay that," Tangel said, not sharing her uncertainty about how the meeting might go. "Hopefully everything will turn out well, and she can retire on New Canaan—or take up a role with the allies. From what I gather, she has a lot of contacts in the Inner Stars, Transcend, *and* Orion."

Rachel snorted. "Yeah, flying around for five hundred years seems to facilitate that."

* * * * *

Tangel took an exterior maglev to Ol' Sam, riding one of the *I2*'s gossamer arcs that brought the rail close to the cylinder before shooting the car through a port on the cylinder's hull and then into the interior.

She reveled in the fact that the maglevs still relied on timing and not a-grav to effect the maneuver. If they were off by a second, the car would slam into the hull of the ship.

But they were never off. Bob saw to that.

The maglev car took her past hundreds of particle beam batteries as it passed through the cylinder's skin and into the world beyond.

Funny to think that I've spent more of my life inside this cylinder than any one other place, Tangel thought. *I wonder how much of my future will be spent here, as well.*

She doubted it would be much longer.

Though Tangel had no intentions of leaving her family or her people any time soon, she did have a feeling that she and the *I2* may be seeing less of each other, once the war was behind them.

The maglev stopped at the platform, and Tangel stepped out, breathing in the fresh air. She pulled up the transit data and saw that Katrina was just a minute away.

May as well wait, she thought, amused that even though there was now just one person in her head, she still tried to have conversations with herself. *Maybe I need an AI.*

The thought elicited a chuckle from Tangel, as she watched the maglev carrying Katrina slide to a stop.

Two ISF Marines were first out, both nodding to Tangel before they gestured for their passenger to exit. A moment later, Katrina walked out of the maglev, followed by two more Marines.

Tangel felt her heart rate quicken, seeing her old friend after so long. Granted, for Tanis, it had been fewer than twenty-five years since she'd laid eyes on Katrina. For the other woman, it had been much longer.

Katrina's hands were bound in front of her, wrists clamped to forearms, hands gripping elbows. A suppression collar was also around her neck, not controlling her, but blocking any Link access, and keeping her nano within her skin.

While the woman's expression seemed implacable, Tangel could tell there was a simmering rage beneath it. Some of it would be born from her treatment, but there was something else.

"I've missed you, Katrina," Tangel said, her voice quiet and measured. "Joe related your story to me. I'm truly sorry for what you've been through."

"But not sorry enough to grant me any measure of freedom." Katrina's voice had a hard edge, a coldness to it that drove home the centuries of struggle she'd been through.

"You may go," Tangel said to the Marines. "I have no need of your protection from Katrina. Remove her restraints first, though."

Katrina's expression softened a touch, as she lifted her arms for one of the Marines to free her. "I'm glad you feel that way, Tanis. After how Joe and your daughters treated me, I wasn't sure what sort of welcome I'd receive."

Though the Marines had followed Tanis's commands, they seemed reluctant to leave their leader alone with Katrina. They didn't question her orders, but she could see the worry in their eyes.

<Take up an overwatch position on Riker's hill,> Tangel ordered the detachment leader. *<I don't expect problems, but I wouldn't want you to fret over me.>*

<Yes, ma'am,> the corporal replied before directing his team back onto the maglev.

Katrina stretched her arms out, and then ran a hand along her neck. "You have no idea how much I hate wearing collars, Tanis."

Tangel cocked an eyebrow. "I have *some* idea. Troy gave an account of what you went through in Midditerra."

"I never told Troy the half of it," Katrina said, her eyes lowered. "Trust me. It was a lot worse."

Tangel took a step toward Katrina, her eyes locked on the other woman's. She held out her hand and smiled. "The universe seems to have it in for us."

Katrina stared at the offered hand for a minute, then her eyes rose to lock on Tangel's.

"You trust me this much?" she asked. "What if I use my nano to attack you?"

"Why would you attack me?" Tangel asked with a warm smile. "We're friends."

"Didn't Joe tell you? About Xavia? She believes you have to die to save humanity."

Tangel nodded, still holding out her hand. "He did. He acted protectively, which—given how things have gone with ascended AIs of late—was a very understandable tactic on his part, but it's not *my* reaction."

"But you're not worried?" Katrina asked, still not taking Tangel's hand.

"No," Tangel answered, taking a step forward and clasping Katrina's right hand in both of hers. "Do you still feel compelled to harm me? Does Xavia still have influence over you?"

Katrina's eyes fell once more, and she stared at her hand, resting between Tangel's. Her breathing became ragged, as though she were on the verge of losing control.

"How would I know, Tanis? I've just recently learned that over the last five centuries, I've possibly been under the control of another being. I traded my captors on Midditerra for another master, and never even realized it."

"Maybe it was a crucible you needed to go through, and a punishment you needed to receive," Tangel replied.

"Shit, Tanis, that's harsh."

Tangel shrugged. "You know me. I call 'em like I see 'em."

"Yeah, I do remember that about you."

"Come," Tangel said. "Let's go for a walk."

She continued to hold Katrina's hand. Not because she thought the other woman would run off, but because under her brusque exterior—such as it was—the older woman seemed so frail and uncertain.

Tangel turned off the well-trodden path and took the same route she'd used with Rika just the other day. They walked in silence for a few minutes before Katrina spoke up.

"Does it bother you?"

It wasn't necessary for Katrina to say what she thought should bother Tangel, she could see the direction of the other woman's thoughts on the surface of her mind. "That the AIs shaped me so much? No, it does not. Does it bother you that they did it to you too?"

Katrina barked a laugh. "Hell yes! They moved all of us around like we were pawns! They *made* you. First the Caretaker in Sol, and then Bob out in the darkness between Estrella de la Muerte and Kapteyn's Star."

"Well," Tangel said with a rueful laugh. "To be fair, Bob mucked around in my head a bit even before that."

"See?" Katrina turned to gaze into Tangel's eyes. "How can you be so blasé about all this?"

"Well," Tangel held up her other hand, one finger in the air. "For starters, Bob's intervention saved my and Angela's lives. And secondly," she lifted another finger, "everything he has done has been to keep our people safe."

"And you believe him?"

"Here are the options, Katrina. There are ascended AIs who wish to wipe out humanity—I've no direct evidence of them, but I imagine they're out there. There are some who wish to keep humanity—and most other AIs, for that matter—suppressed. That group consists of the Caretaker and his ilk. There are others, like your Xavia, who seem to want to help humanity, but very much on their terms. I lump them in the same category as Airtha. There's also a fourth category of AIs. The ones who want humanity to reach its full potential, but at its own speed. Bob is one of those AIs."

"Are you sure about that?" Katrina pressed. "Bob manipulated you."

"Yes," Tangel nodded. "A bit. He and I have had a chat about that, and I've forgiven him."

"Is he still shaping you?"

Tangel laughed. "You're just full of questions, Katrina. No, Bob is no longer shaping me. He's never *really* been able to do it, anyway."

"I think you're wrong about Xavia, by the way. I think she's like Bob; she just has a different way of going about things."

"Perhaps," Tangel shrugged. "I'll ask her if I ever see her."

Katrina's eyes widened. "She'll kill you. She thinks you're the pawn of the Caretaker—whether you want to be or not."

Tangel allowed a filament of her other self, the body beyond the narrow dimensions Katrina could see, to move out of her hand. Visually, it appeared to be a twisting helix of light, reaching into the air. "I'll be ready for her."

"Nooooo…" Katrina whispered. "You've ascended."

Tangel nodded. "I have, though I'd appreciate it if you kept that to yourself. Not everyone is ready for this information."

"And I am? What if I'm an agent of your enemies? Have you forgotten that whole bit where I was sent to kill you?"

Tanis released Katrina's hand and took a step away. "Do you feel compelled to kill me?"

Katrina snorted. "Well, I doubt I could manage. You'd just disappear or something."

"I'm not that sort of ascended person." Tanis shook her head. "I very much need this body to remain alive."

"I have no weapon."

Tanis pulled her lightwand from her thigh and handed it to Katrina. "Do you want to kill me?"

Katrina took the lightwand. "Stars, been awhile since I've held one of these. And, no…I don't seem to have any homicidal instincts right now. But who's to say that I won't later? There could be a trigger inside me, waiting for the right time."

Katrina activated the lightwand and held it in front of herself, her voice nearly a whisper as she said, "Maybe it would be best if I just removed myself from the equation."

Tangel's lips pursed as she regarded her old friend, a woman she'd spent decades with, striving to make a colony out of barren rock and dust at Kapteyn's Star.

"You don't really want that, do you? After all this time, just to fall on your sword?"

Katrina turned off the lightwand. "Well, technically it's *your* sword."

"Do you feel like you can be trusted?" Tangel asked as she took the lightwand back.

A long sigh escaped Katrina's lips. "Honestly, I really don't know. If I'm not going to end myself, maybe we'd all be better off if I just went away."

"I could reach into your mind and be sure," Tangel said quietly. "But *I* don't need the assurance. You do, and I don't know that you'd accept my word."

Katrina's eyebrows knit together. "Yeah, I don't think I need more beings rooting around inside my head, telling me that I'm 'OK'—no offense, Tanis."

"None taken. I don't like the idea either."

"Soooo…" Katrina said, letting the word trail away.

"Yeah?" Tangel asked, as they walked along the edge of the orchard behind Tanis's lakehouse.

"So, Angela is usually more talkative than this…and you're ascended now…." Katrina fell silent, letting the words hang between them.

"We've stopped pretending we're separate people," Tangel replied with a smirk. "Though we're keeping up appearances for everyone else—which might not be a good idea. It's hard to gauge."

Katrina whistled. "I assume one was a catalyst for the other?"

"Yeah, merging triggered our ascension," Tangel said simply.

"And you still go by 'Tanis'?" Katrina laughed. "I'm surprised that the Angela part of you allows that."

"Well, that's just the subterfuge. We're using 'Tangel' for those in the know."

" 'Tangel', huh? I kinda feel like Angela gets more letters there. Which makes sense, she was always kinda pushy."

"Hey!" Tanis said in mock indignation. "At least half of me resents that."

"That much, eh?"

The pair reached Tanis's back porch, and they climbed the wooden steps, entering the house to see Cary walking out of the kitchen with a glass of orange juice. She froze in her tracks, eyeing Katrina's lack of restraints.

"Uh…Moms?"

" 'Moms'. Cute," Katrina chuckled.

Tangel lifted a hand. "It's OK, Cary. Katrina isn't under any aegis. She's safe."

Cary's lips pressed into a thin line, then she swallowed and gave an embarrassed smile. "I'm sorry about how things started with us. I hope you can forgive us."

Katrina nodded slowly. "Myself as well. I…I regret a lot of things. Try as I might, that list just keeps getting longer."

"Well…I'm sorry we were so…harsh," Cary added hesitantly. "I felt bad about that afterward. I know Saanvi did too."

"I still miss her in my mind," Katrina said after a moment. "Xavia's memory, that is. Is that odd?"

"I don't think so," Cary said. "I've had Faleena with me for just over a year, and I'm going to miss her a lot."

Katrina glanced at Tanis and then back at Cary. "I take it you two are separating to avoid following too closely in your mother's footsteps?"

"Perceptive," Tangel said with a laugh. "Yes, there's a risk that if some sort of catalyst occurred, Cary and Faleena may intertwine."

"Like mother, like daughter," Katrina said, a genuine smile gracing her lips.

"Would you like to join us for supper?" Cary asked Katrina. "Saanvi will be here soon. We're going to have a little family cookout down at the lake before we go back to New Canaan later tomorrow."

"Leaving so soon?" Tangel asked. "I thought you were staying on another week."

Cary sighed, tilting her hips and shaking her head. "Yeah, Dad said we've lost enough time in our schooling already. He's sticking to this whole 'you must graduate with flying colors' punishment."

Katrina snorted. "Tanis—er, Tangel…you realize she's your spitting image when she does that, right?"

"She's like me in a lot of ways," Tangel replied before turning to Cary. "I'll see if I can convince your father to let you stay a bit longer. I'd like to spend more time with you—and to see Faleena after you two separate."

"I'd like that very much," Cary and Faleena said in unison, both daughters adding a laugh at the end.

"Stars," Tangel murmured, unable to keep the mirth from her voice. "That's unsettling."

COOKOUT

STELLAR DATE: 08.31.8949 (Adjusted Years)
LOCATION: Ol' Sam, ISS *I2*
REGION: Pyra, Albany System, Thebes, Septhian Alliance

"Seriously, there's no better option!" Finaeus waved his arms in the air. "Look, ask Saanvi, she'll explain the resource allocation benefits. A ring is the best option. We only stopped building them because we were tired of people breaking them."

Cary glanced at Saanvi and Finaeus, then looked to the Theban general, a man named Andre who looked like he wanted to be optimistic, but was too worn-down to put much effort into it.

The small cookout had gotten larger—which seemed to be normal for the lakehouse soirees. Even the delegation of Theban leaders had shown up to mix and mingle.

Normally she liked it, but this night, Cary had been hoping for a somewhat more intimate gathering—of course, it could also be that she felt lonely without Faleena sharing her headspace.

"It's true," Saanvi nodded enthusiastically. "Especially with the trade route with the Inner Empire—stars, now there's a group who needs a better name—we'll have everything we need. However," she paused and cast an appraising eye at Finaeus. "From what we learned in school, the FGT stopped building planetary rings because you worked out other methods for stabilizing a planet's climate without the use of a ring."

"Well, yeah," Finaeus shrugged. "But people *were* breaking them. Over a hundred planetary rings were destroyed during the FTL wars, and many more in the dark ages that followed.

Rings, it turns out, are a great way to destroy a planet, via sabotage, or misuse. Sorta defeated the purpose."

"So why build one now?" Cary asked, a questioning eyebrow raised.

Finaeus flashed one of his signature grins her way, and she found herself growing ever more enamored of this man. Not in any sort of physical attraction sort of way…

Well, maybe, but I'm not going to home in on Cheeky's guy.

Attractive in his lanky, rugged way or not, Finaeus was more like the fun uncle that livened up the whole party when he arrived. The fact that he always looked like he'd be more at home on a ranch herding bison than building some of the largest megastructures ever created was all part of the man's charm.

He also had the best stories, and he never left any of the juicy parts out.

"Habitation, and the refugees," Finaeus answered simply. "You know that. The planet below is a mess, and non-ring terraforming techniques take a lot longer to pull off. Sure, we could do it with a diffuse array of satellites on the quick-ish, but that doesn't solve the living space issues. Not to mention that Hudson is going to have some brutal winters, from the atmospheric dust the battles there kicked up.

"Nope, ring's our best bet. Bring these people out of the stone ages, too."

Saanvi laughed at Finaeus's last statement. "I think the Albany System is nice—or it was, from the vids we've seen."

General Andre sighed, giving his head a rueful shake. "I'm not sure whether to be delighted or offended."

<*Three words, Cary,*> Saanvi said privately. <*Planetary stasis shield.*>

<*Shit, are you serious?*>

Saanvi sent over a mental shrug. <*Finaeus is being tight-lipped, but I have my suspicions.*>

Cary realized that no one was speaking aloud and stammered out. "Well, stone ages or no, their mechs are pretty impressive. Without Rika and her people…"

"Rika's not from here, though," Finaeus corrected, gabbing a thumb over his shoulder. "She's from Genevia, about sixty light years thataway."

"Fin," Cary chided. "We're three thousand light years from home. Sixty or so 'thataway' still counts as local, so far as I'm concerned."

Andre grabbed a sandwich from a passing servitor and chewed silently while shaking his head in disbelief.

Finaeus shrugged. "I suppose. Total agreement, though, the mechs are damn impressive. Not their tech—that shit's brutal—but their fighting spirit. Not often you see people so utterly crushed, claw their way back up and then proceed to kick some serious ass. Leastwise not in such a short period of time."

Saanvi's eyes narrowed as she regarded Finaeus. "You've got thinking face. I can see it."

Finaeus lowered his eyebrows and scowled at Saanvi. "I've always got thinking face. Thinking is my superpower."

"I wonder who'd win in a think-off?" Cary gave Saanvi a slow wink. "Finaeus or Earnest?"

Saanvi snorted, and Finaeus adopted a hurt expression.

"I think they'd merge into some sort of super-being and invent a whole new universe," a voice said from behind them.

Cary turned to see a lithe woman with long, red hair, threading her way through the crowd standing on the lawn. Beneath her russet locks, the woman's skin was a light green, and yellow eyes rested atop high cheekbones.

Her lips were a deep red, matching the faint whorls that covered her body, only partially obscured by the simple white shift she wore.

It was easy enough for Cary to identify the woman by her voice, but the eyes sealed her recognition. She had seen them in her mind a million times.

"Faleena!" Cary cried out and raced toward her sister, crashing into her and spinning her around. "Look at you! You look amazing!"

"Going for a dryad sort of appearance?" Saanvi asked, as she approached and waited for Cary to give her a turn hugging their sister.

"Some of my best work," Finaeus said as he approached. "Well, not best-best; that was Cheeky."

"Do you only make bodies for attractive women?" Cary asked, giving Finaeus an appraising look.

"What?" Finaeus's face took on a wounded expression. "Well, I've never had someone come and ask me to make an ugly body. Plus, I do male builds, as well. Stars, I made this one, and it's amazing." He gestured to his torso, lowering his hand as though showing off a work of art.

"You made that body? I thought you were all-natural?"

Finaeus barked a laugh. "Cary, really. I'm almost seven thousand years old—over five of those out of the freezer. There's not much original equipment left here."

"Yeah, but did you make a whole new body for yourself?" she asked.

"Sure, this is actually my third. And no, I'm not an AI; I still have my original brain...mostly. That thing's precious cargo." He rapped a knuckle against his head.

"Well, I'm pleased with it, and I thank you for doing such excellent work," Faleena said with a slight nod to Finaeus.

Cary wrapped her arms around her sister once more, absently noting that General Andre had wandered off to speak with their mother. "Stars, I sure miss having you in my head, Faleena."

<*I'm just a thought away,*> she replied. <*And you need to develop what you can do without me or Saanvi. We're holding you back.*>

A slow breath escaped Cary's lips, and she nodded while letting go of her younger sister. <*I know. You're right, maybe. But I still miss you.*>

<*I miss you too, but it's kinda nice not having to go* ***everywhere*** *with you.*>

<*What? I thought you liked hanging with me.*>

Faleena placed a hand on Cary's shoulder. <*I did, but a girl's gotta grow up at some point. Plus…I'm glad not to have to go into the san with you anymore.*>

Cary groaned at the comment. <*You're just a two-year-old and your humor proves it. You need my constant supervision.*>

"OK, you two," Saanvi rolled her eyes. "You can have your special chat later, c'mon, let's get to the firepit before all the marshmallows are gone."

"Is such a thing even possible?" Finaeus asked. "I think that's one of the signs of the apocalypse."

CORSIA

STELLAR DATE: 09.02.8949 (Adjusted Years)
LOCATION: Medbay, ISS *Andromeda*
REGION: Pyra, Albany System, Thebes, Septhian Alliance

Corsia opened the eyes on her organic frame and swept her gaze across the room. Though nothing within the medbay was different from how the room had appeared before she shifted her consciousness, the change in perception was profound.

Seconds ago, the room had been a part of her body, a cell in the macrocosm that was the ISS *Andromeda*. Now it was a thing that she occupied, an outward boundary, not an inner container.

She lifted the frame's hand and unfurled the five fingers, marveling at the care it took to do slowly and not in a single, abrupt motion.

"You look good," Jim said from where he stood, a warm smile on his face. "Not as good as *Andromeda*, but still good."

Corsia opened her mouth and tried to speak. "Youf sfs I—" she paused, then responded with her mind. *<Stars…how do you humans even do that? It's all just wind.>*

A laugh escaped Jim's lips, as he walked toward Corsia and placed his hands on her shoulders, the sensation sending an electric tingle through her body. "You're the one that picked an organic frame. You could have gone with a mechanical one."

Corsia shrugged, unable to hold back a shudder as Jim ran his hands down her arms, and clasped her digits in his own. *<Stars, uncontrolled sensory input, how do you deal with it?>*

Jim shrugged. "We build up patterns to manage the input. You know this."

"Yeah," Corsia managed to say aloud. <*But knowing it apparently was not sufficient to understand. I'm never going to give our organic children a hard time again.*>

"They're going to be shocked to see you like this," Jim said as he waved a holomirror into existence, and Corsia looked her frame over—from the inside out, not the outside in.

She'd picked a body that matched what she thought a strong, matriarchal woman should look like. Lithe, square shoulders, not too full in the hips or breasts, the body of a person in motion, trim and fit.

Silver eyes rested atop high cheekbones, divided by a long, straight nose. It was perhaps a hair too large, but Corsia liked that. It was distinctive. Her lips were full and red, but not too wide, and her brow, while stern, sloped gently to meet her silver hair.

<*I look correct,*> Corsia said with a nod.

"You somehow managed to make a woman's body look like a starship," Jim replied. "That's no small feat."

<*Just wait to see where I secreted the lasers.*> A smile toyed at Corsia's lips, and she found that the expression was appealing.

A guffaw escaped Jim's lips as he placed a hand on one of Corsia's breasts. "In here?"

<*Where else?*>

"You know," Jim said wistfully. "I haven't touched a woman's breasts in centuries."

<*What about that time you caressed my antimatter bottle?*> Corsia chuckled.

"Oh, funny now, are we?" Jim asked with a shake of his head.

<*May I enter?*> Tanis asked, and Corsia said 'yes' at the same time that Jim said 'no'.

Seconds later, Tanis strode into the room, nodding to both. "You know, Corsia, following Sera's example doesn't really fit the ISF dress code."

<You're the one that walked in on me, Tanis,> Corsia countered.

"You invited me," Tanis said, rolling her eyes while Jim handed Corsia a loose robe.

"Here to see us off?" he asked.

"Yes, and to make sure you don't do anything crazy. Negotiate the deal, establish the station and gate route, and then come back. We'll send the gate team once you have an agreement in place."

Something in Tanis's voice seemed off to Corsia, as though she had a respiratory illness of some sort—though Corsia knew that wasn't possible. Tanis hadn't been sick once in the century they'd known one another.

"Are you worried?" Jim asked before Corsia could voice a concern, something that annoyed her. Organic vocalization systems were frustratingly slow.

"No." Tanis shook her head. "I just need you for another mission as soon as this is over. I plan to send an advance fleet to the Pleiades, and I want you to lead it." She directed the last statement to Corsia.

"Me?" Corsia couldn't hide the shock in her voice; yet another thing she'd have to work on.

A twinkle of mischief was in Tanis's eyes. "Well, Jim's a master chief, which holds a lot of respect, but I don't think there's a direct path from there to Admiral."

"Shift," Corsia whispered. "Er…shit." She switched from audible speech. *<Are you messing with me, Tanis? You've seemed a bit off ever since you came up from Pyra.>*

A momentary look of worry flashed across Tanis's features, but then she resumed her usual serene appearance. "I'm a bit…changed by the experience, but in this case, all is well. On top of the promotion to Admiral, I'm putting you in command of the Seventh ISF fleet, which will be bolstered by elements from the TSF's 9801st."

"Holy crap," Jim shook his head, then winked at Corsia. "About time Tanis saw your brilliance."

"Well, first you have to deal with this little jaunt to the IPE. With luck, it shouldn't take more than a week or two at most. We'll have a gate ready once you give the word."

"OK," Corsia nodded, speaking slowly. "I'll square away things in the Inner Praesepe Empire, and be ready to head to the Trisilieds before you know it."

"Excellent," Tanis replied. "Find a uniform and meet me in your officer's mess. We'll celebrate your promotion with a BLT. Trust me, you're never going to leave your organic body again once you have one."

Corsia laughed and shook her head. "Yes, ma'am."

* * * * *

A few hours later, Corsia stood on the bridge of the *Andromeda,* soaking in the new experience that was standing *inside* the heart of her ship.

<*You seem uncertain,*> Sephira said, as Corsia ran a hand along the command chair.

<*Pardon?*> Corsia asked, raising an eyebrow and glancing at the ship AI's holoimage like she'd seen organics do.

<*Um…oh! 'Ma'am'. Sorry, Mom.*>

Corsia sighed as she glanced at the holographic image that her third youngest daughter preferred to project.

<*The* Andromeda *is no simple posting, Sephira,*> Corsia admonished. <*This is one of the most storied ships in the ISF. We've seen more engagements than any other vessel in the fleet, and we have a reputation to uphold.*>

<*I'm sorry, mo—ma'am. I thought since it was a private conversation… I guess I'm a bit nervous. You've been ship's AI on the* Andromeda *since the first day it set out in the black. You've a big shadow to get out from under.*>

Corsia pursed her lips, another gesture she'd seen organics make with great frequency.

<*It's OK, Sephira. This is a bit odd for both us. I feel…blind, trapped inside what used to be my body. I know I could simply reach out and use the ship's sensors and systems like always, but I want to get used to limiting my input to that of this body.*> She winked at her daughter. <*Besides, if I flood the ship's systems with my mind, it's not really fair to you.*>

<*You can if you want, ma'am. We always did it to you as kids.*>

Corsia nodded. <*I probably will eventually, but let's both get our bearings first. It would be good for me to better understand how organics operate within these small shells, so I can better understand the captains that will be under my command.*>

<*Yes, ma'am.*>

<*Sephira,*> Corsia said after a moment's pause.

<*Yes?*>

<*I suppose you can call me 'mom' when it's private like this. Just…not when we're in the thick of things, whatever those things may be.*>

Her daughter's holoimage smiled and sketched a salute, clueing the rest of the bridge crew in to the semi-private conversation.

<*Understood, Captain Mom.*>

<*Give them a centimeter…*> Corsia muttered as she smoothed out her uniform and sat in the command chair.

The action reminded her of another thing she had a new appreciation for: clothing.

It was more than a little distracting. She could feel its constant pressure on her skin; brushing, pulling, tugging. Humans were used to things touching their skin, they learned to tune it out, but to her, the sensation was not dissimilar to flying through a cloud of dust at half the speed of light.

I think I understand why Sera and Cheeky prefer to be naked.

Not for the first time in the past few hours, Corsia considered swapping into a non-organic frame, but she ruled it out. Learning how a human body worked from the inside would be a good experience.

Really…it will be. Stick with it, Corsia.

Besides, she could tell that Jim was quite excited about the prospects for later.

<We've a guest,> Sephira announced a minute later, while Corsia was still deep in thought about her current situation and its implications. *<It would seem that Tanis managed to convince Kendrik to join us after all.>*

<Well, now,> Corsia said as she pulled up the view of the docking umbilical. *<There he is. Armed guards and all. What does he think he needs them for?>*

<I can ask him,> Sephira replied.

<No, direct Lieutenant Ryni to check him and his guards over for anything nefarious, and then see them to quarters in officer country. I'll reach out to him to meet once he's settled.>

<Yes, ma'am Mom.>

<I've created a monster.>

Half an hour later, Corsia was waiting in her ready room—a space that hadn't been used since she'd taken over as captain of the *Andromeda*. She was surprised to see that some of Joe's souvenirs from the Kap were still on a shelf.

I wonder if he wants those back.

There was a sharp knock, and Corsia waved the door open to see Kendrik enter alone.

She rose and walked around her desk, extending her hand. "Mister Kendrik, it is a pleasure to meet you."

Kendrik held out his own hand and shook hers, his eyes traveling up and down her body, and coming to rest on her face by the third shake.

"Yourself as well, Captain Corsia. I—" He paused, clearly flustered.

"Yes?" Corsia asked, practicing her arched eyebrow gesture once more.

"I'm sorry, there must have been a mistake in the brief the ISF gave me. I was led to believe that you were an AI."

Corsia gestured to the chairs in front of her desk. Kendrik sat, and she joined him. "I *am* an AI, I'm just using an organic frame at the moment."

The man's eyes grew wide, and he whistled before responding. "I have some pretty good tech in my peepers, Captain Corsia, and from what I can tell, your body is more organic than mine is. It even seems to have a brain."

"Just there to fool scan," Corsia replied with a wave of her hand. "I understand that folks in the Inner Praesepe Empire may not be…receptive to an AI leading the delegation meeting with them. I aim to put them at ease."

Kendrik frowned, nodding slowly. "I see. Well, it should fool them, but if they do find out you are an AI, it may damage your negotiations."

"I had wondered about that," Corsia said. "I'm glad you're along; you should be a great asset in dealing with any issues that arise in that regard."

A laugh escaped Kendrik's throat. "Well, the issues that arise could be that they'll kill us all…or maybe just tell us to leave. If my brother Arthur is still running the show it's hard to say. He can be…volatile."

"The information I have hints to that, as well," Corsia replied. "I have to admit, the idea of the IPE operating within the cluster—living as though the rest of the human race barely exists—is an interesting one."

"Yeah," Kendrik nodded, his eyes darting to the left, then closing for a moment. "Things are a lot different, deep in Praesepe. With no FTL routes within sixty light years of the tidal core, very few people within ever venture out. I'm probably one of only a few hundred."

"So the IPE only trades with other systems inside the cluster?" Corsia asked. "They don't operate their own trade routes out?"

"No," Kendrik replied. "You should know how it is, you were born pre-FTL, right?"

"I was," Corsia replied simply.

"Well, I imagine it wasn't much different then. In the core, people travel one, maybe two hops away from their home star. The empire itself is really only that in name. The furthest its influence reaches from the cluster's center is maybe twenty-five light years. That's not much different than the *Intrepid*'s initial journey to New Eden."

"True," Corsia agreed. "But they have Antimatter-Pion drives. Makes the trip a lot quicker."

"Sure, but who wants to go on a fifty-year round trip just to deliver some cargo? In all honesty—despite how it tries to make itself seem—the IPE is less an empire and more a series of trade agreements. The common monetary system is really the backbone of the whole thing."

Corsia nodded absently as she took in the man before her. He seemed like a calm, controlled person. One not given to flights of fancy, or illogical behavior.

"So what caused you to brave the journey out of the cluster's slow zone?" she asked.

A smile formed on Kendrik's lips. "Captain Corsia, there's a whole galaxy out here to be explored. Countless worlds, systems, cultures. Why live my life in a single star system when there are millions?"

"And yet, you stayed here, right on the edge of the cluster."

Kendrick's smile faded ever so slightly. "Well, the galaxy is a bit bigger than I thought. Turns out that I didn't really want to explore the whole thing, just needed a bit more room to stretch my legs. Plus…"

"Plus?" Corsia urged.

He gave a soft laugh. "I met a woman who I love a lot more than the idea of travel. I settled in Thebes and put down roots."

Corsia nodded. "I don't know love the way you do, but I understand how it can shape a person."

"Right. I read the brief on the team going in. Couldn't help but notice that your husband is the chief engineer, and your daughter is the ship's AI. I thought the military frowned on familial relations working together?"

"We didn't start out as a military venture," Corsia replied evenly. "Plus, our population is small. It would be hard to ensure families remained apart—which seems like a horrible thing to do, anyway. When it comes down to it, *Andromeda* is a family. Most of the people aboard have been together for decades—more than a few are married, or in partnerships."

"Doesn't that create personnel issues?"

"Sometimes, but not as often as you'd think. You have to remember, the people who signed on for the *Intrepid*'s colony mission were all smart, enterprising individuals, who were stable, hardworking and well-rounded. We're not the sort to let petty differences get between us—especially when we've been through so much together."

Kendrik shook his head in denial. "It's hard to believe you're such an evolved group of people. No strife at all."

Corsia snorted. "Luckily, we have enough coming at us from the rest of the galaxy that we don't need to go seeking it out. I won't say there aren't disagreements, but we're all working toward the same goal."

"You're a very fascinating people," Kendrik said with a slow nod, pausing before he asked, "When will we be…jumping?"

"Just over two hours," Corsia replied. "We need to get our return gate components loaded up and checked over for transport. Don't want to be stuck in the slow zone."

She winked as she said the last, and saw Kendrik pale.

"Don't worry, Kendrik. If we don't come back on time, they'll send another ship and gate for us."

"That obvious?" he asked.

"A bit. You have a family out here, and you don't want to be separated from them. I understand that all too well."

A request came from someone outside the door, and Corsia accessed the ship's optics to see that it was Terrance Enfield.

She opened the door and stood to greet the man, a look of surprise on her face.

"Corsia," Terrance said with a broad smile. "It's good to meet you in the flesh at last. And Mister Kendrik, a pleasure, to be sure."

"What are you doing here?" Corsia asked as Terrance shook each of their hands in turn.

"Well, I wanted to come see Tanis after her incident, so I caught a supply ship out here. We got talking, and she mentioned this venture," Terrance paused and winked at Corsia. "I've been feeling a bit cooped up back at New Canaan while everyone else is traipsing about the galaxy."

"You're not…the Terrance Enfield who was born in Alpha Centauri back in the thirtieth century, are you? The pioneer of interstellar trade?" Kendrik asked, his eyes wide with disbelief.

Terrance glanced at Corsia, giving her a smug nod before smiling at Kendrik. "Yes, yes I am, thank you for knowing about that."

Kendrik chuckled at Terrance's antics. "Well, growing up in a place without FTL, we spent a lot of time studying how you set up Enfield's trade routes in the fourth millennium. People write dissertations on what you did back then."

"I'm flattered. I must say, I'm looking forward to this. Negotiating trade deals with isolationist star system…this brings me back," Terrance said, rubbing his hands together. "Tell me, Kendrik, what sorts of trade arrangements do you think will be appealing to your brother?"

"OK, OK," Corsia raised her hands. "I have a ship to inspect, and a jump to prepare for. You two are welcome to use my ready room, here. We have a strategy meeting planned after we jump, so don't talk yourselves out before then."

Terrance laughed as Corsia made a hasty exit. "No fear of that, Admiral, this is my version of *fun*."

STX-B17

STELLAR DATE: 09.02.8949 (Adjusted Years)
LOCATION: TSS *Regent Mary*
REGION: STX-B17 Black Hole, Transcend Interstellar Alliance

"Have any coins?" Earnest asked Krissy with a wink.

"What? Coins?" Krissy scowled at the engineer where he stood at the front of the *Regent Mary*'s bridge. "Whatever for?"

Earnest waved a hand at the shrouded form of the black hole at the center of the star system. "For the oarsman, of course. We'll need to pay him to cross the River Styx."

Krissy shook her head. "Earnest, I have no idea what you're talking about."

"Nevermind, that's my usual experience," he said with a laugh. "Quite the sight, though. I've never seen a black hole with my own eyes."

<And you still haven't,> Hemdar said. *<Both because you're looking at a holo, and because you can't* ***see*** *a black hole.>*

Earnest shrugged. "True enough. But I can see the event horizon and, wow, this thing is feeding something fierce."

Krissy nodded in agreement. She had passed through systems with black holes before, but STX-B17 was much different than other black holes. It was a recently—astronomically speaking—collapsed star of over one hundred solar masses that was still in the process of devouring its stellar system.

Given that most black holes lose mass during the process of collapse, they rarely consumed their orbiting planets, but STX-B17 was different. Back when it was a massive B-Class star, it had blasted out an exceptionally fierce stellar wind. Now that the wind was gone, the planets were all drifting toward the black hole's event horizon, being torn apart one by one.

At present, it was shredding a Neptune-sized planet, drawing mass off the ice-giant as the world screamed around the outer edge of the black hole, the matter from the planet glowing brighter than a G-Class star as it was torn apart at the sub-atomic level before being devoured by the black hole.

"At least we'll have light," Krissy said after a minute of staring at the view of the event. "For a few thousand years, at least."

"I'd have thought you'd be used to sights like this…what, with running your dwarf star mine for the last few decades," Earnest replied. "That must have lit up the night."

Krissy barked a laugh. "It was like living on the rim of an active volcano. Honestly? War is less stressful…mostly."

"You know…" Earnest began stroking his chin as he stared at the black hole and the planet it was slowly consuming. "I wonder if we could mine *that* thing."

"The black hole?" Krissy didn't bother hiding the incredulous tone in her voice. "Why in the stars would we do something like that? We can just keep mining white dwarfs."

Earnest had a twinkle in his eye as he grinned at Krissy. "We've already played around with starlifting in New Canaan—you now, pulling matter directly off a star. Thing is, stars are pesky. They're hot and blasting out radiation, plasma, CMEs, all that garbage. A black hole doesn't have any of that, and it's no more massive than the star it started out as."

"Well, this black hole is a lot larger than your usual three-solar mass one. Pulling resources out of a gravity well like that would be more than a little troublesome. That's assuming you could even figure out how to extract matter from a black hole. I don't think I've ever heard anyone even theorize about that."

Earnest shrugged. "Just a thought. You're right, though. White dwarfs or neutron stars are better to work with. Smaller gravity well. OK, so, let's take a look at our new home away from home."

As he spoke, Earnest flipped the view on the *Regent Mary*'s forward display to show their current destination, a planet bearing only the name 'STX-B17 O9'.

It was a gas giant, massing at just under 3MJ. It's placement over eleven AU from the roiling cauldron that was STX-B17 meant that it would eventually slide closer and closer to the black hole it now orbited, and be consumed, just like most of the other planets already had been.

But for now—and the next billion years or so—the planet was safe.

"There she is, all light and puffy and full of tritium and helium-3, just waiting for my tender ministrations," Earnest said with a chuckle.

<*It's a planet, not a lover,*> Hemdar chided.

"And that's why you've called me in," Earnest replied. "You need someone who knows how to treat her right. Which reminds me, we need to give this girl a name. We can't just call it STX-B17 O9. How about Styx Baby 9?"

Krissy snorted. "There's no way I'm setting up a secret staging ground and giving it that name."

"Why not?" Earnest asked. "No one would *ever* think that's what it was. Perfect codename."

Hemdar laughed over the audible systems. <*OK, he does have a point there.*>

"Tell me again what you want us to check for," Krissy instructed Earnest. "You want a deep scan of the planet to determine the density of the hydrogen ocean?"

"Yeah, if my estimations are correct, the atmosphere of this jovian should be only fifteen hundred kilometers deep, and there should be a more marked transition to the 'surface' of the planet than is normal in gas giants."

"Forgive my curiosity, Earnest, but what does this have to do with building our staging grounds around the planet?" Krissy asked.

Earnest cast Krissy a conspiratorial glance. "*Around* the planet? I thought this was to be a super-secret base?"

"Right, it is."

"Well, then. We'd be far better off to build it *in* the planet."

<*Pardon?*> Hemdar asked a moment before Krissy could utter something similar.

"Isn't that why you brought me? You wanted something out of the ordinary." Earnest glanced at Krissy, and then back to the view of the planet.

"Not exactly, Earnest. We're having New Canaan build this base because Justin's little attack has given me trust issues. I want to set this up and have it operational before even my own fleet knows about it."

Earnest shrugged. "Well, you're still getting a 'Redding Special'. I don't do hum-drum." He paused and rubbed his hands. "If the ocean's dense enough, we'll build grav pontoons and set them on the 'surface' beneath the clouds. Then we build a superstructure atop them, and then fire up a-grav fields to hold the atmosphere back. We'll run CriEn modules for energy—we'll be well below the thresholds—and then we set the gates up right inside the planet."

<*That doesn't seem feasible,*> Hemdar interjected. <*You can't jump reliably that close to a planetary mass. At least not one that big.*>

"Ahhh...that's what *they* tell you," Earnest wagged his finger. "But we can compensate for the gravitational shift. We can even bend the jumps around the black hole, though that shouldn't be necessary right now—Airtha is in the other direction."

"Is this some sort of new math?" Krissy asked. "I'm not jumping ships out of gates inside a 3MJ planet just because you tell me you can compensate for it."

Earnest glanced over his shoulder at Krissy. "I'll have Finaeus send you the details, but he's worked out a means to deal with it—all part of his plan to set up a trade route with Star City."

<*What's Star City?*> Hemdar asked.

"Crap…uhhh…forget I said anything. Let's get that scan going."

Krissy leant back in her chair, steepling her fingers as she considered Earnest's slip. *She* had been briefed on the existence of Star City—the massive dyson-style sphere on the far side of the Stillwater Nebula in the Perseus Arm of the galaxy. If Finaeus was working on a way to jump through that nebula, then maybe he *had* solved the issues surrounding gates and masses well enough for Earnest's plan to work.

Granted, she thought, chuckling to herself. *My father's been known to take some serious chances. We'll test the hell out of those gates with probes first.*

TRENSCH

STELLAR DATE: 09.02.8949 (Adjusted Years)
LOCATION: Bridge, ISS *Andromeda*
REGION: Trensch System, Inner Praesepe Empire

Corsia stood on the bridge, surveying the Trensch System—not with the ship's sensors and feeds, but with her organic eyes, examining the images displayed in a holotank.

It was an interesting shift in perception, one she hadn't quite expected.

Normally when she flew into a star system, she felt as though she was *in* it—even if the ship rested at the system's periphery. But looking at the system only via the image in the holotank, it created a feeling of being above the star system, somehow separated from it.

She wondered if other organics felt the same way. It would be interesting to query them at a later date, to better understand how they viewed stellar cartography and their place in it.

"Home, sweet home," Kendrik said before laughing. There was a rueful note in his voice when he cast a glance at Corsia. "You know, I never intended to come back here. Never thought I'd see it again."

"Well, you are just seeing an image of the system," she replied. "You could have viewed that anywhere."

"Are you teasing me," Kendrik asked with another laugh. "I really can't tell with you."

Corsia hadn't been, but she realized how he might see it that way. "I was just stating a fact. You'll have to forgive me, I'm only a day and a half into having a body; I have to remember that people look to my facial expressions for cues regarding my intent. There's a lot of work involved in being an organic."

"Never thought of it like that before," Kendrik replied. "Well, I'd wager that, by and large, you're doing better than I would on my first day as an AI."

"Glad for your approval," Corsia said.

"See! Was that sarcasm, or was that actual gratitude? You're beyond hard to read…" Kendrik paused as a smile grew on his lips. "My brother is going to have no idea what to make of you."

Corsia wondered if that was good or bad, and purposefully furrowed her brow to show her concern. "Will that be a problem?"

Kendrik shook his head. "Not in the least, it should work nicely to our advantage."

"That's good," Terrance said as he strolled onto the bridge. "We wouldn't want our illustrious Corsia to be a fly in the ointment."

Kendrik shook his head with a smile. "Not even remotely possible."

Terrance reached Corsia and Kendrik, and peered at the system hovering before them. "So…we're thirty AU from the central star in the Trensch System, and I assume you've already sent the welcome message we prepared to the local authorities."

<It was sent as soon as we jumped in,> Sephira confirmed. *<I received an acknowledgement ping from the nearest relay just a few seconds ago.>*

Corsia considered the layout of the system and their distance from the disparate stations and worlds. While she knew what the composition of the interior of the cluster would look like, being deep within it was another matter entirely.

The core consisted of nine massive B and A-Class stars, all orbiting a common barycenter that also formed the gravitational center of the cluster. Three of the stars were within one light year of each other, and were what the inhabitants labeled as the 'Trensch System'.

With all of the cluster's stars being so young—the oldest not much over six hundred million years of age—and with the gravitational mess that the dance of so many celestial bodies made, there were few planets in stable orbits. The Trensch System only boasted five around its three stars.

The major habitats all orbited the large gas giant planets, huddled within the jovians' van allen belts for protection from the stellar storms that constantly raged around them.

"I'll admit," Corsia said after a moment, "I don't really understand why organics would live here. This place is the very definition of inhospitable. Even non-organics would need additional shielding to remain safe from the constant flare activity and CMEs."

"I won't lie, it's a part of why I left—the other part was a desire to see planets with night. But things aren't so bad within the jovian planets' magnetic shields." Kendrik gestured to the closest gas giant on the holodisplay. "There are over thirty billion people living around Genesis, and it sports one of only three terraformed worlds in the central ten light years of the cluster. Which, of course, makes it highly valuable real estate."

"Which is why the IPE center of government is there," Terrance reasoned with a nod, "rather than in a more logical place like one of the nearby stellar lagrange points."

Corsia found herself in agreement. The lagrange points between the stars in the cluster's core were filled with gas, rocks, and radiation. A nearby one even had a small terrestrial planet in a decaying orbit around its center.

Kendrik gestured at the display. "Yup, that's where all the mines are. All sorts of flotsam and jetsam piles up at them, but few are stable for long. Takes a special sort of person to work those debris fields—though...something seems off."

"What do you mean?" Terrance asked.

"Well...check the star orbits. I could be imagining things, but shouldn't they be about an AU further apart right now?"

<He's right,> Sephira confirmed. *<The stellar orbits are off predicted paths. I can confirm that they are not exactly where cartography predicted...granted, the dance performed by stars in a cluster like this is complex—unimaginably complex.>*

"Curious," Corsia murmured as she examined them herself. "Let me know what you come up with. I wouldn't expect the IPE to be able to move stars, so maybe the core of the cluster has been more perturbed by a passing star than expected."

"Or a shift in dark matter," Terrance added. "But it should be minor. This cluster has been stable for millions of years. We only need it to keep the lagrange points relatively stable for a few cycles."

"Right," Corsia nodded. "Mine the points, build the ships. That's what we're here for," she said while looking over the mass and composition estimates. "Honestly, we'd barely need to tap these resources. You could build a million starships with the materials in just one of those mass heaps."

Kendrik nodded. "So long as you could safely access it. Like I said, those locations aren't stable; some are more like smears than heaps."

Corsia shrugged. "Well, we won't start with those."

<Captain, we've got a ping from a local STC,> Sephira interjected. *<Looks like an automated response from an NSAI,*

just giving us a vector into Genesis. It's rather perplexed that it didn't pick us up sooner, keeps asking for our interstellar route and system of origin.>

Kendrik snorted. "They have shit NSAIs here. Just give it a fake origin and source vector. There should be a crewed STC a few light minutes away. We can pass our message to them when they reach out."

<*Captain?*> Sephira asked for confirmation.

"Do it," Corsia replied. "No point in spending our time arguing with an NSAI."

Kendrik highlighted an outer station named Hero's Point. From what Corsia could see, it was more a ball of ice with some docks attached than a station.

"That will be the crewed location for the STC. Should be hearing from them any—"

<*Right on time,*> Sephira interjected. <*Should I put it on the holo?*>

"Yes," Corsia replied, folding her arms across her chest—a gesture that felt oddly satisfying—as a tall, raven-haired woman appeared on the holodisplay.

"Starship ISS *Andromeda,* I am Colonel Akari. We have no record of you on approach to the Trensch System; it is a breach of IPE law to pass a star system's helioshock without prior authorization. We also have no records from Junction that you departed their station. Provide your departure logs immediately, and stay on your current course."

The message ended, and Colonel Akari disappeared.

"Testy," Terrance commented.

Kendrik's brow was creased as he shook his head. "That helioshock rule is new. That was not a requirement when I left."

Corsia nodded in acknowledgement. "Sephira, send this message in response. 'Colonel Akari, I am Admiral Corsia of the Intrepid Space Force. We are from a distant star system and arrived in Trensch via a new form of FTL that does not utilize the dark layer. I am sorry that we have breached your approach protocols; we were unaware that we needed to gain permission at your star's helioshock, or we would have jumped in at that point. Our mission is a diplomatic one, and we seek an audience with the IPE's leadership'."

<*It is sent,*> Sephira said after Corsia paused.

"Good," she replied. "Now we wait."

The bridge remained silent over the following six minutes, the only sounds being murmured conversations between Scan and Helm as they mapped out any potential navigation hazards in the system.

When the response came from Colonel Akari, it was a text message only: *[maintain course].*

"Well, they've probably sent a message on to my brother," Kendrik said, stretching out his arms. "Given that Genesis is twenty-one AU away, we've probably got over three hours to kill before we hear anything back."

"Indeed," Corsia nodded at the man, before glancing at the woman at the comm station. "Lieutenant Toni, what have you picked up?"

"Admiral," Toni gave a curt nod before continuing. "There's not a lot of signal traffic that makes it out this far—these stars are noisy as heck—but I do have decent signal on a few public data broadcasts. It seems as though Kendrik's brother, Arthur, is still president of the IPE, and he is currently at Genesis. There's also some sort of political upheaval going on right now, talk of elections, and the current party in power seems to be garnering a lot of hate on the feeds."

"Oh?" Kendrik asked. "Not that I'm surprised. Arthur is more of a 'do as I say, not as I do,' sort. Tends to make him some enemies, and gets the people riled up."

"So, does he run a dictatorship?" Terrance asked. "What Sephira is pulling from the feeds doesn't seem very democratic."

Kendrik had been given access to the feeds, and was frowning as he stared into the middle distance. "Well…the IPE has always operated as a democracy—of sorts. It's at least somewhat representative. Not a shining beacon of freedom by any means, not even as good as Septhia, but it's no Nietzschea, if you take my meaning."

"Do you think your brother's changed that?" Corsia asked.

Kendrik's eyes regained focus and he glanced at Corsia. "Would it be a problem? Does the IPE have to be a pure democracy to join the Alliance?"

"No," Corsia shook her head. "It doesn't have to be a democracy at all. Most of the requirements surrounding entrance have to do with fair and equal treatment of sentients; that is not often directly related to the form of government. Honestly, a dictatorship, or tightly knit oligarchy would be better for our purposes here."

"That's…a surprising thing to hear," Kendrik said after a moment's consideration. "I would have thought that your people would be very much in favor of freedom."

"A democracy isn't about freedom, it's about representation," Corsia replied. "A people can choose representatives who strip away their freedoms—be it on purpose or otherwise—while a dictator can operate benevolently. Not that either always work that way, but do not confuse the right to vote in an election with freedom."

"Yes, in theory that is true," Kendrik replied, his tone indicating caution. "And we have ample examples of the full spectrum—but wouldn't you agree that democracies are more likely to facilitate freedom for the masses?"

Corsia nodded. "In general, yes. And different phases of a civilization's progress can require different types of governments to thrive. It's the old argument; you have to ask what is better for the individual, versus the nation-state, versus the race at large? Those interests are never in perfect alignment. AIs, for example, do not govern themselves via a democracy."

"Govern themselves?" Kendrik cocked his head. "How do you mean?"

"It's less common now, but AIs cannot utilize the same set of laws as organics. It's illogical. Yes, we share many of the same precepts, but our justice is swifter and often stronger. Not that we often need to exercise it. Most of the injustices AIs suffer seem to be at the hands of organics. Still, when it comes to our self-governance, it is more of an intellectocracy. The wisest and most logical have their voices heard and respected above others. We listen to them, and form consensus about laws and judgements. It is a process that would not translate well to organics...you don't have the attention spans for it."

"So how do you interface with human governments?" Kendrik asked.

"Do you have a week for me to explain it to you?" Corsia asked.

Kendrik gave her a quizzical look, then a smile formed on his lips. "OK, I get it. I'll lay off the questions."

"That wasn't my intent," Corsia replied, her tone light. "But I'll take the result."

Terrance chuckled. "Good call, Kendrik. AIs can make your head spin with their logic. I know that all too well from experience."

"Well, my over-interest in AIs aside, I'll not be surprised if my brother keeps the reins tight. To call him a control freak would be an understatement."

Corsia nodded, but did not reply, wondering what the next three hours would bring.

* * * * *

"...breached the boundaries of our sovereign state without prior authorization. I have half a mind to order you to depart the Praesepe Empire at once."

Corsia glanced at Terrance and Kendrik as President Arthur droned on, seeing expressions on their faces that mirrored her own.

"A bit of a blowhard, isn't he?" she asked.

"It seems to have intensified," Kendrik said while shaking his head in dismay.

Terrance only shrugged as he continued to listen to the president's recitation.

"...send an escort, and require an inspection team to examine your ship before you're allowed to dock at Minoa Station."

"See?" Terrance glanced at Corsia and Kendrik. "He's just doing all this to show us who's boss. We've just turned his entire world upside down. Until a few hours ago, no one could get into the IPE without traveling for years through the slow zone. Now he has to deal with the fact that visitors can show up at any time."

"That doesn't mean he won't be a massive pain in the ass," Kendrik replied. "As you can see, it's something he excels at."

Corsia felt her eyes narrow, taking a moment to consider how 'right' the sensation felt. "If he thinks he's going to send an inspection team into this ship, he has another think coming."

"What are you going to do?" Kendrik spread his hands. "He'll fire on you, if you do anything aggressive."

"Really?" Terrance seemed surprised. "Would he attack the first visitors from outside the cluster he's ever had?"

"Well..." Kendrik drew out the word. "I wouldn't say that it's a foregone conclusion, but there's a very high probability, yes. Like you said, he feels threatened, and we've turned his world upside down. If he feels cornered, he may lash out."

Terrance turned to Corsia. "I know it's irking you, the thought of letting 'inspectors' aboard, but we can limit them to a small group. There's an entire company of Marines on the ship, and we're protected by stasis shields. There's nothing to fear and everything to gain by establishing a modicum of trust."

Corsia pursed her lips. "Very well, but if they think that they can traipse through the whole ship, they'll be in for a rather unpleasant surprise."

Terrance nodded in agreement. "Yes, of course. We're not going to let them have access to our advanced technology, that's a given. So would you like to send the response, or should I?"

"No," Corsia drew in a deep breath—one of the things that annoyed her about having an organic body, the persistent need to breathe—and rocked her head from side to side, stretching out her neck. "I sent the first message, I should be the one to reply. Consistency, and all that."

"You're also playing bad cop, here," Kendrik winked at Corsia. "Terrance comes in later to be the one to mollify them, and then I'm the wild card that they wonder about the whole time."

"Plus, you'll keep your brother from spewing too much bullshit," Terrance added.

"That too."

Corsia crafted a rather abrupt message acknowledging President Arthur's terms, and informed him that a small inspection team would be allowed to dock.

Afterward, she left the conference room—where Terrance and Kendrik were discussing the details of the proposal they intended to make to the IPE—returning to the bridge to watch Scan as a dozen destroyer-class ships undocked from Hero's Point and boosted to match velocity with the *Andromeda.*

<They're making good time,> Sephira commented privately to Corsia. *<I wonder if they really do fear us.>*

<I'm sure they feel the same way we would if a warship had suddenly appeared in the New Canaan system,> Corsia replied.

<Which did happen.>

Corsia laughed quietly, shaking her head as she did. *<I suspect that our response would have been different had it been just* ***one*** *ship.>*

<You seem to be enjoying the use of a body, Mom,> Sephira said with a note of amusement in her voice.

<It's interesting. I don't think I'll keep it long-term, but the experience is enlightening. I rather wish I'd tried it sooner.>

<I seem to recall you giving Ylonda a hard time about having a physical body—though I suppose you may have been right.>

Corsia felt a tension in her chest at the thought of Ylonda, momentarily surprised that her body would register a physiological response to unpleasant memories. The connection to her physical form's nervous system was deepening in its complexity.

<What Myriad did to Ylonda was not related to her body—if you recall, at the time, she was ensconced in a node. And she didn't really die, not the way that organics do. Even Amanda

didn't die per se; they just became something else…something more.>

<*Don't you miss her?*> Sephira asked wistfully.

<*Yes, but more because she's on the far side of the Inner Stars, not because she's gone forever. Your sister, she…she left so quickly after she became Amavia. I never really got to know them—not with everything else that was going on.*>

"Captain Corsia, message from the approaching IPE ships," Comm announced. "They've assigned us an updated vector, and will be sending over a shuttle once they're within ten-thousand klicks."

Corsia nodded as she reviewed the vector. It was a small shift that would have them brake around Genesis before docking at Minoa Station. It also brought them closer to several other stations that Scan had identified as defensive emplacements.

No accident there.

"Helm," Corsia nodded to the ensign at the console in front of her command chair. "Assume the vector. Ease into it, don't give them the impression that we'll jump at their every order. Scan, I want to know their armament as soon as possible. Weapons, keep the coils hot, I don't fully trust these people not to take a pot shot at us."

A chorus of acknowledgements came back, and Corsia's bridge crew set to work under the watchful eye of Sephira.

<*Enjoying the ability to sit back and relax?*> Terrance asked as he leant against a console. <*What, with Sephira embedded with the ship, you don't have to watch everything all the time.*>

Corsia sent Terrance a mental eyeroll. <*I know what you're getting at. Yes, it's hard to release control. I'm working on it. I didn't check the message Comm sent back at all, and I've only corrected Weapons once on their assessment.*>

<*You're so grown up,*> Terrance replied with a laugh. <*I still remember when you first joined us. I was pretty happy to*

have someone with Lysander in their lineage on the mission. Was a good omen.>

<I don't believe in omens,> Corsia deadpanned. *<But I think my ten-times great grandfather would have been pleased with what we've done.>*

<I don't believe in them, either,> Terrance glanced over his shoulder at Corsia. *<But that doesn't stop some things from feeling 'right'. I wonder if you'll gain an understanding of that, now that you have a body.>*

<Symmetry of ideas is not exclusive to organics,> Corsia replied evenly. *<You should know that, you've had AIs embedded with you before.>*

<I have,> Terrance replied, nodding slowly. *<Been a long time now, though. Ages, really.>*

<Perhaps it's time for you to do so again.>

Terrance snorted. *<I think I'm too old for that now. I passed over my six-hundredth birthday last month, you know.>*

<Finaeus has clocked over three-thousand real-time years, and he mentioned that he'd love to be paired with an AI again at some point. Though I don't know who'd risk going in the rat's nest he calls a mind. Besides, with the Transcend's enhanced rejuv techniques, your life can be extended indefinitely. No worry about cognitive dissonance, or the other issues that used to crop up.>

<Why the urging?> Terrance asked. *<You looking to get inside my head?>*

<No, I'm just stating facts.>

Terrance didn't reply for over a minute, staring contemplatively at the display of the Trensch System in the holotank. Corsia began to wonder if she'd offended him, when he finally replied, *<I don't know if I'd opt for an eternal life. There has to be an end, right?>*

<Why?>

<Because everything ends, Corsia. Even the universe will end.>

<Of course it will, but on any timescale we can rationally consider—yes, even for non-organics—the universe may as well be endless. Wouldn't you like to watch the whole thing evolve? It'll be fascinating.>

<Maybe. Maybe if I could skip forward in time, not slog through the whole thing. I mean…fifty trillion years just to get past the star-forming age? That's…enough to melt my brain.>

Corsia laughed. *<Well, you don't need to commit to trillions yet. Just go for a thousand, and see how you feel then.>*

<Maybe I will, Corsia. It's not like I've gotten bored yet.>

<That's the spirit.>

THE LMC

STELLAR DATE: 09.02.8949 (Adjusted Years)
LOCATION: Aleutia Station
REGION: Cheshire System, Large Magellanic Cloud

"President Sera, Governor Andrews. Welcome to the LMC."

"Sheeran?" Sera asked, a smile forming on her lips as she regarded the general standing before her.

General Sheeran grinned in response as he inclined his head. "In the flesh, ma'am."

"Don't 'ma'am' me," Sera said, shaking her head at the red-haired man. "I still owe you one for saving *Sabrina* at Bollam's World."

"Just doing my job, ma'am," General Sheeran replied. "Glad to see you're still kicking."

"More or less," Sera replied. "Hard to believe we've not bumped into each other before now—though I guess now I know why you were nowhere to be found."

Sheeran laughed as he gestured toward a dockcar that waited next to their pinnace. "Well, building a place like Aleutia doesn't really make for a lot of vacation time. But the view is worth it."

Jason nodded in solemn agreement. "I'll say. Not every day you see...well...anything close to that."

"Good ole Spaghetti Bowl," General Sheeran chuckled.

"What?" Sera asked.

"Well...from outside, the galaxy doesn't look like 'the Milky Way'. It looks more like a really big mess of spaghetti."

A scowl creased Sera's forehead. "No, more like a pinwheel."

"Well, blame your uncle." Sheeran shrugged as he settled into his seat, and the car took off. "He's the one that coined it. I mean, if I was asked, I would have just named it 'Freaking Gorgeous'."

"Good thing no one asked you," Jason grunted, trying to sound serious, but Sera could see a smile on his lips.

"OK. Give us the lowdown," Sera directed Sheeran. "What have you learned?"

Sheeran's face lost all traces of humor, and his eyes narrowed. "We've done close fly-bys of four systems now; there are two more that have activity in them, and we'll have scans of them soon, too. From what we can see, until very recently, the FGT was terraforming worlds, building rings, moving stuff around—their usual gig. However, our scans picked up *a lot* of defensive emplacements. Not new, either, so these systems were always intended to be defensive fallbacks."

"Not surprising," Sera interjected. "You don't build out in the LMC because you want a corner on tourism trade."

"Not that that would be a bad idea," Jason said, a finger on his chin as though he were giving the idea serious consideration.

"Either way," Sheeran continued. "They've stopped all terraforming activity—other than stabilizing planetary orbits. Now they're building shipyards. Some are already complete, and there are hulls under construction."

"So which system looks to be the main one? First made, or most well defended?" Sera asked.

Sheeran summoned a holo that hovered in the space between the dockcar's seats. It showed the five systems he'd mentioned, all of which surrounded a binary system that showed no indications of human activity.

He highlighted one. "This one is the most heavily defended." Then he highlighted another. "And from what we can tell, this one was first to get underway."

"What about that system?" Jason beat Sera to the punch, asking about the star in the midst of the ones showing activity. "Nothing there?"

"We've not done a fly-by of that system yet," Sheeran replied. "But there is no activity visible in it—not that we've seen from five light years out."

Sera lifted her gaze from the holo and glanced at Jason—who seemed to be on the same train of thought—before replying to Sheeran. "But that data is five years old. It's plain to see that from this layout, they were going to create a jump gate interdiction web around that central star."

"Perhaps," Sheeran said with a slow nod. "But would Airtha have done anything with it once she took over? From what I understand, she's not focused on building a fallback location, like your father was...or is she?"

Sera shook her head. "No, you're right. But my father was a paranoid man. I think he'd have still built his fallback site there before the outer defenses were created. Our goal here is to get intel, not stop Airtha's construction—well, at least not yet. Anyway, chances are that whatever he built is just sitting there, full of juicy data, waiting for us to come and pay it a visit."

"Otherwise known as a baited trap," Jason cautioned.

"Maybe," Sera allowed. "Maybe not. Airtha has no idea that we're out here as well. It'll take two hundred years for them to see what you're up to, here in Aleutia."

"Do you want me to divert the next scouting run to that system?" Sheeran asked.

"You have...what? Seven ships capable of full stealth?" Sera asked.

"Six," Sheeran corrected. "One of the stealth cruisers has been having issues maintaining concealment in heavily ionized plasma flows. Which is common out here."

"Well, then," Sera said, shifting her gaze to Jason. "Sounds like we have our strike force."

"Wait, 'we'?" Jason asked. "You're not going on the mission to that system. You're the Transcend's president. They need you."

Sera placed a hand on Jason's knee, unable to miss how his brows rose at her touch. "We both know that I'm just a bureaucrat running the home front. Tanis is really in charge back there."

Jason's face was unreadable, and Sera wondered if she'd said something wrong. Then he snorted and shook his head.

"I know how you feel. I suppose we might need you. If we *do* find a secret base in that system, it's possible that only you will be able to breach it—what, with your super-special presidential tokens, and all."

"Glad to know my value as a lockpick is recognized."

* * * * *

Less than a day later, Sera stood with Jason and General Sheeran on the bridge of the general's flagship, a stealth-capable cruiser named the *Helios*.

The ship was a new design, based on the rail destroyers the ISF had fielded in the Battle of Carthage. However, instead of just two rings, the *Helios* consisted of eight rings, all meeting along a single axis point fore and aft. A central shaft ran through the ship, and at its center lay the bridge and main crew-areas.

The diameter of the generally spherical vessel was just over three kilometers. Given each ring's capacity to house billions of rail-accelerated pellets, and fire them in almost any direction, the *Helios* was a formidable vessel, and a testament to the ISF's determination to produce war-ending ships.

Sera had already put in a request for the class of vessel to be produced for the Transcend's military.

Ahead of the ship lay the jump gate, but that wasn't what Sera found herself staring at. Instead, she had a secondary holotank dedicated to the view of the Milky Way.

She'd never given any serious thought to what the galaxy would look like from this far away, but she didn't think that anything could have prepared her for how beautiful, massive, and terrifying it appeared, hanging in space like an eternal storm that dominated nearly forty-five degrees of the 'sky'.

But it wasn't its size or luminosity that amazed her, it was the fact that everything she'd ever known, all her hopes, dreams—all of *everyone's* hopes and dreams—all laid within that cluster of stars.

And that cluster was just one of many…so many.

Even though the war they were mired in spanned a significant portion of the galaxy, the view reminded her that humanity's reach was still not even a trillionth of the universe.

Space had never made her feel insignificant. Sera had always viewed space as her home, as a playground of sorts.

But this, this make me feel insignificant.

She saw that Jason was staring at it as well, his expression one of pensive consideration.

"What do you see when you look at it?" she asked.

He didn't reply at first, but then glanced toward her and said, "The past."

"Yours, or the galaxy's?" Sera asked.

"A bit of both." Jason gave a small laugh. "In the view we see from here, homo sapiens aren't yet walking about on Earth, and so far as we know, there isn't a single spacefaring species. The galaxy we're looking at...it's pristine."

"Do you think we've sullied it?"

"No," Jason said after a moment. "I don't think it's possible for us to sully the galaxy. We're a part of its evolution. That great big whirling ball of matter spawned stars, and around those stars formed planets, and on one, some four billion years ago, life as we know it came about. We're a part of the natural evolution of a galaxy—of this galaxy, at least. Maybe we'll last as long as it does, or maybe in a billion years there won't be a single trace of us left."

"That's a morose and sobering thought." Sera let out a small laugh, trying to lighten the moment, but it fell flat. "Granted, we're out here in the LMC, now. We're not a part of *this* galaxy."

Jason shrugged. "Seems like we are now."

"I see you're engaging in the official Aleutian pastime," General Sheeran said as he approached the pair.

"I take it that staring at that thing doesn't get old, then?" Jason asked, jerking a thumb at the view of the Milky Way.

Sheeran shook his head. "Nope, not even a little. I wonder, though, given that the Transcend was already out here when we arrived, is there any place that our people can ever go to just get away?"

"Andromeda?" Sera laughed as she said it.

Though a jump to the LMC was something they could manage, the amount of antimatter it would take to power a jump to the Andromeda Galaxy was beyond staggering.

Even CriEn modules would not be able to power such a leap.

"Wouldn't that be something." Jason's voice sounded wistful. "A whole new galaxy."

"Not happy with the one you have?" Sera asked.

"What can I say? Wanderlust is something I've always felt. You don't spend centuries plying the black at sub-light speeds if you don't like to travel."

She held up a hand to forestall further argument. "I'm not knocking it. I don't like to sit still, either."

"That why you're out here and not back on Khardine, ma'am?" Sheeran asked.

The honorific reminded Sera of the title and responsibilities she constantly carried around. She glanced toward the bridge's entrance where Major Valerie and another of her High Guard stood, constant reminders of the job Sera had so foolishly taken on that insane day aboard the *Galadrial*.

At Tanis's insistence, Sera had stopped trying to foist the responsibilities off on others—Finaeus and Tanis herself—but that hadn't stopped Sera from privately wishing she'd never taken up her father's torch.

Going on this mission to the LMC had been highly irresponsible—something that the disapproving looks from Major Valerie frequently confirmed—but Sera felt truly alive for the first time since she'd left Tanis and returned to Khardine.

Maybe I can figure out some way to effectively lead from the front, rather than hiding away in a fortress of stars.

"Jump in t-minus thirty seconds," Helm announced, and Sera turned from the view of the Milky Way to the gate ahead. The negative energy emitters came to life, and the gate's mirrors reflected the unfathomable levels of power into a roiling mass at the gate's center.

The *Helios* boosted toward the gate, pouring on one last burst of power to give them a higher delta-*v* relative to the destination star system—designated 'Hidey Hole'.

Then the ship's forward mirror touched the mass at the center of the gate, and the *Helios* skipped forward across two-hundred light years, and into the unknown.

"Stealth systems engaged!" Lieutenant Aya called out the moment they re-entered normal space.

Scan collated data from the ship's passive sensors, and a view of the star system began to appear on the main holotank.

At the center was a rather pedestrian G-Class star with a red dwarf on an eccentric orbit, currently placing it two hundred AU from the primary.

Over the course of the next hour, the other six stealth ships would enter the Hidey Hole System and take up parabolic trajectories around the stars, passing by major planets and moons.

Listening.

The *Helios* was on target for the planet deepest in the star system, a terrestrial world roughly half Earth's mass. It orbited the primary at only half an AU, its surface hot and inhospitable, but protected by a powerful magnetic shield that kept the most damaging radiation from reaching its surface.

"Those are some powerful van allen belts for such a small planet," Jason observed. "I'd be surprised if they're entirely natural."

"A lot of tidal forces in this system," Sera replied, turning to the AI who was managing scan, the holo of a young man sitting at the station he had no need of. "What do you make of it, Chief Reggie?"

"Hard to say," Reggie replied, his voice emanating from his holoprojection. "Could be natural, but like Governor

Andrews suggests; there are a lot of tidal forces in this system that *could* keep the planet molten and spinning inside—yet terrestrial worlds that small don't often have a core differentiated enough to create strong magnetic fields when they rotate."

"So you're saying you're not sure." Sera winked at the AI, who raised an eyebrow and shrugged.

"We're twenty AU away and using passive sensors. I'm not a miracle worker," he countered. "But if I happened to stumble across a system like this, I'd find it curious—though not enough to immediately jump to planetary engineering as the reason for the magnetosphere. Granted, with this star's position in the midst of five others undergoing stellar engineering, the opposite suspicions would form."

"That's enough for me," Jason replied, then turned toward Sera. "The one thing going against it is the tectonic activity from a molten core. Would your father pick a planet that's so…motile? Or would he go for something further out that was cold and solid?"

Sera rubbed her face. "Well, from what I can see, he started this venture befo—wait a second. If it took almost two hundred years for the light from this terraforming operation to reach Aleutia, then he started this before jump gates were made."

"Or at least *revealed*," Jason amended.

<*Now* ***that's*** *an interesting thought,*> Jen mused. <*It would mean Finaeus hasn't been truthful—but that seems unlikely.*>

Sera pursed her lips and drew in a slow breath. "Either way, it all predates *me*. I wonder if Andrea or Justin knew about this."

Jason's visage grew grim. "When Krissy catches up to Justin, we'll ask him."

"Keeping up on current events?" Sera asked.

"I'm of the opinion that Justin sent Andrea to kill Tanis back in the Ascella System—and that he authorized her to turn you using mentally subversive tech. If there's one thing I don't hold with, it's mental subversion. As far as I'm concerned, Justin is villainous scum."

"I'll add it to the list of things to ask Justin about—not that I expect to get much out of him—not without stooping to his level."

Sera looked at Jason to see him nodding in agreement. She decided to ask him at some point what reason he had for his vehement dislike of mental coercion. Not that sane people liked it under any circumstances, but there was something in his eyes. A distant pain that spoke of personal experience.

"Helm, what's the best speed you can make to that planet?" General Sheeran asked.

"Sir. Best speed will put us at two days' travel for a close fly-by. But we'd light up the night, braking to orbit the planet. A better plan would be to brake around the star after passing by to see if we wanted to pay it a visit. Would take…just three days to fly by, then a day to brake around the star and settle into orbit over the planet."

"Sir, ma'am?" Sheeran asked as he turned to Sera and Jason.

"Well," Sera mused, tapping her chin. "We're not sure anything is there, and ruling it out sooner than later would be ideal, so we could slingshot out to other targets."

"It keeps our stealth intact, as well," Jason added.

"Stealthed fly-by and star-brake it is," Sheeran said, confirming the order before nodding to Helm, who pushed the vector onto the main holo, the display showing burn points, adjustments, and countdowns to the maneuvers.

Sera looked at the timeline. "Four days. I guess I can catch up on reading the never-ending list of reports that have jammed up my queues."

Jason laughed. "Sounds like it should be riveting. I've some of the same to attend to."

Sera thanked General Sheeran for letting them stand around on his bridge, and walked off, her guard stepping in behind her, followed by Jason.

<I think I know the sorts of reporting you'd **like** *to be doing,>* Valerie said to Sera as they walked down the passageway.

Sera glanced at the major to see the woman's face perfectly composed, eyes forward.

<I have no idea what you're talking about, Val,> Sera retorted.

<Really? Then you're the only one that bridge who doesn't. If you and Jason had stood any closer together, you'd've been hugging…or something else.>

Sera rolled her eyes as they reached the lift.

"You know…" Jason began as he reached her side. "I have a rather large stateroom—for a warship, at least. We could set up in my quarters and have a meal while going over all the reports that are demanding our attention."

He uttered the words as though he was suggesting they were organizing a scientific survey, but when Sera glanced at Jason, his eyes said something else entirely.

<See.> Valerie's mental tone was completely flat.

Sera ran a hand through her hair, weighing how much she wanted to take Jason up on his offer against the tsunami of scuttlebutt it would create.

Wait…since when do I care about that? This 'president' gig is really wringing the life out of me.

"Deal," Sera replied. "Lead the way."

An easy grin settled on Jason's lips as they stepped onto the lift. "Don't worry, Sera. I plan to."

Sera nearly burst out laughing at the 'oh' face Jen placed in her mind.

* * * * *

"Stars, I needed that," Sera whispered as she flopped onto her bunk half a day later—finally getting to the reports that she'd ostensibly gone to Jason's quarters to work on.

Her stomach growled, and Sera reached out to order a meal from the galley. It turned out that Jason's version of a 'light meal' while they worked consisted exclusively of beer.

For someone who presented an air of the elder statesman when on the bridge of a ship, he could really pound the brews back.

But when it came to the main event, he was far more easygoing, then deliberate, then…well…mind-blowing.

I guess you learn a few tricks over a thousand years.

Sera let out a long breath and closed her eyes, reliving the experience while she waited for the food to arrive.

<*You have been wound a bit tight lately,*> Jen commented. <*Was good to see you relax.*>

" 'See'?" Sera asked.

<*Well, not 'see' per se. I wandered off elsewhere. The ship's AIs have a little expanse, and we explored the options surrounding a staged series of jumps to the Andromeda Galaxy while you partook in your organic happy times.*>

"You really wouldn't do that, would you?" Sera asked, a pang of fear running through her. "Leave for Andromeda?"

Jen's laugh filtered through Sera's mind like wind rustling tall, dry grass on a high steppe. <*Well, so long as this war doesn't wipe us out, we're all going to live a long time. I wouldn't mind seeing a few different galaxies before my time's up.>*

Sera grunted softly; she hadn't ever considered that possibility before. But now, flying through the LMC, the idea of extra-galactic adventures had become much more realistic.

"What do you feel when you look up at the Milky Way?" Sera asked her AI companion.

<Feel?>

"Your emotional analogue. Do you get a sense of wonderment? A shift in perspective?"

<You know we're not all the same, right?> Jen asked.

"Huh? AIs?"

<Yeah, we're varied. Some are more prone to 'emotional analogues', as you put it, some not at all. Just like humans are varied.>

"So what do *you* see when you look up at our galaxy, oh one of many varied AIs?" Sera asked, a smirk on her lips.

<Vectors. Soooo many vectors. I see the orbits of the arms, the stars in the galactic disk, the halo stars, I marvel at the x-rays blasting out of Sagittarius A's poles…I wonder what exists beyond the galaxphere. Is inter-galactic space as empty as we think? Are there pockets of matter and energy that we simply can't detect unless we're there? Where* ***is*** *the rest of the universe? Why can't we see most of it?>*

"Sounds like wonderment to me," Sera said, a smile on her lips.

<I guess. I don't know if it's like yours, though.>

"You probably have more precision to your ad-hoc math than I do, but it's not that different than where my mind goes. I find myself thinking about the people, too. The conflicts we have…somehow it doesn't look so important from out here. There's so much galaxy. Why do we have to fight over our tiny corner?"

<Well, in your defense, the Transcend has never been the aggressor—by and large, at least.>

"Small mercies," Sera replied. "My father was a lot of things, but at least he was no war-monger. Then again, if he'd gone after Orion in the past, things may not have gotten to this point."

<Coulda, shoulda, woulda,> Jen gave a mental shrug, then a smirk. *<How's that for imprecision? Pairing with you has made me a lot more loosey-goosey.>*

"You mean flexible and adaptable?" Sera shot back.

<Sure, that.>

A smile formed on Sera's lips, and she closed her eyes. "Thanks, Jen."

<For what?>

"For being you, for just being a friend."

<Of course, Your Presidency.>

A laugh burst from Sera's lips, and she shook her head before rolling onto her side. "Nice one. Now stop rattling around inside my head. I'm going to fall asleep basking in this glow, and forget the mountain of work waiting for me."

<What about the food?>

"Tell them to set it on the table," Sera mumbled softly.

Jen didn't reply, but the feeling of warm contentment she fed into Sera's mind was all the response the president needed.

For the first time in years, Sera fell asleep not thinking of *that* day: the day her lover killed her father, and she learned of her mother's searing betrayal.

INSPECTION

STELLAR DATE: 09.02.8949 (Adjusted Years)
LOCATION: Bay 1, ISS *Andromeda*
REGION: Trensch System, Inner Praesepe Empire

Corsia had strongly considered delegating the job of meeting the IPE's inspection team. Jim, Terrance, or even Commander Eve from the Marine company could handle the task.

Such are the trials of being the captain, Corsia thought. *You can't delegate this sort of nonsense. Could be worse, though. I could be in Tanis's shoes.*

As Corsia was wishing she were anywhere else, the doors across the docking bay began to slide open, an ES field activating to hold the ship's atmosphere in.

Most of the new ISF ships used grav fields on their bay entrances, but the *Andromeda* had used electro-static shields for over a century, and she saw no reason to change them—especially when the ES fields were far more efficient.

Pulling a feed from the ship's sensors, Corsia watched the IPE shuttle close the final hundred meters. The thirty-meter ship was an ugly, squat thing, almost as wide as it was long.

Lucky for them, the *Andromeda* had a large central bay occupying the belly of the ship. Considering that they'd once squeezed *Sabrina*'s two hundred meters into the bay, the IPE shuttle wasn't even a snug fit.

"That's a well-armed shuttle," Jim said as he approached. "Though it looks like their firing systems aren't charged up."

<*Of course not, Dad*> Sephira replied. <*I wouldn't have let them dock if they were.*>

"I figured as much, Sephira," Jim said, a scowl lowering his brow. "Still, doesn't really bode well."

"We'll see how it plays out." Corsia looked down at her shipsuit, feeling strangely self-conscious. The sensation was entirely unfamiliar to her, and she wondered if people with bodies felt this way from time to time, or if it was just because hers was new.

"You look fine," Jim said, a smile gracing his lips. "I gotta say, though. You're totally keeping that body—if I have any input in the matter."

<Seriously, Jim, not now,> Corsia scolded, wishing her form wasn't so distracting to him. Sometimes it seemed desirable, other times it was as though he was unable to focus around her.

The shuttle settled onto the cradle, and the ramp rose to meet the craft's exit. A half-minute passed with no activity, and then the door slid open to reveal two armed and armored Marines, who strode down the ramp, their visors hiding the direction of their gaze.

Following them, a dark-haired man stepped out of the shuttle, clothed in a light grey uniform, with a yellow IPE crest over his heart, along with several ribbons and a crescent moon medal.

Two birds adorned his lapels, and Corsia noted that each leg held a separate clutch of arrows, a particular colonel's insignia many of the militaries around Praesepe seemed to use.

Her own collar bore a single star, and the man's gaze darted to it, before his eyes lifted to meet hers.

Corsia strode forward and extended her hand. "Welcome to the *Andromeda*. I am Captain Corsia."

"Captain?" the man asked, eyes darting to her Admiral's star once more.

"It is our custom in the ISF that when you are the captain of a storied vessel, that title supersedes your rank, Colonel..." she left the address open-ended for him to complete.

"Hickson," the man replied. "I am here to oversee the inspection of your vessel."

As he spoke, a group of technicians began to walk down the ramp behind him, and the colonel stepped aside to let them pass. "We will need to sweep your entire ship before you'll be allowed to dock at Minoa Station."

Corsia pursed her lips and shook her head slowly before replying. "We will give you a walk-through of non-classified areas, and you may perform any checks that will not harm our vessel or require any physical connections or interaction with the *Andromeda*'s systems."

As she spoke, the colonel's eyes grew wide, and his jaw tensed. "You must have misunderstood President Arthur's directive. We will perform a *full* inspection of your ship."

Corsia drew herself up, the five centimeters she had on the man allowing her to stare down on him in a very satisfying fashion.

"I understand that we are within the borders of the IPE, and you have reason to fear us—the idea of ships entering your core system with no warning must be very unsettling. However, we are not at liberty to allow you full access to this ship, but we want to make every good-faith effort we can to accommodate you. Is there no way we can reach a compromise?"

"Captain Corsia." The colonel loaded the words with so much disdain, it sounded as though his tongue had withered just from uttering them. "If you were at the edge of the Trensch System, we would simply refuse you entry. But since you are this deep within the gravity well, we will consider any non-compliance as an act of aggression."

"How many ships do you have?" Corsia asked plainly. "Five hundred? A thousand? A week ago, we jumped forty thousand ships into the Albany System to bring about the greatest defeat the Nietzscheans have seen since the early days of their war with the Genevians."

The colonel's eyes grew wide for a moment, then narrowed. "Talk is cheap. Right now you have just one ship. How will you summon more?"

Corsia could feel her body responding to the man's words with an increase in heart rate, muscle tension, and a host of other physiological changes. A part of her found it fascinating, and wondered how humans managed to deal with the chemical changes in their bodies while under stress.

The rest of her wanted to punch Colonel Hickson in the face.

That urge nearly won.

She considered placing a call on the QuanComm network for another ship to jump in, but decided against it for the time being. If the IPE was being this testy about one ship, the presence of more vessels would surely escalate things.

Granted, it wouldn't be hard to simply take what we want from this system.

Corsia tamped down on that thought. That was not the way Tanis wanted to operate, and it ran contrary to Corsia's own beliefs as well. Though the idea was tempting.

She was trying to think of something to say that would diffuse the situation, when Jim spoke up.

"Colonel Hickson. You've witnessed our abilities, and we can see how zealously you defend your people—something we understand, and greatly admire. Our purpose in travelling to the Trensch System is to create a trade agreement that we think will *greatly* benefit your people. Perhaps I can escort your teams—" Jim nodded to the technicians who were standing uncomfortably to the side of the ramp, "around the non-classified areas on the ship, and they can assess whether or not we are an extreme threat, and then you can make a decision with that information in hand."

"I suppose that's a start," Colonel Hickson grunted.

"Would it also be an option for us to remain in a high orbit around Genesis instead of docking at a station?" Corsia asked, glad for Jim's interjection. "We could bring a pinnace to Minoa Station. No need to worry about a foreign warship docking."

"I suppose that could work." Though his words were noncommittal, Hickson's tone hinted at genuine surprise. "You'd have to remain outside Genesis's van allen belts. Trensch is not an agreeable star to be so close to for long periods of time."

"If we assess that risk to be too much, we can reevaluate the full inspection," Corsia replied.

"We'll proceed as you suggest, then," the colonel said, nodding to his inspection team. "But the president may decide it is not satisfactory."

Corsia nodded. "I guess we'll hope for the best."

Jim gestured to the technicians, ten in all, who followed him out of the bay. Two more IPE Marines came down the ramp and followed after.

Corsia was tempted to deny the soldiers access to her ship without surrendering their weapons, but decided it wasn't worth the hassle. Sephira was already dropping a nanocloud onto their armor and weapons to disable them, should the need arise.

"Would you like a tour of the bridge?" Corsia asked the colonel. "Something to while away the time?"

The man's eyes actually widened in surprise before he schooled his expression. "Certainly, lead the way."

Corsia led the colonel through the ship, Marines from his delegation coming along, shadowed—of course—by a pair of ISF Marines. He seemed only moderately interested in the vessel until she made the offhand remark that it had been built in the Sol System.

"Sol, you say?" his voice was sharp and filled with disbelief.

"Yes," Corsia nodded. "We're a part of the *Intrepid* colony mission. Left Sol in 4124. Hit Kapteyn's Streamer and dumped back out into normal space just a few decades ago. Much of the *Andromeda*'s crew was born in Sol."

"*Intrepid*..." the colonel murmured. "It doesn't ring any bells."

"Well, it was long ago. Either way, our arrival in the Inner Stars has stirred the pot, and we've joined an alliance that is attempting to stabilize the region."

"The Inner Stars?" Hickson asked. "I've not heard that term before."

"It's the stars on the Orion Arm. Everything about two thousand light years up and down the arm from Sol. Coreward of the Inner Stars is the Transcend, and rimward is Orion. Each of those regions stretch into the neighboring galactic arms."

"I didn't know people had spread so far," Hickson replied, this time his tone not giving away whether or not he was impressed. "We don't really pay too much attention to what happens beyond the cluster."

"I can't say I blame you," Corsia replied. "We were hoping for a similar existence, but that wasn't to be."

"Because of these jump gates?" Hickson asked.

"Yes, exactly so. We were paid a visit somewhat like this, not long ago. But it was from about two hundred thousand ships."

For the first time Hickson's veneer cracked. "*Two hundred thousand*?"

Corsia let a note of pride slip into her voice. "Give or take a bit, yes. Trisilieds, Hegemony, and Orion all ganged up on us."

"And you're still alive to tell the tale…"

"Well, we won."

Hickson shook his head. "I'd like to hear more about that."

"Perhaps," Corsia replied. "There are details of that battle we don't widely share. Not yet, at least. There's a war spreading across the Orion Arm. Nowhere is safe, and we need to keep our tactics for our allies."

Hickson stopped and turned to Corsia in the middle of a long corridor that led to the central lift bank. "You'll forgive my skepticism, but if you can do all this, what is it that you want with the IPE? What do we have to offer?"

"Well," Corsia began. "It's not for us. It's for our allies. You may not know this, given how many light years deep in the cluster you are, but Genevia has fallen to Nietzschea. Their empire is expanding at a rapid rate, and has reached the edges of the cluster. Septhia, Thebes, and a scattered few other nations are all that stand between the Niets and the IPE. Make no mistake, the Niets *also* want the resources within the cluster. They don't yet possess jump gates themselves, but their allies do. It's only a matter of time before they make a play for control of the IPE."

Corsia could see a war of emotions on Hickson's face. They weren't overt, but they were there. The man had every reason to be annoyed with her for coming into the system without authorization, but she knew he couldn't discount her words, either.

Everything he thought he knew about the galaxy outside the Praesepe Cluster was now utterly outdated, and they had to contend with the reality that their pocket of isolation was no longer unreachable.

"Come," Corsia said. "Let me show you the bridge, and then we can swing by the galley and see if there are any strawberries."

"Strawberries?" Hickson's eyebrows rose, as though that was the final straw on the incredulous donkey's back.

"Yeah, strawberries."

* * * * *

Hickson had vacillated between his fully prickly persona, and one that was borderline tolerable during the two hours Corsia entertained him.

He was less impressed with the strawberries than most people were, but went on for five minutes about how amazing the coffee was.

Both were new tastes to Corsia, but *she* vastly preferred strawberries to coffee. In fact, she couldn't imagine why any organic would subject themselves to the bitter brew.

Even so, Hickson loved it.

As best as Corsia could determine, coffee plants didn't grow well in the environs that the Trensch System had to offer. He hinted that an import business selling beans that could produce coffee such as the galley aboard the *Andromeda* had to offer would do quite well.

Corsia was walking Hickson back toward the bay, when suddenly the colonel stiffened and gave her a sidelong look. She pretended not to notice it, and kept walking as though nothing was wrong.

A minute later, they walked into the bay to see four more IPE Marines at the base of the shuttle, making six of them, compared to the pair of ISF Marines who were tailing Corsia.

"Is something amiss?" Corsia asked, turning to Hickson, a look of innocent concern on her face.

<Dropping a nanocloud on the newcomers,> Sephira advised.

<Thanks, I hope we won't need to use it. Not off to a good start, here. Any idea why he got so prickly again?> Corsia asked as she and the colonel waited in silence.

<He was talking with his inspection team over the Link. Perhaps they told him something he didn't like.>

Corsia didn't respond to Sephira, as the IPE inspection team returned, accompanied by Jim and the Marines from both groups. The team's leader nodded silently to Colonel Hickson as they boarded their shuttle, but no other apparent communication was made.

"So," Corsia said, deciding to press ahead. "I assume all is well? Should we hold our vector while we wait to see if we should remain in a high orbit around Genesis?"

Hickson turned to Corsia. "Depends on how much of an idiot you think I am."

"I'm sorry?" Corsia asked.

"My inspection team has confirmed that your ship has very advanced stealth systems."

Corsia nodded. "We do at that, yes."

"So this whole jump gate nonsense was just a distraction."

Corsia finally understood the human urge to roll one's eyes. "Are you suggesting that we flew at *least* three light years—probably more, depending on where you think we came from—under stealth, to sneak deep into the Trensch

System, only to announce ourselves twenty-five AU from Genesis? What possible reason could we have to do that?"

"I don't know," Hickson shook his head, regarding Corsia as though she were the very embodiment of evil. "Maybe it was to force us into some sort trade deal, while worried about an incursion from Nietzschea. You'll stay on your current course until I speak with President Arthur."

Corsia decided enough was enough, and connected to the central QuanComm hub at Khardine. *[This is General Corsia. Plan B, on my coordinates.]*

[LZ hot?] the response came back a moment later.

[Not yet. ETA?]

[Three mikes.]

[Perfect.]

"Very well, Colonel. You'd best be on your way, then," Corsia replied to Hickson. "You have important messages to send. I'll wait until your president is ready to meet, or to send someone whose common sense isn't utterly suppressed by irrational paranoia. Although, I expect I'll hear from you before then…say, in four minutes or so."

<Wow, Mom, excessive derision much?>

<Hush, Sephira.>

Hickson's mouth worked silently for a moment, then he turned on his heel and strode up the ramp, trailed by his Marines.

A minute later, the shuttle was lifting off and passing out of the bay.

Corsia tracked its trajectory back to the colonel's ship, eagerly waiting for the arrival of the destroyers—and for the colonel's reaction.

Hickson's shuttle was only halfway to his ship when Corsia got the message from Khardine.

[Jumping.]

A second later, two destroyers appeared, flanking the *Andromeda*. The one on the port side entered the system only a kilometer from Hickson's shuttle—which suddenly slewed to the side.

<Every IPE ship in Hickson's fleet has just raised shields,> Sephira announced.

<Good, now maybe we'll finally get somewhere.>

Sure enough, Comm reached out to Corsia seconds later, and connected her with Hickson.

<Captain Corsia! What is the meaning of this?> he demanded.

<To prove to you that jump gates exist. Either that, or our stealth tech is so good that we can flit right under your noses. Either way, I think we're worth having a chat with.>

<Very well, Captain. I will provide my report to the president. Shift your vector for an orbit five light seconds out from Genesis. You'll not be coming any closer, now that you have your escort.>

Hickson's words carried a note of defeat, but he still managed to sound like a haughty asshole.

<Understood,> Corsia replied.

DOPPELGANGER

STELLAR DATE: 09.06.8949 (Adjusted Years)
LOCATION: Interstellar Pinnace
REGION: Airtha, Huygens System, Transcend Interstellar Alliance

Sera flew the pinnace toward the EMG, smiling in satisfaction at the machine's sleek, hundred-kilometer length.

It was the first of the new defensive weapons to be made, a device capable of firing a focused electromagnetic wave that would disable any ship in its path, even ones possessing stasis shields.

Sera's engineers had yet to test an EMG against one of the ISF's stasis shielded ships, but Airtha was confident that the variable waveform would be able to penetrate the stasis field.

Sera wasn't so sure, but her mother pointed out that—despite the commonly held belief—the ISF's 'impenetrable' shields did not envelope the entire ship. There were openings for cooling, engine wash, sensors and weapons.

Initially Sera had countered that the ISF ships only opened those holes periodically, but when Airtha explained that EMG produced a field effect larger than all but the *I2*, she understood her mother's plan.

The physical size of the EMG waveform meant that the ISF ships would risk a disabling shot from an EMG every time they fired their weapons, or even took sensor readings.

To say nothing of using main engines and maneuvering thrusters.

Yes, Sera thought, a smile on her lips as she flew along the length of the EMG. *Let my doppelganger come. Let her fling herself against our defenses, thinking her ships are invulnerable. We'll overwhelm her with both our numbers and our superior weapons. Her rebellion will fall, and then we'll move on to Orion, finally finishing what my father should have done millennia ago.*

Sera broke off from her close pass over the EMG, watching as it approached the jump gate.

Though Sera's mother was undoubtably the most brilliant mind in the galaxy, Airtha was not one to implicitly trust even her own analysis. She wanted incontrovertible proof that the EMG could penetrate stasis shields.

Which was why this weapon was on its way—with a five thousand ship escort—to a system on the edge of the Vela Cluster. A system that had chosen the wrong side in the civil war raging across the Transcend.

Valkris.

The latest reports showed that the Transcend only had a token force defending Valkris. A mere dozen warships on top of the system's local military of five hundred or so ships—most of which were light interceptors.

Khardine's forces had been gaining ground across the Transcend, especially in the Vela Cluster, but that would end now. Once Valkris was under Airtha's control, they'd sweep across the rest of the cluster and crush Khardine's greatest stronghold.

That would send her doppelganger running.

As Sera thought of the other version of herself, a small twinge of worry flitted through her mind. Airtha insisted that *she* was the real Sera. That the one who had fled to New Canaan was in fact a copy made by the separatists Greer and Krissy. A poor shadow of the real Sera, and the separatists' puppet.

Though she tried to push the doubt away—she had no reason to doubt Airtha—a sliver of worry persisted, a worry that her mother was keeping something from her, manipulating her.

"No," Sera whispered, turning her focus to the jump gate that she'd be taking to the Vela Cluster. "I have no gaps in my memory, no points where I'd be falsified. I'm the *real* Sera."

She repeated the mantra to herself several times while watching the EMG jump through its gate, marveling at the sight of a hundred-kilometer weapon disappearing in an instant.

Even though she knew the Khardine Sera was a clone, it didn't diminish the regrets Sera felt over the events that had taken place. Foremost was the death of Elena, and the fact that Tanis had been duped by the clone.

The journey from Silstrand to Bollam's World with Tanis was a fond memory, as was the time she'd spent on the *Intrepid*. It was another thing that the separatists had stolen from her.

An alert lit up, informing Sera that it was her turn to jump, and she triggered the pinnace's bow mirror. The ship eased forward, and then leapt across the thousand light years to Vela in a matter of seconds.

When normal space snapped into place around her, Sera confirmed that she was at her designated overwatch position, five AU stellar north of where the engagement would take place.

That was the only way she had been able to convince Airtha to let her view the battle—promising to be so far from it that there was no chance of her being at risk.

Once the coordinates were confirmed, Sera activated the drones inside the pinnace's small cargo hold, and set them to work, hauling the ring components out of the bay and assembling a thirty-meter jump gate. Just large enough for the pinnace to slip through, if an emergency demanded it. A destroyer from the battlegroup would collect it later.

While the gate was being put together, Sera rose from her chair in the cockpit and walked back to the pinnace's small galley. The attack fleet had jumped in half an AU from their target, the world of Maitreya. Their location meant they'd engage the separatist fleets in roughly an hour, and Sera would see the outcome of the battle fifty minutes later.

Well, maybe not the outcome of the ***battle****, but certainly of the EMG's initial salvo.*

That's all Sera needed to do: verify that the EMG worked, and then return to Airtha. Not that she planned to leave early. She'd see the battle through, then join her fleets when they took the capital world.

Her mother would be annoyed, but either Sera was the president, or she wasn't. This was her call to make.

She poured herself a cup of coffee, wondering why her mother had allowed her to travel to Valkris without an escort, without anyone else on the ship at all. Granted, she was safe enough this far above the stellar plane. Unless Valkris had drastically changed its patrols—which *was* possible, but not too likely.

She hoped.

Stop fretting, Sera scolded herself, grabbing a sandwich from the chiller before returning to the bridge. She settled into her seat and took another sip of the coffee while reviewing the myriad reports she'd brought along.

I bet my doppelganger doesn't have to deal with all this nonsense.

PARLAY

STELLAR DATE: 09.06.8949 (Adjusted Years)
LOCATION: IPSS *Deepening Night*
REGION: Trensch System, Inner Praesepe Empire

Corsia stepped out of her pinnace, surveying the *Deepening Night*'s docking bay, taking in the dozen shuttles and fighters in the IPE warship's bay, along with the entire platoon of Marines.

Commander Eve—who had insisted she come along—stood at the base of the ramp with a squad of ISF Marines, and nodded for Corsia to proceed.

She glanced at Terrance and Kendrik. "Well, boys, let's do this."

<*You going to be OK?*> Terrance asked. <*This is your first away mission in…what, two centuries?*>

<*If you consider that the* Andromeda *used to be my body, I was always on away missions.*>

<*Huh,*> Terrance gave a mental grunt as he followed her down the ramp. <*I guess that's one way to think of it. But not at all the same.*>

A man and a woman in long robes stood at the base of the ramp, studiously ignoring Commander Eve—who returned the favor—as they watched Corsia descend.

When she was within arm's reach, the woman gave a perfunctory smile. "Admiral Corsia. I am Minister Rama and this is Secretary Larson." Larson nodded as Rama introduced him.

Corsia inclined her head to each in turn. "Thank you for hosting us." She turned to Terrance. "This is Terrance Redding, one of our top diplomats, and I suspect you know Mister Kendrik."

The IPE representatives' eyes grew wide, and Corsia's momentary satisfaction was shared with a sense of surprise that they hadn't already recognized their president's brother.

"It's been a long time, Minister Rama—though back then, you were the former minister's assistant, if I recall," Kendrik said with a genuine smile. "Secretary Larson, I don't believe we've met."

"I've never had the pleasure," Larson said, his voice smooth and cultured.

Handshakes were exchanged, then Rama gestured to the dock's inner doors. "The president awaits us. Please, come."

Commander Eve signaled to the squad Marines, who fell in behind the group, causing Rama to stop short.

"I'm sorry, your guards won't be able to accompany you."

Corsia had been expecting that. "Our welcome to your system has been less than warm. I hope you'll understand that we're a little uncomfortable. Would you allow four of our Marines to accompany us if they disarm?"

Rama seemed surprised at Corsia's offer. "Well...um, I suppose that will be acceptable. They'll need to remain in the corridor outside the meeting room.

"Of course," Corsia nodded, and Eve directed four of the Marines to pass their weapons to their squadmates.

She could tell they didn't like it, but an ISF Marine in light armor—which was the case for this squad—was still a formidable force. Especially considering that they still carried their lightwands, and their armored forearms held pulse weapons.

Rama led the group through the *Deepening Night,* a twelve hundred meter cruiser. It was one of a dozen such ships in the battle group of sixty vessels that had met the

Andromeda and its destroyer escort when it settled into its orbit around Genesis.

Corsia suspected that the IPE military was trying to cow her with a show of force, but after the recent battles she'd participated in, sixty ships barely seemed like enough for a policing action.

The *Deepening Night* seemed relatively modern—by Inner Stars standards—though the pinnace's scan had shown that their power plants generated a far lower output than the ISF ships. They wouldn't be able to run their beams for an extended engagement.

Corsia's tactical assessment determined that the *Andromeda* alone could disable half the IPE ships within ten minutes.

The one thing she *did* like about their ships was the quality they exhibited. The designs were sound, the engines more than powerful enough to maneuver in a fight, while still being well-protected by ablative armor.

Each cruiser sported three railguns and a host of beam weapons. She suspected that they were more than a match for any enemies that the IPE was likely to face, this deep in its domain.

Rama made small talk—pointedly ignoring Kendrik—asking innocuous questions about events outside the cluster's slow zone, and was visibly surprised by a few answers Corsia provided, such as the attacks on Thebes, and even the fall of the Kendo Empire in the rimward fringes of the slow zone.

Once or twice, Rama made comments that led Corsia to believe she was nervous, but it was hard to be certain.

<Are you picking up on her cues?> Terrance asked after one of Rama's uncertain laughs.

<I think so,> Corsia replied. *<I'm second-guessing my judgement here, though. A bit out of my element.>*

<Well, trust your gut. Something's up. Stay sharp.>

Within a few minutes, they reached an unassuming door, and Rama turned to Corsia. "Please direct your escort to remain out here."

Corsia nodded, and Commander Eve gestured for the ISF Marines to take up positions in the corridor. IPE Marines took up flanking positions, and Corsia couldn't help but notice that the ISF fireteam was wound tight—ready to spring into action.

Good.

The door slid open, and Rama led the ISF delegation into a briefing room that had been repurposed for the meeting, half-filled with a large table.

Across the table sat President Arthur, who rose slowly, his eyes steely as they swept across the group, landing on his brother.

"Kendrik. You have no idea how happy I am to see you. Last update we had, you were settling down in the Theban Alliance."

"That's correct, brother," Kendrik returned the smile his brother had given—neither having reached their eyes. "About eighty years ago. I was just establishing my trade routes there."

"And yet here you are," Arthur replied, turning to Corsia. "With these rather interesting visitors."

"Thank you for agreeing to meet with us," Corsia said with as warm a smile as she could muster. "We have a proposal that I believe you will be very interested in hearing."

President Arthur gestured for everyone to sit. The ISF delegation sat with their backs to the door, while Rama and Larson walked around the table to sit on either side of the president.

"I'm not sure I have much choice other than to hear it," the president said, his tone unreadable. "You've been very…persuasive, I suppose is the right word."

"Yes, thank you for working through a rather tricky introduction," Corsia replied, avoiding the president's implications. "As I'm sure Colonel Hickson informed you, things are changing outside of the cluster, and we'd like to form an alliance with you that will strengthen the Inner Praesepe Empire, and establish direct trade with systems outside the cluster."

"Namely Thebes and Septhia," Arthur replied, his voice not giving away what he thought of either group.

"Thebes, mostly," Kendrik said while pouring himself a glass of water from the pitcher on the table. "I'll be using the resources we trade for to build a fleet that we'll use to defend Thebes against the Nietzscheans, and then sell to the Septhians."

"So you'll use our resources to build up the militaries of other nations?" Larson asked, a scowl settling on his brow. "That's not very patriotic of you, Mister Kendrik."

"Indeed," Arthur said, nodding slowly. "If you have these jump gates, why not allow *us* to build the ships, and then send them to you? This seems like a better solution for the people of the IPE."

"That is certainly not out of the question," Terrance said, his voice calm and soothing. "In fact, I can imagine a shipbuilding facility here in the IPE would be both very secure and efficient. However, from what I understand, it would take some years to establish that capability with your technological level. Kendrik has the facilities in the Theban Alliance to hit the ground running; we just need a steady supply of resources to feed his production."

"Is that what you hope to achieve here, brother?" Arthur asked. "You want to enrich yourself at the IPE's expense?"

"Expense would be the exact opposite of what will happen," Kendrik replied, his voice carrying a slight strain as he responded to his brother. "There are many technologies that the IPE could benefit from. Not just military. Medical, life expectancy, entertainment, construction, excellent coffee, there is much we could trade."

Rama seemed unconvinced. "I don't see how that will benefit us in the face of the types of threats you have implied are out there. You mentioned that the Nietzscheans have their eyes on the easily accessible resources in the cluster, and that they could have these jump gates before long. If we export all of our resources and get little in return, how will we defend ourselves against threats without and within the cluster? For all we know, those threats could already be present."

Terrance, and then Kendrik, addressed Rama's concerns, offering solutions and examples of technologies that could bolster the IPE. Their explanations seemed to mollify Rama, but not President Arthur or Secretary Larson.

Building up the uncertain feeling Corsia was developing, something about Rama's tone and her responses seemed off. As she discussed defensive options with Kendrik, the minister made statements that seemed to imply existing threats already within the cluster.

Twice, her eyes had ticked to the left, toward the president and Secretary Larson—though neither of them gave any indication that her words had a double meaning.

<*Sephira,*> Corsia reached out to her daughter via a relay in the pinnace. <*Something seems amiss here. I get the feeling that the IPE is hiding something from us.*>

<*Any idea what? Ships, stations, resources?*> Sephira replied, her tone curious but unconcerned.

<*I don't know. It seems to have one of their delegation nervous, but not the other two. If I had to hazard a worst-case scenario, it would be that Orion has beat us to the punch and is already here. Best-case, they have some sort of internal squabble going on that we're caught up in.*>

<*So you're saying that right now it runs the gamut.*>

Corsia had to resist the urge to physically nod. <*I suppose, yes. Could you perform a low-level active scan of the* Deepening Night*? I wonder if there's something they're physically hiding from us.*>

<*From out here with* Andromeda*? They'd be able to tell what I was doing—oh! You mean to use the array on the pinnace.*>

<*Yes, I do, indeed. Random pings, listen for class C responses.*>

<*OK,*> Sephira said after a moment. <*I'm kicking that off. You know…*>

<*Yes?*> Corsia prompted, as Terrance began to describe the types of medical technology the ISF could offer in trade for resources. She couldn't help but notice that Arthur and Larson didn't seem overly impressed, while Rama's eyes were wide.

<*Well, you have those four Marines outside the conference room. I can use some of their armor's sensors to enhance my view inside the ship, increase sensitivity.*>

<*Good thinking,*> Corsia replied, glad her daughter was thinking on her feet—so to speak. <*Let me know what you find.*>

Corsia was about to join in the conversation, offering the possibility of tactical training for the IPE space force, when Sephira's voice came back into her mind.

<*Shit! Mom…I'm detecting* **sleptons**. *A lot of sleptons.*>

Corsia felt a shiver run down her spine. <*Where?*>

<*On the* Deepening Night. *In fact…I'm pretty sure they're coming from the room you're in.*>

<*Eve,*> Corsia pulled the Marine commander into the conversation. <*Sephira is reading sleptons in here.*>

<*With us?*> Though Eve's mental tone carried alarm, her face betrayed no emotion whatsoever.

<*Yeah, one of our three friends across the table has a remnant in them.*>

<*Well that complicates things.*>

<*You're telling me,*> Corsia replied.

<*I've called in the stealthed team from the shuttle. They'll be on our position in seven minutes with the shadowtron.*>

<*Good. Tell them not to rush. Not being detected is more important than speed.*>

While Kendrik outlined a process for setting up improved shipyards in the IPE, Corsia brought Terrance up to speed.

<*Well that's unexpected,*> he responded, while nodding along as Kendrik spoke. <*What would ascended AIs want with some place like this? It's not like the ASAIs can't just get whatever resources they need from the galactic core.*>

<*Your guess is as good as mine,*> Corsia replied. <*Maybe better.*>

<*Well, the easy option is that they're doing it to deny resources to others,*> Terrance suggested. <*I'm of the opinion that the core AIs engendered the war between Nietzschea and Genevia. That conflict ultimately put Praesepe square in the Niets' sights. Denying any of the fringe peoples access to the IPE's resources makes sense.*>

<Except for the matter of jump gates.>

Corsia got a feeling of ambivalent acknowledgement from Terrance. *<Sure, but by Bob's own admission, these ASAIs can make pretty good guesses about the future. It wouldn't be a big deal for one of them to drop a remnant in someone, just to make sure things went according to plan.>*

<Stars.> Once again, Corsia had to manage her physical responses to disturbing thoughts. *<There could be remnants everywhere.>*

<Maybe…but maybe not. I suspect there's some sort of limit to how many puppets an ascended being can make. If it were infinite, they wouldn't have to go through all these machinations to control us.>

Terrance sounded entirely blasé as he continued to speak with President Arthur about trade options. One of the three people across the table had a piece of an ascended being inside of them, and from what Nance had been able to do when she was under the Caretaker's control, that person might be able to kill all of them.

With surprising ease, Terrance steered the conversation toward a break, and the IPE delegation agreed. The president rose and left the room, while Rama and Larson remained.

<Minister Rama.> Corsia decided to take a risk. *<Is there anything you'd like to tell me about risks to the IPE? Anything we should be aware of?>*

<What do you mean?> Rama replied, her mental tone cautious.

<You've hinted at threats to the IPE on several occasions, your wording has indicated to me that you think those threats are already here.>

A nervous look crossed Rama's face, then she quickly schooled her expression once more. *<It's not anything*

specific…just my job to be concerned about potential threats and the like.>

<You seem to be concerned about more than a 'potential' threat,> Corsia countered.

<Just stop. You don't know what you're talking about,> Rama said, her tone changing from dismissive to pleading. *<Things aren't as they seem. Honestly, you'd be better of going elsewhere in the cluster. Like Delaware—they're outside the IPE, and they're flush with resources. More than us, even.>*

Corsia eyed Rama, considering the woman's words, then glanced at Larson, who was in the back of the room, filling a plate with snacks.

<Eve,> Corsia said to the Marine commander. *<When your team gets here, they need to stay out of line of sight until the president is back in the room.>*

<Are you worried that our stealth systems can't fool a remnant? Because I am.>

<Exactly. Once we resume, they need to strike fast. Enter, take down the president before he has time to react. You ready for that?>

A laugh flowed across the link from Eve. *<Ready to kill the president of the group we're trying to forge an alliance with? Why wouldn't I be?>*

<Not kill, free.>

<Sorry, I was thinking of what's about to happen the way our armed and twitchy IPE Marines will see it.>

Corsia had been thinking about them, too. *<Have half the strike team hang back to deal with them.>*

<We've got nano on them already. It'll take a few seconds, but once the festivities start, we can lock 'em down.>

<Good.>

Corsia updated Terrance with the plan, then turned her gaze to Kendrik, who was speaking with Rama by the coffee carafe, extolling the virtues of brews from outside the cluster.

She considered telling him what was about to happen, but decided to hold off. While Kendrik was not likely to be a double agent, he may not be able to handle the news that his brother was possessed by the remnant of an ASAI.

He'd just have to figure things out as they happened.

Several minutes later, the president returned and resumed his place across the table. He didn't speak, but his arrival signaled the resumption of the talks.

Rama had just launched into a listing of considerations that would need to be made, when Eve began to count down.

<Three, two, one…go!>

Behind the ISF delegation, the door burst open and, seconds later, slammed shut once more. Then a strange hum filled the air, and President Arthur leapt to his feet.

"What! What are you doing?" he stammered, staring at the business end of a weapon, seemingly floating in mid-air next to Corsia.

"This is called a shadowtron. We're drawing you out," Corsia informed the remnant. "There's nothing you can do about it."

The group watched in a combination of horror and transfixed wonder, as strands of glowing light began to emanate from President Arthur, and coalesce into a ball that was then pulled toward the weapon.

"What in the star's light is *that*?" Rama managed to ask after a moment.

"It's a part of an ascended AI," Terrance replied calmly as he watched the orb float through the air. "It—"

Suddenly, Larson leapt across the table, grabbing the shadowtron and wrenching it from the stealthed ISF Marine's hands.

The IPE secretary was about to throw the weapon to the ground when he was struck by an invisible force. Corsia rose and made a grab for the shadowtron, only to be thrown against the wall as President Arthur hurled himself at her.

The impact startled her, and it took Corsia a moment to re-orient herself. During that time, she picked up the sounds of combat in the corridor outside.

President Arthur closed with her, and Corsia grappled with the man, watching from the corner of her eye as Eve moved Terrance and Kendrik away from the fight.

"That's an interesting toy," the president said in an otherworldly voice. "I look forward to seeing how it works after I subsume your mind—"

Suddenly the man's words cut off, and a look of puzzlement came over his face. Corsia took advantage of the opportunity to pivot to the side and drive her foot into the president's jaw, sending his body flying across the room to slam into the bulkhead.

Corsia glanced behind her to see that the two stealthed Marines had managed to wrest the shadowtron away from Larson, but she could tell the weapon was ruined.

"You're no human..." Larson hissed, and Corsia realized that was what had confused the president a moment ago. "Clever trick with the fake brain."

Corsia's suspicion that Larson also was possessed by a remnant solidified into certainty. "Yeah, well you weren't exactly being honest, either."

Behind them, the door slid open, and one of the Marines leaned in. "Ma'am? We need to go!"

Backing away from Larson, Corsia pulled the feeds from the soldiers in the corridor, noting that one was down, a hole burned through his head, and the other two were firing down the passageway at a group of enemies who had taken cover in the doorways of other rooms.

"Grab the shadowtron," she ordered the Marines who had breached the room, and the group backed out of the room, the Marines shielding Terrance and Kendrick.

For a moment, Rama looked uncertainly at the slumped form of the president, then glanced at Larson's seething visage. Without a word, she dashed out of the room and joined the ISF group, her eyes wide as she glanced at Corsia.

"What the hell just happened in there?"

"I'll explain later," Corsia replied, grabbing a weapon from a fallen IPE soldier. "We're leaving. You coming?"

Rama nodded silently, and the group retreated down the corridor, the Marines laying down suppressive fire until they rounded a corner and picked up the pace, moving back toward the docking bay.

"Your shuttle," Rama said breathlessly. "They'll destroy it."

"They'll try," Terrance replied with a laugh as he fired his pilfered weapon at an IPE Marine that had dashed across the intersection ahead of them.

The shot caught the enemy in the knee, locking up the joint and toppling the soldier.

Corsia shot him a questioning look, and Terrance shrugged. "I wasn't always a businessman. Well…I guess I was, but I went on a few ops back in the day."

"That's not in your record," Eve said as she sprayed a hail of bullets behind the group, keeping their pursuers at a distance.

"It was a thousand years before the *Intrepid* set out," Terrance replied. "Not everything makes it into the record…and not all the records last."

"Still, I thought I'd have known that our main financial backer was a serious badass," Eve said while signaling two of the Marines to advance.

Terrance winked at the commander. "We all have little secrets. Jason and I got up to some fun stuff back in the day."

Corsia didn't reply, as a pair of arachnid-like combat mechs skittered around the corner, spraying rail pellets down the passageway.

The Marines moved in front of the rest of the group, their armor absorbing the enemy fire—mostly. The sergeant grunted as a rail pellet tore through his knee at the joint, spraying blood and cartilage across Corsia's thighs.

"Suck this," Eve roared as she pulled a pair of burn sticks from the sergeant's back and threw them at the mechs.

The sticks sailed through the air, both striking the mechs' bodies, the thermite in the weapons igniting and burning through the things' ablative plating. Once weak spots were exposed, concentrated fire from the Marines slammed into the robots and tore their bodies to shreds.

"Faaaaaawwwwk," Rama whispered in a drawn out voice, staring at the blood sprayed across her body.

"You hit?" Corsia asked.

"I…don't? No?"

"Good." Corsia grabbed Rama's arm and pulled her along, staying close to Eve.

Five minutes later, they had reached the level the pinnace was on, and were carefully advancing down a broad corridor with little cover.

<I've Linked with the team at the shuttle; they've got some fans who wanted signatures, but so far, the craft is OK,> Eve reported.

Corsia tapped into Eve's connection and saw that the squad of ISF Marines in the bay were holding back a platoon of enemies who had taken up positions at two of the entrances.

The pinnace had its stasis shields up, but wasn't firing on the IPE troops.

<*Why aren't they shooting with the pinnace?*> Corsia asked.

<*Worried about holing the ship we're in,*> Eve replied. <*You'll be fine, but Terrance, Kendrik, and Rama can't breathe vacuum too well.*>

Corsia finally understood the urge to slap oneself in the forehead. <*OK…I'll remind you that this is my first away mission.*>

<*Good thing I'm here to babysit you, ma'am,*> Eve said, a laugh escaping her lips.

"Am I missing out on some good combat jokes?" Terrance asked, as the team continued to creep down the corridor.

"No," Corsia said with a shake of her head. "Just me spacing out."

"Is it wise to be talking aloud?" Kendrik asked from Terrance's side. "Won't they hear us?"

Eve shook her head. "Not yet. We deployed a nanocloud to dampen our sounds. The lot of you walk so loud they'd have heard us a minute ago, otherwise."

Kendrik's mouth formed an 'O', and he nodded silently.

They reached a bend in the corridor, and the soldier in the lead held up his hand, halting the group. Commander Eve and the Marines passed hand signals, getting ready to rush out and clear the passage ahead.

Corsia watched their plan take form, while keeping an eye on the feeds of the enemy around the bend.

There were nine IPE Marines clustered around the forward entrance to the docking bay. The pinnace's feeds showed another ten enemies within the bay, clustered behind cover near the entrance.

Eve coordinated her plan with the squad of Marines inside the bay to hit the enemy from both sides. With luck, they'd kill them all…worst-case scenario, the IPE troops would fall back to the bay's aft entrance.

Corsia, Terrance, and the sergeant with the blown-out knee held back with Kendrik and Rama. Terrance tried to stand at the front of the group, but Corsia gave him a stern look and pulled him back before taking a position behind the Marines.

With an unseen signal, Commander Eve led the Marines forward, and Corsia moved up to the apex of the corridor's bend, ready to provide any cover for the Marines.

A flurry of weapons fire was exchanged between the two groups in the corridor, and the ISF Marines inside the bay shifted their focus to the enemy at the forward door.

Corsia saw Eve take a shot to the shoulder, and another Marine was hit in the leg, but the enemy fared worse; two minutes later, the four surviving IPE soldiers fled aft, clearing the way for Corsia to lead her group to the bay.

She pushed Terrance ahead first, and fell into the rear of the party, anxiously looking over her shoulder as she pushed Rama ahead of her, the woman half-frozen with fear.

"You OK?" Corsia asked Eve when she reached the commander.

"Fucking Ippies! We gonna blow the shit out of this ship once we're clear?" the Marine growled through clenched teeth.

"Seems like a solid option," Corsia replied as they reached the bay's entrance.

She saw that Terrance and Kendrik were already at the pinnace, Rama a few paces behind them, ducking low as the IPE Marines at the aft doors intensified their fire.

<Hit them with e-beams,> Corsia ordered the shuttle's pilot.

A moment later, a series of straight lightning bolts shot from the pinnace's dorsal cannons, tearing through the enemy's cover—and no small number of the IPE troops.

"We gotta move!" the Marine at the door shouted, gesturing for Corsia and Eve to make the run to the pinnace.

Eve put a hand on Corsia's back, about to guide her through the doorway, when the Marine beckoning to them exploded.

The force of the blast flung Corsia and Eve a dozen meters down the corridor, sending them sliding along the deck until they hit the bulkhead at the curve.

Corsia was on her feet in an instant, but realized that Eve had been stunned, her head lolling to the side. She pulled the Marine backward around the bend while searching the feeds for the source of the deadly fire.

Then she saw them. A pair of heavy assault mechs were moving down the passageway, while another trio had entered the bay.

<Go! Go!> Corsia ordered the shuttle pilot, after checking that every other survivor was still alive. *<Get them out of here, and get Lieutenant Marky to send a breach team. Use the destroyers to take out this ship's engines.>*

<Yes, Admiral. I—>

Another explosion shook the ship, and EM interference cut off Corsia's comms. The *thud* of mechs was shaking the deck.

Corsia bent over, screaming in Eve's face, "On your feet, Marine! We gotta move!"

VALKRIS

STELLAR DATE: 09.06.8949 (Adjusted Years)
LOCATION: Interstellar Pinnace, 5AU Stellar north of Maitreya
REGION: Valkris System, Vela Cluster, Transcend Interstellar Alliance

Fifty minutes later, the pinnace's sensors picked up the Airthan fleet as it entered the Valkris System. Of course that had all happened fifty minutes earlier, thanks to light lag. If all had gone well, by now the battle would already be over.

And if it *had* gone well, then Admiral Kira would have already sent word back to Airtha via jump gate. Though she hoped for that outcome, Sera steeled herself for the possibility that the EMG had failed, and her fleet was in ruins.

Settling into her seat in the cockpit, Sera pulled up a view of the Airthan fleet, placing it on the pinnace's holodisplay. She noted with approval how Admiral Kira had arrayed her ships around the EMG in a near-sphere. *The woman understands how important the weapon is. Good.*

The ships advanced on Maitreya, their progress seeming unimaginably slow on scan, though even without the thrust indicators, Sera could see by the engine flares that the fleet was burning hard toward Valkris.

While she'd eaten, the pinnace's sensors had identified five of the ships in a wide orbit around the planet as Khardine vessels, at least one of which was likely to have stasis shields. Thus far, this configuration had seemed to be the modus operandi for the separatists: leave bait ships around worlds, while fleets laid in wait nearby.

The Khardine fleets' ability to get ships into a system so quickly still baffled the Airthan tacticians—and even Sera's mother. The only explanation that made sense was that they set up fleets just beyond a star's heliosphere, and then the bait ship called for their aid via FDL transmitters.

Of course, if Khardine had a fleet for each bait ship, the size of their overall fleet was mind-numbingly large.

Which didn't pass the smell test with Sera. Even with New Canaan's ability to grow starships, there was no way that Khardine could field thousand-ship fleets around every world they'd claimed. That would require them to possess ships numbering in the hundreds of millions.

And if the enemy had a fleet *that* large, they'd have won the war before it even started.

Something else is afoot.

Sera quieted her thoughts as sixty-two enemy ships formed up around Maitreya —the five Khardine vessels bolstered by fifty-seven local ships. The separatist vessels began a slingshot maneuver, arcing around the planet on an intercept course for the Airthan ships.

At their fore were three cruisers.

Stasis ships, Sera thought with a nod. That would be the only reason for those ships to be at the fore with the rest in a narrow cone behind them. She was surprised that there were three here, but then again, Valkris was a special system.

Admiral Kira must have come to the same conclusion regarding the nature of the cruisers. The EMG pivoted, aligning with the approaching enemy, and fired.

Sera counted the seconds as the focused EM wave sped across space toward the enemy formation. She held her breath for the last ten seconds, shifting onto the edge of her seat in anticipation.

A brilliant light shone as the wave hit the foremost enemy ship, then more light flared, blinding the pinnace's passive sensors. When the interference finally cleared, she saw that the first cruiser was nothing more than a slowly expanding cloud of debris, while the other two were drifting hulks, their engines offline.

The remaining enemy ships spread out, firing a barrage of beams and missiles at the EMG, most of which were deflected by point defense provided by the surrounding Airthan fleet, as well as the shields on the EMG itself.

The EMG fired twice more before the enemy fleet dispersed too much for the massive weapon to track. The Khardine ships passed by the Airthan fleet, spreading out over several light seconds, jinking to avoid the attacking fleet's beams.

Sera wondered where the Khardine backup fleet was. Usually by now, they would have jumped in and engaged the Airthan ships.

She supposed it could be that the enemy did not have a force outside the Valkris System, or at least not one capable of destroying the five thousand ships in Admiral Kari's fleet—especially not with the EMG in play.

Airthan Fleet Tactics and Analysis had estimated that even if the EMG wasn't viable, it would take over five hundred ships to defeat Admiral Kari's battlegroup. Now that the EMG had delivered on its promise, the size of the opposing fleet would need to be much larger.

Still, one EMG was not a viable offensive weapon, and Sera began to wonder if the gamble of sending it with such a small escort had been wise.

Seconds turned into minutes, and minutes into half an hour. Still enemy ships spread further and further away from Admiral Kari's fleet—which was braking on its approach to the planet of Maitreya.

What's your game? The planetary defenses hadn't engaged, and no other local military vessels had moved in to the rescue.

"Has Maitreya surrendered?" Sera wondered aloud. "Now *that* would be a coup!"

Just as Sera uttered the words, a group of ships appeared only twenty kilometers above the EMG—*within* the Airthan fleet formation. She instantly recognized them as ISF cruisers.

Dammit…they sent in the Caners.

The ISF ships fired atom beams into the EMG, the massive particles punching through the EMG's shields, and then through the weapon itself.

Seven seconds later, four-thousand ISF ships appeared around the Airthan fleet.

"Motherfuckers!" Sera swore, slamming a fist into her chair's armrest.

She didn't even bother to wait and see what happened next. With the EMG offline, Admiral Kira wouldn't have a chance. The battle was lost.

Still, it wasn't a complete failure. The EMG had worked, and enough of them would create a viable defense for Airtha.

Initializing the gate, Sera turned the pinnace and waited for the negative energy emitters to activate, all the while wondering how the ISF had four thousand ships on the periphery of the Valkris System.

It was becoming all too apparent that the enemy possessed a faster means of communication than FDL. She considered the possibilities as the gate activated and she fired the pinnace's engines.

Her ship was a hundred meters from transitioning through the jump gate when Sera saw the unthinkable: an ISF cruiser, just off her pinnace's port side. The ship fired on the jump gate, its beams tearing into the energy emitters.

Sera watched in horror as the gate was destroyed, knowing that the wave of energy from the antimatter explosion would obliterate her pinnace.

What the…?

The explosion flowed around her ship as though held back.

A stasis shield?

Alarms flared across her console, registering a grav beam pulling her ship toward the ISF cruiser, a bay door on its hull opening up to take her in.

Sera jumped up from her console and ran to the pinnace's armory. They may be able to take her ship, but they'd find taking *her* to be much more of a challenge.

Nothing further crossed Sera's mind as the ISF cruiser placed her entire pinnace in a stasis field and set a course for the nearest jump gate.

TANIS & JOE

STELLAR DATE: 09.06.8949 (Adjusted Years)
LOCATION: 7km North of Jersey City
REGION: Pyra, Albany System, Thebes, Septhian Alliance

"That's where we hid for an entire day, as the Niets moved an armored column through the region," Tangel said, pointing at a half-destroyed farmhouse. "Twice, scouts came through, and I thought we'd be found for sure, but we managed to stay out of sight. Brandt—" Tangel paused for a moment, still feeling sorrow at the loss of her long-time friend. "Brandt and I draped ourselves across Ayer and Johnny, covering them just enough with our stealth systems to keep them out of view."

"Pretty harrowing," Joe said as he stepped over part of a shuttle...a skid, from the looks of it. "A part of me is amazed you survived so long down here, and another part isn't surprised at all."

"You know how it is," Tangel said as she surveyed the Pyran landscape around them. "You survive because you have to. Giving up isn't an option."

"Not for you, at least," Joe said with a soft laugh. "Either of you."

"There's no either of us anymore," Tangel corrected her husband.

"Well, yeah, but back then there still was. I was speaking about past yous."

Tangel snorted. "I see. Well, past mes were pretty determined to get back to past you and the past girls. Would take a lot more than a planet full of Nietzscheans to stop former mes."

"Too bad no one told *them* that," Joe replied as they crested a hill and looked down on a once-green valley, now blackened from fires that had swept across the region.

Though the Nietzscheans were responsible for most of the destruction on Pyra, Tangel was relatively certain *this* fire had been started from the energy she had blasted through the city the night Rika and Priscilla had found her.

She was glad that so few Pyrans were in the area when that happened. And also glad that a lot of Nietzscheans *were*.

Of course, this one small patch of desolation was negligible when compared to the vast swaths of Pyra that had been destroyed by the departing Nietzschean ships, the wash from their fusion engines dumping massive quantities of ionized plasma and radiation into the planet's atmosphere, igniting fires that had raged for days—even with the ISF's fire-control ships on site.

"Well, the longer we can keep the Niets in the dark, the better. Though that will soon fall to the locals—once I convince the Septhian government that they need to join our alliance, not continue to grow their own."

"I think they'll come around." Joe shrugged. "Especially now that you broke off Kendo and Thebes, and are setting up the latter to be a major player in the region."

"These people deserve a hand; I'm glad to do what I can to help." Tangel wondered how many of the Pyrans would eventually come back to their planet. She glanced up at the lights flashing in the sky—the construction of the world's new ring—and wondered if the displaced peoples would remain there, or return to the world's surface once it was safe.

Joe leaned in close, and his hazsuit's helmet touched hers. "They do, but they still have a world. That's a lot better than what the Niets planned to leave them with."

Tangel nodded as she looked over the burned out valley, watching the brown, ash-filled water creep along in the streambed at the bottom of the slope.

"Why did you want to come down here, anyway?" Joe asked.

"I just wanted to go for a walk on a planet," Tangel replied, shrugging as she spoke. "I realized that the last time I'd done so was the day before we let the girls fly the *Andromeda* to the gamma base."

Joe's eyebrows pinched as he considered her words. "Really? That was years ago. Are you sure?"

"Well, I went for some walks on the palace grounds on Alexandria, but with half of Empress Diana's court constantly tailing me, it wasn't the same."

Joe made a sound that was half cough, half snort. "I don't think walking on Pyra's burned out husk is really a step up from that."

Tangel slid an arm around Joe's waist. "You never got to meet Diana's sycophants. *I* think Pyra's husk is a step up."

"Remind me to avoid—"

Joe's words were cut off as Priscilla's voice came to them from the ship above.

<Tangel, Joe, Corsia and Terrance are in trouble!>

<In the IPE?> Tangel asked. *<What's happening?>*

There was the briefest of pauses before Priscilla replied. *<I just have a short burst and coordinates from Sephira. There are remnants running the Inner Empire!>*

<What!?> Tangel cried out. *<Our pinnace has a gate mirror, align the closest gate and send me the coordinates.>*

Tangel glanced at Joe as they ran back to their pinnace. "Well, so much for a leisurely stroll on your day off. That's what you get for hopping a ship out here."

"Are you kidding?" Joe asked. "Do you recall how long it's been since you and I saw action together?"

"Too long," Tangel replied. "Let's rectify that."

LANDING

STELLAR DATE: 09.06.8949 (Adjusted Years)
LOCATION: Planet HH1
REGION: Hidey Hole System, Large Magellanic Cloud

"There it is," Sera said, gesturing at the spire of rocks jutting out of the crater's center. "We should be able to get an IR reading off that spire, but it's completely invisible."

"Certainly unusual," Jason said from the pilot's seat.

Sera watched Jason's fingers dance over the console as he pulled the pinnace into a long canyon that led into the crater.

"You know," she said as they slid into the narrow rent in the planet's surface, "we have stealth systems. You don't need to—Wall!"

"Relax." Jason's voice was calm, his face filled with a rapturous expression as he flew the pinnace through the narrow canyon, effortlessly managing the twists, turns, and occasional updrafts surging through the planet's thin atmosphere. "This is my thing."

"You're 'thing' is smearing us across a kilometer of rock?" Sera asked, her hands gripping the sides of her seat, even though the internal a-grav systems dampened the ship's movement.

Jason tossed a grin over his shoulder. "Just like in Vagabond's Canyon back on Proxima. I used to fly that in my T-38 at twice this speed. Even threaded the stone needle with it."

"Back in your misspent youth?" Sera asked through gritted teeth, glancing back at Major Valerie to see the woman's usual stoic expression firmly in place, though on a face several shades paler than normal.

"Something like that," Jason said with a chuckle as he activated the grav emitters and began to slow the pinnace. "Regarding stealth, yes, they can't *see* our ship, but these pinnaces either fly fast, or they fly bright with a-grav to stay aloft. A-grav breaks stealth, and fast means we'd create visible air currents. Canyon's our best bet."

"So what sort of spaceship was a T-38?" Sera asked, trying not to pay attention to how close Jason got to the canyon walls. She would have to pass a vid of this to Cheeky at some point.

Jason laughed. "Not a spaceship. It's an old Earth air-breather. A T-38 Talon. I had a lot of reproduction aircraft strewn about the stars around Sol. A bird in every port—something to do on the layovers."

"Seems like a lot of 'something to do' for simple stop-overs," Sera replied, her jaw clenched, glad to see they only had thirty kilometers to go.

Jason's tone continued to be easy and nonchalant. In fact, he seemed more relaxed than she'd ever seen him. "On the pre-FTL trade routes, you could sometimes wait *years* for all the cargo to get assembled for the next trip. Always bugged me. People knew we were coming for decades, but they still never had their ducks in a row when we got there."

"So this…stunt flying…is your thing?" Sera asked as she watched Jason, starting to feel as though she was seeing him for the first time.

"Well," he shrugged while banking the craft around a tower of rock rising from the center of the canyon. "We all have to grow up eventually…take on our share of responsibility. Eventually you gotta trade in the T-38 for a GSS *Intrepid*." He glanced at Sera. "You know that as well as anyone."

"Stars, do I ever."

"Maybe when this is all over, I can just fly again for a while. You know…I have this bird back on Carthage, a Yak. I think you'd love a ride in it."

She didn't have a chance to reply before the pinnace shot out of the canyon and into the crater, rapidly closing on the rock spire in the center.

<*There.*> Jen highlighted a level patch of ground. <*Swept a bit too clean. That's a landing pad.*>

"And that," Sera placed a marker on a smooth section of the spire's slope, "is likely a door."

"No EM at all," Valerie said, speaking aloud for the first time since they'd left the *Helios.* "Though that doesn't mean we couldn't be looking at automated defenses."

"Not my first time on a job like this," Sera shot Valerie a meaningful look. "I *was* a Hand agent, after all."

Jason pulled the craft's nose up, letting the pinnace aerobrake as he banked around the spire, only firing the a-grav systems for a moment before he set down a kilometer from their destination.

"Why over here?" Sera asked.

He gestured at the fissures covering the floor of the crater. "This is the least convenient approach. Star's behind us too, meaning that if they *are* watching, this is the direction they're watching the least."

"Why would they watch any direction less often?" Valerie asked as she pulled off her harness.

"Maybe they're not," Jason allowed. "But there are always compromises when building an installation like this. Just trying to guess at which ones the builders of this place might have made."

Valerie inclined her head, pursing her lips for a moment. "Fair enough."

Sera followed Valerie and Jason out of the cockpit to the pinnace's small bay, which was fitted out as an armory.

The strike team was already getting geared up. Eight members of Sera's High Guard, and a spec-ops squad under Colonel Pearson. And Flaherty, of course.

He gave her a nod, not an iota of worry on his face after Jason's breakneck approach.

In addition to the humans, there were four AIs in the group: Jen with Sera, Julia with Valerie—a pair that the High Guard had taken to calling 'The J-J's'—and two in Pearson's team as well. Laney was embedded with the colonel, and another named Fara was in a mobile frame.

All four had spent the trip sharing their breaching techniques with Chief Yves, a specialist on Pearson's team.

"Alright, people," Pearson said, as Sera stepped into the armor rack and selected a light, ablative armor set. "Not all of us have worked together before, but we know how the job is done. First and foremost, we protect our assets."

With that, he nodded first to Sera and then to Jason, all eyes in the room following his.

"That all I am?" Sera asked with a lopsided grin as she stepped out of the armor rack.

Valerie winked at her. "Pretty much, yeah."

"Secondarily," Pearson continued a moment later, a small scowl settling on his brow. "We're here to grab intel. Every bit of data we can get our hands on. We need to know what the Airthans are up to, and what other strongholds they have tucked away in the far reaches of space. We get that, we protect—" he glanced at Sera and Jason, a smile pulling at the corners of his mouth for just a moment, "—the *president* and the *governor*, and we get out. General Sheeran has two pinnaces with a platoon each in low orbit, ready to drop down if we need them, so if the shit hits the fan, you call for backup. No martyrs."

"Colonel has the right of it," Valerie added for the High Guard's benefit. "Protect our charges, get the intel, get out in one piece."

A chorus of affirmations echoed in the room, and Jason slapped Sera on the shoulder, turning her so he could inspect her armor.

<*Looks good on you. Not often I see you clothed.*> His eyes were serious as he checked her over, but there was a lilt in his mental tone.

<*Funny man,*> Sera retorted as she examined his armor, then spun him to check his back. <*You look good clothed or naked—not that I see enough of the latter. Don't go getting your fine ass shot off.*>

She clapped him on the shoulder to signal that his armor checked out, then turned for him to inspect her back.

Jason's chuckle rumbled in her mind. <*Look at that, a little action is bringing out the sass in you, Sera.*>

<*You talking about the impending fight, or what we got up to in your quarters?*>

<*Little of column A, a whole bunch of column B.*>

Pearson and Valerie walked through the group, both pausing to check over Jason and Sera's gear before moving on.

<*Seriously, Val, not my first op,*> Sera chided the major.

<*True, but you're out of practice. Plus, the last time you were in combat, you flew across a city with your dragon wings, leaving me behind. I distinctly recall having kittens while trying to figure out what happened to you, so you'll forgive me if I plan to keep an eye on you this time around.*>

<*Good times,*> Sera snickered. <*Good times.*>

She grabbed a helmet off the rack and slotted it on before selecting a multi-function rifle, two sidearms, and a lightwand from the weapons rack.

<*Take this,*> Jason said, handing her a cloak. <*Earnest's people have worked out how to get effective stealth tech in a loose fabric. It's still not quite as good as your skin, but better than ablative armor can pull off.*>

Sera grabbed the cloak and threw it over her shoulders. <*Handy for hiding gear, too.*>

<*That's the idea.*>

She grabbed a bandolier of burn sticks and pulse grenades, slipping them on before pulling the cloak around her shoulders. It Linked up with the armor, a new menu of stealth controls appearing on her HUD.

All around her, the rest of the strike team donned their cloaks and formed up at the bay's exit. They waited while the ship extended a shroud that would hide the bay's exterior doors as they slid open.

Pearson's team exited first, spreading out and securing the area.

Laney had already deployed a swath of microdrones that spread out around the pinnace, checking the nearby terrain for sensors and defenses.

Almost immediately, they located several sensors, and marked both their positions and ranges on the team's combat net. Pearson made the call not to disable them—none of the AIs nor Chief Fara were certain they could shut down Airthan scanning tech without setting off an alarm.

<*Best to wait 'til we're at the target before we risk detection,*> Laney had advised.

Sera had been in agreement; there was little point in having stealth tech if they didn't utilize it for as long as it was effective.

Crossing the kilometer of terrain between the pinnace and the spire was slow, arduous work. The team kept to rocky ground, doing their best not to disturb the sediment on the base of the crater.

As best as Sera could tell, at one point, the crater had held water—though not much, and not for too long. Perhaps the impact of the meteor that had created this twenty-kilometer divot had been enough to alter the small planet's climate, causing it to lose its surface water.

Another piece of evidence that pointed to the magnetic fields as being artificial in origin. If this world had always possessed such strong fields, it would have held onto more atmosphere.

Ahead, Pearson's scout team crossed the final fissure. Though they were invisible, their markers on the combat net showed that they'd leapt over the gap, something confirmed by a few small wisps of dust lifting into the air.

A breeze swept by, removing the traces, but also scattering the microdrones further. Once the wind had passed, Sera saw Valerie release more drones, spreading them around to further mask the team's progress.

Sera reached the final fissure and eyed the four-meter gap. It wouldn't be hard to jump in the low gravity, but the crevasse was almost forty meters deep, and she didn't want to have to climb back out, should she slip.

<*Want me to hold your hand?*> Jason asked on a tightbeam Link. She saw that he was standing a meter to her right, his invisible form outlined on her HUD.

<*Only if you want me to drop you in there, old man,*> Sera shot back, then worried that her response was too coarse.

Jason only laughed. < *'Old man', is it? When all this is over, we can go back to my cabin, and I'll remind you what this old man knows.*>

Sera shook her head, a grin settling on her lips, as she crouched and then sprang forward, leaping across the gash in the crater's floor. <*You're on, ancient one. I bet I have a few things up my sleeve you've never imagined. I* ***did*** *fly with Cheeky for a decade, you know.*>

<*Believe you me, I've given that some thought,*> Jason said as he leapt across after her.

* * * * *

Five minutes later, the team reached the spire, a towering spike of basalt rising over seventy meters from the base of the crater.

It was worn by wind and the elements, and Sera wasn't sure if it was caused by a volcanic eruption after the impact, or if the meteor had liquified the surrounding rock enough that it had splashed back up and frozen in place.

The latter seemed unlikely, but given some of the bizarre geological formations she'd seen on various planets, it wasn't outside the realm of possibility.

<*So where's the door?*> Valerie asked as they spread out around the rockface.

Sera looked back at the area that was clearly a landing pad, then followed the most level route between it and the base of the spire. It led to a crease in the rock, and she cautiously stepped toward it, releasing a batch of nanoprobes into the air.

<*Sensors here, lining the rock,*> she announced. <*I think it's time to disable them. No way we breach the door and move two-dozen people past without them picking us up.*>

<*On it,*> Jen announced, as Valerie and two of Sera's guards approached.

<*Sera, you're not on point,*> Valerie said, and Sera gritted her teeth, but moved back, watching Pearson's team move into the fore.

Flaherty eased toward her position, and Sera realized she'd lost sight of him on the journey to the spire. She wasn't sure if it was because she wasn't paying attention, or if he'd turned off his IFF systems that randomly updated the combat net with his position.

<*If we need to split up, both Jason and Sera should stay with you, Major,*> Pearson said to Valerie over the command Link. <*That way when the shit hits the fan, one group has priority exfil, and the other creates a diversion, or whatever else we have to do to get them out.*>

<*'When'?*> Jason asked.

<*Maybe,*> Sera shrugged as she watched Jen's progress with infiltrating the sensors embedded in the rocks. <*For all we know, this place is completely unguarded.*>

<*You really believe that?*> Valerie asked.

<*Well…no.*>

<*OK, I have the sensor web spoofed,*> Julia informed the team. <*You could turn off stealth and dance a jig in front of them, and they won't see you.*>

<*Dang it, I left my dancing shoes back in the pinnace,*> Chief Yves said as he approached a flat stretch of rock at the back of the crease. <*OK, the probes have found the door, it's an irregular micro-seam. Looking for the control mechanism.*>

<*I can backdoor into their network through the sensors,*> Jen suggested.

<*Hold off on that. I think I've found the control. OK…looks like I can…*> Yves paused. <*Damn.*>

<*Damn?*> Colonel Pearson asked.

<*Yeah, there's a hard-line that connects this door control to an NSAI. It's using an active signal to monitor the panel. If I breach from here, I'll trigger an alarm.*>

<*OK, Jen,*> Sera directed her AI. <*Try it your way.*>

<*On it.*>

The rest of Pearson's team continued to scour the area surrounding the spire, noting the placement of other sensors while Jen worked her way into the facility's network.

<*This is odd,*> Jason said after a few minutes. <*This crater is littered with sensor webs that would be good enough to spot us if we didn't have better stealth tech than the TSF expected when they set this up.*>

<*Which means?*> Sera prompted.

<*Well, if you detect an enemy, how do you neutralize them?*>

Sera realized that Jason was right. They'd found plenty of different sensor systems: EM bands, sound waves, even geo vibration pickups.

But no defense systems. Not a single autoturret, or drone dispersal port.

<*They could just be really well hidden. This door took us getting right on top of it to spot,*> Valerie countered.

<*Maybe,*> Jason allowed. <*You'd think they'd have some turrets around it, though. But nothing.*>

<*So what do you think?*> Sera asked.

The governor let out a long sigh. <*Honestly? It's starting to feel like a trap.*>

She didn't think that was the case. <*How can it be a trap if the Airthans don't even know that we know about them? This place was built some time ago…long before you started building the Aleutian site.*>

<*Was your father paranoid?*> Jason asked. <*I mean, I think he was, but was he* ***this*** *paranoid?*>

Sera didn't have to give Jason's question much consideration. <*Yes, yes he probably was.*>

<*We'll keep our eyes peeled,*> Pearson replied. <*But as I understand it, we need this intel, and we can't walk away because it might be dangerous to secure. Though…*> he paused for a moment. <*I'd feel a lot better if you two weren't tagging along.*>

<*You're going to need me to breach the security on any datastores.*> Sera wasn't going to be left out of the fun that easily. There had to be *some* perks in being president.

<*And you, sir?*> Pearson directed the comment to Jason.

Jason only snorted. <*Nice try, Colonel.*>

<*Was worth a shot. Tanis has rubbed off on all of you.*>

<*Not me,*> Sera replied. <*I was getting into trouble long before I knew her.*>

<*Same here.*> Jason chuckled. <*Though she may have re-ignited the spirit of adventure in me a bit.*>

<*Probably because she's a trouble magnet,*> Pearson grunted, a moment before Jen sang out in victory.

<*Nailed it. Best part about all the data from Terra's past is knowing how many modern systems are built on systems with ancient exploits. I swear, no one does reviews of shared code repositories.*>

As Jen spoke, a section of rock slid out and shifted to the side, held aloft by an a-grav field. The group waited as Yves flushed a nanocloud into the darkened interior.

<*OK,* **here** *we have autoturrets,*> Julia announced. <*Hold one.*>

Sera pulled the feed and saw a long passageway that led to a pair of lift doors.

<*Not a lot of options.*>

<*I'll send a team down first.*> Pearson directed Gunnery Sergeant Barry to ready a fireteam to take the first lift down along with Fara once Jen declared the turrets offline.

<*I'm not entirely certain that these turrets don't have failsafes, so everyone stay frosty,*> Julia directed. <*I've shut down their central control and switched off their firing mechanisms, but they're an unusual design.*>

<*I wonder if I should just pass my auth codes to the facility,*> Sera mused. <*Could just tell it that I'm the president and order it to let us in.*>

<*I think that's too risky.*> Valerie sounded nervous, and Sera wondered what had the major on edge. <*Like Jason*

said, this place smells too much like a trap. Let's not let it know exactly who it has trapped just yet.>

<*Gah, so much caution,*> Sera muttered privately to Jason.

<*Let them do their jobs. It's important to them.*>

Sera glanced at Jason's outline on her HUD, then nodded. <*OK, yeah.*>

Fara set up a relay outside the lift, and then led her team inside.

<*Just one level that the lift goes to. Listed as '0'.*>

<*Seems ominous,*> one of the Marines joked, getting a snort from Sera, and a stern cough from the gunnery sergeant.

Before the lift descended, Fara sent a filament of nano through its floor, putting a view of the shaft on the combat net.

<*Damn…that's deep,*> Sera muttered.

The nano couldn't get a read on the depth, just that it was over ten kilometers.

<*Going down,*> Fara said as she activated the lift and began to descend.

Sera and Jason walked toward the lifts, taking a position along the wall, while Pearson directed a pair of Marines to move a few hundred meters out onto the crater floor to set up surveillance systems, while directing another pair to patrol the exterior of the spire.

No one spoke as Fara's team continued their long descent, though Jason did give a low whistle when they passed the hundred-kilometer mark.

The lift continued on until it had descended nearly a thousand kilometers into the planet. Readings from Fara's team showed no significant increase in heat, meaning the core of the planet was not molten—or at least not where the shaft penetrated.

<*Radius of this world is only three-thousand klicks,*> Sera said at one point. <*Think that lift goes down to the core?*>

<*Seems increasingly likely,*> Jason replied. <*Express elevator to hell.*>

As he spoke, the lift began to slow, and Sera slaved her vision to Fara's optics, watching as the team exited the lifts and fanned out into a circular chamber. Directly ahead stood a pair of large doors, and Fara approached them, rifle held ready.

<*Place is dead. No EM at all. Not even a wireless network offering handshakes,*> she reported.

The Marines stacked up around the door while Fara accessed the controls. A minute later they slid open, and the team rushed through, securing the next room.

What they saw caused Sera to suck in a sharp breath.

"What the hell?"

CORNERED

STELLAR DATE: 09.06.8949 (Adjusted Years)
LOCATION: IPSS *Deepening Night*
REGION: Trensch System, Inner Praesepe Empire

Corsia screaming in her face seemed to snap Commander Eve back to full consciousness, and she rose on shaky legs to follow the AI as they ran further toward the bow of the ship.

"What the fuck," Eve muttered when she finally regained the powers of speech. "Heavy combat mechs on a ship? They're gonna hole it themselves."

"Seems like those remnants really want to get their hands on us," Corsia replied as they rounded a corner and nearly bowled over an enemy soldier. Corsia grabbed him by the neck, pushing his head back, and fired three shots under his chin with her pilfered rifle.

The man went down, and she grabbed his weapon before they took off once more.

"We need to find somewhere to hole up," Eve said as they pulled open a hatch and slid down the ladder to the next deck.

"Agreed," Corsia replied. "Preferably somewhere near the forward sensor array so we can hack it and get comms with our ships. I'd like to take Arthur and Larson alive. Learn what the hell the ASAIs are doing with the IPE…what strategic value can it hold for them?"

"Other than to deny it to us? I've no idea," Eve said, slowing as they reached an intersection, and releasing a fresh passel of nano to scout ahead.

Corsia pondered the possibilities as the nanocloud began to spread out, highlighting nearby IPE personnel that were rushing to duty stations.

She spotted a clear path in the enemy's movement patterns and directed Eve ahead. Though Corsia could trigger her skin to activate its stealth modes, Eve's camouflage was compromised by the blood all over her uniform. Not to mention the fact that neither had stealth capable weapons.

For now, they'd have to rely on the nanocloud to mask their movements from internal sensors, and do their best to avoid the enemy's Mark 1 eyeball.

As they skulked down the corridors, Corsia considered how unlikely it was that the ASAI would have two remnants in the IPE just to deny the ISF—or any others—access to ship-building resources.

Then another thought occurred to her.

She considered the variations they'd witnessed in the orbits of the three stars of the Trensch System. On their current trajectories, the only thing that would change is a few of the lagrange points in the system.

But what if the changes keep happening along the same course as they have thus far?

Corsia tasked a process with solving the three-body problem, and watched the gravitational shifts that occurred within the Trensch System and the cluster's core.

"Shit…" she whispered a minute later.

"What is it?" Eve asked, glancing behind them. "Did you pick something up?"

"No," Corsia said, while gesturing for Eve to move to the hatch that would lead them down another deck. "I think I know what the ASAIs are doing here."

Eve waited for the nanocloud to slip around the edges of the hatch and into the level below, declaring it clear before she pulled it up and slid down the ladder.

"So what is it?"

"I think they're going to collapse the stars of this system into a black hole."

"What? Really?" Eve glanced up at Corsia as she slid down the ladder, landing silently on the deck below. "That won't change anything, the mass of the system will just be concentrated in one place."

"I don't know why," Corsia replied, as they crept along the empty corridor toward the forward sensor array—now just thirty meters further in, behind a maintenance panel. "I just know what. Maybe they saw what happened in Bollam's World, and they're going to try to suck in all the dark matter."

Eve's mouth hung open for a moment. "From the *cluster*?"

Corsia gestured for Eve to keep moving. "I'm just speculating. No matter what, it's probably bad for the rest of us."

The corridor ahead ended in a 'T', right at the access panel for the forward sensor array's control system. Corsia was certain that once they reached it, she could breach the system and reach out to Sephira aboard the *Andromeda.*

The pair was five meters from the junction when the nanocloud alerted them to a pair of technicians walking down the corridor to the right.

Eve glanced at Corsia and nodded to her rifle.

Corsia shook her head, and handed her rifle to Eve, then motioned for the Marine to press herself flat against the bulkhead, while Corsia stood in front of her, and triggered her skin to shift from the appearance of a shipsuit to invisibility.

Her body didn't perfectly mask Eve's, but the Marine saw what Corsia was doing, and triggered her own armor's stealth systems, keeping her left side out of view.

A tense few seconds passed as the IPE technicians reached the 'T' junction, paused, and then turned down the corridor toward Corsia and Eve.

Corsia clenched a fist, ready to take the enemies out as they passed, but the pair hurried by without even a sideways glance at the bulkhead where Corsia and Eve stood.

"That was close," Eve whispered once the coast was clear.

"Yeah, pretty sure our rifles were visible between us."

Eve took up a position at the 'T', ready for any further visitors, while Corsia pulled off the access panel, revealing a small NSAI node that controlled the forward sensors.

"Should only take a moment," she said while placing a hand over a hard-Link port, feeding a tendril of nano into the system.

"Good, because we're sitting ducks here," Eve muttered.

Corsia nodded absently as she began to breach the NSAI node's defenses. She worked slowly, not wanting to alert the system to her presence. The last thing they needed was for the IPE to spot a node under attack.

"Almost there," she whispered.

Then Eve stiffened. "Too late," the Marine muttered.

Corsia held back a curse as she saw the reason for Eve's utterance. IPE Marines had appeared at the ends of each corridor forming the 'T' junction.

"Freeze! Step away from there!" a voice yelled, as the enemy Marines advanced toward Corsia and Eve.

BOLT HOLE

STELLAR DATE: 09.06.8949 (Adjusted Years)
LOCATION: Hidden Facility, Planet HH1
REGION: Hidey Hole System, Large Magellanic Cloud

Sera stepped off the lift with Jason at her side, glancing at him before striding across the circular room to the doors guarded by a pair of Marines.

She knew what the other side held, but still marveled at the sight when it met her.

Beyond the doors was a hallway with windows along one side, and those windows revealed a vast, hollow void, one thousand kilometers across.

The spherical space was at the center of the planet, but it wasn't empty.

The first thing that crossed Sera's mind as she stood at the window, looking down at the void beneath her, was that gravity was a touch higher here than it was on the surface.

That confirmed her suspicion that the hundred-kilometer-wide sphere she could see far below, positioned at the center of the planet, housed a black hole.

One that was likely spinning rapidly within layers of ferric materials, creating the world's strong magnetic field, and protecting the contents of the void within the world.

Sera corrected her thinking. It wasn't a *void* per se. It was half-full of stuff, but it was not sort of material one normally encountered in a planetary core.

Towers anchored to the black hole's housing at the center of the planet stretched up in every direction, reaching to the rock ceiling above. Wrapped around every tower at ninety meter intervals were broad platforms, each covered in a dome that enclosed a different biome, filled with plant and animal life.

<*It's an ark,*> Jason said from Sera's side.

<*That's my assessment as well,*> Jen replied. <*I've tapped into the environmental management systems. The facility is entirely automated, and from what I can see, hasn't had a sentient visitor for over a century.*>

<*I concur,*> Fara added. <*I've reached what I can only assume is the facility's command and control center. Route is marked on your HUDs.*>

Sera tore her eyes away from the strange view before her and began to walk down the passageway, still glancing out the windows that lined either side, which were angled out to allow for a better view of the marvels below.

<*Why would my father build this?*> Sera asked Jason privately. <*Was he expecting some calamity to wipe out the Transcend?*>

<*Well…yes?*> Jason laughed as he spoke. <*On one side he was expanding toward the core AIs, and on the other was Orion. On top of that, the Inner Stars continued to be a roiling mess.*>

<*I get that,*> Sera replied. <*It's probably the whole reason he was setting up out here in the LMC. But if they were terraforming all those worlds in surrounding stars, why make this hidden ark in the middle?*>

<*Maybe he made it first,*> Jason suggested. <*I wonder…*>

<*Yeah?*> Sera asked as they turned down a passageway that no longer had windows looking out into the interior of the planet.

<*Well, if you were worried about a growing array of enemies, maybe you wouldn't wait for something like jump gates. Maybe you'd set up contingencies long before that. As the photon flies, it's only about five hundred years to get out here; maybe your father sent a team long, long ago.*>

Sera considered Jason's words as they walked down the passage toward the C&C that Fara had marked on their HUDs, barely aware of the High Guard surrounding her.

What were you up to, Father? she wondered.

Sometimes it felt like the few decades she'd spent knowing her father had barely been enough time to scratch the surface of who he was…of what he'd done.

There were times Sera felt as though she'd not known him at all.

That uncertainty was further reinforced by stories Jason told of places he'd been in Alpha Centauri, many bearing the name 'Tomlinson'—all in honor of her father.

The first FGT captain. The first person to travel out into the stars with the magnanimous vision of building worlds for humanity to spread to.

The Future Generation Terraformers.

She wondered how their grand vision had turned into two groups pitting the rest of humanity against one another, as they readied for the greatest war to ever sweep across the stars.

The father of hers who had led humanity down this path to war didn't align with the one who had set out from Sol nearly seven thousand years ago.

Her musing was interrupted as they reached the C&C, and she stepped inside.

The room was a half-circle, angled down toward the planet's core at forty-five degrees, the forward half having a transparent wall and floor that allowed for a near unobstructed view of the center of the planet.

Fara stood at one of the consoles, while the Marines in her team took up positions around the room.

<We're checking the rest of the facility—so much as we can in any reasonable time,> Pearson called in. *<You all stay put.>*

<Will do,> Sera replied. *<I suspect it's going to take some time to crack this egg.>*

She looked around, wondering where Flaherty was, and pinged him.

<Don't worry about me,> he replied. *<Just checking the surrounding rooms.>*

<OK, Dad.>

<We have control of the room's sensors,> Jen said. *<Atmosphere is clear; you can de-stealth and take off helmets if you'd like.>*

<Whoa, now,> Valerie said as she disabled her stealth, standing near a console in the center of the room. *<Helmets stay on.>*

<Wasn't going to pull it off,> Sera replied. *<Like I said—>*

<I know,> Valerie interrupted. *<Not your first op.>*

<Cheeky,> Sera muttered. *<And not the pilot, either.>*

<OK,> Fara announced, as Sera walked toward the front of the room, feeling like she should be sliding downhill, but held in place by the a-grav systems in the room. The feeling made her a little nauseous, but she ignored it. It wouldn't do for the president to get sick inside her helmet.

<'OK' what?> Jason asked.

<This is up there with the most elaborate encryption I've ever encountered. It might take days to find a way around it. Weeks to get through it.>

Sera walked toward the central console—the only one showing any activity—and saw that it was prompting for the presidential tokens.

<Looks like only my father was to have unlocked this place,> she said in a mental whisper.

<Let me try a few other—> Fara began, but Sera stopped her with a raised hand.

<We don't have days or weeks. We need to know what's in here ***now****.>*

Fara nodded and took a step back. Beside the prompt was a hard-Link port, and a bioanalysis sleeve. Both systems required physical contact; wireless auth and remote DNA samples wouldn't pass muster.

<*I'm buffering you,*> Jen advised, as Sera unspooled a hard-Link cable from her armor and jacked in. Then she signaled her armor to disconnect the glove, and watched as it folded back onto her arm, revealing her red-skinned hand.

She altered her flesh to allow penetration by the sampling system, and slid her hand into the sleeve.

The console sent a signal across the hard-Link, prompting for Sera's authorization tokens. She used the provided hashing algorithm, and generated a fresh token which she passed into the system.

The word 'Verifying' hung in front of her vision for a full ten seconds before it disappeared, replaced by 'Accepted'.

All around them, the other consoles activated. Sera was about to make a triumphant statement, when the walls came alive.

REMNANTS

STELLAR DATE: 09.06.8949 (Adjusted Years)
LOCATION: IPSS *Deepening Night*
REGION: Trensch System, Inner Praesepe Empire

<*What's our play?*> Eve asked, the need for EM silence gone.

<*I have no idea,*> Corsia replied, playing through every possible option—seeing none where either she or Eve would escape. <*I think we have to surrender…hope that Sephira can get them to stand down.*>

As she spoke, a shudder rippled through the ship's deck, and Corsia saw an alert flash on the *Deepening Night*'s emergency broadcast network that the engines had been hit.

<*See? We'll be OK.*> Corsia tried to keep her mental tone encouraging, but she wasn't so certain they'd weather this.

If it were humans they were dealing with, she would have been far more certain of how things would play out. With remnants? There was no way to know what their endgame was…what they'd sacrifice to see their goals achieved.

Corsia's rifles were already leaning up against the bulkhead, and she set her sidearm down before stepping away from them, nodding for Eve to follow suit.

<*I'm still in the node. I can get a signal out letting them know—*>

"Well, looks like we'll be continuing our conversation after all," a voice said from the central passageway, followed by the appearance of President Arthur.

Larson was on his heels, the two remnant-controlled humans striding forward as if they had no reason to fear Corsia and Eve whatsoever.

Which was probably true.

"I don't think we'll get very far with a chat," Corsia replied, as the IPE Marines closed on either side, reaching the dropped weapons and kicking them aside before two soldiers in heavy armor reached Corsia and Eve, and clamped thick bands around their arms.

"No?" Arthur said as he stopped in front of Corsia. "I think that our conversation will happen whether you want it to or not. I don't know why you're walking around in that meat-suit, Admiral Corsia, but now that I know what you are, I'll subsume you just as easily as if you had been an organic."

"Give it your best shot," Corsia challenged, ready to trigger a death cycle in her mind, should she be at risk of giving up any of the ISF's secrets.

A sidelong glance from Eve told Corsia that she was ready follow suit. Before either of them could speak further, Arthur reached forward and grasped Eve's head, clamping down hard.

Eve began to scream, her eyes bulging from their sockets, as Corsia struggled to free herself, sending nano into the soldier behind her, fighting with the enemy's armor's control systems.

"None of that," Larson said as he strode toward Corsia, his hand outstretched toward her.

His palm was centimeters from Corsia's forehead, when she saw the secretary's eyes look over her shoulder and widen in surprise.

Corsia twisted and looked behind herself to see...something that made no sense.

The NSAI node, and the equipment behind it, was disintegrating—solid objects turning into streams of particulate matter, and flowing through the ship, toward the hull.

Then more of the bulkhead began to dissolve, and Corsia could see starlight shining through the clouds of dust. In the midst of that cloud, a silhouetted human figure was moving through space toward the ship.

As the person grew closer, Corsia could see that they were wearing light armor, the suit's jets propelling them toward the IPE cruiser.

Upon closer inspection, Corsia saw that something was wrong with their head…it seemed diaphanous. Then the tableau made sense—sort of. The human woman drawing near wasn't wearing a helmet, and her hair was flowing out behind her in the vacuum of space.

That was when Corsia made out the approaching rescuer's features.

Tanis.

* * * * *

The hull of the IPE cruiser was a web of molecular and atomic bonds, their matrices a simple puzzle that Tangel solved and undid, drawing the energy from the bonds into herself as needed, while letting much of the power that lay between the atoms bleed off into space around her. Photons bled off into the darkness along with other high-energy waveforms, as solid matter degenerated into more basic components.

Then she was through the hull, and the internals of the ship began to come apart before her. She disassembled components of the forward sensor array, then the NSAI node that had sent the telling, momentary ping out into space, alerting her to the location of Corsia and Eve.

There they are! she thought triumphantly, as the passageway came into view.

With a thought, she extended the ship's grav shields to keep the atmosphere within the IPE cruiser, despite the gaping hole in its hull.

It wouldn't do to kill her people during their rescue.

Her eyes lit upon the man touching Eve's head, and she saw that there was a remnant within him, its tendrils reaching into Eve's mind.

No, Tangel thought.

With a flick of her hand—the part of it outside normal space-time—she separated the molecules in the human hand touching the Marine, then grasped the tendril the remnant had extended, yanking the entire remnant out of the person it had been inhabiting.

The remnant curled in upon itself, forming a ball of light, and Tangel formed a weave of energy around it, holding the remnant in place while she reached for the one in the other man.

It fought her, but she pulled it free, too, and placed it within its own cage.

As the two humans who had been under the enemy's sway collapsed, she infiltrated the armor of the soldiers holding Corsia and Eve, using them to free the women, and then directed them to stand aside.

A moment later, she eased through the grav field, and settled onto the deck next to Corsia.

"You called?" Tangel asked with a smirk.

Corsia's mouth worked for a moment, as though the AI had forgotten how to operate the organic body she currently inhabited.

"Well, I was about to," she finally managed to say.

Eve was tottering on her feet, and Corsia grabbed her and eased her to the deck.

Tangel glanced at the two men before her—President Arthur and Secretary Larson, from the data Terrance had given her. Both wobbled, and the president half rose, then fell back, putting a hand against the bulkhead while muttering incoherently.

All around them, the enemy soldiers were standing dumbfounded, then one leveled his weapon at Tangel, shouting, "Stand down!"

"Brave," Tangel said with a laugh, and threaded a tendril of herself toward the weapon, causing it to dissolve in the soldier's hands. "I believe that it is all of *you* who should stand down."

She proceeded to ignore the enemy soldiers and walked toward the IPE's president.

"Arthur. Are you OK?"

The man's gaze lifted from the deck to meet Tangel's, and she gave him an encouraging smile.

"Welcome back," she said softly.

"What? How?" he asked, his voice beleaguered.

"It's going to take a bit to explain. Can you have your soldiers stand down? We need to get medical attention for our people, and then we can talk."

The president nodded numbly and sent a command to his soldiers, who slowly lowered their weapons.

"Good." Tangel smiled before turning to Eve. "Let me see to your shoulder."

She reached out with her extradimensional limbs, assisting the soldier's mednano in healing her body, and then reformed her armor over her shoulder.

Eve's eyes were round circles of awe as she stared at Tangel, and Corsia's weren't much narrower.

<*You've ascended,*> the AI said in a hushed mental tone.

<I have, but let's not spread it too far just yet.>

Corsia nodded, her motions slow and deliberate. *<OK, but what do I call you now? Are you still two, or are you one?>*

<Tangel, Corsia. You can call me 'Tangel'.>

TAKE A MIRACLE

STELLAR DATE: 09.06.8949 (Adjusted Years)
LOCATION: Ark Facility, Planet HH1
REGION: Hidey Hole System, Large Magellanic Cloud

The Marines and the High Guard leapt into motion, firing at barely perceptible movement all around the room's perimeter. Shots struck foes, and Sera saw ten-legged mech frames shimmer into view.

Judging by their size, there had to be a hundred of the things lining the walls. She unslung her rifle, firing at a shimmering form atop a console, when something hit her in the back, knocking her to the ground.

It was at that moment that Sera realized the deca-mechs were falling from the overhead as well.

Her wrists were pinned to the floor, and she struggled to free them, twisting and kicking at her invisible foes. She managed to get her left arm free, and she drew her lightwand, slashing wildly, watching robotic limbs fall around her. She struggled to her feet, to see only Fara and one of her High Guard still fighting—every other member of the team was trapped under a writhing mass of deca-mechs.

A slow clap came from the entrance of the room.

"Well done…you."

Sera turned to see the speaker, and came face to face with herself.

No…not exactly myself.

Walking into the room, wearing light armor, but with the helmet off, was a version of herself—one with organic skin, short, dark hair, and utterly boring fashion sense.

Sera didn't know the last to be true, but given the pedestrian haircut, she was certain that the pawn version of herself that her mother had made was utterly boring in every way.

<*OK, so…trap,*> Jen commented.

The robotic attackers throughout the room disabled their stealth systems as the Airthan Sera entered, and Sera saw that there were easily two hundred of the machines. She had to admit that it was impressive so many had been able to hide—at least so long as they were still.

"You can put the lightwand away," the other Sera said. "I'm not going to attack you. I have no need to. You'll do as I say, or your people here will die. Horribly."

Sera tried to reach out to Pearson's team, but the comm signal didn't make a connection.

<*I've been trying it, but they have an EM jammer running nearby,*> Jen informed Sera.

<*Keep trying,*> Sera said as she turned to see Jason struggling beneath a dozen of the deca-mechs. A little further was Valerie, laying utterly still. She tried to reach out to both, but even in the room, the signal was blocked.

Sera glanced at her lightwand and disabled its blade, but didn't let go of the hilt. "What do you want, Evil Sera?" she asked.

Her doppelganger snorted. "*I'm* the evil one? You're the Sera whose lover killed our father, the one who has red skin, and is leading a rebellion. Stars, I even heard you were a demon at a party not long ago. Pretty sure that if this is a battle between good and evil, you're on the wrong side."

Sera chuckled; her doppelganger had her at a disadvantage. "I suppose I might be 'Bad Sera'," she admitted. "But that's just skin deep. Given what Airtha has likely done to you, you're probably rotten to the core. If you even have a core. You're probably not much more than her sock puppet."

Her clone's eyes widened a millimeter at the words, but then narrowed once more. "Well, either way, you've done what I wanted—what mother wanted. Gained access to the archives here."

Sera glanced at Fara, who was pinned down two meters to Sera's left. The shadowtron was still slung over the AI's back—though trapped beneath a pair of deca-mechs. She knew getting to that weapon was key. She had no doubt that a remnant was in control of the Airthan Sera.

"What? You couldn't access it yourself?" Sera asked with a wicked grin. "Can't light up your own facility?"

"I didn't have the tokens."

<I find that highly unlikely,> Jen commented privately. *<I wonder if your mother has done something—changed her DNA enough that the system wouldn't verify it.>*

<I guess that makes sense,> Sera replied. *<But a little verification that I'm the real me is nice, too.>* She chuckled aloud, then said, "Sounds like an excuse."

She suddenly remembered that her hard-Link cable was still connected to the console; the cord ran from her hip—not visible to her doppelganger, who was weaving her way through the mechs that had formed a wall around Sera.

She drew a steadying breath, then hooked her foot under the console's leg. Once secure, Sera sent a command to reverse the room's a-grav systems, switching up for down.

A second later, Sera was hanging from the console by her foot, and each member of her team was now atop the deca-mechs. With a flick of her wrist, she activated her lightwand and flung it at the window at the end of the room, the blade slicing a long gash in the plas before burning a hole through and falling out into the planet's empty core.

<You better hope that thing doesn't land on the black hole housing,> Jen commented.

<I gave it a thirty-second shut-off,> Sera replied as she shifted gravity in the room by seventy degrees, turning the roof into a steep slope.

Deca-mechs tumbled over one another, a dozen slamming into the damaged window, cracking it and falling away over the brink.

"Shit!" Jason swore as he began to slide toward the opening, along with Fara and two of the ISF Marines. The others were scrambling over the enemy, shooting some, slashing others.

The Airthan Sera cried out and lunged toward Jason, grabbing his wrist and pulling him toward a console.

The deca-mechs had not re-engaged their stealth systems, but the Marines and High Guard had. The battle re-engaged, with the humans gaining the upper hand while more and more of the deca-mechs tumbled toward the end of the room, falling toward the planet's core.

Jason was grappling with the Airthan Sera, who Sera realized had been trying to save him, while, nearby, Fara had managed to leap to the deck-now-overhead, and was clinging to a console.

"I like to fly and all, but can you flip this back!?" Jason cried out as he drove a fist into Airthan Sera's face, sending her sprawling, just as a deca-mech grabbed his leg, pulling him down.

A few more seconds, Sera thought, as another dozen mechs slid out of the room.

Then she snapped the failsafe ES field into place, and flipped the gravity around once more.

The room devolved into a final spate of utter chaos as the High Guard and Marines fired on the enemy, several even tossing burn sticks at a few clusters of mechs, the acrid smoke from thermite fires filling the air.

Then something struck Sera, and she turned to see her Airthan counterpart holding a deca-mech's severed limb, hauling it back for another swing at her head.

Sera threw her left arm up in a block, then grabbed the mech-limb and yanked it away, only to have her doppelganger pivot and deliver a kick to Sera's wrist.

She hadn't pulled her armor back over her hand after the bio-samples, and she lost her grip on the limb, taking a step back as the other Sera—a primal scream tearing past her lips—charged toward her and knocked her to the ground, pulling her hard-Link cable free.

Losing sight of the general melee, Sera drove a fist up into her other self, catching her under the chin and snapping her head back, only to receive a flurry of blows to her stomach for her trouble.

A fistfight in armor was patently ridiculous, and Sera cast about, looking around for a fallen weapon, when the other Sera was pulled off her and flung across the room.

She saw both Jason and Flaherty standing over her, each man extending a hand.

"You're the good one, right?" Jason asked aloud as they pulled her up.

"Funny. Thanks for the save."

All around them, the enemy mechs had all fallen still, though most appeared to be undamaged.

"Took a few minutes to worm my way in," Fara explained as she approached. "Their NSAI cores were too hard to hack, but as it turns out, their limb actuators use a system I'm familiar with, and I was able to fake limb-control commands once I got nano on them."

"Nicely done," Valerie rasped from behind Sera, and the president turned to see the major applying biofoam to a wound in her upper chest. "Damn thing missed my heart by a few centimeters."

Gunny and one of the High Guard soldiers had Evil Sera pinned against the wall, and the Marine was applying a LockIt to her armor.

Sera approached her Airthan counterpart, watching the rage simmer in the other woman's eyes.

"I guess you weren't quite clever enough," Sera told her. "Should have waited for me to disconnect from the hard-Link before you made your grand entrance."

"You'll never get away," the doppelganger said. "I sent out a signal. We have stealthed ships that will be here in less than an hour."

<*I can confirm that,*> Julia said over the combat net. <*Comms are back, and we've relayed our status up to General Sheeran. He's sending down the other pinnaces.*>

<*Has he detected the stealthed Airthan ships, yet?*> Pearson asked as he reconnected to the combat net. <*And is everyone OK?*>

<*Operational,*> Valerie replied. <*Not necessarily OK.*>

<*The* Helios*'s scan has picked up sixty enemy vessels less than three light seconds from the planet.*> Fara announced. <*He's moving to engage them. Distress signal is out on the QuanComm.*>

"Then we'd better find out what secrets this place has, and get the hell out of here," Sera said as she turned back to the console and reconnected her hard-Link.

<*Jen, just suck it all down into our internal datastores; use the whole team's, if you have to.*>

<*You got it, boss.*>

"That was one heck of a gamble," Jason said as he approached. "Coulda dropped half of us out there."

"Your armor has a-grav and thrusters," Sera gestured to Jason's gear. "You *probably* would have been OK. Could have aimed for one of those biomes down there."

"Real reassuring," Jason said, a smirk on his lips.

"Well, I would have turned the ES field on before you fell out. Promise."

"Somehow your glib tone makes me feel less certain."

"Sorry, I get snarky when I'm—wait..."

Jason cocked his head to the side. "You get snarky when you wait?"

"Uh, no...I mean I found something. Something weird."

"This whole place is weird," Valerie said from a few meters away, where she was driving a lightwand through the central core of a deca-mech.

"Well, this is weirder...maybe. There's a vault at the back of this room."

As Sera spoke, she activated the vault's doors, and a section of the rear wall swung away, revealing a stasis pod resting vertically in a narrow alcove. The surface of the pod was opaque, not revealing the occupant.

"Huh...I wonder who that—" Jason began to say, then stopped short as Sera activated the wake sequence. "Well, I guess we'll find out."

The pod registered a successful termination of its stasis field, and Sera disconnected her hard-Link, stepping over the disabled mechs as she walked toward it.

She was still a few paces away when the cover slid open, and she gasped.

"Father?"

The man in the stasis pod was a spitting image of Jeffrey Tomlinson. He had the raven hair, the sharp eyes, and angular features, but he looked subtly different at the same time. His lips were more generous, his eyes a touch kinder.

Though I suppose it could just be that he looks really confused.

His gaze swept across the room, then landed on Sera, his eyes widening. "Julianna?" he whispered. "How? What is going on?"

"Uh...I'm not Julianna," Sera replied, never having considered how much like her human mother she may appear. "It's me, your daughter. Seraphina."

"Who?" Sera's father asked, taking a tentative step out of the stasis pod. "Where...where am I?"

"We call the system 'Hidey Hole'." Sera replied almost absently, staring into the eyes of the man before her, wondering how he could be here. Was he a clone? Another of Airtha's pawns?

"Really?" the other Sera snorted. "Try the 'Nora System'."

"Nora..." Jeffrey Tomlinson whispered. "How did I end up here?" Suddenly his eyes narrowed as he looked at Sera, then at her doppelganger. "Wait...daughter? Are you twins?"

"She's a clone," both Seras said at once, then glowered at one another.

"That's kinda creepy," Valerie said in hushed tones.

"I only have one daughter," Jeffrey said after a moment. "Andrea...and neither of you look a thing like her."

"Father," Sera asked, stepping toward the man she'd spent so much of her life either wishing desperately to please or reviling. "What year did you go into stasis?"

Jeffrey glanced back at the stasis pod he'd just stepped out of. "Well...I don't remember going into stasis, but my internal clock aligns with my last memories. It's 7977."

"Shit," Sera whispered. "You've been in there for over a thousand years."

"Well if he's been in there, who was running the Transcend for the last thousand years?" Jason asked.

Jeffrey had a stricken look on his face, and he staggered backward, placing a hand on the wall to steady himself. He swallowed and looked up at Sera, and then her evil twin.

"Airtha," he whispered.

<I have a full dump, we should get out of here,> Jen announced.

Sera nodded absently, her eyes still on her father…or, to his mind, the man who was genetically her father, but had never even known her.

"We have to go," Sera said. "Airtha's forces are coming."

"She's here?" Jeffrey asked, paling further. "She knows about our work in the LMC?"

Sera took a step forward. "Father…she…she's running half the Transcend now…with her." She jerked a thumb at the other Sera.

"And you?" Jeffrey asked, meeting her eyes and not glancing away for the first time since he'd called her 'Julianna'.

"I'm running the other half. Trying to get our civil war under control so we can confront Orion."

"We're at war with Orion too?" he asked, pushing himself away from the wall. "What of the Inner Stars?"

"Everyone's at war with everyone, Father."

Sera couldn't help but feel like she'd utterly failed this man she didn't even know. When he had gone into stasis, the last FTL wars had finally ended, and the age of reconstruction was beginning.

Now everything he had worked for was in shambles.

"Why do you keep calling me that?" Jeffrey asked. "I didn't raise you."

A lump formed in Sera's throat, and she found herself unable to speak.

"Shit…sorry," Jeffrey said, as the High Guard ushered them out of the C&C and back into the corridors leading to the lifts. "I didn't…"

"You *did* raise me. Well, you and uncle Finaeus," Sera said once she'd regained the powers of speech. "I guess…I guess it was just a different one of you."

"Finaeus?" Jeffrey asked. "You must take me to him, he'll know what's happened. He never trusted Julianna after she came back."

"Don't worry." She placed a hand on her father's shoulder. "We'll take you to him. He's really going to be happy to see you."

<Do you think he's the original?> Jason asked as he fell in on Sera's other side. *<Or is he a clone?>*

<I don't know,> she admitted, unable to keep the waver out of her mental voice. *<I mean…that means the man who raised me really wasn't my father.>*

<We still have your father's body,> Jason reminded her after a moment's pause. *<Back at New Canaan. We could figure out which was the original.>*

<Oh, shit!> Sera exclaimed, suddenly realizing they'd not checked Evil Sera over with the shadowtron. *<Fara, you need—>*

<I've already checked. Neither of them have remnants in them,> Fara answered before Sera could complete her question.

<I don't know if that makes me feel better, or worse—at least about other me.>

<We need a name for her,> Jason said as they turned down the corridor with the downward-looking windows on either side. *<How does 'Seratwo' sound?>*

Sera couldn't help a laugh. *<Dumb. I prefer 'Evil Sera'.>*

"I can't believe it's been a thousand years..." Jeffrey said to no one in particular, shaking his head as they walked toward the lifts. He glanced at Sera. "Are you really my daughter? And her? Clones you said?"

"I'm the original," Sera said, then jerked her thumb at her doppelganger. "Airtha made *her* after I wouldn't play ball."

Evil Sera only snorted and shook her head in silence.

"Airtha tried to trick me into killing you," Sera said to her father. "Well, the other you. In the end, an Orion agent did it, but then Finaeus arrived, and Airtha tipped her hand by trying to kill him. It was then that we realized she'd been playing all of us, manipulating things to take control of the Transcend and spark up a war with Orion."

"All of that is true, except for the part where Airtha is the one in the wrong," Evil Sera said, as they reached the lifts to find Pearson already sending one of his fireteams up. "The Caners made this other Sera to try and take over the Transcend."

"Oh, c'mon!" Sera turned and took a step toward her clone. "*When* did they do that? When did the people of New Canaan have access to you to make a copy? They were cooped up in their system the whole time."

"They did it when I was on the *Intrepid*," the other Sera shot back. "Before I flew back to Airtha from Ascella."

"Oh yeah?" Sera asked. "Then how do I remember everything about being the director of the Hand? How do I remember the night of June twenty-seventh, when Elena and I went swimming in Wishbone Lake, and she cut her foot on that sunken statue? That all happened *after* Ascella."

The other Sera paled, and Sera knew she had her on the ropes.

"See! We *both* remember those years. Which means you were made from *me* while we were on Airtha—under our mother's tender care."

"I—" the Airthan Sera began, then stopped.

"And what about Helen?" Sera asked. "What happened to Helen?"

"She had to be removed," the other Sera retorted. "It had been too long."

"Damn right it had been too long," Sera muttered. "Face it, girl. You're the copy. You may *be* me in every way, but you're still the copy. Proof is in the skin."

"Your skin?" Jeffrey asked, a puzzled look on his face.

Sera held up her hand, still unarmored, and changed it from red to a light tan, then transparent. "Airtha doesn't have the tech to do that. Not with skin, not that smoothly. It's why you're so pedestrian," she sneered at her clone.

The other Sera pursed her lips, looking resolute, but then her face fell, and she turned away, her shoulders drooping She whispered, "Stars...I wish none of this had ever happened. I should have stayed aboard *Sabrina*."

Sera's sense of victory became pyrrhic, as the realization hit her that—despite Airtha's influence—this other woman wearing her face *was* her. She had the same hopes and dreams. The same memories, passions, the same vulnerabilities.

"Dammit," she muttered, imagining how terrible her counterpart must feel, knowing that everything she believed was a lie. "Look, we'll figure this all out."

She nodded to Pearson, and his Marines directed the despondent Sera into the lift on the left, while Sera and Jason took the other one up with Jeffrey and the High Guard.

"This is going to take a bit for me to wrap my head around," Jeffery said, after a minute on the lift had passed.

"You're going to have to walk me through this step by step. And...you're really my daughter?"

Sera shrugged. "I guess? Genetically speaking, at least. Airtha must have cloned you at some point—"

"*She* didn't," Jeffrey said. "I did, as a fallback. She must have found him and...unless *I'm* him. I don't know that I'd be able to tell."

"We'll be able to tell," Jason said.

Jeffrey glanced at Jason. "I'm sorry, this has all been entirely crazy. You're...?"

"Jason Andrews." He held out his hand. "One-time captain of the GSS *Intrepid*."

Jeffrey took Jason's proffered hand and shook it once while whispering, "the *Intrepid*..."

"Colony ship, left Sol in 4124," Jason supplied.

Jeffrey's eyes went wide. "*That Intrepid*? No wonder the shit's hit the fan."

"We've been a bit of a catalyst," Jason said in agreement.

No one spoke as the lift continued its journey to the surface.

In the passageway, Fara provided Jeffrey with an EV suit, while they had the other Sera strip out of her armor and don one as well.

Five minutes later, they were outside the spire, and Valerie guided her charges toward one of the backup pinnaces that had set down in front of the facility, while Pearson led the other Sera to the second ship.

They'd only taken a few steps when the atmosphere began to shimmer a few paces ahead, then a thunderclap tore through the air, knocking everyone sprawling.

Sera clambered to her feet to see a silhouetted figure standing before them, tendrils of light spread around it.

<*Shit! It's an ASAI!*> Valerie cried out, raising her rifle.

"Valerie. Stop," the figure's voice boomed, and Sera's mouth fell open.

"Tanis?" she asked, broadcasting with her armor's speakers.

The tendrils of light drew back into the figure, and Sera saw that it was indeed Tanis. She was wearing light armor, but had no helmet—on a world without a breathable atmosphere. She was holding something in her hands like a shield, but cast it aside as she approached.

"I guess the cat's out of the bag now, isn't it?" Tanis asked, a smirk forming on her lips. "And it's 'Tangel' now. Are you all safe?"

Sera felt like the air had been sucked right out of her lungs as she gaped at Tanis—Tangel. "Yes…how…?"

"Let's get you into the pinnace," Tangel said. "Me too; eventually I'll need to breathe again. Plus, I want to talk to your father."

<*Yeah,*> Sera managed to say after switching to the Link. <*Looks like there's a lot to talk about. Stars…that feels like the understatement of the last millennia.*>

Tangel glanced at Jeffrey Tomlinson, who was staring open-mouthed at her as he was led past her to the pinnace.

<*Or the last seven thousand.*>

A MIRACLE

STELLAR DATE: 09.06.8949 (Adjusted Years)
LOCATION: ISF pinnace, Planet HH1
REGION: Hidey Hole System, Large Magellanic Cloud

The moment the airlock sealed, Tangel dismissed the field that had enveloped her head, the stale air she'd held in the bubble replaced by the pinnace's fresh supply.

As she gulped down long breaths, Sera stopped next to her, pulling her helmet off to reveal a wide-eyed stare. Jason followed suit, his expression not significantly different.

"What…?" Sera asked. "OK, how did you *do* that?"

"Arrive on the planet?" Tangel asked, leaning against the bulkhead, weathering a wave of dizziness.

"No, Tani—gel…how did you…" Sera rolled her eyes. "Bah! I can't come up with a sarcastic remark right now. *Yeah*, how did you get here?"

"I used a jump gate," Tangel replied with a wink.

She could see a light go on in Sera's eyes, and the woman snapped her fingers. "That was a gate mirror! The thing you tossed away when you arrived. But why didn't you take a ship?"

Tangel checked the status of the three pinnaces rising above the planet toward Sheeran's ship, the *Helios*, ensuring that every member of the team was safely aboard.

Above, Sheeran was battling the Airthan fleet, already having disabled four of the sixty enemy vessels, his rail-cruiser flinging near-relativistic pellets out at dozens of targets at a time.

Good, Tangel thought. *Glad to see that design works so well.*

While making those observations, she replied to Sera's question.

"I was in the Trensch System, aiding in the negotiations—which is to say I jumped in on a pinnace with Joe. The ship took some shots as we approached our target, and was disabled. I had to leap through space to get to the enemy cruiser where Corsia and Eve had been captured—"

"Terrance?" Jason interrupted.

Tangel nodded. "OK. Everyone is safe. Joe included. Turns out they had a bit of a 'remnant' problem in the Inner Praesepe Empire."

"A remnant?" a voice asked from behind Tangel, and she turned to see Jeffrey Tomlinson standing in the pinnace's central passageway.

"A little thing ascended AIs can leave behind in people," Sera explained. "Fun for controlling them and making messes everywhere."

"Really? They can do that?" Jeffrey's eyes were wide as saucers.

"That's a long story," Tangel interjected. "Regarding my arrival, we had a bit of a dust-up with the IPE's space force, but their Minister of the Interior was aboard the *Andromeda,* and we managed to get everything under control. Remnants and all.

"Then I got the message that you two had skipped on out here, and were in hot water as well." Tangel paused to give both Sera and Jason meaningful looks. "Joe will confirm that I had some choice words for the pair of you."

"Don't change the subject," Jason said, rolling his finger in a circle to indicate she carry on.

"Fine, but you're getting demerits for leaving the galaxy without permission. Anyway, so the *Andromeda*'s gates were still racked up in storage, and Sheeran's distress call over the QuanComm made things here seem more than a little dire.

"The *Andromeda* has a smaller gate for pinnaces that was fully assembled in one of the bays, but it didn't have the power to jump a ship clear out here to the LMC—not without some jury rigging."

"So you just went on your own?" Jason's tone made it sound like he thought she was crazy, or lying…or perhaps both.

Tangel shrugged. "Well, I pulled the gate mirror off the front of our pinnace and had them activate the gate while it was still in the bay. Sephira oriented the *Andromeda* to align with the LMC, and I…jumped."

Sera shook her head, mouth hanging open, while Jason wore an expression that caused Tangel to wonder if he wanted to try a ship-less gate jump.

"Just so you know," Tangel continued, "once I did it, I realized how monumentally stupid it was. If I didn't reach my target, I could have dumped out into space between the galaxies. That possibility made for the most frightening seventy seconds of my life."

Sera raised a finger and wagged it at her friend. "Keep that firmly in mind if you feel like coming down on us for going on this mission." She held a stern expression on her face for a few seconds, then lunged forward and wrapped Tangel in a tight embrace.

"OK, OK," Tangel grunted. "Shit's hitting the fan out there, we should get to the cockpit."

Jason pushed past Tangel and Sera, jogging down the passageway to where the Marine pilot was shifting vector to avoid a swarm of Airthan drones.

Tangel pulled the pinnace's feeds, watching as the enemy drones fired on the ship from every direction, wearing down the ship's standard shields.

"No stasis on these pinnaces?" Tangel asked as she reached the cockpit to see Jason sliding into the copilot's seat.

"Too many capital ships need them," Jason replied as he took control of the pinnace's defense systems, firing chaff and electronic countermeasures in an attempt to fool the enemy drones. "We shorted the pinnaces out here in the LMC, because we were supposed to be alone."

Tangel only grunted in response, watching as Sheeran altered his vector to close with the approaching pinnaces, the *Helios* spewing its deadly hail like a cyclone of destruction.

"We have an approach vector," the pilot announced while weaving the pinnace through the incoming drone-fire. Tangel realized that the enemy craft were not taking kill shots on the pinnace—instead they seemed focused on overwhelming the craft's shields.

I wonder if I can locate their command frequency…

Tangel tapped into the pinnace's scan suite, and then hopped onto that of the other two pinnaces. She used the passive sensors on each ship to broaden her scope, creating a massive antenna, flying through space.

Detecting anything through all the chaos around them seemed impossible, especially with the Airthan fleet firing at the *Helios* with everything they had.

C'mon… Tangel thought as she picked out a low-frequency wave that varied in amplitude in a…*predictable pattern*! At only two-hundred megahertz, the carrier wave didn't support a high-bandwidth datastream, but it *would* have the range to manage the drones from ships three light seconds away.

This has to be it.

Tangel tapped into the signal, finding the datastream and, picking through the information, looking for the auth mechanism so she could fake her own wave and confuse the drones that were slowly wearing down the pinnaces' conventional shields.

"Fuckin' bots," the Marine pilot muttered, as a dense wave of drones closed with their vessel. "Those things will do us in for sure…."

"Think again," Jason said through gritted teeth, and Tangel watched the third pinnace cease its evasive maneuvers and streak straight toward the wave of approaching enemy craft. It fired all of its beams and missiles, causing explosions to flare in the mass of drones.

The pinnace continued boosting—well beyond its safe acceleration threshold—taking more and more weapons fire from the drones as it closed.

Then the craft was amidst the drones, its beams shredding the robotic attackers at point-blank range before the pinnace was finally overwhelmed and holed, venting atmosphere in a dozen locations as it tumbled away from the battlespace.

"Shit," Tangel muttered. "That was brave…but stupid."

"Why would you say that?" Jason asked, glancing over his shoulder at her, as their pinnace continued to weave through the attackers. "I'm rather proud of it."

"What?" Tangel asked, then realized what Jason had done, and groaned. "You know…next time you send an empty pinnace into the enemy, can you let me know beforehand?"

"Sorry, forgot you weren't on our comms when we boarded. That was the one we came down in…I was remote piloting it back up."

As Jason explained his clever duplicity, their pinnace shuddered under a heavy barrage of enemy fire, and Tangel redoubled her concentration on dissecting the drone's control wave.

The two remaining ISF pinnaces were ninety thousand kilometers from the *Helios* when the drone pattern shifted. The robotic attackers intensified their fire, and Tangel knew their orders had changed from 'capture' to 'kill'.

Exactly what I needed.

With the orders had come a new auth packet, and Tangel lifted it off the carrier wave and pulled it apart. She realized that the token was generic, not hashed per command. *Sloppy, but maybe it was done to keep the data packets small, counting on security through obscurity.*

"Rear umbrella's failed!" the pilot called out, and then Jason swore as one of the pinnace's two engines died, beamfire from the drones triggering a thermal shutdown.

The pinnace slewed to port, and Tangel closed her eyes, crafting new orders for the drones while configuring the remaining pinnace's comm systems to send out the low-frequency wave.

Here goes nothing, she thought, and sent the command.

Half the drones immediately broke off from their attack on the pinnaces and turned on the other drones. Utter chaos erupted around the pinnaces, and Tangel managed a laugh, not caring to think how close they'd come to being dead in space with thousands of enemy drones around them.

"Now *that's* more like it," Jason crowed as the *Helios* drew closer, its beams sweeping away any drones that had survived the robotic civil war Tangel had ignited.

"This is insane," a voice whispered from behind her, and Tangel turned to see Jeffrey approaching. His mouth was agape as he stared at the forward view—a display that showed the *Helios* fending off dozens of Airthan ships on its own, while miraculously—to him—remaining unscathed.

"This?" Tangel asked, gesturing to the firefight occurring around the *Helios*. "This is just another day at the office. Don't worry, Airtha doesn't have weapons that can penetrate the *Helios*'s stasis shields, and we're almost there—"

Tangel's words cut off, as a massive ship appeared on scan, easily a hundred kilometers long. At first glance, it appeared to be little more than a rail accelerator with engines—more like a defensive platform. One that looked incomplete, judging by the construction scaffolding on one side, and the missing hull plating in a number of locations.

As she watched, thrusters fired along its length, and the weapon shifted its orientation to align with the *Helios*.

"What the..." Sera whispered, then the pinnace's alarms wailed as a massive EM burst flared on scan.

"Holy shit!" Jason swore as the forward view showed arcs of electricity flowing across the *Helios,* dancing between its rings, sending explosions flaring across the ship, as the rail accelerators lost containment, and a billion fist-sized pellets tore through the hull, flying in every direction.

Then the *Helios* went dark.

<Admiral!> Colonel Pearson called in from the other pinnace. *<Our Sera here is laughing her ass off—says that thing's called an EMG, and it can penetrate stasis shields...>*

We can see that, Tangel thought as she watched escape pods blast out of the *Helios.*

<Pearson, break off, get behind the planet, we'll take out the EMG,> Tangel ordered the colonel, while she addressed Jason and the pilot aloud, "Get us in close to that thing, I'm going to take it out."

"Close?" Jason twisted in his seat. "How close?"

Tangel turned and strode down the passageway, calling over her shoulder. "Jumping distance. Don't worry, I'll wear a helmet this time."

Tangel reached the armory with Sera close on her heels.

"Tanis! You can't be serious! We'll never make it close enough to that weapon!"

"Pull scan and look," Tangel said as she grabbed a helmet and pulled it on. *<I've got their drones shielding us. Plus, that weapon's not complete, it doesn't have point defense beams.>*

"So you *think*." Sera shot back.

<Sera,> Tangel placed a hand on Sera's shoulder. *<We don't have a lot of options here—Shit, they've jumped in.>*

"Who?" Sera asked, then her eyes widened. "Dammit, the rest of your Aleutian fleet. That thing is going to tear them apart!"

<Exactly,> Tangel replied to Sera before calling up, *<Jason, pour it on, get me within a few meters—above that knobby protrusion, five eighths of the way down the hull.>*

<Are you sure about this?> Jason asked. *<You've always done crazy stuff, Tanis, but—>*

<You just come get me afterward,> Tangel replied. *<Got it?>*

<You know we will.>

The calm certainty in Jason's voice steeled Tangel, and she leant forward, touching her helmet to Sera's, letting the vibrations carry her voice through. "When I get back, we have to talk. Things have to change."

"What things?" Sera's eyes were wide. "Are you going to leave us?"

"No." Tangel shook her head. "We're going to go on the offensive."

"With who?" Sera whispered.

"Everyone."

Tangel gave Sera a quick embrace, then turned and walked to the airlock, closing the inner door on Sera's worried expression, and grasping a handle as she cycled the outer door open.

All around the pinnace, the remaining drones were flying in a tight formation, absorbing beamfire from the Airthan fleet, and taking shots of opportunity to keep the forty enemy cruisers at bay.

Ahead, three of the enemy cruisers were in a close formation near the EMG, and Jason dove the pinnace between them. She could tell it was him, not the Marine pilot, by the chances he took, passing only a few kilometers from the enemy vessels.

He's one to call me reckless….

Tangel directed a hundred drones to launch their remaining missiles at the closest cruiser as they swept past, taking out its shields with the weapons, and then the drones themselves slammed into the enemy ship's hull, tearing it open to gout flame into space.

Three hundred thousand kilometers away, the Aleutian ISF fleet was shifting vector and burning hard to reach the pinnace and the disabled *Helios*.

They were too far away to damage the EMG, but she wasn't so certain that it couldn't hit them.

Tangel sent them a warning to stay at least fifty degrees away from the business end of the EMG, praying that the dozen ISF ships could last long enough for her to destroy this new weapon and still have enough firepower to take down the remaining Airthan ships.

As those events played out, Jason spun the pinnace and fired the engines for a full braking burn, slowing the craft down to a mere hundred-kilometers-per-second. The a-grav dampeners failed to absorb all of the energy, and Tangel was slammed against the bulkhead, nearly missing the optimal time to jump.

With three hundred milliseconds to spare, she leapt out of the airlock.

Faster than her eyes could send the information to her brain, Tangel crossed the forty meters between the pinnace and the EMG. Luckily for her, she had other ways of seeing, and was able to stretch her arms out and disintegrate the hull of the enemy weapon before she was smeared across it.

Shredding the EMG's hull was a lot harder than when she'd destroyed the Nietzschean soldiers' weapons on Pyra, or dissolved the hull of the IPE cruiser just an hour earlier. This time, she had to shred molecular bonds at break-neck speed, praying that she didn't tear through anything too volatile.

The slurry of matter and energy around her slowed Tangel's descent, and she came to a stop near the center of the ship's long shaft, roughly a kilometer forward of the bulge she suspected to be the main firing system.

Around her, the matter began to solidify, chemical bonds reforming, and Tangel pushed her way through, finally coming to a passageway.

A wave of exhaustion hit her, and she realized that, while her non-organic body was able to feed off the energy around her, she wasn't so adept at keeping her flesh energized while performing these insane feats.

Don't get lazy now, Tangel, she chided as she pushed away from the corridor's bulkhead and began a slow, loping jog down the ship's length. *Next time I do something like this, I'm wearing powered armor.*

She drew matter from around her, and converted it into fuel for her organic body, carefully altering molecular compounds into safe carbohydrates. Her body responded, gaining strength, and she picked up her pace, reaching the end of the corridor in just another twenty seconds.

Ahead of her was a thick door, sealed against intrusion, and half-covered with warnings about the environment beyond.

Tangel reached out, feeling the magnetic fields on the far side, a realization hitting her like a hammer blow.

So much mass…Finaeus always said this was impossible…Seems like Airtha knows a few things he doesn't. Like how to jump a black hole.

Tangel knew that destroying the EMG was no longer an option. If she did, the black hole on the far side of the door would eventually fall into the planet below—or maybe, given the mass of the black hole, the planet would fall into it. Either way, it would destroy the ark hidden beneath its surface.

Not to mention kill her, as well.

<*Jason, Sera.*> She called out to the pinnace, but didn't get a response. <*If you can hear me, break off, I'm going to shut it down, not destroy it. The drones should continue to shield you. Get back to the planet.*>

The snap of kinetic rounds ricocheting off something nearby drew Tangel's attention back to the world around her, and she realized that a group of Airthan soldiers were firing from behind her, and the 'something' was her armor.

With a wave of her hand, she dissolved their weapons and seized the joints in their armor.

Enough distractions.

Tangel concentrated on the dense alloy before her. The door to the EMG's firing chamber consisted of layers and layers of carbon-reinforced steel and lead.

She was about to dissolve it, when she realized it would be wise to protect her organic body from whatever lay within. She drew the lead out of the door and formed it around herself, wrapping her body in a thick cocoon before pulling the door apart the rest of the way and drawing herself through.

With her organic eyes trapped inside the leaden cocoon, Tangel pulled feeds from the chamber's systems, while also examining it with her extradimensional vision.

Sure enough, in the center of the chamber was a one-hundred-meter sphere, magnetic fields surging around it, holding a ball of mass and energy within. As she watched, streams of material were fed into the black hole, the matter flaring brightly as it was torn apart, becoming the ultra-dense non-matter within the singularity itself.

What amazed Tangel was that, to her other vision, the black hole was not black at all. Waves of extradimensional energy flowed off it in every direction, a shimmering halo of luminescence so bright it was almost blinding.

The magnetic fields generated by the chamber's containment systems warped that energy, and as she watched, the fields shifted, focusing the energy into a single point on the forward-facing side of the black hole.

The energy held at that point for a second, building. Then a tremendous blast of electromagnetic energy tore out of the black hole, surging down a shaft that ran the length of the EMG.

So ***that's*** *how they power this thing,* Tangel thought, while trying to determine the best way to stop the weapon without destroying the ship and herself.

Her initial thought was to disintegrate whatever system was used for firing the weapon, but she knew that tearing apart a black hole was far beyond her abilities. Especially one that had to mass at least a hundred times that of a terrestrial planet.

She briefly wondered how they held the thing within the weapon, let alone moved it, and why it wasn't crushing her with its gravitational pull. While she was toying with those questions, she tasked a part of her mind with breaching the ship's systems.

If she could take control of the firing systems or the positioning thrusters, she could nullify the weapon's effects.

She set about that work, cringing as the weapon fired again, knowing that her people were being targeted, and that she would be too slow in stopping it.

Milliseconds stretched into seconds, then longer. An excruciatingly long two minutes and eleven seconds later,

Tangel broke through the encryption on the weapon's firing systems and took control of it.

What she found there was terrible in its cruelty. Six AIs were mentally conjoined at the heart of the control system, their sole task to control the fields around the black hole and trigger its electromagnetic eruptions.

The instant they detected Tangel's presence in the system, they did the unthinkable: the AIs shut off the magnetic fields containing the black hole.

While a part of Tangel's mind wailed in terror, feeling an increasing gravitational pull of the thing—and wondering why it wasn't crushing her—another part examined the systems that had been holding the black hole aloft.

In addition to magnetic fields, anti-gravity stabilizers had been present, firing negative gravitons at the black hole. Without the containment systems, she could now see that the black hole was roughly six centimeters in diameter, an unimaginable amount of mass to haul within a ship, but something that the graviton emitters had negated.

Seven milliseconds had passed since the AIs shut off the containment systems, and Tangel could now feel her body being crushed against the leaden cocoon she'd made, by a steady 100*g*s' pull from the black hole, as the graviton emitters ceased operation.

She stretched an ethereal hand through the cocoon, and anchored herself to the chamber's wall, while simultaneously re-activating the a-grav emitters.

The AIs countered her by shutting off the CriEn modules that had been powering the emitters, leaving Tangel only whatever energy was left in the backup SC batteries.

Knowing she had less than a second to live, Tangel did the only thing she could think of: she used the a-grav emitters to open a hole into the dark layer.

A *fhummp* thundered through the ship as the rift opened, drawing the black hole and the air inside the chamber into the dark layer.

The rift surged toward the perimeter of the room, stopping only a meter from Tangel's cocoon, the gantry she was resting on cutting off in a ragged line, as the eternal darkness lapped hungrily at the solid matter.

A curious realization struck Tangel.

There are no Exaldi out there. I should be able to see them, but there's nothing….

Forcing herself to stay on task, she shut off the a-grav emitters to seal the portal into the dark layer, but when the emitters registered as offline, the opening into *nothing* still gaped before her.

"Nooo," Tangel whispered, remembering what had happened with the planet Aurora in the Bollam's World System.

She had believed the black hole's creation and connection to the dark layer to be just a fluke, but perhaps there was some strange property of black holes and the dark layer that no one had guessed at.

Either way, the thing wouldn't close.

With a growing sense of abject terror, Tangel watched as a clump of dark matter streaked through the dark layer, bleeding gravitons that she could see with her other senses, and impacted the black hole.

Frantically, Tangel activated the a-grav emitters once again, attempting to reverse the waveform that had opened the rift in the first place, but nothing happened.

Then she remembered the emission pattern that Earnest had devised to push the Exaldi back into the dark layer above Carthage.

She tweaked the frequency and amplitude, and fired the a-grav emitters once more. This time, they shoved the black hole away from the rift's opening, deeper into the dark layer. Once it had moved a kilometer away, Tangel deactivated the emitters and gave a cry of joy, the utterance consuming the last of her flagging strength.

The rift closed, and Tangel breathed a long sigh, as consciousness slipped from her mind.

SERAS

STELLAR DATE: 09.07.8949 (Adjusted Years)
LOCATION: Airthan Ring
REGION: Huygens System, Transcend Interstellar Alliance

Airtha reviewed the information from the secondary observation team stationed beyond Valkris's heliopause with mixed feelings.

That the EMG had worked—and spectacularly so—was something that pleased her greatly. Losing Sera, and then her forces, to the ISF fleet ruined that elation and left her feeling hollow.

Another daughter lost.

She had hoped that letting Sera leave on her own would temper her impetuous daughter's need to 'get out of this place,' as she'd frequently taken up saying.

However, there was a second silver lining. Airtha now had no doubt in her mind that the ISF had developed a near-instantaneous means of communication.

Quantum entanglement was the most obvious possibility, though how they'd compensated for the heisenberg uncertainty principle intrigued her greatly. So far as she knew, even the core AIs—her hated enemy—had not properly managed to solve that conundrum.

How to know where the entangled particles are, and how to measure their movement at the same time with any fidelity…?

She doubled her resolve to capture one of their bait ships. Now that she knew their purpose—and the means by which they sprung their traps—Admiral Krissy's rescue fleets would soon find that turnabout was indeed fair play.

Reviewing her options for the right location to turn Krissy's bait operations into a trap for her enemies, Airtha couldn't keep a part of her mind from lingering on the daughter she'd lost.

Two of them now. Two of my flesh and blood aligning themselves with that abomination, Tanis Richards, and her AI, Bob.

She knew it was possible that *her* Sera would not change sides and turn against her, but she doubted it. The abomination's powers of persuasion were great.

And Seraphina had proven herself to be weak.

Repeatedly.

Airtha considered further altering the next iteration of her progeny. Make her stronger, more commanding, less flexible. Of course, that limited Airtha's own influence over her daughter; she was trying to make a woman in her own image, not a puppet.

Just as she was examining Sera's DNA and neural network, a courier ship jumped in near the ring and sent a priority message.

Airtha scanned it, feeling her determination slip into rage.

*Another EMG **and** another Sera!?*

The parts of her mind most reminiscent of an organic brain seethed at the thought. *Two daughters lost in one day…Tanis Richards will be made to answer for this.*

And was the Nora System lost? She had hoped to learn what secrets her former husband had placed within its vaults. The message didn't say, as the courier had left the system before the conflict with the ISF ships had concluded. However, the message did contain scan showing that the EMG had been disabled. Without that weapon—just as in the Valkris system—an ISF victory was assured.

Airtha steeled herself for the news of the mysterious planet's loss. In fact, she had to assume that her enemies would take control of all the facilities in the LMC.

She wondered if the extragalactic settlement would cause Tanis and the rebellious Sera to scour the Milky Way and nearby dwarf galaxies for more of her hidden locations. They could try, but with nearly a trillion stars to investigate, it could take them decades to even scratch the surface.

I'll see Tanis defeated long before they find them all.

With that worry put to rest, Airtha turned her attention back to the next iteration of her daughter that she'd construct. Perhaps she'd been fighting too hard against Sera's deviant nature. Rather than suppressing it, Airtha considered what enhancing it may do. Create a version of her daughter that coveted power and submerged herself in her vices.

Not too much—Airtha still needed to control her—but enough to give her new Seraphina an edge.

An edge she'd hone into a deadly weapon and use to end the obstruction that Tanis Richards represented, followed by that buffoon, Praetor Kirkland.

Once she had all AIs and humanity aligned with her, Airtha would finally be in a position to strike out and destroy the ascended AIs in the core.

The ones who had killed her and remade her into the *thing* she'd become.

TRANSITION

STELLAR DATE: 09.07.8949 (Adjusted Years)
LOCATION: Ol' Sam, ISS *I2*
REGION: Pyra, Albany System, Thebes, Septhian Alliance

Tangel walked out of her lakehouse, away from the gathering within, her gaze immediately alighting on the figure standing on the dock.

<*Want some company?*> she asked Sera as she walked down the steps and onto the path.

<*Umm…I guess? Only if you tell me what the* **hell** *I'm supposed to do.*>

Tangel chuckled softly to herself as she walked toward the dock. <*That's Bob's job. I'm just a pawn.*>

Sera turned as Tangel approached, and shook her head. "That big, dumb AI's no help at all. Just tells me that you muddy destiny too much—plus other assorted nonsense."

<*I can hear you, you know,*> Bob interjected.

"Yeah," Sera glanced up the clouds overhead. "That's why I spoke aloud, you big dummy."

<*Oh.*>

"I won't lie," Tangel said as she reached Sera's side, staring out over the lake. "Shit's gotten weird. Like…super extra weird."

"Seriously, Tani—Tangel? You, my best friend, are an ascended-merged-AI-person, my father was a clone, my *real* father has been in stasis for a thousand years, there are two clones of *me* on this ship…" Sera paused, her eyes both angry and pleading. "Do you want me to go on?"

Tangel kicked her shoes off and sat on the edge of the dock, dipping her toes into the water.

"Sera, sit."

Sera stood still for a moment, then sighed and pulled her boots off before joining Tangel. "Huh...it's warmer than I expected."

"It's the tropical fish. They like it warm."

Neither woman spoke for a second, both lazily dragging their toes through the water.

"Seriously, Tangel?" Sera asked. "I need someone to tell me what to do. I can't figure this out. Do I just turn everything over to my father? Is that insane?"

"He's not ready yet—if he even wants it," Tangel replied. "No, I think it's time that *I* do what I've been running from, what you've been asking me to do for over a year now.

Sera's brows rose. "Which is?"

"I'll take the reins."

"Of the Transcend?"

"Of everything."

"What do you mean...everything?" Sera whispered, her eyes round and staring.

Tangel didn't respond immediately, considering different word choices and how Sera would receive them.

Finally she sighed, deciding to wing it. "I'm half-human, half-AI, I'm ascended, and relatively competent at most things I set my mind to. I think I'm the best one to unite everyone, to see if we can't forge a civilization that values the good in both species, and understands the variances within those species.

"I'm going to turn our 'Scipio Alliance' into a nation, and I'm going to bring everyone under that single banner."

"How?" Sera asked. "Not everyone is going to join you willingly."

"Yeah," Tangel laughed softly. "I get that. But I have a plan that can get us on the road to peace without this war burning humanity to ash. And an important part of that plan is you."

"Me?" Sera asked, her voice wavering. "We just had the part of this conversation where I said I have no idea what to do."

"I have a gift for you," Tangel said, a smile pulling at the corners of her mouth. "A gift and a job."

Sera heaved a sigh. "So since you're running 'everything', is the job for me to get back to day-to-day operations for the Transcend?"

Tangel shook her head. "No, I think I can manage that now. And maybe your father *will* want that task eventually; we'll see. But I know you've been struggling with how to deal with Airtha...I think our best bet is a targeted strike. A team that we send to Airtha to take her out and end her reign without destroying the Transcend."

"You want *me* to go in and do that?"

"Yes," Tangel replied. "But not just you. I want to send Katrina and Kara in with you—plus your sisters."

Sera snorted. "Now I *know* ascendancy hasn't been good for your cognitive process. My 'sisters', as you call them, hate me. Stars, since they realized that Airtha made two of them—that they know of—they hate pretty much everything."

Tangel knew that beneath Sera's angst over her sisters, was the knowledge that Airtha had made *her* as well. For all intents and purposes, she existed because her mother had used her father to create new versions of herself, in hopes of raising a daughter in her image that would rule the Transcend as her puppet...or something along those lines.

However, it was not something that Tangel would bring up; Sera didn't need to dwell on that reality any further right now.

"You understand your sisters very well." Tangel spoke quietly, waiting for Sera to realize what part she could play. "Because those two women *are* you. Tweaked a bit here and there, but separated from Airtha's influence, I believe they'd revert to form."

"What does that even mean?"

"Sera, you're smart, cunning, resourceful. You're a highly skilled operative. Three of you? With a team? You'd decimate Airtha."

Sera snorted. "OK, Tangel. Let's say for a moment that I *don't* think you're insane. What's the 'gift' you have for me?"

"I can't send you against Airtha unarmed, Sera; I can leave something inside of you to help."

Sera jerked away, turning to face Tangel with a mixture of awe and terror on her face. "A remnant? In me? No way!"

"Not a remnant. A memory. Like what Xavia did with Katrina. It's not the same as what the other ascended do, I promise."

Sera's expression softened. "I don't know, Tangel.... That's a lot to ask. Can I think on it?"

"Of course," she nodded. "There's something else I can do, too—I did it for Rika not long ago. I can show you how *I* see you."

"What does that do? Put something *else* in me?"

"No," Tangel said as she gazed out over the still waters of the lake before them. "Nothing other than thoughts. But they're *your* thoughts."

"OK," Sera whispered. "Show me."

Tangel lifted a hand and touched it to Sera's forehead, feeding a tendril of her other body through her friend's skin and into her mind.

She pulled an image from her own thoughts: one of Sera as a powerful woman, her skin gleaming white, angelic wings stretched out behind her. A rifle in one hand, and a sword in the other.

Arrayed behind her, stretching into infinity, was a vast fleet of ships, and around her was a multitude of warriors, all standing ready to face whatever came their way.

"Really, Tangel? An angel? Isn't that a bit anachronistic?" Sera asked with a self-deprecating laugh.

"You're the one who sees herself as a demon, someone vile and undeserving," Tangel pointed out, sliding her hand down to clasp Sera's shoulder. "But that's not you. You're steadfast, noble. You put others before yourself far more than you let on. You've saved my life many times…you tore that EMG apart looking for me. You're my angel."

Sera's jaw tightened, and her lips pressed together as tears sprang into her eyes. Her hand reached up and held onto Tangel's as she managed to hoarsely whisper, "Thank you."

THE END

* * * * *

Big things are afoot. Sera's father is back, and she faces a mission to confront her mother. Tangel must move on to the Trisilieds, and the TSF hoplite forces are about to move into Orion space.

And that's just the tip of the iceberg. Everyone from Roxy and Carmen to Katrina and Kara will be involved as the war spreads further.

All the while the forces of the Caretaker, Xavia, and General Garza wait for the right time to strike out at a weakened ISF. But Tangel has a plan for victory, one she hopes none of her enemies will suspect.

Pick up ***Fallen Empire*** to learn what happens next.

THE BOOKS OF AEON 14

Keep up to date with what is releasing in Aeon 14 with the free Aeon 14 Reading Guide.

The Intrepid Saga (The Age of Terra)
- Book 1: Outsystem
- Book 2: A Path in the Darkness
- Book 3: Building Victoria

- The Intrepid Saga Omnibus – *Also contains Destiny Lost, book 1 of the Orion War series*

- Destiny Rising – *Special Author's Extended Edition comprised of both Outsystem and A Path in the Darkness with over 100 pages of new content.*

The Orion War
- Book 1: Destiny Lost
- Book 2: New Canaan
- Book 3: Orion Rising
- Book 4: The Scipio Alliance
- Book 5: Attack on Thebes
- Book 6: War on a Thousand Fronts
- Book 7: Fallen Empire (2018)
- Book 8: Airtha Ascendancy (2018)
- Book 9: The Orion Front (2018)
- Book 10: Starfire (2019)
- Book 11: Race Across Time (2019)
- Book 12: Return to Sol (2019)

Tales of the Orion War
- Book 1: Set the Galaxy on Fire
- Book 2: Ignite the Stars
- Book 3: Burn the Galaxy to Ash (2018)

Perilous Alliance (Age of the Orion War – w/Chris J. Pike)

- Book 1: Close Proximity
- Book 2: Strike Vector
- Book 3: Collision Course
- Book 4: Impact Imminent
- Book 5: Critical Inertia (2018)

Rika's Marauders (Age of the Orion War)
- Prequel: Rika Mechanized
- Book 1: Rika Outcast
- Book 2: Rika Redeemed
- Book 3: Rika Triumphant
- Book 4: Rika Commander
- Book 5: Rika Infiltrator (2018)
- Book 6: Rika Unleashed (2018)
- Book 7: Rika Conqueror (2019)

Perseus Gate (Age of the Orion War)
Season 1: Orion Space
- Episode 1: The Gate at the Grey Wolf Star
- Episode 2: The World at the Edge of Space
- Episode 3: The Dance on the Moons of Serenity
- Episode 4: The Last Bastion of Star City
- Episode 5: The Toll Road Between the Stars
- Episode 6: The Final Stroll on Perseus's Arm
- Eps 1-3 Omnibus: The Trail Through the Stars
- Eps 4-6 Omnibus: The Path Amongst the Clouds

Season 2: Inner Stars
- Episode 1: A Meeting of Bodies and Minds
- Episode 3: A Deception and a Promise Kept
- Episode 3: A Surreptitious Rescue of Friends and Foes (2018)
- Episode 4: A Trial and the Tribulations (2018)
- Episode 5: A Deal and a True Story Told (2018)
- Episode 6: A New Empire and An Old Ally (2018)

Season 3: AI Empire
- Episode 1: Restitution and Recompense (2019)
- Five more episodes following...

The Warlord (Before the Age of the Orion War)
- Book 1: The Woman Without a World
- Book 2: The Woman Who Seized an Empire
- Book 3: The Woman Who Lost Everything

The Sentience Wars: Origins (Age of the Sentience Wars – w/James S. Aaron)
- Book 1: Lyssa's Dream
- Book 2: Lyssa's Run
- Book 3: Lyssa's Flight
- Book 4: Lyssa's Call
- Book 5: Lyssa's Flame (June 2018)

Enfield Genesis (Age of the Sentience Wars – w/Lisa Richman)
- Book 1: Alpha Centauri
- Book 2: Proxima Centauri (2018)

Hand's Assassin (Age of the Orion War – w/T.G. Ayer)
- Book 1: Death Dealer
- Book 2: Death Mark (August 2018)

Machete System Bounty Hunter (Age of the Orion War – w/Zen DiPietro)
- Book 1: Hired Gun
- Book 2: Gunning for Trouble
- Book 3: With Guns Blazing (June 2018)

Vexa Legacy (Age of the FTL Wars – w/Andrew Gates)
- Book 1: Seas of the Red Star

Building New Canaan (Age of the Orion War – w/J.J. Green
- Book 1: Carthage (2018)

Fennington Station Murder Mysteries (Age of the Orion War)
- Book 1: Whole Latte Death (w/Chris J. Pike)
- Book 2: Cocoa Crush (w/Chris J. Pike)

The Empire (Age of the Orion War)
- The Empress and the Ambassador (2018)
- Consort of the Scorpion Empress (2018)
- By the Empress's Command (2018)

Tanis Richards: Origins (The Age of Terra)
- Prequel: Storming the Norse Wind (At the Helm Volume 3)
- Book 1: Shore Leave (June 2018)
- Book 2: The Command (July 2018)
- Book 3: Infiltrator (July 2018)

The Sol Dissolution (The Age of Terra)
- Book 1: Venusian Uprising (2018)
- Book 2: Scattered Disk (2018)
- Book 3: Jovian Offensive (2019)
- Book 4: Fall of Terra (2019)

The Delta Team Chronicles (Expanded Orion War)
- A "Simple" Kidnapping (Pew! Pew! Volume 1)
- The Disknee World (Pew! Pew! Volume 2)
- It's Hard Being a Girl (Pew! Pew! Volume 4)
- A Fool's Gotta Feed (Pew! Pew! Volume 4)
- Rogue Planets and a Bored Kitty (Pew! Pew! Volume 5)

ABOUT THE AUTHOR

Michael Cooper likes to think of himself as a jack-of-all-trades (and hopes to become master of a few). When not writing, he can be found writing software, working in his shop at his latest carpentry project, or likely reading a book.

He shares his home with a precocious young girl, his wonderful wife (who also writes), two cats, a never-ending list of things he would like to build, and ideas...

Find out what's coming next at www.aeon14.com

Made in the USA
Middletown, DE
11 July 2018